'With this, I can conquer the world,' said Heenmor.

He was talking about the stone egg which sat on one corner of the table: a sullen grey weight lit by dull light from the twelve firestones which studded the walls of this chamber high in the Tower of the order of Arl. The everlast ochre cast no shadows.

'Aren't you interested?' said Heenmor, in a voice which mocked his opponent.

Elkor Alish, warrior of Rovac, said nothing, but studied the wizards and the warriors arrayed on the chess board. In chess, as in real life, a wizard had a hundred times the power of a warrior – but wizards could still be killed.

'Aren't you interested?' said Heenmor again. 'Believe me: the death-stone has power enough to conquer the world.'

Alish raised his eyes.

'What exactly does it do?'

Also by Hugh Cook

THE WORDSMITHS AND THE WARGUILD
THE WOMEN AND THE WARLORDS
THE WALRUS AND THE WARWOLF
THE WICKED AND THE WITLESS
THE WISHSTONE AND THE WONDER WORKERS
THE WAZIR AND THE WITCH
and published by Corgi Books

THE WIZARDS
AND THE WARRIORS

Hugh Cook

CORGI BOOKS

THE WIZARDS AND THE WARRIORS
A CORGI BOOK 0 552 12566 0

Originally published in Great Britain by
Colin Smythe Limited

PRINTING HISTORY
Colin Smythe edition published 1986
Corgi edition published 1986
Corgi edition reprinted 1987 (twice)
Corgi edition reprinted 1988
Corgi edition reprinted 1989
Corgi edition reprinted 1990

This book is set in 10/11pt Times

Corgi Books are published by Transworld Publishers
Ltd., 61–63 Uxbridge Road, Ealing, London W5 5SA, in
Australia by Transworld Publishers (Australia) Pty. Ltd.,
15–23 Helles Avenue, Moorebank, NSW 2170, and in New
Zealand by Transworld Publishers (N.Z.) Ltd., Cnr. Moselle
and Waipareira Avenues, Henderson, Auckland.

Printed and bound in Great Britain by
Cox & Wyman Ltd., Reading, Berks.

The Salt Road, which offers travellers a route that is safe from pirates, is a major trade route, even though much of the way is mountainous. Goods traded along the Salt Road include Stokos steel, keflo shells, sponges, sugar, Ashmolean jade, leeches, furs, dried fish, antlers, shark teeth, slaves, Selzirk silk, Narba leatherwork, pearls from Ebonair, crocodile skin from Geris, silver from the mines of Dalar ken Halvar, glass, copper, tin, lead, amber, pottery, wine, wool, spices and wheat

THE WIZARDS AND THE WARRIORS

CHAPTER ONE

Name: Phyphor.
Birthplace: Galsh Ebrek.
Occupation: wizard.
Status: Master wizard of the order of Arl, with powers over light and fire.
Description: very old gentleman with scarred beardless chin, bald pate, black skullcap, sheep's teeth, grey robes, iron-shod wooden staff, leather boots.
Residence: Sunside Chambers, Prime Tower, Castle of Controlling Power, near Drangsturm.

* * *

It was Phyphor's birthday.
He was 5736 years old.
He saw no cause to celebrate.
It was windy; it was raining; he was wet; his boots were leaking. The sheep's teeth set in his jaws by enchantment were aching. He was a long, long way from home. And he was advancing into danger.
'We should reach Estar today,' said Phyphor to his travelling companions. 'So be prepared!'
His two companions were his fat, slovenly apprentice Garash, and a youngster named Miphon who had less than a century to his credit. In Estar, the three of them hoped to find the renegade wizard they had been sent to kill.
They were not in pursuit of any ordinary renegade, such as the lord of the sea dragons, the notorious Hostaja Sken-Pitilkin, wizard of Drum. No, they were after a far more dangerous quarry.

11

In defiance of the Confederation of Wizards, the maverick Heenmor had looted an artefact of power from the Dry Pit in the Forbidden Zone.

Phyphor's party had to seek out Heenmor, kill him, recover whatever he had stolen from the Dry Pit and present it to the Confederation in the Castle of Controlling Power.

Their chances of success and survival were, in Phyphor's estimation, about ten per cent.

*　*　*

Name: Miphon.

Birthplace: Driftwood Islands.

Occupation: wizard.

Status: Minor wizard of the order of Nin, with limited powers to hear and control the minds of wild things.

Description: slender man of youthful appearance with green eyes and a ready smile; dressed in woollen underclothes, waterproof leather outers, well-greased boots and a broad-brimmed feathered hat.

Residence: lives as a travelling healer with no fixed abode.

*　*　*

When Phyphor's little band encountered the evil wizard Heenmor, Miphon's only task would be to charm away the lethal copper-strike snake which always accompanied Heenmor.

Even so, he stood a good chance of getting killed.

After the catastrophic wars of antiquity known as the Days of Wrath, the Founders of the Confederation of Wizards had written this:

'Know that the Dry Pit contains power sufficient to destroy the world. As you value your lives and the world which supports those lives, preserve our absolute

12

ban on the Dry Pit and the Forbidden Zone which surrounds it.'

Heenmor had defied that ban.

Heenmor had raided the Dry Pit.

Heenmor might be ready – even now – to destroy the world.

So how could they hope to defeat him?

Miphon did not worry about it at all, but wondered, instead, what new delights awaited him in Estar. Right now, he was enthralled by the rugged landscape they were travelling through. He made no mention of his pleasure to Phyphor and Garash, as both had grown dour and sour on their long journey north along the Salt Road.

Miphon wished the other two could share his joy in the wild and wonderful array of landscapes, vistas, cities, towns, villages, rocks, animals, seascapes, trees, foods, smells, songs and languages which they had encountered on their journey.

But the two wizards of Arl were immune to Miphon's enthusiasms. They were always at their worst when it was raining. And right now it was raining quite heavily.

So, as they went north along the Salt Road, with overbearing mountains on the right, and the grey tumult of the Central Ocean on the left, Miphon contented himself by singing songs of love and wonder to the donkey.

It is worth noting that Miphon, thanks to his sensible dress, was more or less waterproof, whereas both Phyphor and his apprentice Garash were soaking wet.

*　　*　　*

Name: Smeralda.
Status: beast of burden.
Description: patient grey four-legged animal burdened with books, blankets, manuscripts, herbs, tent,

13

quilts, cooking pots, fish hooks, fishing lines, mosquito nets etc. etc.

Musical taste: severely limited, despite Miphon's best efforts in this direction.

* * *

Late in the day, the three wizards – with their donkey in tow – reached the southern border of Estar. There a flame trench stretched for a thousand paces from mountain cliffs to the sea, which steamed where the trench continued for another hundred paces underwater; waves surging up the trench toward the mountains boiled away to nothing before they travelled half the distance.

Phyphor had been here before.

In the days of the Long War, Phyphor and other wizards had defeated the Swarms, here on the southern border of Estar. They had defeated the Swarms, but only with the help of a storm that had raged in from the Central Ocean – a storm so fierce that the legends later made said it had shaken teeth from jawbones and set the mountains to creaking. Certainly it had scattered the Neversh, breaking their strength.

It had been so close.

Only the storm had saved them.

If the Swarms had broken through, they could have spread north to the continent of Tameran and west to the Ravlish Lands. As it was, the Swarms had been driven back to the Deep South, where the wizards had built the flame trench Drangsturm and the chain of castles where the Confederation kept watch, and was pledged to keep watch forever if need be.

Though he had been here before, Phyphor scarcely recognised the place. The trench had not been maintained since the Long War, though the rubble, rubbish and erosion of four thousand years had not sufficed to fill it. A rutted track plunged to a greasy wooden

14

duckwalk laid across the steaming mud at the bottom, then climbed the steep slope on the other side.

Nearby was a small, ruinous fort which had once guarded the southern side of the trench. On the far side, scattered blocks of masonry showed where men had once built something which the years had since pulled down.

'We'll cross tomorrow morning,' said Phyphor, who saw no need to risk that breakneck slope in the failing light, where an old wizard might miss his footing in the gloom and end up waist-deep in ovenhot mud. 'Tonight we'll shelter in the fort.'

'A damp, ugly ruin if ever I saw one,' said Garash.

'Sleep in the rain if you don't like it,' said Phyphor.

Miphon said nothing. Trying to play peacemaker between these two was, he had discovered, singularly unrewarding. Phyphor, having trained Garash, was deeply disappointed with his pupil, who had turned out to be reckless, power-hungry and amoral; Garash, for his part, bitterly resented Phyphor's refusal to release him from his apprenticeship, despite his mastery of his art.

The wind, kicking up ripples in the puddles, found no gate to bar the way as it whirled into the fortress. Entering, Garash dared a Word of Location:

'Onamonagonamonth!'

He was richly rewarded.

From half a dozen different directions, bell-like notes rang out. As the deafening noise died away, Garash cried, in great excitement:

'There's magic here! There's power!'

'Of course, fool!' roared Phyphor. 'My fire-iron, my staff of power, that oddment slung around your neck. Quite apart from all that, there's the power sources for the flame trench.'

'Oh,' said Garash, crestfallen.

'Honestly,' said Phyphor, 'Sometimes you're so stupid I feel like kicking you from here to breakfast.'

Garash did not take that criticism well.

'Let's explore,' said Phyphor.

There was little to the fort but a courtyard, a crumbling wall surrounding it, and one squat tower. Wooden stumps, the remains of floor beams, were embedded in the towerstones at three levels. A separate, steadily rising curve of stumps showed where the stairs had been. Saba Yavendar must have seen similar things in the years of chaos after the fall of the Empire of Wizards, for he had written:

Where wind may walk but men no longer,
Stairs rise in easy stages to the vaults of air;
Our lives have become to climb them.

From the tower, strong stone steps curved away downwards, into the unknown.

'I wonder what's down there,' said Garash.

'Would you care to investigate?' said Phyphor.

Garash wiped a drop of rainwater from the end of his nose.

'I'll leave that honour to you,' he said.

Cautiously, Phyphor started downwards, ready to blast any lurking monster with fire. He went quietly, but not silently. Rainwater dripped from his cloak and water squelched in his boots. Entering the darkness, he whispered a Word. His right hand began to glow with a cold light which glimmered on spider webs and damp stone.

He turned a corner: and found treasure.

A stack of firewood, lumped up in a cellar.

It was damp, true, and colonised by woolly grey mould, but it was richness all the same. Small bones marked the cellar as an animal's lair, but no fur and fangs contested possession.

'Treasure,' muttered Phyphor, kicking the firewood.

He said a Word, and the glow from his hand died away. Standing there, breathing darkness, he longed to be back in the Castle of Controlling Power, which commanded the western end of the league-wide flame trench – the Great Dyke, some called it, while others named it Drangsturm – which reached from the Central Ocean to the Inner Waters in the east, so dividing the continent of Argan in two.

'Hey, it's wet up here,' shouted Garash. 'Can we come down? Can you hear me? Is it safe?'

'Come on down,' said Phyphor.

Garash joined him, but Miphon stayed outside to hobble the donkey. By now, it was so dark that he was almost working by touch; the mountains were dissolving into mist. His job done, he took the heavy saddlebags down to the cellar and heaped some wood together for a fire. Phyphor threw a fire-iron onto the wood and muttered a few words. The wood steamed as winter damp dried out, then kicked into flame.

'I could have used my tinder box,' said Miphon.

Phyphor made no answer, not wanting to confess how badly the rigours of this latest march had chilled him. He was too old for this kind of expedition: that was the truth of it.

The fire made them feel better; as Saba Yavendar said:

Fire is always friendliest in a world of foes,
Poor man's dancer, widow's warmer, child's enchanter;
Always, even in the winter chill, as summer warm
Toward my autumn bones, my widower's rest.

While Garash grumbled about the smoke from the fire, Miphon cooked. They ate. Then they sat apart, mumbling through the Meditations of Power which allowed them to gather the strength they needed for sorcery, and the Meditations of Balance which prevented that strength from spontaneously destroying them.

Then they fell asleep, to dream their separate dreams.

17

Phyphor had nightmares about the Swarms. He dreamt of twisted shapes against the sky, twisted screams in the noon-day sun in the days when the Neversh flew. He dreamt of the Stalkers and the lowly scuttling keflos, of the double-hulled Engulfers, the green centipedes, the Wings, the tunnellers, the blue ants, and all the others – the fearless myrmidons of the Skull of the Deep South.

Miphon pillowed his head on a stone, ignoring, as he settled to his dreams, its distant grinding curses; the stone still remembered the pain when men, for their building, had split it to its present size.

Once asleep, Miphon dreamt the dream of the stone. (Lamentations: 'Lemarl! Lemarl!')

Dreamt the dream of the stone, lay in the dreamtime which is neither Lemarl nor Amarl, lay in the dream-time which is the nothing time, chaos in which the mind can be creator. 'Lemarl,' said the stone. Not weeping, not wishing it could weep: whatever it remembered, it had forgotten both tears and laughter.

Miphon woke once to hear Garash in a corner, grunting, straining. Why can't he go outside? Because it's raining, that's why. Again he woke, finding water dripping from the cellar rocks onto his face. He shifted to a place dry but less comfortable. He renewed his stone dreams.

Garash, for his part, dreamt of food.

CHAPTER TWO

Name: Garash.

Occupation: wizard.

Status: apprentice to Phyphor, though his training is completed.

Description: stout grey-robed individual with bulging eyes, small scruffy beard and smallpox-scarred face of indeterminate age.

Career: reputedly served the Silver Emperor of Dalar ken Halvar for two centuries before fleeing Parengarenga after participating in an unsuccessful coup. Began but did not complete apprenticeships with both a wizard of the order of Varkarlor and a wizard of the order of Ebber before taking service with Phyphor.

* * *

'Wake up!'

Garash, kicked awake from a banquet, opened his eyes to darkness.

'By the seventh hell!' he growled, his eyes full of sand, his mouth full of stones, 'What is it?'

His dreamtime banquet had disintegrated, but he could still remember the tantalising smell of roast pork. Or was it long pig? One was as good as the other, in his experience.

'Up!' said Phyphor. 'Up!'

'Alright, alright,' said Garash. 'I'm on my feet. What now?'

'Come on, Miphon.'

'No need to use your boot like that,' said Miphon, searching for his feathered hat. 'I'm ready.'

'Hurry then. Up the stairs.'

'What is it?' said Garash. 'Tell us!'

'Outside! Now!'

Miphon groped for his boots, could not find them. Went barefoot. Floor wet, rain dripping through stones, pools in concavities, stairs wet. Garash stumbled, cursed, slipped, swore.

'Hurry up,' said Phyphor.

Up the curve of the stairs – faint phosphorescent gleam from Phyphor's cloak – up the stairs and out into the courtyard. Garash lubbered along last, panting. Rain fell steadily. Waves crashed against the shore.

'Look!'

On a hillside two leagues north, a stand of trees was blazing. Other conflagrations glowered in the distance.

'What are they?' said Garash. 'War beacons?'

The sky answered him with a bellow of rage and pain.

'Dragon,' said Phyphor.

'It sounds as if it's gone mad,' said Garash.

'Perhaps it has,' said Phyphor.

Now they understood his urgency. Their donkey, Smeralda, was out there somewhere in the darkness. If the dragon happened to chance upon her, it would know there were people here.

'How far's the donkey gone?' said Phyphor.

He did not know what he asked. It was one thing to listen for Smeralda's thoughts, and quite another to decide distance and direction. Miphon was equal to the task: but only just.

'South,' said Miphon. 'Two hundred paces, maybe less.'

'Get it!' said Phyphor. 'Hurry! Then we'll take shelter.'

'Why kick me up here for this?' grumbled Garash.

Phyphor said nothing, but watched as Miphon splashed away into the night.

'Phyphor!' said Garash.

Phyphor looked up. Overhead, a red spark reeled

through the sky, like a bit of burning straw spinning in the wind.

'Hold!' shouted Phyphor. 'It's overhead! Back to the cellar!'

The three wizards stumbled down the stairs and stood together in the darkness, wet and panting.

'Call the donkey to you,' said Phyphor.

'I'll try,' said Miphon. 'But it takes time. It's hard work. I can't guarantee success.'

'Try.'

Miphon blocked out the sounds of falling rain, surf-echo, dripping and trickling water. His mind listened for Smeralda's mind. And heard, instead, the dragon's mind – a senseless chant of pain, rage, hate, fierce as the warrior who wrenches a spear from his side and turns it on the enemy.

Then all heard the rush of wings pitched to a scream as the dragon plunged down, down toward the fortress, down with such reckless rage that Miphon thought it would hit the earth. It wrenched out of its dive, blasting the fort with fire as it skimmed past fast as falling. The cellar entrance flamed orange-red.

'It saw nothing,' said Garash, shaken. 'It looked, but it saw nothing. There was nothing for it to see.'

'Hush,' said Phyphor.

'It can't hear us!'

'Hush! Let Miphon listen.'

Miphon listened. The dragon was . . . gaining height . . . gaining height . . . disappointed . . . circling . . . circling . . . rage spent, rage gathering . . .

'It doesn't know we're here,' said Miphon.

'Of course not,' said Garash. 'There was nothing. Nothing for it to see.'

'What does the dragon do now?' said Phyphor.

'I think – I hope it'll go and blast something else,' said Miphon.

Then heard: recognition! The dragon saw something! Then they all heard the scream as wings plummeted down, one tortured protest from Smeralda, then the wings of the dragon seeking height again, seeking height with a batblack labouring which overpowered the sound of the surf, conjuring visions of a huge leather bellows wheezing out volumes of air.

The dragon was triumphant because now . . . now it knew!

'It knows there are people here,' said Miphon flatly. 'A donkey means people. It'll quarter the area till it finds us, if it takes all night. If we stay here it'll sniff us out, then fry us alive.'

'Flame can't reach us here,' said Garash.

'Flame can't but heat can,' said Phyphor. 'Outside!'

They hastened up the stairs to rejoin the rain. They scanned the dark sky. High above, a fire-spark circled slowly. Underfoot, the courtyard stones were still faintly warm from dragon fire. The monster circled, once and again, and then:

'It sees us,' said Miphon.

'You kill it,' said Phyphor to Garash.

'I'll try,' said Garash.

Miphon and Phyphor retreated to the top of the steps. Garash stood alone, licking his lips anxiously. His bulging eyes watched the spark. Red spark. So high, so high. And now . . . and now it dipped. Garash raised his right hand. He must wait.

Down came the dragon.

Garash waited, trembling.

He could hear the wings.

The spark was a fire, a bonfire, a furnace. Close, closer, too close!

Garash screamed a Word.

White fire flared from his hand. The dragon, way off to one side of the blast of power, slewed sideways and went gliding away into the darkness.

'What were you trying to do?' said Phyphor. 'Fry eggs?'

'It wasn't where I thought it was.'

22

'Get into the cellar, you. I'll kill it myself.'

Garash stumbled away, having wasted the accumulated strength of four hundred and seventy-nine days of the Meditation of Power on turning raindrops into steam.

'Where's the dragon?' said Phyphor, blinded by the flare of light. 'I can't see anything.'

'The dragon's thinking,' said Miphon. 'Making a plan.'

'I thought it wasn't in any state to make plans.'

'Near-death can sober up anything, even a raging dragon. It's cautious now. It's thinking.'

'What?'

'I can't tell.'

As Phyphor's night-sight recovered, he scanned the sky, blinking against the rain.

'Is the dragon moving?'

'No. It's on top of the cliffs.'

'Doing what?'

'Searching and finding.'

'Finding what?'

'I can't tell. Phyphor, it's in the air again. Up there!'

'Where? Where?'

'Above us.'

'But I can't see it!'

No red spark betrayed the dragon, which was not forced to show fire as it flew if it chose not to.

'If I try to blast it, can you guide my hand?'

'I can't pinpoint the dragon,' said Miphon. 'That's too hard.'

'Then I'll wait till it dives,' said Phyphor. 'I've stood against the Neversh. I can stand against a dragon.'

They heard something falling.

A rock shattered beside them.

'The cellar!' yelled Phyphor.

They ran. The dragon plunged down, dropping rocks as it swooped. They heard its wings cutting the air. A rock shattered at the head of the stairs, but they were already in the cellar, bleeding from a dozen rock splinters. The fort shook as the dragon crashed to earth. It bellowed. It blasted out fire. Flame filled the stairwell. Rainwater boiled to scalding steam. A flush of heat hit the cellar.

'Blast it!' screamed Garash.

'It's not in line of sight, fool,' said Phyphor.

Another blast of fire. The stink of dragon. The scrabble of talons. More fire. More steam. They were being cooked alive.

Phyphor stepped forward to try for a clear shot at the dragon. A blast of fire sent him reeling back, beating at his burning cloak. He had been singed by just the last fraction of that blast: any closer, and he would have been killed. Miphon pushed past, but Phyphor grabbed him.

'Where do you think you're going?'

'To stay is to die,' said Miphon. 'If it gets me, it may think there's nobody else.'

'Wait,' said Phyphor.

He raised his staff and hammered it down.

He spoke a Word.

The earth trembled and shook.

Phyphor spoke a Word and a Word and a Word. There was a roar louder than any dragon, or any clan of dragons. Garash screamed, throwing himself to the ground. Miphon listened.

– pain, pain, pain –

'The dragon's hurt,' said Miphon. 'It's going.'

They heard it bellow.

(Distant. Fading.)

Miphon ran upstairs. Phyphor followed close behind, panting as they burst out into the night air. The walls of the fort lay in ruins. Blocks of stone had been flung through the air as the flame trench, exploding, cleansed itself of the debris of four thousand years in a single convulsive spasm. Now the flame trench was alive, flames raging for half a league between mountain and

24

sea. Heat beat against their faces. The clouds above smouldered with bloodlight reflections.

'Are you hurt?' said Miphon.

'My hands are burnt a little,' said Phyphor.

'Over here,' said Miphon, leading him from the fort to find water where he could cool his singed hands.

'Where's the dragon?' said Phyphor.

'Far away now,' said Miphon. 'Far away. It won't be back. It's hurt. The rocks thrown by the blast hurt it.'

'Will it die?'

'I don't know. But it won't be back. It won't be back.'

The ground trembled underfoot; they smelt torn earth, the stink of dragon, the dust of splintered rock; heat and light from the fire dyke beat against their faces. They heard the roar of flames, the hiss of rain boiling as it struck fire, waves from the sea exploding into steam.

Garash joined them.

'The dragon?' said Garash.

'It's gone,' said Miphon.

'How long will the flames burn for?' said Garash, who knew the answer – fifty days at least, and maybe longer – but half-hoped that someone would tell him different.

'Too long,' said Phyphor. 'We'll have to find a way over the mountains.'

Where the flame-trench ran out into the sea for a hundred paces, the waters seethed and boiled. Lacking a boat strong enough to venture out into those turbulent waters – lacking, indeed, any boat at all – the wizards could not outflank the flame trench on the seaward side.

'Mountains!' said Garash, spitting out the word with disgust.

'We could swim,' ventured Miphon.

'You could, perhaps,' said Garash. 'I've never learnt to play fish.'

Garash, having wasted all his accumulated power in trying to kill the dragon, felt weak and exhausted. He felt, obscurely, that Phyphor had somehow tricked him. After all, Phyphor had finally driven off the dragon simply by calling out the Words which had made the fire dyke erupt. Garash could have done as much, if he had thought of it. He was comforted by knowing he still had power stored in the shrivelled twist of wood hung round his neck, power he had stored there during dull days in the Castle of Controlling Power.

'I couldn't venture the swim either,' said Phyphor. 'So it'll have to be the mountains.'

CHAPTER THREE

Name: Heenmor.

Occupation: wizard.

Status: Master wizard of the order of Arl. A renegade wanted dead – most definitely dead – by the Confederation of Wizards.

Description: a massive, troll-shouldered giant, twice the height of any ordinary mortal. Black eyes, blue beard and ginger hair. Robes of khaki, boots of white leather.

Career: most notable exploit was his organisation of an expedition to loot an artefact of power from the Dry Pit in the Forbidden Zone. His companions either died in the Dry Pit or were murdered by Heenmor afterwards; notes found in their archives alerted the Confederation of Wizards to Heenmor's misdeeds.

* * *

'With this, I can conquer the world,' said Heenmor.

He was talking about the stone egg which sat on one corner of the table: a sullen grey weight lit by dull light from the twelve firestones which studded the walls of this chamber high in the Tower of the order of Arl. The everlast ochre light cast no shadows.

'Aren't you interested?' said Heenmor, in a voice which mocked his opponent.

Elkor Alish, warrior of Rovac, said nothing, but studied the wizards and the warriors arrayed on the chess board. In chess, as in real life, a wizard had a hundred times the power of a warrior – but wizards could still be killed.

27

'Aren't you interested?' said Heenmor again. 'Believe me: the death-stone has power enough to conquer the world.'

Alish raised his eyes.

'What exactly does it do?'

* * *

'I'd love to know what Heenmor's taken from the Dry Pit,' said Garash, stumbling along a punishing mountain trail. 'I'd love to know what it does.'

'We'll find out soon enough,' said Phyphor.

'I only hope it's something worth risking our lives for.'

'We're not in this for personal gain!' said Phyphor sharply.

'No, no, of course not,' said Garash hastily.

Then went sprawling as a stone slipped beneath his feet.

'Test each stone before you trust it,' said Miphon.

Garash swore, and ignored him.

'I'd still like to know,' said Garash, 'Just what it is and what it does.'

* * *

'So you'd like to know?' said Heenmor.

'Yes,' said Elkor Alish.

'Ah,' said Heenmor, 'That's . . . that's a secret.'

And Heenmor smiled.

When Alish had been initiated into the Code of Night, they had told him this: remember that the wizard, scorning us, is apt to forget how fast your sword can end his life. Alish had never forgotten – which was why, face to face with the ancient enemy, he matched Heenmor time and again at chess, enduring the wizard's contempt.

But what was the death-stone? What did it do? Why

28

was it so important? Why did Heenmor boast about it?

'Why do you invite me here so often?' said Alish.

'Perhaps I just like a game of chess,' said Heenmor.

'There's more to it than that.'

'You're right. There is. The truth is, I want to recruit a bodyguard. You, perhaps. I want the best. They say you're the best. But is it so? They call you the man who does not shed blood. That's a strange name for a Rovac warrior, isn't it?'

'My name is Elkor Alish.'

'The man who does not shed blood.'

Yes, that was what they called him now. But in the Cold West, men had known him by other names: Red Terror, Bloodsword, He Who Walks, Our Lord Despair. In the Cold West, he had been a great mercenary leader, until the day when, sickened of the slaughter, he had chosen to commit himself to the vows of the Code of Night: to destroy the ancient enemy and take the continent of Argan for the people of Rovac.

'I can kill if I have to,' said Alish.

'I've seen no proof of it,' said Heenmor.

Alish focused on the chess pieces: castles, merchants, sages, wizards, warriors, hell-banes, battering rams – and the Neversh, each with six wings, each with two feeding spikes reminiscent of the tusks of the mammoths of the Cold West. He remembered hunting mammoths with Gorn, Falmer and Morgan Hearst. Falmer was dead now: may the deep hell be gentle on his soul.

'Why are you telling me about the death-stone?' said Alish.

'To tempt you to my service,' said Heenmor. 'Believe me: the stone egg gives me power enough to conquer the world. Serve me, and you'll be richly rewarded.'

'With such power, what do you need me for?'

'To protect me from my enemies. Certain wizards are on my track. Jealousy makes them murderous. They wish to kill me for the death-stone.'

29

'If it makes you so powerful, what do you need me for?'

'When my enemies come, I'll have to flee,' said Heenmor. 'I need time yet to perfect my mastery of the death-stone. Till then, I need a bodyguard. It takes more than one pair of eyes to watch out the night.'

'I have a job already.'

'What? Guarding Prince Comedo? Guarding that little smear of excrement that vaunts itself as a prince of the favoured blood? Is that the height of your ambition?'

'How can you, a wizard, dare recruit a Rovac warrior?'

'I dare anything,' said Heenmor smoothly. 'I know your oath will bind you, if you enter my service.'

Heenmor's lethal copper-strike snake was coiled on one side of the table, watching. The death-stone sat on the other side. Alish knew himself fast enough to kill the wizard or the snake. But not both. Reaching to the chess board, he moved one of the Neversh to confront one of Heenmor's wizards. Heenmor moved the threatened piece out of range.

'Perhaps Morgan Hearst will accept my offer,' said Heenmor. 'He's a warrior's warrior. I've watched him matching swords with that peasant, Durnwold. Training troops for the spring – and the war Comedo's promised him. He's a killer, isn't he? You can see it in his eyes. Maybe he's my man.'

'Ask him and see,' said Alish.

Would Hearst yield to temptation? Surely not. A Rovac warrior could never pledge himself to a wizard. Alish studied the chess board, trying to work out how to kill Heenmor's two remaining wizards.

'Alish,' said Heenmor, 'All I need is a little time. Then I'll have perfect control of the death-stone. That means power. Enough power to rule the world – or destroy it. Join me. Serve me. What's the choice? To stay here? In Estar? Here is almost like being nowhere.

Winter's ending. My enemies are coming – I'm sure of it. Make your choices, Alish!'

Alish smoothed his hands over his long black hair, thinking carefully. If he struck at Heenmor, the snake would kill him, but what if he grabbed for the stone egg sitting so near to hand?

Heenmor gestured at the stone egg.

'The man who rules this rules everything,' said Heenmor. 'Even if he can't rule himself.'

Alish hesitated – then snatched up the death-stone.

Heenmor laughed.

'So,' he said, 'You do have ambition.'

The stone egg felt cool and heavy.

'See the script on the side of the death-stone?' said Heenmor. 'Any wizard can read it. Raise the death-stone above your head. Say the Words. Do it!'

Alish looked at the characters cut into the stone egg: cursive scrolls, loops and hooks, shapes that imitated worm-casts or the convolutions of the intestines. They meant nothing to him.

Heenmor laughed again.

Suddenly the death-stone kicked, as if it was a living heart.

'Use it now,' said Heenmor. 'Use it – or if you hold it any longer it will kill you.'

Alish threw down the stone, scattering the chess pieces. The snake raised its head and stared at him.

'One day I'm going to kill you,' said Alish. 'One day I'm going to kill every wizard in the world.'

Heenmor laughed, as one might laugh at a child.

CHAPTER FOUR

Salt Road: main trading route serving the continent of Argan, the Ravlish Lands and the Cold West.

Starting at the Castle of Controlling Power by Drangsturm, runs north through the cities of Narba, Veda, Selzirk and Runcorn, through the lands of Chorst, Dybra and Estar, then into the Penvash Peninsular.

Turning west, reaches the Penvash Channel then proceeds through the Ravlish Lands to the city of Chi'ash-lan and the Cold West.

Goods traded along the Salt Road include: salt, silk, slaves, animals, hides, gold, silver, lead, copper, bronze, keflo shell, linen, hemp, glass, crystal, wood, wool, quernstones, lodestones, leeches, sponges, olive oil, lemons, citrons, coconuts, rare birds, amber and ambergris.

News, rumour, gossip and slander also, of course, travel the Salt Road.

*　　*　　*

'Phyphor, it's too much for me,' said Garash. 'Can't we rest? Can't we stop?'

Phyphor trudged on, in silence, his eyes downcast. His walk was little more than a survival stagger. The long days spent labouring over the mountains then navigating across open country to regain the Salt Road had worn him to his bones.

'Slave driver,' muttered Garash.

That was about the worst insult one wizard could offer another. When Phyphor did not respond, Miphon took his hand. It was cold, like a bit of dead wood.

'Phyphor . . .''

The old wizard did not resist as Miphon drew him to the shelter of a clump of roadside trees.

'What's his problem?' said Garash.

'Too much wet, wind and road,' said Miphon.

Acutely aware that there would be nobody to help them if Phyphor began to slip into a death-stupor, Miphon gathered wood, lit a fire, heated a little gruel then fed it to Phyphor, who mumbled it down without resistance. It was the last of their food. They had eaten scarcely enough to warm their skeletons over the last few days.

Phyphor recovered quickly with the help of campfire warmth and gruel. Wizards had resources not given to ordinary men; though he had reached the edge of death, he was soon insisting that they press on. As they tramped north, Miphon engaged him in conversation from time to time to gauge his condition.

Phyphor was still holding up well when late afternoon brought them to the hamlet of Delve – a collection of squatdwellings crouching in the wetrot shadows of trees that choked a narrow gully. No dragon could have seen the hamlet from the air; it was almost invisible from the road.

The wizards knew what they would find: doors that stooped as low as the aching curve of rheumatism, rooves of sodden thatch, dark interiors cluttered with animals, floors of septic mud and manure, and people with the similar squinting eyes and chinless faces that come from generations of drunken fathers ramming their daughters against the walls.

First to greet them was a small black dog which raced through the mud so full of teeth and fury that Miphon at first thought it was rabid. It flung itself at them. Phyphor caught it with his staff, knocking it sideways into a tree. It lay in the rain as if stunned, then slowly crawled away, dragging its hindquarters.

People began to appear in doorways: old women with faces like those of smoke-shrivelled shrunken heads, young men picking at their teeth in a meditative way, a young woman with the bulging belly of a pregnancy near term. None of them said anything. They stood in the doorways as if they had been there all their lives staring out into the rain.

Finally a girl-child came splashing through the mud.

'Galish?' she said.

'No,' said Miphon, in the Trading Tongue.

'Not Galish, what?' said the girl.

'Wizards,' said Miphon.

The girl laughed. She flicked mud at them with one of her small bare feet. Garash growled; Phyphor hushed him.

'Where can we get a bed for the night?' said Miphon.

'Where?'

'A bed? For the night? Where?'

'Where what?'

'Where sleep,' said Miphon hopefully. 'Where sleep.'

'Sleep. Oh, sleep!'

The girl rocked up and down on her toes in the mud, which had splashed up her legs to her knees. She stuck the tip of her tongue between her teeth and waited. Miphon brought out a small coin, a bronze bisque from the Rice Empire, with the crescent moon on one side and the disc of the sun on the other. He held it out. The girl snatched it, quick as a frog whipping a fly from the sky. She smuggled it through layers of rags till it lay in some secret hiding place next to her skin.

'Sleep,' she said, and led them to one of the houses, stamping occasionally so that mud and water flew through the air around her. 'Sleep.'

Peering into the house, the wizards saw a smoking fire and a big wooden table in which hollows had been gouged into which soup could be ladled – this household was too poor to afford food bowls. A man lumbered out of the interior gloom and placed himself in the doorway.

'Galish?' he said.

'No,' said Miphon. 'Are you an innkeeper?'

'Certain, yes.'

'We'd like to stay here for the night if we may.'

'Who might you be then?' said the man, checking the size of his nose with his thumb.

'We're from the south,' said Miphon.

'South is where you're from, but who are you?'

'My style is Phyphor, master wizard of the order of Arl, which has rank among the highest of the eight orders,' said Phyphor.

Phyphor had learnt the Galish Trading Tongue from a wizard who had learnt it from a book; he had let Miphon do most of the talking on their journey north.

'Are we in understanding?' said Phyphor.

'I understand,' said the innkeeper, 'And you?'

He pointed at Garash.

'My style is Garash. Have a care, lest my wrath breed toward destruction. Stand ajar to let us in; spread straw overhead the mud.'

A woman inside the house, who was tending the smoking fire, cackled. Garash swung his head toward her. His protuberant eyes peered suspiciously at her gloomy corner.

'Why is that wet crack laughing?' he said.

'It's a joke to think we've got straw to throw on the floor at this end of a hard winter and a wet spring,' said the innkeeper. 'You now, young one. Who are you?'

'E'parg Miphon,' said Miphon, naming himself with the immaculate Galish of a constant traveller. 'We'd be grateful to have the pleasure of your fireside.'

'Gratitude is all my soul, as the crel said to the egg,' quoth the innkeeper. The word 'crel' was unknown to the Galish Trading Tongue, but Miphon did not ask for a translation, for the innkeeper made his meaning clear enough: 'You, my pretties, must pay with a pretty, for what costs a pretty isn't bought with a word.'

35

'We've got money enough,' said Garash belligerently, thus compromising their position for the subsequent bargaining.

The innkeeper, standing dry inside the doorway, got the better of the haggling; the wizards, outside in the rain, were eager to get under cover. With money paid, they went in and pulled up stools by the fire. Phyphor pulled off his boots, which were starting to tear apart, and stuck his wrinkled feet close to the fire. It burnt too low for his liking, but he knew the innkeeper would not want to burn more wood than he had to.

'We have more money,' said Miphon, 'If you can get us bread and wine.'

They settled the price: a small dorth, a coin with an ear of wheat on each side, which had travelled with the wizards all the way from Selzirk. The innkeeper spoke to the old woman in Estral, the native tongue of Estar – unintelligible to the wizards – and the two went out into the rain.

No sooner had they gone than Phyphor shoved his staff into the fire and muttered. Flames shot up. The chimney blazed briefly as soot caught fire, then Phyphor muttered again and the flames dampened down a little.

When the innkeeper and the old woman returned, the innkeeper grunted when he saw the fire, and looked suspiciously at the wizards.

'Your fires,' said Phyphor, 'It burns well.'

'Yes,' said the innkeeper. 'Here be food. Here be drink.'

The bread was hard and unleavened; the wine tasted like vinegar. Even so, the wizards ate ravenously and drank deep, sating their hollow hunger.

'You've had many fires along the Salt Road,' said Miphon casually.

'The hills are burnt, yes. The dragon ran amok – no man has asked it why. Hearsay tells the dragon breathed on the steamer to south to fire it up. A hunter gone south saw the steamer spit lightning at the dragon. Next thing, the steamer was all in flames. Blocks the road. Bad for trade, that. Did you venture the mountains?'

'Yes,' said Miphon. 'It was a long journey. But wizards are used to long journeys. We heard of another wizard who's been this way. Heenmor's his name.'

'Heenmor, eh?' said the innkeeper. 'It's not a name we know much of in these parts . . .'

'Oh,' said Miphon, and that was all he said.

Miphon took off his boots and massaged his feet slowly, working some warmth into them.

'Midwinter we heard a tell of Heenmor,' said the innkeeper. 'Not that I believe a word of the tell.'

'What you don't believe we won't trouble you for,' said Miphon. 'Pass the wine, please.'

Midwinter tales were not worth the money: it was the beginning of spring, and winter tales would not tell them if Heenmor was still in Castle Vaunting.

CHAPTER FIVE

Name: Morgan Gestrel Hearst.

Birthplace: the islands of Rovac.

Occupation: bodyguard to Prince Comedo of Estar.

Status: a hero of the wars of the Cold West, veteran soldier of Rovac, Chevalier of the Iron Order of the city of Chi'ash-lan, blood-sworn defender of Johan Meryl Comedo of Estar.

Description: lean clean-shaven man of average height, age 35, hair grey, eyes grey.

Career: going off to the wars at age 14, served variously in lands north and south of Rovac, then spent 10 years in the Cold West under the command of Elkor Alish. Subsequently followed Alish to Estar.

*　　*　　*

The day was dying. In Hearst's room in Castle Vaunting, the fire had not been lit; it was cold.

'What do you want?' said Hearst, as Alish entered.

'I'm here to see how you are,' said Alish.

'Oh? And what concern is that of yours?'

'Don't be likc that,' said Alish. He picked up the goblet Hearst had been drinking from. 'What's this?'

'A drink.'

Alish sniffed it, tasted it.

'Ganshmed!' he said, naming the vodka by its Rovac name, which translates literally as deathwater.

'So?'

'This is no night for boozing.'

'It's not night yet.'

'Morgan . . . it's a hard enough climb for any man

under any conditions. Drunk, you won't have a chance.'

'It's my life.'

'Listen, Morgan! You were a fool to dare this challenge. That can't be denied. But with that said – why condemn yourself to death before you start. Get to bed. Rest. Sleep. You'll need all your strength tomorrow – and we start early."

'Give me my drink,' said Hearst.

'Morgan, aren't you listening?'

'It's my life.'

'Your life, yes – but the honour of Rovac lives or dies through you.'

'Alish, I'll be dead by noon tomorrow. A piss on the honour of Rovac! Now give me my drink. Come on, give it! By the hell! By the hell, Alish, did you have to hit me so hard?'

'Get up,' said Alish. 'Get up. See? You're halfway legless already. How much have you drunk?'

'Enough,' said Hearst. 'But I can walk straight, talk straight and stick it up straight. Now give me my drink.'

'No. I'd sooner kill you here than see you fall tomorrow because you're drunk.'

'Kill me?' roared Hearst.

And lugged his sword Hast from the scabbard. That sword was a miracle of metalwork, but the hands that held it were in no condition to wield it.

'Draw!' growled Hearst. 'Draw, you god-rot hero!'

But Alish kept his blade, Ethlite, sheathed. Slowly, deliberately, he poured Hearst's vodka onto the floor. Hearst lunged for him. Alish sidestepped neatly, then helped him on his way with a shove that sent him crashing into the wall.

Hearst collapsed to the floor, groaning. Alish's resolve hardened: if necessary, he would kill Hearst in the morning rather than let him make a fool of himself in front of Prince Comedo and his minions. Once they

39

had been friends: but Hearst had long since lost the right to Alish's friendship.

Alish opened the door, slipped outside and beckoned to the man who stood waiting in the corridor.

'Durnwold,' said Alish, 'You were right to call me: he's in a bad way. But I can't do anything for him. You try. If he stops drinking and gets to sleep, he'll have a chance tomorrow. Otherwise . . . '

'I understand,' said Durnwold, nodding. 'I'll do what I can.'

Alish left; Durnwold entered Hearst's room.

Morgan Hearst sat on the bed, hands supporting his head. He looked up, then looked away.

Durnwold picked up the sword Hast and turned it over in his hands. It was a true battle-sword, forged generations ago by the smiths of Stokos. It was made of firelight steel, which, consisting of interwoven layers of high carbon and low carbon steel, is light, strong and flexible, and will never fail in battle.

'It's a fine blade,' said Durnwold.

'A fine blade, yes,' said Hearst, his voice dull.

The steel had been etched with vinegar to bring out the grain; patterns as various as the shapings of the sea snaked along the blade as Durnwold displayed it to the last of the daylight.

'I held that blade at Enelorf,' said Hearst.

'You told me.'

'I've no fear in battle, you know.'

'I know it.'

'We've been through many battles together, blood-sword Hast and Morgan Hearst.'

'Yes,' said Durnwold. 'It's a fine blade indeed. A warrior's weapon. A weapon too good to leave for a prince'.

'Yes,' said Hearst, his face now lost in shadow. 'Far too good for a prince.'

'We ride to war soon,' said Durnwold. 'You've trained me. I was born a peasant, but, given free choice,

40

I'd rather be your battle-companion. Tell me, am I good enough?'

Hearst did not answer for a while. Then he spoke, out of the darkness:

'You have the makings of a warrior. All you need now is the battles to harden you. And I could wish no better companion than you to ride with me. But I've heard so much of your talk of the sheep, the farm, the peat, your brother Valarkin, your sisters spinning wool – I thought yours was a peasant's heart forever.'

'I can't help my past,' said Durnwold, 'But I have the will to help my future. My future lies with yours.'

'Give me my sword then,' said Hearst, reaching from darkness to darkness. 'Strength and steel, hey? Yes. I'll do it. The climb and the kill. I'll do them both.'

CHAPTER SIX

Pox: vernacular name used for a number of diseases characterised by eruptive sores, but in particular for syphilis.

Pox doctor: one who heals or purports to heal venereal diseases such as syphilis, gonorrhoea etc. etc.

* * *

In Castle Vaunting, night brought sleep to the warrior Morgan Hearst, who was due to face his doom on the morrow.

In the hamlet of Delve, night brought sleep also to the wizards Phyphor and Garash, who ensconced themselves in a loft. But Miphon stayed awake, for he was needed for doctor work.

Even here in Delve, the people had heard the legends of the Alliance of wizards and heroes four thousand years and more before, the Alliance which had fought so long and hard against the Swarms. However, whatever legend, song or rumour might say, most folk credited wizards with no magic. Their standing was low, for they were best known as pox doctors. Most people had no chance to unlearn their ignorance, for wizards came seldom to Estar, and, though Delve knew of Heenmor, it was only by hearsay.

The last wizard to visit Delve had been a young apprentice discarded by his tutor because of his poor scholarship and his inability to build and control power through the Meditations. He had been scraping a living as a healer, though his studies of the healing arts were far from complete.

Such incompetent failures were the wizards most frequently seen by men, and, encountering such a novice, a young man blinking behind wire-rimmed spectacles, shuffling his feet, stuttering, travelling burdened with herbs, leeches, divining rods, poultices, eye of newt and ear of bat, it was hard to credit the seventh oldest profession with any importance.

Phyphor, however, was powerful, dangerous, and, of course, very old; the ages of wizards, though measured in fewer years than the ages of rock, outshadow the mayfly lives of common men. Garash was younger, but still very dangerous.

These two did not lance boils, perform abortions, repair hymens or draw teeth. They had not devoted themselves to the High Arts in order to labour over ingrowing toenails. Their hands held the powers of thunder; they had mastered the Names and the Words; they had learnt the Four Secrets and the Nine Mysteries; they had the harsh pride of those who follow the most rigorous of intellectual disciplines. They were meant for greatness: but wherever they went, young men would come slinking up to them to beg cures for oozing chancres, and furtive young women would bring them their tears and fears. They would never shake the appellation of pox doctor, even though they had done nothing to earn it.

Of the three, only Miphon had really studied the gentle skills of healing; only he was humble enough to put himself at the service of the common people.

That night, there was a birth. As the local midwife had lately died of septicaemia, Miphon served as accoucheur, delivering the child with aplomb. It was the easiest birth he had ever attended – and he had seen many in the families of the Landguard of the Far South. As always, he felt joy at this most common yet most profound of all miracles. As it has been Written (in Kalob IV, quilt 9, section 3b, line xxii): 'The greatest Heights yield to those who stoop the Lowest'. Miphon, reaching those Heights, was amply rewarded.

The people credited him with the easy birth, though in fact he had done little except be there to catch the baby. He was honoured by being asked to name the perfect girl-child who had just joined humanity.

'I name her Smeralda,' said Miphon, giving her the nicest name he knew.

'May we know who she is named after?'

'A good person,' said Miphon, thinking quickly. Who'd choose to be named after a deceased donkey? He improvised: 'A princess of Selzirk, pride of the Harvest Plains.'

This satisfied everyone.

Miphon got little sleep, for Phyphor woke in the early-early, and forced them to set off down the road by darkness. Proper food and a proper bed had rejuvenated him; he was eager to close with Castle Vaunting and finish their business with the wizard Heenmor.

And so it was that three Forces left Delve by night, all Powers in the World of Events, Lights in the Unseen Realm, Graduates of the Trials of Strength, Motivators of History, masters of lore versed in the logic of the Cause and the nature of the Beginning. And the peasants of Delve, despite their gratitude for the successful birth, told rude pox doctor jokes when the wizards were gone, then returned to the pleasures of seducing their sisters and scratching the boils on their backsides and the lice in their hair.

CHAPTER SEVEN

Dragon: large scale-armoured egg-laying fire-breathing carnivore, not to be confused with the sea serpent of the Central Ocean or the taniwha of Quilth. Dragons are not related to the colony creatures of the Swarms but are related – distantly – to the phoenix and the basilisk, and – very distantly – to the platypus. There are three types:

1. Common or land dragon: very large, inimical, extremely destructive aviator of limited intelligence, typically leading a solitary, cave-dwelling existence;

2. Sea dragon: flightless, intelligent, gregarious creature noted for vanity and promiscuity. Robust swimmer, but mates on land – frequently. Properly flattered, is relatively harmless, but if scorned becomes extremely dangerous;

3. Imperial dragon: lithe, sinuous, domesticated flying dragon of Yestron, where it is famed for its gentle nature and plaintive song. Extremely susceptible to all those diseases which affect bees, it also swiftly becomes alcoholic if exposed to temptation.

* * *

Alish, watching the rising stars, judged the night half gone. It was time to set out. Hearst, roused from sleep, was soon asleep in the saddle; he did not wake again until they were nearly at Maf, ten leagues south of Castle Vaunting.

Waking, he found that words already dared by Prince Comedo's jester began to nag through his head:

45

Sing now the song of Hearst the dung,
A drunkard with a braggart's tongue.

Now Hearst he thought that pigs could fly,
When wine-cups he had gundled,
So pumped his loins and puffed his boasts,
Then off to Maf he trundled.
But Hearst found pigs can't reach the sky:
No dragon had he fondled
When slipped his foot to fill his mouth,
And screaming he fell down to land,
Spread wide across the grinning rocks:
The place which now the seagull mocks.

Sing now the song of Hearst the dung,
Unmastered by his pride and tongue,
Split from his crutch to his boasting lung,
No prettier than what the seagull done.

The song had found popular appeal with Comedo's
men, a rag-tag rabble of bandits, pirates, assorted thugs
and deserters. Later, no doubt, they would have time to
make a longer, bawdier, funnier song.

Their drinking doggerel would tell of how, a few
days after the dragon Zenphos raged across Estar, the
wizard Heenmor fled the castle. Prince Comedo,
desiring revenge for insults and injuries the castle had
suffered, sent Morgan Hearst out wizard-hunting with
nineteen mounted men. But when his horse fell lame,
he missed the kill – and it was the men who died, not
the wizard.

Hearst's temper – never a steady beast, that temper –
had grown stormy in the days of lame-foot limp-foot
jokes that followed, leading him to drink more than he
should have to ease that temper to its nightly sleep.

Finally Morgan Hearst, scourge of the Cold West,
had sat at the card table with a full skin to lose money,
shirt and sword to the young fool Prince Comedo.

Hearst – drunken, boastful, vain – had made one last gamble: 'This one last wager I'll make with you on the turn of the next card, and if I win I'll reclaim all I've lost, and if I lose . . .'

– Ah yes, you lost, didn't you, bird-dung, and that's why you're here.

For this was the wager: 'If I lose, I'll go to Maf to scale the cliff that daunts the eagle's wing; I'll raid the lair where the dragon Zenphos lives; I'll bring you the red ruby of legend which the wizard Paklish set in the dragon's head, after the sage Ammamman tore the left eye from its socket.'

Thus the wager.

– So. It's done. Now for the death.

He had known the wager for madness even as he made it, but he had been too proud to retract it. They would have laughed at him. He was strong, and brave, but a laugh could wound him to the marrow.

– They would have laughed at you, and made rude jokes about you, and talked for generations about the wager Morgan Hearst made in his cups, and had to retract in shame.

– But they'll joke away regardless, after you fall. They'll call you a zany fool, a drunken clown.

– They'll be right.

Already, he could imagine, in precise detail, the disaster which lay ahead of him. He knew that he was doomed. He was sober for the climb, but he was sure it would make no difference.

In the half-light before sunrise, they saw the bones of men, cattle, a small whale, a juvenile sea serpent. The horses, picking their way over the stony ground to the southern face of Maf, grew uneasy; finally Durnwold's baulked, and he had to dismount and lead it by foot.

All too soon, they were there.

'Rise, sun!' cried Comedo.

The sun obeyed.

'Your sword,' said Comedo to Hearst, as the sun

splayed their long shadows across the ground.

Hearst yielded the blade.

'But remember,' said Hearst, 'I regain it if I succeed.'

'If?' said Comedo. 'You venture an If? You disappoint me.'

Hearst grimaced, but said nothing as the prince brandished the battle-sword Hast, a weapon as famous as the warrior Morgan Hearst. Avor the Hawk had dared many battles with that blade, never finding any man to match him. A woman had killed him in the end – his seventh wife had poisoned him when he discarded her for an eighth. After that, the sword had come to Hearst, who had carried it year after year in the Cold West, till it was as much a part of him as his arm.

– Hast, my sword, my strength, my half-brother, my brother in blood.

'Why linger, friend?' said Comedo. 'Remember, up is hard, but down is easy – all you have to do is jump.'

And he laughed. For Comedo, life was full of occasions for merriment. His executioner provided him with many of them.

– He laughs. He laughs at you, Morgan Hearst, leader of men. Yes. But with good reason.

Durnwold came to Hearst.

'I'll wait for you,' said Durnwold.

'You may have to wait a long time.'

'I'll wait. Trust me.'

'I do,' said Hearst.

Then glanced at Alish, who sat silently on his horse. The sun shone on his long black hair, his embroidered cloak, his golden jewellery. Hearst knew Alish could have shinned up this mountain, making the climb seem effortless. Only a face of sheer ice or sheer glass could have defeated him. But then, Alish was not afraid of heights.

'We're waiting,' said Comedo, who was getting bored.

'I know, my prince,' said Hearst.

48

And turned to face the mountain.

*   *   *

The wide world turns. The entire continent of Argan now lies in sunlight; the edge of dawn moves slowly westward across the Central Ocean toward Rovac and the Cold West. While Hearst labours up the rockwalls of Maf, an isolated mountain spike in the north-west of Argan, the cities of the continent are waking in the morning light.

In the free port of Runcorn, the Common Gates are opened; in Androlmarphos, dominating the delta of the Velvet River, the harbour chains are removed; in Selzirk, the kingmaker Farfalla – named for the moth – rises to her daily rituals.

Further to the south, in Veda, stronghold of the sages, the Masters are at study; the troops of the Secular Arm man Veda's battlements and drill on the training grounds. Further South again, Landguard patrols prowl the Far South. By Drangsturm, the turrets and towers of the spectacular upthrust of the Castle of Controlling Power mass against the light; beyond the Great Dyke, in the Deep South, small bands of Southsearchers in the land of Swarms settle down to wait out the dangers of the day.

Hearst climbs, his danger increasing from moment to moment, but the life of the world will continue whether he gains the heights or falls. Win or lose, succeed or fail, the world will go on without him, and well he knows how little he matters to the world as he struggles up the cliff face.

It is the loneliest hour of his life.

*   *   *

There was a crack up there. It would give him a handhold, if he could reach it.

49

– Can you reach it, little man? No. It's out of reach.

– Look down. Come on. I dare you. Look down. Yes, yes, that's right. Down.

He looked down, to see a flash of white sliding through the air far below his feet. A gull. On the rocks below the gull, a few small specks dotted the rocks: men. His comrades.

– So they're waiting. Some of them, at least. But what does it matter? You'll never see them again unless you reach that handhold.

He was exhausted. It was too far to climb back down.

– You'll never reach that handhold.

Never.

The sweat from his last exertions had dried on his body. The wind which had harried him earlier in the day had gone to torment some other place, but the air was still cold. He was cold.

– Colder still when dead, no doubt.

He could not reach that stronghold, that handhold, that griphold which would secure him against that five-scream fall. It was impossible. This was the end.

– Any regrets? Many. But at least nobody else will die because of this foolishness. None other was fool enough to join this climb. Not even Durnwold.

He was facing his end. And he was facing it alone.

– Bereft of strength, and far away my friends.

His legs were trembling. If he let go it would all be finished. It would be so easy to let go. He would slip back into the air that was softer than feathers. He would fall.

So easy.

His head hurt where a falling rock had clipped it earlier in the climb. The short-cropped hair there was stiff with blood. He had dried blood on his fingers, torn by grappling with the cliff.

He was so tired.

So cold.

If he let go, no more pain. No more fear. It would all be over. But they would make rude songs about him.

They would liken him to spattered bird dung.

– Look up.

– Look up, arse-wipe. Up!

– How far?

– Only thirty paces.

Only thirteen paces to the dragon's lair. There were ten leagues to a march - twenty thousand paces – and often he had made two marches between sunrise and sunset. Would thirty paces defeat him now? If he had been a man-sized fly he could have walked those thirty paces on a single breath of air.

– Look up.

– The only chance is up. Will the left hand hold you?

The left hand held him. He stretched. The handhold was out of reach. But only just. Should he jump? It wasn't far. But when a man is on a cliff-face where even to flex his knees may be precarious, when he has climbed so far, with so much pain, with so much fear . . .

– But there's no other choice.

– So jump!

Hearst boosted himself up, to find his fear had previously cramped him to a crouch even when he thought he was at full stretch. He gained the handhold. One hand on. Two!

Easy.

His feet slipped, scrabbled, then found their resting place. Then slipped again. Then half his handhold crumbled away to nothing. His left hand clawed at the air. He was hanging by one hand only. His fingers began to slide.

Then his flailing hand found a crevice.

– Hold me, woman-rock.

It held.

His feet found purchase. Two hands on. Two feet on. And he could see his next handhold. He reached for it, gained it. Up. To the next. The next. He climbed, animated by a burst of fury, raging at himself for letting

51

fear trick him into thinking he needed to jump for that crucial handhold – appalled at how close he had come to throwing his life away.

Climbing with a furious effort which threatened to burst his heart, he reached a crack running vertically to the gaping cleft which was the entrance to the dragon's lair. The chimney widened; he wedged his body inside it, and rested. His rage died away, replaced by shuddering exhaustion.

– Cling to the rock. Cling to the rock. Like darkness, like mother. Like warmth and hot milk after cold rain; like mother. Is that part of the warrior's way? Longing for milk and for mother? Is it? What are you, Hearst?

– I'm here. And it's not far now. Not far.

– But what about climbing down again? What about that? Look down.

– No. Don't look down. Not now. Climb.

He climbed. Past a trace of green moss. Past a tract of crumbling rock. Up now, up. And what was that stink? Dragon, surely.

– And what if he roars out now, in his fury, Zenphos with his wings unfurling and gouts of flame hurling from his mouth? Then that will be the end, man-leader, that will be the end.

– But at least the climb is finished.

He gained level rock, and collapsed in the mouth of the cave. Some men called him fearless, and certainly he would dare all and any, sword against sword. Many challengers had died with his cold eyes watching them. In battle he seemed tireless; his voice never faltered, even when the battle went against his forces. So he was called fearless: but he had his fears, and heights was one of them. The first stretch of the cliff had almost brought him to collapse, and by now he had been climbing for more than half a day.

For some time, he lay in the mouth of the dragon's lair without the power of sight or thought. When he recovered, the sun was still riding in the sky; his first thought was to look down.

– That would be a mistake.

– But if you don't look down, you will always remember that you were afraid to look down.

He looked down.

Beneath his feet the sky dropped away to the barren land: rolling country stretching south for thirty leagues to where the Barley Hills smudged the horizon. Sun flashed on water; Estar, with its peat soils and heavy winter rains, was a country of tarns, pools, brooks, streams and swamps. He could see the Salt Road running on a north-south line to the west of Maf; he could see the Central Ocean leagues beyond, and the charred remains of burnt trees, looking no larger from this height than little black beard bristles.

If he had slipped, his body would have crunched to a bloody skinful of offal when it hit the rocks. Spasms shook his body as memories assailed him. He knew he could never climb down. He closed his eyes.

– Open your eyes. The time is now.

It was time to die. The sayings had it that a man facing a dragon was as an infant confronted by the strength of an armed and armoured adult, like a leaf in the face of a forest fire. Hearst did not doubt it. He unshipped the spear from his back. A short spear, not man-high but child-high. No weapon for a warrior: but what else could he have carried up that face of terror? His sword, of course: but Comedo had his sword.

His stomach was empty, his mouth dry; he had carried nothing to eat or drink. At least he would not be spattered like bird-dung on the rocks. At least men would know that he had met his end as a warrior. There would be no jokes: only speculation, bad dreams and dread.

He advanced, breathing heavily though the air stank. What was that sound, like the sea yet unlike? What was that sound, like the sighing in a shell, yet louder? That must be breathing.

53

His eyes adjusted to the gloom.

He saw it.

'Ah,' he said. 'Ah . . .'

– So that's a dragon. That's a dragon. By the purple flames and the singing knives of the fourth hell, the songs don't do the fire-spawn justice. I thought the fear of heights to be my worst, but if I had any water in me I'd be losing it now. I'd say it was big as a longship, except it's bigger. I'd say its talons were like scythes, except they're longer.

– But it is asleep, it is asleep, and you have a chance, Morgan Hearst, son of Avor the Hawk, warrior of Rovac, song-singer, sword-master, leader of men. You have a chance.

He slipped through the gloom. The dragon bulked in mountains above him. Darkness rendered all its colours in grey. Discarded scales the size of dinner plates slithered underfoot as his feet disturbed them. The sound of breathing crowded his ears.

He approached the head. It was hot, it was hot. The vast lips were slightly parted, as if in a snarl, revealing fractions of the razor teeth. Through chinks between the teeth he could see the glow of inner fires, red as a bed of hot coals. One casual belch from that mouth would send him reeling back in a blaze of burning hair and flaming clothing, crisped like bacon.

He looked up. Above and out of reach, gathering light from the shadows, glowed another red light: the huge ruby that filled the empty eye socket. He looked for the other eye. The right eye. There. Only small, weak scales covered the flexible eyelid.

Now.

He took the spear. He sighted. He cast. The spear smashed into the eye. There was a pause. There was the regular sound of breathing. Then the spear was driven back out. It fell on the ground. A torrent of black pus vomited from the hole. Hearst dodged to one side.

The flow eased to a trickle, then to a dribble, then to

nothing. Then from the sunken black sac of that decayed eye came a white worm thick as a man's arm. It quested blindly in the air, then retreated to the death it was feeding on, the body days dead, the stinking corpse which lay there with its mouth full of dying fire.

And still there was the sound of breathing.

*   *   *

The wide world turns. For the continent of Argan, it is late afternoon; in fact, the eastern edge of the continent already lies in darkness. Soon that darkness will cover the entire continent; while Hearst rests in the dragon's lair high in the mountain of Maf, a fang of rock in Estar, the cities of the Argan prepare for sleep.

On the road, travellers – Galish merchants, hunters, pilgrims, wandering musicians, questing heroes, vagrants, lepers and similar riff-raff – are making camp. The wizards Phyphor, Garash and Miphon are half-way between Delve and Maf.

In Selzirk, pride of the Harvest Plains, the kingmaker Farfalla attends to the day's last rituals; in Veda, the Masters of the sages practice Silence. Still further south, Landguard patrols prepare for night and sleep; elsewhere, Southsearchers dream on for a little longer before waking for the night.

The world knows nothing of the ordeal which has tested Morgan Hearst, yet he allows himself the thought that in time he will be known to the whole world that worked its way through these hours of daylight, not knowing they were different to any others.

*   *   *

Hearst grunted, and toppled the ruby into the gulf of evening air. It fell, glimmered briefly, then dropped from sight. Men would know him as a hero now, to be spoken of in the same breath as the dragon Zenphos,

55

the wizard Paklish and the sage Ammamman. The generations would rank him with the heroes of the Long War – or above them. That was some comfort, but not enough to reconcile him with death. Not nearly enough. He could not climb down, but he was not finished yet.

He stretched. His joints ached. He had wintered by the fireside, safe from the cold. He hoped the day of exposure to the wind and chill would not make his joints stiffen. He would be lost if his bones locked up, as they had on occasion in the Cold West. He turned back into the cave, navigating by the sullen glow still smouldering between the jaws of the dead dragon.

Behind the corpse were tunnels through which the air channelled, creating that sighing sea-shell sound of breathing. He would explore methodically, taking every left turn when the tunnel forked. One wrong step might drop him to the bottom of a hidden chasm, so he went shuffle by stoop into the worm-blind darkness, feeling his way.

– Don't fight the dark, seduce it.

The gut-twisted tunnels knotted themselves through the dark. They rose, fell, and corkscrewed sideways. He climbed at least as often as he descended; every down he found turned up. Dehydrated, exhausted, ravenous with hunger, he began to hallucinate, to hear voices, to see lights. He paused to rest, sucking on a small stone to ease his thirst. Then lectured himself onwards.

– On your feet, son of Avor, on your feet.

A derelict wind chanted through his skull. In the wind, he heard the voices of ghosts. He clapped his hands to drive them away. Up ahead, he imagined he saw a star.

– Go away, star.

Another step, another star.

Then a dozen. A hundred. A thousand. The tunnel widened until his arms could not span it. Hearst stepped out under the night sky.

– So we're out.

– We've made it.

– Hast, my half-brother, my brother in blood, we are to be reunited.

But where were the rocks? The trees? Where, for that matter, was the horizon?

Belatedly, he realised that he was not, after all, at the foot of Maf: he was on the summit. He swayed with exhaustion. Stars lay in water in small pools on the mountain top; Hearst, his mouth as dry as ashes, knelt and drank deep. Then, from the edge of a cliffdrop, he surveyed the darkness, which was featureless except where, somewhere, a fire burnt.

Hearst, taking bearings on the stars, judged the fire to lie in the direction of the temple, from which Prince Comedo had withdrawn the traditional protection of his guards after the temple priests, declaring they would kill the dragon, had instead aroused its fury and sent it raging up and down the Salt Road. Was the temple burning? What did he care?

– Sleep, Morgan, sleep. Sleep, and see what the sun has to say. No more walking in the darkness until we have seen the face of the sun at least once more. That will be enough, to see the face of the sun. That will be enough.

He retired to the tunnel, which would shelter him if it rained. Then, exhausted, he slept.

CHAPTER EIGHT

Name: Valarkin (brother of Durnwold).
Birthplace: Little Hunger Farm, Estar.
Occupation: priest of the temple of the Demon of Estar.
Status: acolyte.
Description: a young man with face and nose both narrow; mouth small and teeth sharp; hair and eyes both ratskin brown.

*   *   *

The day after leaving Delve, the wizards passed the brooding cliffs of Maf, which lay east of the Salt Road. The people of Delve had told them of the dragon's lair.

'Can you tell if the dragon's at home?' asked Phyphor.

'At this distance, no,' said Miphon.

One league further north, they came upon the ruins of Estar's temple. Amongst the charred rubble they found one living man, squatting in the ashes by a fire-scarred idol. His clothing, designed for ceremony rather than for use, was dirty and torn. His hands were blistered by the labour of uncovering the idol from the wreckage. One fingernail was bruised sullen black-red.

'Who are you?' asked Phyphor in Galish.

The stranger said nothing, but stared blankly at the idol. It had huge eyes which focused on nothing, broad lips parted to suck and absorb, a vast sagging chin; its fingers were tipped with claws.

'Name yourself!' roared Garash.

The young stranger rocked backwards and forwards, humming words without meaning.

'Stranger,' said Miphon quietly, fingering the idol. 'May we know your name? Please.'

'Valarkin,' murmured the man.

'Who burnt this place?'

'Those who did,' said Valarkin.

Which, though true, was unsatisfactory.

Bodies, many half-cremated, littered the ruins. From one, Garash salvaged an amulet.

'The spider,' said Phyphor, as Garash weighed it in his hand. 'Collosnon soldiers have been here.'

'This has no power,' said Garash with contempt, tossing the amulet to one side.

Miphon fielded it. The amulet was an oval ceramic tile with a neckcord – or the charred remains of one – threaded through a small hole. On the front was a black spider on a green background; on the back was a diamond made of a hundred curious hieroglyphs.

'Can you read this?' said Miphon to Phyphor.

'No,' said Phyphor. 'But only Collosnon soldiers wear those things. I know that much.'

Miphon let the amulet fall. Since they lost the donkey, he had learnt to carry essentials only.

'So the Collosnon have reached Estar,' said Garash. 'Perhaps in time we'll see the master of Tameran march his troops to the Great Dyke.'

Phyphor thought of all the northing they had made – through territory watched by the Landguard, by way of Narba to the Rice Empire, past Veda to the Harvest Plains, then to Selzirk, then Runcorn, then through the mountain kingdoms into Estar.

'No,' he said. 'Never.'

'We fought hard,' said the young Valarkin, speaking up unexpectedly. 'We did our best. But they were too many.'

'Do the Collosnon rule Estar now?' asked Phyphor.

'Not yet,' said Valarkin. 'They attacked here, but

59

they were only a raiding party. The prince's soldiers caught them at it. There was a fight. The Collosnon lost – but all our people were dead by then. Saving me.'

'Were you a priest here?'

'Yes,' said Valarkin. Then added: 'I fought in the defence of the temple. I fought well.'

That was a lie. He had fled when the attack started, hiding in darkness until Comedo's troops had arrived to destroy the Collosnon invaders.

'Valarkin,' said Miphon, 'Can you tell us if the wizard Heenmor is still at Castle Vaunting?'

'We've not talked with the castle since the dragon ravaged the land,' said Valarkin. 'The castle hates us. Because the dragon burnt the country. They blame us for that.'

The dragon, yes. Phyphor looked at the sky. It was almost dayfail.

'Don't worry about the dragon,' said Valarkin. 'You can stay here – many travellers did. Our god kept the dragon away. Anyway, it's dead now. Our god destroyed it.'

'When?' said Garash.

'The night it burned the countryside. That was the night of its death-agony. Are we to blame for that? Gods are for the care of the dead, not the killing of dragons. The prince was warned.'

'About what?' said Garash.

'That there would be dangers. He's to blame. Comedo. We warned him – but he insisted. So the dragon died a noisy death – what difference does it make? Our god killed it. Not instantly – but it's dead all right.'

'Why is the prince angry then?' said Miphon.

'Because it burnt Lorford,' said Valarkin, looking at him with angry eyes gimlet-sharp. 'It burnt the palace stables. He can only seat twenty men on horseback now – there was plenty of roast horsemeat the night the dragon flew.'

60

Hoping the dragon was indeed dead, the wizards began to make camp. Another day should take them to Lorford.

Elsewhere, after a day spent crawling and climbing through mountain tunnels, the Rovac warrior Morgan Hearst emerged into the evening air at the foot of the mountain of Maf. Soon he found Durnwold, who had been keeping vigil, waiting for a sign. Durnwold had kept Hearst's horse with him, as well as his own. As the two men rode toward the Salt Road, they saw a campfire burning in the temple ruins.

Gaining the road, they headed for Lorford; they did not stop to investigate the camp fire, and those warming themselves by its flames thought it wisest not to challenge the two horsemen passing in the night.

CHAPTER NINE

Name: Johan Meryl Comedo, prince of Estar.
Occupation: ruler of Estar.
Status: Class Enemy of the Common People.
Hobbies: preservation of traditional royal prerogatives by way of rape, torture, looting, arson, sundry oppressions of peasants, incarceration without charge or trial, etc. etc.
Description: not quite the man his father was.

*　　*　　*

Ten leagues is an easy day for an army, but the twenty thousand paces from the temple to the town of Lorford taxed the wizards severely. Garash, unwilling to drive himself, slowed them up; it was evening when they reached the town – too late to seek entry to Castle Vaunting.

Valarkin, travelling with the wizards, showed them round this strange town which had been built half by optimists above ground, and half by pessimists below. The pessimists had survived the dragon; the rest of the town was in ruins.

They took shelter in an underground tavern crowded with drunks celebrating the death of the dragon. This excuse for boozing had already lasted a night and a day, but enthusiasm still ran high. The dragon's death meant peace and prosperity – promising beer money for everyone.

The dragon had been killed – or so went the story – by Morgan Hearst, a hero from the west. When Valarkin stood up to dispute this, he was jeered at, then beaten

62

up and thrown outside to lie in the street in the company of a few blind drunk gross green Melski males.

The wizards learnt that some Collosnon soldiers – preparing for an invasion, perhaps? – were raiding in Estar. Nobody lamented the lost temple and its dead priests, but the wiser heads realised that the Collosnon, by burning the temple, had destroyed one of Estar's most powerful defences. Still, they were sure Castle Vaunting could stand against any invaders. What worried them was the flame trench on the southern border, which must delay any Galish convoys coming from that direction.

One man longing for the Galish to arrive was a drunken sea captain from the Harvest Plains. In the autumn, he had sailed from Androlmarphos with a cargo of luxuries for the Ravlish Lands. Attacked by pirates, his ship had escaped, only to be severely damaged by a storm. He had brought it up the Hollern River for repairs, anchoring just below the fords of Lorford.

'My troubles were only starting. My screwrot crew deserted to take service with the prince. This end of winter – the winter cost me pretty, never doubt it – the prince seized my cargo's cream. Six boys – six! The best – young slave boys, trained to service. The temple wanted them for sacrifice. To persuade a god to kill a dragon. We all know what killed what in the end. The prince donated them. Easy for him to give, wasn't it?

'There were women, too – but those went to the prince. He's a fine one for taking. And he's not the only one! The Melski have torn the nails from my ship, working underwater. It's grounded on the riverbed. So here I sit till the Galish come so I can sell what's left – then I'll barefoot back to Runcorn and beyond.'

As an introduction to the habits and practises of Johan Meryl Comedo, this was hardly promising; other stories the wizards heard did nothing to advance him in their favour.

Come morning, they walked up Melross Hill to the black battlements of the castle dominating the heights above Lorford. Although it was spring, the cold wind sang a joyless, bitter song as it cut through chinks and gaps in the walls of the hillside hovels of the servants who worked in the castle but were refused shelter there.

Comedo and his fighting men – and their women – occupied only the castle's gatehouse keep; nobody dwelt in the eight towers of the eight orders of wizards, still sealed against men as they had been through all the centuries since wizards had deserted them. Darkest and tallest was the tower of the Dark Order, the order of Ebber, the order of Shadows, the commanders of dreams and delusions.

Comedo refused to share his keep with his servants, and would not let them build inside the flat area enclosed by the long battlements as he did not want vernacular elements spoiling the classical flow of his castle's interior. Hence the hovels on the hill. Fleabite children stared from shack-shanty doors as the wizards laboured uphill, buffeted by the wind.

'The dragon missed what most needed burning,' said Garash.

The hovels had been built right to the edge of the flame trench which moated the castle. Unlike the fire dyke on Estar's southern border, this trench had never filled with rubble, despite lack of maintenance; it dropped so deep that one could count a falling stone from one to ten before it hit bottom. Where water and wastes were discharged, sprawling green moss followed the moist trail downwards, but far before the bottom of the trench it was too hot for moss to grow.

Writhing red and orange flames simmered at the bottom of the fire dyke. It had been built to last even should the Swarms besiege the castle for five thousand years on end; the passing centuries had not quenched those flames, and, if the right Words were said, they would blaze upward to fill the entire trench for fifty days or more.

Though the flame trench was at its most passive, it was still hot enough for the shack-dwellers to be able to cook meals in metal pots descending on chains a fraction of the way into the depths. A woman emptied a tub of washing water to the gulf; falling, the water boiled to steam.

'I suppose the schtot find living so close to the heat makes infanticide easy,' said Garash; 'schtot' was a pejorative from the Galish Trading Tongue, which he was trying hard to master.

'I suppose so,' said Phyphor, not really listening – he was thinking about the love-labours wizards had lavished on these fortifications built for their personal protection, and what shoddy work they had done on the barriers made during the Long War to stop the northward spread of the Swarms.

'Let's go and test this prince's temper then,' said Garash.

'We'll do no testing unless we have to,' said Phyphor. 'And I'll do the talking. Remember that.'

As they crossed the drawbridge, the wind tried to strip them naked. Ahead rose the seventy levels of the gatehouse keep, pierced by narrow windows and garnished with an eclectic array of corpses in various states of decomposition.

'What charming taste!' said Garash, eyeing the dangling bodies.

'What did you expect?' said Phyphor. 'Sophistication?'

'I expect nothing,' said Garash. 'But I mark the prince is a butcher. Perhaps it might amuse him to add a couple of wizards to his corpse collection.'

'Only two?' said Miphon.

'Make it two wizards and a pox doctor,' said Garash.

'If you want to draw distinctions,' said Miphon, 'Make it one of Nin, one of Arl, and one fat slobbery greedbox.'

'I eat to my best because I've got a mind to nourish,' said Garash with dignity. 'Unlike some.'

'Enough,' said Phyphor, for they had reached the archway at the end of the drawbridge.

Coming in out of the wind, the wizards smelt the stench of rotten meat, decayed vegetables and sewerage, a first token of the squalor of Comedo's court. Looking through the archway – which, though it could be sealed by portcullises, ran the length of the ground floor of the gatehouse keep – they saw some men rebuilding charred wooden buildings in the central court, where the dragon had fired stables, kennels and a banqueting hall.

'Well well,' said one of two guards, stirring himself to stand erect. 'What's this now, walking in on its hind legs?'

'Let me pass,' said Garash.

'Not so hasty,' said the guard. 'Not so hasty.'

'My companion may be hasty,' said Phyphor, 'But he has reason. We do have business which should not be delayed. Let us pass.'

The guard rubbed his nose.

'Let you pass? Indeed I'll let you pass, pass left or right or pass back the way you came, or pass water if you wish, but if you try to pass me by you'll pass beyond the sight of men, right quickly, unless you've got the password or some other passable credentials.'

'I am a wizard,' said Phyphor, letting his iron-shod staff thud against the flagstones.

'A wizard, hey?' said the guard. 'Well, by the Skull of the Deep South, a wizard. I'm sorry to tell you, though, we've got no pox for curing. We've had poxy weather and poxy food, a poxy dull winter and the spring not much better, but the actual smelly little article we don't have in quantity.'

Phyphor thumped his staff again on the flagstones.

'Man,' said Garash, pushing forward, 'Man, do you know – '

Phyphor put out an arm to hold Garash back.

'Well, by my grandmother's sweet brown eye,' said the guard, 'We do have a windy temper here, don't we Bartlom?'

'Yes,' said Bartlom. 'We'll see some magic if we're lucky. I've heard of pox doctor magic. The pox doctors, you see, turn sheep into lovers and pigs into whores.'

'We did have a real wizard once,' said the first guard. 'His name was Heen or Hein or Hay, or some such, if you please. Twice my height, yes, his face as white as ice, his eyes as black as night. He had a snake which killed with a single bite. You're not wizards. You may be pox doctors, but we've no requirement for quacks today. So you can't come in, unless you care to turn me into a frog or a fish.'

'Why change you?' said Garash. 'Nature decided you should be born a pig, so who are we to interfere?'

'That's not nice, Mr Pox,' said the guard, frowning. 'He's not nice at all, is he, Bartlom? Would his tongue improve with cooking, perhaps?'

Phyphor lost patience. His staff swung through the air: once. No exercise of magic could have inflicted a worse injury. Bartlom started to lug out his sword. Phyphor felled him with a blow to the head. He went down and stayed down.

'You did that nicely,' said Garash. 'Like swatting flies.'

'Was there no other way?' said Miphon.

'Why worry about scum like that?' said Garash. 'Their lives are worthless anyway. Time only teaches them to waste time.'

'Come!' said Phyphor, venturing in under the first portcullis.

Somewhere, someone was shouting, his voice echoing in the distance:

'Andranovory! Get your drunken arse up here!'

They were now well and truly in Prince Comedo's domain.

CHAPTER TEN

Rovac (noun): a group of 27 islands in the Central Ocean; inhabitant(s) of those islands; their nation; their language; (adjective): of or concerning the said islands, inhabitants, nation or language.

The Rovac nonsense: dismissive term used by wizards to describe the long-standing historical dispute between the nation of Rovac and the Confederation of Wizards.

Rovac staunch (noun) (obsolete): ritual drink formerly employed by the warriors of Rovac during initiation rituals, consisting of equal parts of blood, cream, alcohol and water.

* * *

Taking directions from a serving boy whom they woke from a drunken sleep in a slovenly guard room, the wizards climbed to the seventh level of the gatehouse keep, occasionally disturbing rats; these first seven levels alone could have housed a thousand people, so probably the upper levels were deserted.

On the seventh level, a door opened to a hall where three men sat guarding Comedo's chambers: two at chess, one watching. Ignored by the guards, the wizards looked around the room, which doubled as an armoury.

On the walls were weapons: swords double-edged and single, stabbing and slashing, sparring and dueling; cutlasses, broadswords, claymores; dirks, stilettos, skinning knives, throwing knives and foreign dueling daggers with one edge deeply serrated to catch and break a rapier blade. There were quivers, arrows, quarrels, stave bows, crossbows, composite bows. And also: spears, javelins, halberds, pikes, battleaxes, knuckledusters, cut throat razors, maces, billhooks, throwing stars, morning stars and dissecting kits. And armour: chain mail, scale mail, breast plates, greaves, gauntlets, helmets round or horned or spiked. And shields: from bucklers to full-length body shields.

The collection indicated how rich Castle Vaunting had become from centuries of taxing the Salt Road in money and in kind.

'I have you,' said one of the chessplayers.

Or, to be precise, he spoke a word known to all chess players: damorg. The same word in all languages, it must have spread with the game.

The other player conceded defeat, and the three guards turned their attention to the three wizards.

'Name yourself,' said one of the guards, a haughty man with an elegant cloak. His square-cut beard was black, as was the oiled hair he held in place with combs of whalebone.

'Where's Comedo?' said Garash, before Phyphor could speak.

'Where he chooses to be,' said the guard. 'And you'll be out on your arse unless you can give a good account of yourself. I'm Elkor Alish, captain of the personal bodyguard of the prince of Estar, so I'll ask the questions here. Those who will not answer to me must answer to my sword, Ethlite. Be sure that Ethlite has a sharper tongue than I do.'

'Don't threaten us,' said Garash.

'Who are you then?'

'My style is Garash. A wizard of the order of Arl. Power is at my readiness to diminish you from the face of the sun with a single blast of fire.'

Alish threw his chair at Garash. As Garash ducked, Alish drew his sword. Garash snatched at the chain round his neck. The sword was faster.

'Drop your hands,' said Alish, holding steel to

Garash's throat. 'Drop your hands, or you'll feel the sharp edge of some poetry in motion.'

As Garash obeyed, Alish sidestepped, then ducked round behind the wizards. Phyphor laughed.

'Well, Garash,' said Phyphor, turning. 'You certainly – '

'Don't move!' shouted Alish.

Phyphor froze.

'Now remember I'm behind you,' said Alish. 'Man, wizard or sage, you can die whatever you are. The fat one says he's a wizard, so I'll call you all wizards. Any movement – any mumbling – any chanting – and my sword will have your heads.'

'You can't keep us here forever,' said Garash.

'Yes, fat one: a problem. My blade can trim that problem down to size, if necessary. What did you say your name was?'

'Garash.'

'Garash who? Garash what? What is your family? Your clan?'

'Garash is all the name I have.'

'Well then. Your name, young one?'

'My name is Miphon. I bear you no ill.'

'Steel would say it bears no ill, but it kills all the same. You, old one, who are you?'

'Elkor Alish, my style is Phyphor, a wizard of Arl. I seek audience with Prince Comedo to ask for help in hunting down the wizard Heenmor. We wish to punish him . . . to kill him.'

Alish laughed.

'Find Heenmor? Kill him? We'd help if we could, I'm sure. He ate here at his pleasure all through the winter. And killed here, too. When he left, twenty followed. He lost them in forest too dense for horses. But they tracked him, closed with him on foot – and died. Where he's gone to, nobody knows.'

'Elkor Alish . . .'

'Yes, old one?'

70

'Phyhor is my style, as I have told you.'

'Then speak, Phyphor.'

'Elkor Alish, we come to kill Heenmor. You would enjoy to see him dead. Where is our quarrel?'

Alish paused. By striking now, he could kill three wizards. He was fast enough. It would be a step to fulfilling his obligations to the Code of Night and the destiny of Rovac: a glorious start to a spring that would see Hearst lead Comedo's army on a conquest of Dybra which Alish saw as the start of a long campaign that might eventually take their armies to the wizard strongholds in the Far South.

He could strike now: or wait.

If he let the wizards live, perhaps they would find Heenmor and secure the death-stone. Then Alish could kill them at leisure, taking the death-stone for himself.

'Swear not to harm me or any other in the castle,' said Alish, 'And there will be no quarrel between us.'

'Why must we swear?' said Garash.

'Because Ethlite is hungry,' said Alish.

'Elkor Alish,' said Phyphor, 'I swear by the Rule of Law to honour the lives of this castle, providing none hinder my pursuit of the wizard Heenmor. By the Rule of Law I swear it.'

'And you, wizard Garash?'

First Garash then Miphon swore the same oath. Alish sheathed his sword.

'So you've sworn the oath,' said Alish, walking back to join his two comrades. 'For what it's worth.'

'You question the value of a wizard's oath?' said Garash angrily. 'No wizard ever breaks an oath.'

Alish laughed at him.

'How dare you laugh!'

'Peace, Garash,' said Phyphor. 'This is not the time or the place.'

'All right,' said Garash. Then, abruptly: 'Who are those people?'

He pointed at the other guards, who had sat silent

71

throughout the confrontation. One, a short pink man with a smirking mouth, looked remarkably like a pig dressed in chain mail. A battle axe hung from his belt, a knife at his side and a helmet within easy reach.

'The short one is Gorn,' said Alish. 'The tall one, the swordsman, is someone else again.'

'Tell that, that Gorn,' said Garash, 'Tell him to take us to Prince Comedo. Now!'

Alish, allowing himself an enigmatic smile, re-arranged his embroidered cloak so the hilt of his sword showed. He had sworn no oath that would protect the wizards.

'Are you threatening me?' said Garash.

'Garash!' said Phyphor. 'Favour us with your silence. Elkor Alish, if you would be so good, kindly take us to Prince Comedo.'

'Unfortunately,' said Alish, 'That worthy is out hunting.'

'What?' said Phyphor. 'With armed invaders on the loose?'

'Most are fled or dead,' said Alish. 'They're no match for the fighters here. There was never a proper invasion – just a few men sent from Tameran to burn the temple and scout out the land.'

'If the prince isn't here,' said Garash, 'Why are you guarding his chambers?'

'Within is a fortune worth murdering your mother for. Morgan Hearst slew the dragon on Maf. He's a hero. He gouged a giant ruby from its eye socket, as proof. That's what we're guarding.'

'Is that Hearst?' said Miphon, indicating the tall swordsman.

The swordsman laughed. He looked like a fighting man's fighting man. Big grappling hands; a barrel chest; a face scarred and beer-battered, marked by a network of broken red veins. The left ear was missing. He was older than Alish or Gorn; when he spoke, his voice was deep, and slightly hoarse:

'No,' he said, accenting the Trading Tongue strangely. 'I'm not Morgan Hearst. I have the pride and pleasure of being Volaine Persaga Haveros, lately Lord Commander of the Imperial City of Gendormargensis, but now out of favour with our lord Khmar, who has placed a price on my head.'

'A Collosnon soldier!' said Phyphor, with surprise.

Volaine Persaga Haveros bowed, slightly.

Gendormargensis, as all the world knew, was the ruling city of Khmar's empire – a city by the Yolantarath River commanding the strategic gap between the Sarapine Ranges and the Balardade Massif, deep in the heartland of Tameran, far north of Estar.

'Are all three of you Collosnon soldiers?' said Phyphor.

'No,' said Haveros. 'Just me. Alish and Gorn have never set foot in Tameran. They're from the west. Rovac warriors.'

Phyphor's face registered shock. But it was Garash who spoke first:

'What? Those two? Rovac warriors? A runt with the face of a pig and a fop in a pretty cloak?'

Alish put his hand to the hilt of his sword, then restrained himself. His pleasure would come later. He made a promise to himself: sooner or later, he would see the green of this wizard's spleen.

'What did you expect?' he said. 'We're only men, whatever the legends say. But when you meet Morgan Hearst, then you'll meet a hero.'

'It's not Hearst we're after,' said Phyphor. 'It's the prince.'

'All in good time,' said Alish, carelessly. 'His hunt should end by evening. Come, we'll find you quarters.'

'We'll sleep in our towers,' said Phyphor. 'We'll be quite comfortable there.'

'Of course,' said Alish. 'Do you know the way?'

'I've been here before,' said Phyphor.

He was glad to get away. So there were Rovac in

Estar! Never before had he met the ancient enemy face to face. Despite his laughter at the time, he was rather shaken by the speed with which Alish had attacked and mastered Garash. And he was appalled to think that a Rovac warrior now had the protection of his oath.

Well, despite what Garash had said, oaths could be broken . . .

CHAPTER ELEVEN

Arl: one of the most powerful of the eight orders of wizards, having power over light and over fire.

* * *

From the fifth level of the gatehouse keep the wizards exited onto the battlements, which were twenty paces wide, with the flame trench moat on one side and a four-storey drop to the flagstones of the central courtyard on the other. Overhead the gatehouse keep towered skywards for another sixty-six levels, terminating at the seventieth floor.

'You should have killed him when he attacked me,' said Garash, speaking of Alish. 'He might have killed me.'

'And I might have been grateful,' said Phyphor.

'You need me! You can't kill Heenmor on your own!'

'I could use help – but you were no help at all when the dragon attacked us.'

'Neither was that wizard of Nin,' said Garash.

'Please allow me – ' began Miphon.

'Quiet!' shouted Phyphor.

For once, they obeyed – the word came out as a howl of anguish, shocking them to silence.

Phyphor stood there, trembling. With an unaccustomed sense of hopelessness, he remembered so many similar situations from the past, when wizards, ranting, raging, burning white-hot with unreasonable fury, had embroiled themselves in their own little melodramas, while about them empires fell and the world rode down the wide road to ruin. Without a word, he led them on.

Five hundred paces took them from the gatehouse keep to the tower of the order of Seth, pierced with a gateway which anyone could use – though only a wizard of Seth could enter the tower. Next came the tower of Arl, where they stopped; beyond lay the tower of Nin.

'Miphon,' said Phyphor. 'Come inside with us.'

'Are you mad?' said Garash. 'We can't have a wizard from another order in our tower.'

Phyphor turned a cold eye on his apprentice.

'For the last time,' said Phyphor, 'remember your place.'

'I won't stand for it! The order of Arl has never – '

'Garash! Enough!'

'You may be the master here and now,' said Garash, heatedly, 'but what will our order say if they hear you've let the order of Nin into our tower – the order of bird-callers and fish-ticklers? There's no precedent for such a thing.'

'I've heard you out,' said Phyphor. 'Now you hear me. There's no precedent for our mission. Never before has a wizard ventured to the Dry Pit. Who knows what Heenmor found there? Who knows what he left in the tower? Maybe twenty different kinds of death. The more of us and the more skills we have between us, the better. And while I'm about it, don't despise bird-calling and fish-tickling – that talent has fed us often enough on this mission.'

Garash nodded as if he agreed – then grabbed for the chain round his neck.

Phyphor's staff thwacked against his fingers. Then he jabbed Garash in the ribs. Garash squealed. The staff chopped into his kidneys. Garash fell to the ground. The staff swept back for another blow.

'No,' said Miphon, restraining Phyphor. 'You'll kill him.'

'Perhaps I should,' said Phyphor, breathing heavily. 'My best efforts to teach him – and he turns out like this. Kill him, yes. It's not a bad idea.'

76

But he did not strike.

Garash, curled up in pain, moaned.

'On your feet,' said Phyphor. 'Come on! Up! Now! Up up up! Stop snivelling! Get up! On your feet, yes, that's better. Now look me in the eyes. In the eyes!'

Garash could not or would not meet his gaze.

'What was your plan?' said Phyphor. 'Kill me, then go home? Listen. There's no excuse for going back. Our mission is too important for that. We'll follow Heenmor if we have to track him all the way to Chi'ash-lan. If we've lost his trail, we'll search until we pick it up again, even if that means quartering the Ravlish Lands and searching Tameran entire.

'If I offend against protocol, you can prosecute me in front of the order when we return. But if you return to the Castle of Controlling Power without completing this mission, the order will kill you on arrival.'

'I'll be pissing blood for a week,' moaned Garash. 'I'll be pissing blood for a week.'

'Pox doctor, heal thyself,' said Phyphor, without sympathy. 'Now let's go in. You first. Now!'

He shoved Garash toward the wall. Garash stumbled, tried to turn, and fell backwards. The wall parted like mist around him.

'Come,' said Phyphor, 'Take my hand.'

Taking Phyphor's hand – to get into the tower of Arl he needed physical contact with a wizard of Arl – Miphon walked through the wall as if through fog, and was inside.

Garash was on the floor.

'I'm blind!' screamed Garash. 'Blind!'

The air stank of burnt hair. The back of Garash's head had been singed and the back of his cloak had been scorched.

'You were lucky you fell backwards,' said Phyphor. 'Heenmor must have set a blast trap here. If you'd walked in facing forward, you might have lost your eyes.'

77

'Don't you hear me? I'm blind.'

'It's only flash-blindness,' said Phyphor. 'You'll get back your sight in a day or two.'

'Help me up,' said Garash.

Phyphor laughed at him.

By the ochre everlast light of the firestones of the tower of Arl, Phyphor's mouth showed heavy brown sheep-teeth in a mirthless grin. Standing there, tall figure in robes and skullcap, scars on his chin and lines of age seaming his face, he looked like a deathmessenger.

'Upstairs,' said Phyphor. 'You first, Garash. If there's any surprises, they're yours.'

At first Garash demurred – but soon yielded to Phyphor's blunt methods of persuasion.

The tower of Arl rose from the battlements in fifty levels. The first thirty, windowless, held nothing but clasp-sealed jars of water and urns of siege dust. The next twenty were bare but for some stone furniture. As they climbed, Miphon and Phyphor followed Garash at a distance. The stairs were shallow, as wizards might have to climb them through thousands of years of frail old age. The stairway walls were covered with strange markings: glyphs and star-symbols which Miphon had never seen before. He did not like to ask what they were, but Phyphor volunteered the information.

'All that you see is written in the Inner Language of the order of Arl,' said Phyphor. 'It's used for saying that which must not be overheard. You're probably the first wizard of Nin even to hear of its existence. Does Nin have anything like it?'

'No,' said Miphon.

He was not telling the truth. His order did have a special method for secret conversations. Theirs was the only order able to speak to and hear animal minds, so they would use the slow, clear mind of a tortoise. They would sit it down on a table, with a few lettuce leaves so it would not wander, then one wizard would put a thought into its mind for the others to pick up. The thought would fade swiftly, allowing questions, answers or elaboration. Miphon kept this secret, guessing wizards of any other order would find this ceremony ludicrous.

'We've no great secrets like the other orders,' said Miphon. 'Everyone knows that.'

'Everyone presumes that,' said Phyphor. 'But I'm not so sure. Hurry up, Garash! You're not crippled, only blind.'

The murderous fifty level climb exhausted all of them. However, there were no more traps. In the uppermost level, they found a table, a couple of chairs and a chess set. On the floor was a stone relief map of the lands of Estar, Trest, Dybra and Chorst. The map showed the flame trench on the southern border of Estar throbbing with red light.

'That's new since I was here last,' said Phyphor. 'It would have told Heenmor the southern fire trench was burning again. The day we reached the border, he must have known it.'

'What are you talking about?' asked Garash, from his blindness.

'Nothing that need concern you,' said Phyphor.

Garash yelped.

'That's a chair,' said Phyphor. 'There's a couch to your left.'

Garash groped his way to the couch, then lay down. With a grinding-grating, the stone conformed, at least approximately, to the curves of his body. Phyphor frowned at the ugly noise: it suggested that time's decay was telling even on the tower of Arl. Garash, lying back, went limp, as if unconscious.

'What if his sight doesn't come back?' murmured Miphon.

'There's a drop-shaft on every level of this tower,' said Phyphor. 'They have their uses.'

Miphon hoped he was only joking.

CHAPTER TWELVE

Name: Durnwold (brother of Valarkin).
Birthplace: Little Hunger Farm, Estar.
Occupation: soldier.
Description: a strong, swarthy young man who looks rather stupid but actually has all his wits about him.
Career: since leaving his father's house, has served Prince Comedo. Has trained with the sword under the tutelage of Morgan Hearst, warrior of Rovac.

* * *

Footling – knocked from his horse by a branch – fell with a cry. His horse, dismounted, stopped. But the chase went on.

Durnwold urged his horse: 'Ya! Ya!'

Hearst rode silent and intent, bent low beneath the whipping branches. The trail swung into undergrowth too thick to ride through. Durnwold and Hearst swung down from their horses. Bent low beneath branch and bough, they ran with swords drawn.

One of their quarry turned at bay. Durnwold was at him first. Sword clashed with sword as Hearst slipped past to follow the trail. Durnwold, on his lonesome, fought the Collosnon soldier.

The earth was damp. Their boots slipped and stumbled. Their mouths were open: breathing harsh. In the dim underbranch light they thrust and countered. Fear for fear they matched each other. The Collosnon soldier dared a cut which Durnwold only half-turned. The blade ripped his flank. It hurt! He parried another blow then hacked for the head.

Metal bit metal. The Collosnon sword shattered. The soldier looked at it – shocked, astonished. Durnwold's blade bit to the bridge of his nose. Durnwold sliced, thrust, hacked, chopped, grunting, sweating, swearing, butchering his enemy to a bloody mess of gore and bone. Then dropped his sword and staggered to the support of a tree, where he rested, clutching his wounded side, panting, gasping.

It was a while before he realised he was only lightly wounded, and not likely to die yet.

Meanwhile Hearst, now far out of sight, ran on along an easy trail of broken twigs, footprints, torn branches, and, once, a vivid red wound where a boot had ripped the skin from an exposed tree root. He saw marks where his exhausted quarry had slipped and fallen. Bursting into a clearing, Hearst saw his quarry: sprawled full length with an arrow in his chest. Hearst saw the archer: a dark-haired weatherbeaten man of middle years, and behind him . . . what? It fled, leaving him with a vague impression of large eyes and fox fur.

'Who are you?' demanded Hearst, speaking Estral.

'Blackwood,' said the archer.

'And what was that thing that ran away?'

'A fodden.'

'What's that? Paw and claw? Or thumb and fist?'

'Thumb and fist,' said Blackwood. 'But it lives like paw and claw. It finds game for me.'

Blackwood spoke the language of Estar well enough to assure Hearst that he was a native of the land. Hearst switched to the Trading Tongue, in which he was more fluent.

'Do you claim the head?' said Hearst.

'The head? Mister, I'm not that hungry.'

'The prince will want to see it,' said Hearst, chopping down on the corpse with his sword.

He gave a quick look round, sheathed his blade, then set off at a jog, holding the head by a fistful of hair. He did not look back.

*　　*　　*

Blackwood wondered about that warrior who had demanded his name before leaving without giving his own, who had cropped grey hair, cold eyes, and a brutal way with human flesh. He hoped they would not meet again.

The dead Collosnon soldier had discarded his sword, helmet and cuirass to be able to run faster, but the spider amulet at his throat told the world which master he served. Sighting that amulet, Blackwood had shot without hesitation. The arrow had caught the soldier just to the left of the breastbone; he had spun round and fallen dead.

The fodden crept out of the undergrowth and began to lick the blood. Blackwood nudged it aside with his boot.

'No,' he said.

'Why not?' said the fodden, lisping, hissing, spluttering. Practice let Blackwood understand its distorted speech easily.

'It's not for eating.'

'Blood is blood. It was a bad man. It's sorry now, isn't it?'

'It's still not for eating,' said Blackwood.

The fodden swiped at the corpse with one fox-fur hand. Blackwood kicked it away. Hissing, the fodden shrank back into the trees. Blackwood knelt by the headless body and cut out his arrow, which had the barbed broadhead he favoured for hunting; its three flight-feathers were yellow for easy retrieval.

'Murmer,' said Blackwood. 'Come on.'

The fodden lingered, hunched in shadows.

'Come on!'

The fodden followed reluctantly. It was short, bandy-legged and covered in red fox fur but for its bald-bone head. Its eyes were green slits; its teeth suggested it was a carnivore with a vicious bite. Breeding colonies of foddens lived only in the Penvash Peninsular; this one was old, and young male foddens would have killed it if it had not left. It was always moody and foul-tempered for weeks after waking from hibernation, and liable to do ugly and spiteful things; this far into spring it should have got past that stage, but there was no sign of its temper improving.

Blackwood followed the track of smashed vegetation and leaking blood. He went slowly, not wanting to overtake the warrior. The fodden followed at a distance.

Blackwood was burdened with a roll of waterproof canvas as an emergency weather shelter; a quiver of arrows; a composite bow of wood, sinew and horn; a small food pouch; and, strapped to his belt, a case of black leather holding his hunting trousse: a large chopper, a small chopper, a saw, an awl, a knife and a sharpening stone. Many animals had been dismembered by that useful collection.

He discovered a second headless body, badly hacked about. A shattered sword-stump lay nearby. Obviously there had been a fight: the soft ground was scuffed and gouged where the combatants had braced and slipped.

'Another,' said Murmer.

'Yes,' said Blackwood. 'Don't touch!'

'So starve me then,' said Murmer, idling past, tongue touching greedy lips.

The dead did not shock Blackwood; he was familiar enough with mutilated bodies. He had not wept for the dead since the time when he had held in his arms the last of his stillborn children. At tax time, which began on the full of the Harvest Moon, Comedo's soldiers would hunt down defaulters and slaughter them. Blackwood had seen it. He knew all about the bloat and stink of corpses, the disintegration of the human face, the collapse of the body to scum and bones.

'Heel!' said Blackwood, as Murmer lagged behind.

Blackwood expected the hunters, who had betrayed themselves to him earlier by sounding horns when a kill had been made, would be gone by the time he reached the forest edge – but they were still there. He should have guessed: he had heard sounds of fighting when they had been ambushed, and should have known they would be delayed.

Crouching in the forest, he watched. Some of the men sat on horses chatting to each other; some were still searching corpses for anything worth taking. Two were exercised in keeping the dogs from tearing at the bodies of dead men and two dead horses.

Prince Comedo, laughing, sat high on a white horse with retainers around him. He wore a plumed helmet but no armour. He carried a spear on which a head had been mounted; the ears and nose had been sliced away, the eyes gouged out. Red stains from the prince's bloody hands had stained the mane of his horse where he had stroked it.

One Collosnon soldier, still alive, had been slung over the saddle of a horse and tied there for the journey back to Castle Vaunting. He had taken a scalp wound, but it was not bad enough to threaten his life – worse luck for him.

Laughing, smiling, Comedo gave the signal to head for home. Horns blared, men cheered. They set off with a jingle of harness, a racket of dogs. When all were gone, Blackwood ventured forth. Flies already buzzed around the corpses. He looked back at the forest. The fodden was nowhere to be seen.

'Murmer? Come here! Murmer!'

No answer.

Blackwood looked at the sky. He was running out of daylight. He started to walk east. The hunt had come from the east, as a cursory glance at their tracks made plain. Every step took him nearer to home; it was disturbing to have hunters come so close to his house. He always feared that on his return he might find the door smashed open and blood on the floor and the walls . . .

When Blackwood was out of sight, Murmer slipped from the forest to disturb the flies. He stooped to a wound-gash, and drank, deeply.

* * *

It was almost dayfail; a tarn near the forest edge already held the colour of the night. It was that time of evening when the black slugs emerge to soothe through the cool air; the wind, which had long ago lost its morning strength, was dying. Twilight was settling in the creaking branches as Blackwood stalked into the forest with anger on his heavy-jowled face.

'Softly now,' he said. 'Soft!'

But the animal strung up by wire and iron jaws kicked and strained in panic, tearing its lacerated body still further. Blackwood, knife in hand, saw horror in its eyes. The creature looked so human that it crossed his mind that perhaps it was more than mere deer. But in any case he could not save it. The knife glinted, striking, as he did the deer a kindness. Blood dripped down from the body Comedo's yahooing huntsmen had hung high with wire and trap-jaws. Blackwood cursed the prince:

– Blood in your mouth, you rat-rapist.

This traditional felicity eased his feelings. He had cursed Comedo many times before – though never, not even in his bedrock dreams, did he consider abandoning curses for action.

The tracks – a child could have seen it – showed horses and dogs had been here. Those dogs were big brutes kept hungerfed; they would have put the deer out of its misery soon enough, if their masters had not whipped them off. The prince enjoyed watching suffering. People used to think his father was bad, but the father's faults had lain in overlarge appetites, not in calculated sadism.

Blackwood had been the father's huntsman. Later, Comedo had employed Blackwood to organise hunts for him. However, Comedo's joyful slaughter had swiftly thinned the game away to almost nothing. Blaming Blackwood for the dearth, Comedo had turned him out of the castle, ordering that no man in Estar feed or shelter such a useless mouth, on pain of death.

Blackwood, surviving for years in a house hidden away in Looming Forest, guessed he would fare just as well under Collosnon rule, but still had no compunction about killing the invaders if they came his way. From talks from the Melski of the river, Blackwood had learnt of Collosnon atrocities against poor fishing folk living near the river. The Collosnon had no taint of royalty to protect them from his anger.

Now, as evening faded to night. Blackwood gralloched the deer, then washed his knife in the tarn. A sudden splash shattered the night calm. Blackwood peered into the darkness and spoke sharply:

'Murmer! Stop throwing rocks!'

The fodden said nothing, but Blackwood knew it was there. Another rock splashed into the water.

'Murmer!'

Spluttering laughter from the darkness. Was the fodden going mad in its old age?

Perhaps.

* * *

As the moon rose, Blackwood shouldered the carcass and set off for home. It was death to touch the prince's meat, but the prince never claimed his kills. And though it may be death to break the law, it is death to be poor and keep it.

Tramping through the darkness, he indulged himself with smoky memories of the aftermath of other hunts. Horns announcing the return to the castle. Groaning banquet tables. The hall flushed with heat. Jugglers, singers, music. Tankards hammering on the table as the songs roared out. Good meat and greasy fingers.

Had it really been like that, in the old days, before Comedo came to power and the dragon came to Estar? Perhaps. Certanly things were different now. Hard times, hard times . . .

Blackwood came to a stream, which he followed into the forest; water would wash away footprints and any leaking blood, leaving no trail for men or dogs. His boots kept out the water, but it chilled his feet. The fodden splashed along noisily behind him. Blackwood turned and hissed angrily; Murmer sat down on the bank and sulked.

Deep in the forest, Blackwood left the stream and followed a minimal trail to the clearing where stood his house, outhouse and woodshed. The buildings were hidden in darkness, but there was the smell of wood-smoke in the air, the smell of a hearth-fire. Blackwood hung the deer carcass where no ground-life could gnaw it, then went inside.

Mystrel, his wife, greeted him quietly: touch of hand against hand, touch of forehead against forehead. She smiled; he could see her smile by firelight and rush-lights. She said nothing, but brought him some soup; they were in no hurry to exchange words. After years of living in isolation together, a touch could do all their greeting.

She was now thirty-five. Time had been hard on her face, but her body was still strong enough for its purpose. Two months gone, and seven months to go.

– I will have a son. And my son will have a better life than this.

A child. The renewed promise of a future. They had not expected it. Why not? Simply because they were too accustomed to disappointment. But it was happening. With fresh meat outside, a warm fire inside and a future to plan, Blackwood was happy.

   * * *

Murmer killed a lamb that night.

– Ha! Have you, have at you, womb-warm. Shlust shroost! Kick then, saast, kick. Bog-cold soon, womb-kick. Warm, ha, yes, mother me, warm one, saas-sister. Where's your high-stride hook-crook watching one then, womb-warm? No help now, ha? Dreams now, womb-kick. Dreams. Saaa!

The lamb was dead.

Murmer ate.

He was thumb and fist, but anyone who saw him feeding there by moonlight, glancing round suspiciously from time to time, would probably have classed him as paw and claw, savagery akin to wark and wylie.

After feeding, Murmer was on his way.

His destination was Castle Vaunting.

CHAPTER THIRTEEN

Name: Blackwood (husband of Mystrel).

Occupation: woodsman.

Status: once a hired lackey of the ruling class, but now a victim of the Class Enemy of the Common People.

Description: a dark-haired heavy-jowled man of middle years, looking, incidentally, remarkably like Shen Shen Drax, the leech-gatherer of Delve.

*   *   *

The executioner – such was his title, though he was a gaoler as well – was masked with grey mud. Clay was his face, but his voice was gravel. Shadows lurched as his head swung to face Blackwood. His eyes were black pits.

'Who are,' said the executioner, 'Who are you?'

His breath stank, like dead meat softening underground. Torchlight showed clumsy thumbmarks in his clay mask, from which bits of straw protruded.

'My question was not, was not to exercise my throat. Who are you?'

The executioner's assistants, who were holding Blackwood's arms, shook him. They wore featureless strawman masks.

'Blackwood's my name.'

'Blackwood,' said the executioner. Thoughtfully, he rubbed at bits of straw bristling from his mask, as another man might have rubbed his beard. 'Blackwood. The name has a past, even if it doesn't have a future.'

'I was head of the hunt. Years ago.'

'A hunter. From the sun? How is the sun? These

shadows have held me thirty years, you know.'

The executioner lurched toward Blackwood, who pulled back from the stench. The assistants wrenched his arms to agony. The clay face brushed his. Bristles scraped across his skin.

'So. So. How is the sun? Is it thaw yet?'

'It's spring.'

'Ah, the green. What have these bones been doing this green that the dark should claim them? Well?'

Blackwood was silent. Then his arms were twisted. He cried out.

'Don't,' said the executioner, weaving his clay face from side to side, 'Don't try silence. Or excuses. We're all born guilty, all guilty, so don't cry innocent. We've just one newborn today: yourself. Save yourself today and tomorrow may save you yet again. Now answer. What did you do?'

'I took meat the prince had killed.'

'Meat. We have a place for meat. Bring him!'

The strawmen forced Blackwood to a room of jaws, hooks, breakers, crunchers, claws. Here was the Warm Mother, the Sharp Sister, the Iron Maiden. And three abandoned bodies.

'Let him look,' said the executioner.

Blackwood was released. He was free, for the first time since his house was raided. Now was his chance to grab a branding iron and run amok, slashing and stabbing until they cut him down. But Mystrel was their prisoner, unless she was dead. He could not die yet! He was not yet free for death.

'Collosnon corpses. They deserved. We'll feed them soon. We'll show. Bring him!'

The strawmen hustled Blackwood through winding dungeon darkness, following the clay man, who sometimes paused to kick the bars of a cell till something inside woke and whimpered.

'Not time,' said the executioner. 'The work, not time enough. So kick the door. In the end, in the end, we do the work. The first year we let them walk. The prince might want them. If there's no call that year, he's forgotten. They're ours. The second year, the second we break them to a crawl. Then the third. Down to their bellies in the dirt. The fourth year is the last. Will the prince remember you? Do you want him to?'

Blackwood said nothing.

Their footsteps roused snarls from certain cells; others held only stinking silence. This was the underside of Castle Vaunting: stale air, dripping water, rot, fear, decay.

'We feed,' said the executioner, halting where the tunnel opened to an engulfing drop. 'Here! Feed bodies. Listen.'

Listening, they heard nothing.

'It's not moving,' said one of the assistants.

'Silence! Silence! Tongues can be taught silence if they don't teach themselves. Thirty years I haven't seen the sun, but I still have eyes, ah yes. Tongues and eyes – lost if they're not deserved . . . but you're right. It's not moving.'

The executioner took a torch from a wall bracket and tossed it to the pit. They glimpsed a mountainous gelatinous mass disfigured by warts, craters, ridges. The torch splashed into water and went out. Darkness shifted: sucking, squelching.

'Lopsloss,' said the executioner. 'Lopsloss. It's moving. It's moving now. Now you've seen it. Now into a cell. Wait, wait for us. We'll for you, come for you, soon, not yet, but soon. Wait for us.'

*   *   *

Down on your bones. Down on your knees.

Down on your bones in the dark.

They can break anything they care to. Ribs, collarbone, elbow. They can pick and choose. Knee, ankle, crutch.

Crouched in the darkness, he waited for them to come and choose. Sometimes something coughed, or a chain clinked. Far down a cellblock corridor, a torch guttered low, then out.

Finally, he realised they had no special plan for him. Showing him the torture chamber had been a working routine. It meant nothing. Showing him the lopsloss had been another working routine. That meant nothing, too.

They would remember him in a year.

* * *

'Blackwood. Black . . . wood.'

It was Mystrel.

Blackwood sat up on the straw where he had been lying for half of eternity. He listened.

'Black . . . wood.'

The voice was distorted by echoes. Faint as the beat of the wings of a bat deep underground.

'Black . . . wood.'

He tried to shout – but fear was strangling him.

'Black . . . wood.'

He bowed his head and breathed the damp, fetid air, till fear was overcome and he was able to shout:

'Mystrel!'

He had not seen her since a soldier from the raiding party had knocked him to the ground. He had feared her burnt in the blaze when the soldiers had fired the house.

'Blackwood!'

'Are you all right?'

Right ight ight . . . echechecho through hollow stone, through dank places black as the wing of the bat, the scaffold's drop-hole.

'Yes!'

Suddenly there was a hoot as if from an owl, then a bark as if from a dog, and soon the whole line of cells

92

was clamouring as prisoners jeered, mocked, barked, howled and hammered against the bars. The sound only died away when one of the executioner's assistants arrived, bearing a new torch.

The torch prowled up and down.

Tread of iron-shod boots on stone.

Boots which halted. In front of Blackwood's cell.

Saying nothing.

'Mister,' said Blackwood. 'The woman . . . the woman is my wife. Can you . . . can you . . . can you bring me my wife?'

The strawman mask studied him in silence.

Then it nodded.

Blackwood waited . . . and waited. Then the straw-man came back, unlocked the door and threw inside the battered bloody body of Murmer the fodden. Then locked the door and went away again.

*   *   *

Someone was asleep; Blackwood could hear mutter-ing, and teeth grating together. He sat in shadow, becoming shadow. Murmer huddled silently in one corner of the cell. Blackwood knew the fodden was watching him. What did it expect? To be pulped to death? He was tempted, truly – but knew the fodden was old, its mind addled by age and hibernation. It couldn't help itself. So help it into the darkness, then. Kill it! Yes? No . . .

Not yet, at any rate.

For if he killed the fodden, the guards might hurt Mystrel. And if he didn't? What then? What would they do to her at the end of a year? He knew the answer. His eyes were hot, hot and burning. The best they could hope for was to die. But, thinking of his unborn child, he knew he could not permit himself to hope for that.

93

CHAPTER FOURTEEN

Nin: one of the weakest of the eight orders of wizards, having power over the minds of wild things.

* * *

Miphon woke to sunlight streaming through the stained glass windows of the top room of Nin's four-storey tower. Wondering why he had slept so well, he remembered that the castle stones had no voices. For once he had slept without hearing stones, rocks and mountains grumbling and complaining. The process used to build the castle had killed all life in the rock thus employed, letting Miphon sleep without that mournful cry always in his head:

'Lemarl . . .'

A broken windowpane allowed him a clear view across the glitter of the Hollern River and the trees of Looming Forest to the distant northern mountains of the Penvash Peninsular rising high and steep under the blue vault of the heavens.

Momentarily, he remembered an ocean-going canoe of the Driftwood Islands which had been named The Blue Vault of the Heavens. But that was long ago and far away . . . and he could never go back. It was too late for that. Years too late.

He slopped out, making use of a drop-shaft which overhung the flame trench. He ate some siege dust, through it almost choked him – they would have to arrange rations with the castle. He would see if he could sort something out with the cook or quartermaster before hc saw Comedo.

* * *

'Enter,' said Prince Comedo.

Miphon went into the prince's room. The first thing he saw was a girl - small, thin, pale, hairless and almost breastless. There was blood on her thighs. She parted curtains, vanishing into an adjoining chamber.

Miphon bowed, and tried a few courtesies on the prince, inwardly lamenting the deficiencies of the Galish Trading Tongue. Designed for haggling, it permitted few flatteries. Translated into Galish, words like 'Greetings, my lord' meant, literally, 'Hi, camel master', while 'I am at your service' suggested something like 'I'm willing to bargain'.

Miphon need not have worried. Prince Comedo, having received much homage in Galish, believed that phrases such as 'Hi, camel master' were tokens of great respect. All his life, Galish had been, to him, a formal, courtly tongue; he was completely ignorant of the irreverent, vernacular life the Trading Tongue lived in the marketplaces of the Salt Road.

Abruptly, Comedo demanded how one became a wizard. Miphon was taken aback, but, recovering swiftly, spoke in generalities about Venturing, Testing and Proving.

'Heenmor said as much,' said Comedo, apparently irritated. 'But he never told me precisely what makes a wizard.'

'You wish to know, my lord?'

'Yes!'

'The heart of the matter is service,' said Miphon. 'One works as a humble apprentice for many years. One studies with humility. One serves another who is prepared to teach.'

'Is that the only way?'

'Yes. One must serve.'

'For a long time?'

'Yes, my lord.'

'I would not serve. Others serve me. That's the way things are supposed to be. Heenmor served me. He's gone now, of course. I miss him. I was the only ruler in the known world to own a wizard. I owned him, but he made too many demands. He was . . . so tall. His shadow was too long.

'I told Morgan Hearst to kill him. We were eating chestnuts at the time. But the wizard fled. He made a magic to kill my men. I can show you one who didn't die. He wants to die, but I keep him. He's unique. I'll show you . . . but not today. Not today. But believe me, I have him. The only one.'

'Did Heenmor say where he was going? Do you know where he went?'

'Don't drop questions so, like hail on my head. Remember, I own the dandelion. One puff, and you're dead. My servants – they told you about my foot?'

'Yes, my lord,' said Miphon.

And was soon at work.

Comedo, walking barefoot to bed, had stepped on a needle, which had broken off in his foot. After some days, his heel was now red and inflamed, yellow pus swelling the skin round the puncture site. Miphon heated a needle in the flame of a candle to kill 'the life which feeds on the eye which cannot see it'. He broke open the skin, expressed globs of pus and wiped them away. Then began to dig.

Comedo's hands knotted together, his mouth twisted, and sweat broke out on his brow, though Miphon doubted if he was hurting more than a fraction, if at all. Finally Miphon saw the black stump of the broken needle. He coaxed it to the surface and drew it out. It was black, corroded, rotten. Miphon exhibited his prize.

'Here it is. See.'

'No,' said Comedo, shielding his face. 'I don't want to see. I don't, I won't. You're finished, you can go.'

'Not yet,' said Miphon calmly. 'A hot poultice comes next, to draw out the corruption.'

He prepared and placed the poultice. Comedo complained of the heat of it, but Miphon soothed him as one might sooth a child, and Comedo allowed himself to be soothed.

'They tell me,' said Comedo, while the poultice did its work, 'that you'll hunt off shortly after Heenmor. He always feared pursuit . . . I don't know why.'

'We can't follow him unless we know where he is.'

'You came from the south.'

'Yes,' said Miphon. 'He won't have gone south.'

'He could have gone north . . . the Melski would know. But the Melski are animals, they'd never tell us. Perhaps he went east to my cousin Jeferies . . . that's a long way, though.'

'How far?'

'From here to the High Castle in Trest . . . about a hundred leagues.'

'Ten marches.'

'Yes,' said Comedo. 'You take the Eastway. For the first fifteen leagues, that's a road. Then you reach Sepik. After that, there's a path. It goes through the swamps.'

'My lord,' said Miphon, 'Before we set out, we'd like to see the place where Heenmor used magic to kill the men chasing him. If that's no trouble . . .'

'It's in deep forest. You'd never find it. There's nobody here who'd dare guide you there.'

'Surely a prince so wealthy as yourself, a prince able to maintain such a magnificent retinue – I am impressed to find even Rovac warriors in your service – must surely have, somewhere, within the wide bounds –'

'Enough,' said Prince Comedo, holding up a hand for silence. 'I will think on it. Thinking will do me no harm. Perhaps I will think of someone for you. In the meantime: you may go.'

'Yes, my lord.'

Exiting from Comedo's chambers, Miphon heard a distant, echoing voice shouting:

'Andranovory! Let him go!'

He still hadn't arranged about rations.

CHAPTER FIFTEEN

Name: Elkor Alish.
Birthplace: the islands of Rovac.
Occupation: captain of Prince Comedo's bodyguard.
Status: a famed army leader of the Cold West, known variously as Red Terror, Bloodsword, He Who Walks, Our Lord Despair; a leading member of the Code of Night, the secret organisation dedicated to the death of all wizards.
Description: a wiry man of 37 noted for haughty demeanour, elegant dress and a taste for golden jewellery; hair long and black; beard square-cut and black.

* * *

On a fine spring morning, a small party left Castle Vaunting for the place in Looming Forest where Heenmor had killed with magic. With the wizards Phyphor, Garash and Miphon went two Rovac warriors, Elkor Alish and Morgan Hearst. Prince Comedo, in a fit of generosity, had insisted on providing these bodyguards. The wizards had been unable to think of any diplomatic way to refuse this favour; Garash had suggested several undiplomatic ways, which Phyphor had vetoed.

The party was guided by a native of Estar introduced by Comedo as 'a man from the woods, a thief, a criminal, one of the creatures of darkness'. The wizards had paid little attention to Comedo's claims: by now, they had his measure.

Descending Melross Hill, they went through Lorford.

Galish merchants were in town; the locals would tell them nothing of Collosnon raiders, only that a hero named Morgan Hearst had scaled the cliffs of Maf and killed the dragon Zenphos. The Galish convoy would have only good news to take along the Salt Road.

The little expedition crossed the Hollern River and headed into Looming Forest. At first, the forest was airy and open, as it was thinned regularly by people from the town cutting firewood.

'Why so troubled, Rovac warrior?' asked Garash, noting Hearst's expression. 'Are you afraid?'

'No,' said Hearst, and that was all he said.

This was where his horse had fallen lame. Killing the dragon had silenced talk of that episode, but the memory still troubled him. When his horse went lame, he should have commandeered a mount from one of his men. A commander had a duty to be to the fore in a crisis.

'You do look worried,' said Garash, pushing his luck a little.

'Maybe he's trying to decide where to bury you,' said Alish, annoyed that Hearst took that meekly. 'There's plenty of choices.'

'What about you?' said Garash, turning on Blackwood, the easier target.

Blackwood, their guide, looked at him.

'The forest is my home,' said Blackwood. 'In any case, I have no choice. My wife is held hostage against my return. I must guide you to pay for my crime.'

'What crime is that?' said Miphon, curiosity aroused.

'Stealing one of the prince's kills,' said Blackwood. 'He abandons them, but he is jealous of them.'

'How can he find out who takes abandoned meat?'

'He spreads his wings at night and flies around watching.'

'Oh,' said Miphon, not at all sure what to make of that.

The forest grew dense, the trees huge and gnarled.

100

Once they paused, conceding the right of way to a wark, one of the big, lumbering bears of the Penvash Peninsular, seldom seen so far south. At noon they halted for a bite to eat, then pushed on.

'How much further?' said Phyphor.

'Not far,' said Blackwood. 'We'll be there soon.'

'Have you actually been there yourself?'

'No. But the Melski told me the way.'

'The Melski?' said Garash. 'Those animals are dangerous.'

'I've made them my friends,' said Blackwood.

'Then more fool you.'

Blackwood made no answer.

Pebbles began to crunch underfoot: a few at first, then many. They were fragile and light, like pumice; they were the size of tears.

'That was rain,' said Blackwood. 'Falling through the sky, it turned to stone. Water on the ground became black glass.'

'Who said so?' said Garash. 'The Melski?'

'Yes,' said Blackwood. 'They called it the black rain.'

'If it rained stones, the leaves would've been shredded.'

'The stones are very light,' said Blackwood. 'Besides, the leaves weren't out when Heenmor worked his magic.'

Further on, they passed a huge rock which had splintered several trees.

'It looks as if a giant threw it here,' said Phyphor. 'Are there giants in Estar?'

'Mister, there's no such thing as giants,' said Blackwood. 'The rock walked here.'

'You're wrong about giants,' said Garash. 'And about rocks. Rocks don't walk.'

'This one did. So did the others. After Heenmor did his magic. Some died after they walked into the river – the Melski saw them.'

'Rocks don't die,' said Garash. 'They're not alive to start with.'

'They walked,' insisted Blackwood, firm in his faith in the Melski. 'They talked.'

'I see,' said Garash. 'Did they go into town to ask for a mug of beer and a bed for the night?'

'No, mister,' said Blackwood. 'They didn't have the money to buy such.'

'No money?' said Garash.

'It's true.' said Alish, taking up the story. 'They had no money, for Heenmor picked their pockets. These rocks, you see, they're not well up on the ways of wizards and the world.'

'Pockets?' said Garash, outraged. 'That can't be true. Rocks don't have pockets!'

'I've read of such things,' said Miphon quietly. 'They're dealt with in the Terminal Texts. All walking rocks have three pockets at least. Surely you remember that from your own readings?'

That was a barbed thrust. The Terminal Texts were a set of notoriously difficult manuscripts owned by the Confederation of Wizards, and Garash was not one of the world's greatest scholars.

'What kind of pockets?' said Garash slowly.

'Green ones,' said Miphon promptly. 'Each big enough to hold two and a half sticks of tobacco.'

'Miphon!' said Phyphor, annoyed to see Miphon joining this demented Garash-baiting. 'That's enough about rocks and pockets for today and forever!'

'You mean it's not true?' said Garash. And then, with rising anger: 'It's not true?'

'Of course it's true,' said Alish. 'Any drunk will tell you.'

At that moment, they came upon a leafless tree with grey twigs. Garash snapped one off. It was stone. His protruberant eyes stared at it. He started as Alish drew a knife – but the warrior only wanted to pry at some bark. Turned to stone, it flaked off to show wood beneath.

'It's only on the surface,' said Phyphor.

'Still,' said Miphon, 'It killed the tree. Look – the very ground is stone.' He kicked a hole in it. Stone snapped beneath his heel. 'Again, the surface only. But what's that, there?'

'A puddle,' said Blackwood.

Miphon knelt down and dug it out of the ground. Whatever it had been, the 'puddle' was now a thin plate of obsidian. Miphon passed it to Phyphor, who turned it over in his hands then gave it to Garash. Hearst had no wish to handle it, but Elkor Alish reached for it; after a moment's hesitation, Garash yielded it.

Alish was fascinated. Here was power indeed, a weapon that destroyed all living things without exception, leaving the land barren and uninhabited. Nothing else could do that – except fire, a chancy weapon easily affected by wind or rain. A man commanding such power would be hard put to conjure up ambition to match his ability.

'Let's go on,' said Hearst.

They went on through a forest of stone. Many of the trees had collapsed under their own weight, shattering to shards. Their feet went crunchy-scrunchy over the stones. This, Alish knew, was what Heenmor's death-stone had done; the garbled reports of survivors who had run fast enough to escape its action had not captured the terrible magnificence of the destruction.

Further on, they discovered the body of a man. It had been turned to stone.

'This is one of the ten who died,' said Blackwood.

'Did the Melski see them die?' said Phyphor.

'The Melski shadowed them,' said Blackwood. 'They keep a watch on intruders in the forest. But when the rain started to turn to stone, the Melski ran. They said there was a grinding sound in the sky; the sun grew dark. Those who ran survived: those who lingered died. They did not get much time to run.'

'Where was Heenmor?' said Phyphor.

'He was at the centre,' said Blackwood. 'Everything around turned to stone except in the place just around where he was standing. When the Melski first went to see, rocks chased them.'

'But walking rocks aren't real!' howled Garash, provoked beyond endurance. 'We settled that! They're not real, understand? They're like – like sleeping pictures.'

'He means dreams,' said Miphon.

'Dreams? Mister, I dreamt of the sky last night. If dreams aren't real, what then?'

Garash, not agile enough for this debate, made no answer. He took out his frustrations by kicking at the stonemade man. A fold of clothing splintered. He kicked again, snapping a thousand fine threads of what had once been hair. He trod on the face. The stone curve of an eye broke under his boot, revealing an eyesocket empty but for a bit of stone the size of a pea, as if the eyeball had shrivelled up to that little bit of rock.

Blackwood looked up at the sky.

'It's getting late,' he said. 'Unless we turn back, we'll have to camp somewhere among the stones.'

'Rocks,' muttered Garash.

Could rocks really walk? He didn't like the idea at all.

'I say we should press on,' said Alish, seeing that Garash was discomforted. 'The more we learn about this the better.'

'We know enough,' said Garash.

'We don't yet know the truth about walking rocks,' said Phyphor. 'Let's go on.'

They did – with difficulty, as many branches had fallen from the trees, covering the ground with shattered stone.

'Elkor Alish,' said Phyphor.

'Yes?'

'This magic . . . some men died, some escaped. Did any escape with their lives but with . . . consequences?'

'Maybe,' said Alish.

'Tell him,' said Hearst.

'He's a wizard,' said Alish.

'Yes,' said Hearst, 'and we're living men, not the incarnation of the wrath of the dust of history.'

'You speak too lightly of blood matters,' said Alish.

'If you don't tell him, others will,' said Hearst. 'Plenty know. Two survivors didn't run as fast as the others. Bits and pieces of them turned to stone. One died quickly; the other still lives. Prince Comedo keeps him as a toy.'

Both Hearst and Alish had seen that last living victim when Comedo put him on display. His skin was mostly grey; his hands had thickened to useless chunks of rock; one leg was paralyzed and the other had turned to stone below the knee. Stone lips kept his mouth forever open; his tongue licked round uneasily in the warm darkness within. One eye blinked; the other, together with most of the face, had turned to stone.

'The survivor,' said Phyphor, 'Will he live or die?'

'I don't know,' said Alish. 'I don't think he cares.'

'I think he envies the dead,' said Hearst.

'Look,' said Blackwood, 'There's water ahead.'

The rain had filled a dip in the ground where Heenmor's magic had turned the earth to stone. The water was dark, still and silent. They came to a halt by the sinister dark waters. Grey stone. Dark water. The sky above was turning grey. And no bird sang.

Blackwood coughed, loudly, and spat. The march had wearied him. These last few years, he had not felt as fit as he used to. Maybe it was the famine-hungry winters which had sapped his strength; it could hardly be old age.

'This,' said Garash, with satisfaction, 'is where we turn back.'

'We've come this far, we might as well go to the end,' said Alish, unbuckling his sword and wading in boldly until the water rose to his waist.

'Do you like it in there?' said Garash.

'Come on in,' said Alish. 'The water's wonderful. You're not afraid, are you?'

'I'm too old for children's hero-games,' said Garash, dismissing his challenge with contempt.

Alish saw he had lost this round. Nobody else cared to play fish, so Alish, putting a brave face on it, went on alone, raising his sword above his head as water rose to his neck. Ahead was a tree: dead, but made of wood, not stone. Reaching it, he scraped the bottom with the toe of his boot, stirring up mud. Investigating carefully with his feet, he found that stone gave way to mud within a circle about as wide as his outstretched arms. This was the area of safety when the magic was at work.

When Heenmor had used his death-stone, anyone bold enough to close with him could have killed him and survived within that circle of safety – if Heenmor's snake did not take revenge. Alish was satisfied. He had learnt something. He made his way back, toward the others.

'Well,' said Garash, 'did you enjoy yourself?'

'Yes,' said Alish, 'I feel refreshed.'

Emerging from the water dripping wet, he set off, leading the way at a cracking pace which soon had all but Hearst stumbling far behind him. Marching, Alish counted paces to determine the distance from the centre of safety to the outer fringes of the circle of death. Five hundred paces back the way they had come brought them to a place where several large trees lay in pieces; nearby lay a large rock. The shattered trees were half stone, half timber; the stone fell away easily from the wood when Alish kicked it.

He laid a fire, then Blackwood went to work with flint and steel and lit it; soon, for the first time in generations, warriors of Rovac were bedded down by the same camp fire as wizards from the Castle of Controlling Power.

CHAPTER SIXTEEN

Name: Miphon.

Mission: the quest to encompass Heenmor's death and recover whatever magic Heenmor stole from the Dry Pit.

Duties: officially, only to distract Heenmor's copper-strike snake in any confrontation; in practice, he has been donkey-master, cook, healer, translator and diplomat, and has already once had to intervene to keep Phyphor from beating Garash to death.

Appearance: as he is currently rolled up with Blackwood in a length of waterproof canvas – it is too cold to be coy – his appearance cannot be checked, but, when last seen, he proved himself a slender, youthful, green-eyed man sturdily dressed in wool and leathers.

*   *   *

Blackwood woke, untangled himself from canvas and from a stranger's warmth, and went to take a piss. The night was giving way to song-light, but no bird sang. His body was aching from the march of the day before, but he whistled as he gathered wood and conjured life from the ashes of the fire. He was happy. They would be returning to the castle today, and Mystrel would be waiting for him.

Blackwood was careless about the amount of noise he made, guessing that the two soldiers, Hearst and Alish, would sleep on regardless. And he didn't trouble his head about the wizards, as he had scant respect for pox doctors.

He smiled at the crackling fire, and the fire beamed back.

*   *   *

Miphon had not woken properly when Blackwood roused himself. He lay half-submerged in sleep, lubbery as a sodden old boot. He could hear the grumbling discord of the thoughts of a nearby rock, thoughts which he could understand as the language of stone was one of the secrets known by the order of Nin.

Those thoughts, stronger than any he had ever heard before from rock or stone, or even mountain, were bitter as the face of a widowed bride, bitter as the torment of a young warrior who has lost both eyes from the wounds of his first battle, bitter as the snarl of a hostage whose king – his brother, no less – has by the breaking of a treaty doomed him to lose both his hands and his feet. Miphon lay there, half asleep, listening, piecing together the lament of the rock:

Time was time when the seven-octave wind,
Lighter than year-first frost,
Lighter than Tremulo's touch, than Vyvan's
    reverberation,
Could through me funnel, shaping latelments:
When my desire could fist my thought to form
Or race the daylight to the night's delight –
Stars to calm tentharow aftermath, half-dreaming
    trance
That followed passion –

Passion we had in days of then
When mountains, garrulous and strong,
Desired the thunder, fought with lightning
For favour and delight –
Lemarl! That world where I had sight!

Years faded brightness to an echo of remembered
    echoes,

108

Till only echoes we remembered –
Not the glitter-diamond light of crystal Tremulo,
The stride and pride of Vyvan's march,
And Lemstol's flight –
Far less the actual face of Wathnamora,
The songs of Telemornos
And the jokes the mountains told.

Gone for ages, as if forever: then given!
No brief surge of strength, strong, but false and
    failing,
That earthquake brings:
This was animation to outpace the wind!
Berserk in exultation,
My balance spun to frenzy. Joy!
My eyes seventy
Blazing to the sun!
The world of pulp rolled under as my onslaught
Rolled the day to night while the wide earth
    rolled,
And overhead the stars succumbed to sun,
Renewed, and then were sun again.

Then gone: the world smashed down to darkness.
A shuffle, then a final jolt.
The sun went blind.
Now silence pits dark against nothing.
Weight renews forever.

There is no death for us: no hell: no resolution.
Only the substance split and folded from the
    substance,
Halving, and, again, halving,
Till strength and intellect lie sharded into sand,
Too small to think, remember or compute:
Pinhead specks of hatred, loss and sorrow
Where half-words fractured from millenium memory
    echo.

It happens.
Truth is bitter as stamagan's taste: bitter
As the stretch of sun, the ice contraction,
Season's wedge which splits my substance open.
Lemarl: that world
Had no shadows.
No grind of seasons.

The mortal creatures of the pulp have shadows:
Vague, to match their mist.
And I today so low that I
Envy their mortality . . .

Miphon, half asleep, listened . . . floating . . . heard
the lament begin again. The repetition reminded him of
an animal pacing the bars of its tiny cage. Perhaps the
rock would recite the same words for another thousand
years, without change: they were all more or less mad,
those voices of stone, and with good reason. He knew
the rock might change its tune if it became aware of the
creatures of pulp camping beside it, but that would take
days to happen if it happened at all. Rocks sensed the
world slowly, vaguely, or not at all.

Miphon opened his eyes, blinked at the sunrise, and
sat up. He could still hear the rock, but only dimly. If he
wished, he could start a dialogue with it – but that
would probably be an unkindness. Let it go on
repeating – perhaps forever – the lament it had made in
moments of agony when it had been at least partly sane
and coherent. It had adapted to its condition; Miphon
had no wish to cause it harm.

Passion we had in days of then
When mountains, garrulous and strong,
Desired the thunder, fought with lightning
For favour and delight –

That had been in the world created by the Horn,

when stones, rocks and mountains had been entities free to love, to shape and to build – passionate, careless and immortal. Then the great god Ameeshoth had fought and killed the Horn. Why? Who knew? The sages claimed to know, but much of their teaching was pure invention.

Whatever the reason, after destroying the Horn, Ameeshoth had built this world – the world known as Amarl – over the world of Lemarl. Stones, rocks and mountains had become gross matter, their minds doomed to stasis for all time. If Miphon had been in Ameeshoth's place, he would not have been so cruel: but then, he could not judge the motives of gods.

'Breakfast?' said Blackwood.

'Please.'

'It's not much.'

'It's welcome, whatever it is.'

Breakfast was some small barley meal cakes; they would eat properly when they got back to the castle. Shortly, with all woken, breakfasted and packed, they moved off, glad to get moving to get some warmth into their bones.

'I heard a stone thinking today,' said Miphon.

'We settled the question of stones yesterday,' said Garash with a growl; he thought he was being baited again.

'Your thinking doesn't stop theirs,' said Miphon. 'This one thought most prettily.'

'Really?' said Garash. 'Did it ask your hand in marriage?'

'It said that Heenmor's magic made it free to move for a time.'

'Magic cannot create life,' said Garash, reciting an ancient dogma. 'So how could the stone come alive?'

'It was alive to start with,' said Miphon. 'From the minds of mountains, we of Nin know that they and all their kin have been alive from the beginning of time.'

111

'What is time then, if you're so clever?' said Garash.

'Time is that which permits,' said Miphon, giving the traditional answer, which is, of course, no answer at all. 'Forget about time, because –'

'Because what? Will forgetting time make me immortal?'

'Garash,' said Phyphor, sharply, 'Hear him out.'

'As you wish,' said Garash. 'I'm sure it's good therapy for him to air his delusions.'

'Let's talk about what you've seen with your own two eyes,' said Miphon, considering and then abandoning the idea of a lecture on the inner life of rocks. 'You've seen stone trees, smashed trees, smashed trails, rocks at the end of the trails. How did the rocks get there? Giants didn't throw them there, and rocks don't fall from the sky.'

'They do, you know,' said Blackwood.

'Shut up!' yelled Garash, sick of this impertinent woodsman who dared to intrude on the debates of wizards.

'Mister,' said Blackwood, with dignity, 'I've seen it myself. A rock fell from the sky when I was a child. In the Barley Hills, it was. As big as a house. Big, and hot as fire.'

'If you believe that,' said Garash, 'you're in your second childhood already.'

'You don't know everything,' said Blackwood. And then, voicing something which sounded like a venture into the field of metaphysics, but was actually an expression of contempt: 'You can't.'

Garash stopped, and turned on Blackwood.

'The woodsman is under our protection,' said Hearst swiftly; he liked Blackwood's mettle, and did not wish to see him come to harm.

'Step back, old man,' said Blackwood, fearless as he was ignorant of his danger. He gave Garash a little shove. 'Back! I don't want to hurt you.'

'Please!' said Miphon.

Garash breathed heavily. He was angry, but not too angry to think. He had lost most of his power trying to blast the dragon on the southern border. If he used the rest to kill Blackwood, he would be helpless in any confrontation with Phyphor.

'It pleases me,' said Garash, 'to let him live. For the moment.'

'Thank you, mister,' said Blackwood. 'I'll do you the same courtesy in return.'

As their march had come to a halt, Phyphor decided to settle the question of rocks and stones before going any further. He asked a question:

'Miphon, what's this argument about rocks in aid of? What are you trying to tell us? From looking around us, we know that Heenmor's got power enough to destroy a city at a single blow. That's a cruel thing to know – but it's simple. We can all tell its significance, so we don't need lectures. Apart from that – is there anything else to know?'

Miphon hesitated, looking round at his listeners: the wizards Phyphor and Garash, the Rovac warriors Alish and Hearst, and the woodsman Blackwood. He had to make them understand! He spoke, choosing his words carefully:

'Heenmor has stolen magic from the Dry Pit,' said Miphon. 'I can now guess the nature of that magic. When used, it destroys part of the world created by the great god Ameeshoth – the world in which we live. The creatures of the Horn, meaning rocks and stones, are set free.

'So far, Heenmor can only command a temporary destruction of a small part of the fabric of the world. But if he could learn to control this magic well enough to destroy the fabric of the world of Ameeshoth and then the world of the Horn, he could uncover the original Chaos.

'And if he could learn to shape and control that, then he could make himself into a god. That, I think, could

113

well be what he's planning. Even if he fails, he might destroy the entire universe just by trying. Against such danger, we need all the strength we can muster. I ask all of you here today to join with me in pledging yourself to a common cause.'

Alish laughed, harshly:

'A common cause? Between wizards and the Rovac? Forget it!'

Blackwood looked blank.

'What have gods got to do with it?' asked Blackwood, who hadn't followed the argument at all.

'Miphon,' said Phyphor, with unaccustomed gentleness, 'Even if what you say is true, you can't make instant diplomacy between wizards and Rovac.'

'And it can't be true,' said Garash, 'because rocks don't walk, think or talk.'

'Come on,' said Hearst, eager to quit this forest where men under his command had suffered and died.

And, yielding to his initiative, they resumed their march. Warm skies fared above them as they walked; reaching the region of living things, Blackwood murmured:

Sky, blue sky, the colour of my lover's eyes;
Leaf, young leaf, her hands no softer.

Miphon, delighting in the forest of spring, and remembering the forest of stone they had left behind, thought for the first time in a long time of the sleeping secrets. Heenmor had a power greater than any other known – but the order of Nin also had powers. Great powers. The sleeping secrets. Was this the time to recall those secrets, to open, as the saying went, the book of Nariq?

No.

Only those who sought life, peace and understanding joined the order of Nin. None joined for power – but when they were initiated, the sleeping secrets were

114

revealed to them, giving them powers too terrible for human beings to be trusted with. In the depths of the Shackle Mountains, in the shadow of thunder, in the place between darkness and light, they were taught by the Book of Nariq, and then they were taught to forget.

None dare start the rites of recall except in the most dire emergency. 'What is known must be unknown; what is revealed must be hidden.' Miphon, tempted, controlled himself. The sleeping secrets could not help them find Heenmor. And once they found him, a knife in the back or an arrow in the heart would serve their purpose. Yet, all the way back to Lorford, he thought of the secret powers which needed only the rites of recall to be his.

CHAPTER SEVENTEEN

The Galish: the traders of the Salt Road. Their language, the Trading Tongue (known often simply as 'Galish') serves as a lingua franca for every market place from the Castle of Controlling Power to Chi'ashlan.

Galish, of necessity, is the unifying language of the polyglot pirate community of the Greater Teeth. Dialects of Galish are also spoken in Sung (in Ravlish East) and on the fishing islands of the Lesser Teeth, both areas first colonised by Galish traders.

*   *   *

The sky was clouding over as they neared Lorford. Arriving, they found Melski rafts moored in shallow water upstream from the bridge. Galish – hostile, angry and determined – were loading the rafts. Even two of their pregnant women were hard at work. Right now, camels were being herded into custom-built pens on the rafts.

A man – the wizards recognised him as a sea captain from the Harvest Plains – was trying to negotiate a deal with the Galish. They were not interested. When he grabbed one by the shoulder to remonstrate with him, he was knocked unconscious by an elbow jolt. A ragged cheer went up from locals looking on.

'The Melski,' said Phyphor. 'You seemed to know them well. Ask them if they know where Heenmor went.'

But Blackwood was eager to get back to his wife.

'Mister,' he said, 'It's no good talking to the Melski.

116

They're animals. They can't be trusted. A certain pox doctor told me so.'

'The prince has made peace with these people,' warned Hearst, who did not want to see Blackwood get into trouble. 'Do what they want.'

'Mister,' said Blackwood, 'your orders command me.'

And he obeyed.

One of the Galish demurred when Blackwood tried to board a raft, but a Melski he knew, seeing his predicament, summoned him.

'You see,' said Blackwood. 'He slaps his thigh. He calls me.'

'Go to him then – but keep out of the way.'

'Thank you,' said Blackwood, and went to the Melski.

The Melski, a male, was named Hor-hor-hurulg-murg for short, and more pretentious things for long. He was leaning against a sweep-oar; he had been out of the water for a long time, and the webs between his green fingers were dry and wrinkled.

'Greetings,' said Blackwood in the Melski tongue, a language which lent itself to sonorous formality. 'Greetings in the hour of the sun, greetings from the land to the water.'

'Greetings, Bla-wod,' said his friend. 'Greetings from the water to the land. May our days lie downstream together.'

'One may hope the cycle permits it,' said Blackwood.

'Indeed, one may hope. One may always hope. We hoped for you, Bla-wod, though the river said your house was ash, your bones the same.'

'The house, yes,' said Blackwood. 'The bones, as you see, still need picking.'

Then they began to talk in earnest. Hor-hor-hurulg-murg told how the Galish, finding out about the Collosnon raids, were cutting short their stay in Estar. Their convoy would leave before nightfall, Melski muscle labouring it upstream against the Hollern River to Lake Armansis, deep in the Penvash Peninsular; from there, the Galish would cross a mountain pass to the coast then make the short sea journey west to the Ravlish Lands.

Asked about the wizard Heenmor, Hor-hor-hurulg-murg said he knew nothing.

'Me and mine have wintered in the far of the river, north by north from Lake Armansis. Our southing has given us some of the news, but not all. I will ask the river for you; when we meet again, I will have the answer.'

'Thank you,' said Blackwood.

And returned to the bridge, where the wizards and the warriors were waiting for his return.

'You took your time!' said Garash. 'Why so slow?'

'Mister,' said Blackwood, 'The Melski think before they speak. Try it some time – you'll find it slows the speech remarkably.'

'What did they say?' asked Phyphor, as Garash sought for a suitable retort.

'They don't know. That's all. But they'll ask.'

'Ask what?' said Garash. 'The sky? The trees? The river? Or your precious talking stones?'

'They'll ask their kin,' said Blackwood. 'Then answer us.'

'Till then,' said Hearst, 'we can organise patrols to search north, south, east and west. North in case he's in the forest far from the river and the Melski. South in case he's doubled back on you. That's what I'd do – hide where you'd searched already. West, the river meets the sea. He may have taken a boat from Iglis. East, in case he's fled to Trest. I'll talk to the prince about putting out the patrols.'

'This doesn't mean we're making a common cause with you,' said Alish. 'Just that we all want Heenmor dead.'

Alish disliked Hearst's enthusiasm for working with

118

the wizards, but Alish did want Heenmor's head – and the death-stone. One thing was for certain: wherever Heenmor went, he would have been noted. Twice the height of any other man, he had no hope of hiding himself in a crowd. That made their task easier.

Unknown to Alish, their task was shortly to be complicated by war. Enemy troops were already within the borders, and were closing swiftly on Lorford.

CHAPTER EIGHTEEN

The Collosnon Empire: realm of the Yarglat horsetribes
and their subject peoples.

Capital: Gendormargensis, ruling city of Tameran.

Ruler: the Lord Emperor Khmar, a warrior ferae
naturae.

Religion: no state religion, though the horse cult of
Noth is powerful amongst the Yarglat.

Language: Eparget (the ruling Yarglat dialect);
Ordhar (the command language of the armies);
sundry minor tongues.

History: like most imperial histories, a tale of blood
and ashes; the dominant theme is conquest.

*   *   *

By nightfall, the day which had begun so brightly
had turned to heavy pounding rain that fell without
relief. Through this rain, the first refugees began to
arrive from the countryside, bearing confused tales
of attack by night, pursuit, swords and slaughter,
armies on the march. At dawn, people began to
evacuate Lorford, seeking safety in Castle Vaunting;
the central court soon filled with the clamour of
homeless citizens, their animals and their bewildered
children.

Shortly before noon, Collosnon cavalry attacked
Lorford, claiming many victims: people who had
delayed leaving, being sceptical of the reports of
invasion. Prince Comedo ordered the drawbridge
pulled up. Some half-hearted smoke ascended from
parts of Lorford; the town had been too badly dragon-

damaged for the enemy to have much success in burning it.

While the cavalry were still completing their kill, infantry marched in from the east, from Trest, so now everyone knew Trest had been conquered by Khmar, the Red Emperor, ruler of the greater part of Tameran. Red he was called, because that was the colour the rivers ran in the lands his armies marched through.

Alish watched from the battlements, feeling a strange sense of exultation at the sight of enemy soldiers swarming over the land. He estimated five thousand stood against them, as opposed to a few hundred able-bodied men within the castle.

'Beautiful,' he murmured, as he watched.

The old excitement possessed him. What better sight than the coherent power of thousands of men unified by a single will? He remembered his days of greatness. Elkor Alish, Our Lord Despair, had been a famous commander in the Cold West. But those days were behind him. His conscience – rare flower among Rovac warriors, that conscience – could not sanction any more killing of the innocent.

But even so, watching the men out there, he yearned for an excuse to campaign. To satisfy his conscience, it must be a pure campaign against an enemy of unmitigated evil. Alish knew of a war which would fulfil those needs: a war against the wizards, the ancient enemy which had once committed a monstrous crime which only wizards and Rovac warriors knew of.

Given possession and control of Heenmor's death-stone, Alish could become a world conqueror. Armies would follow him. They would march south in glory to sack the wizard strongholds, fighting a war where every action would be justified by their cause. Alish knew this to be his duty: for he was a member of the Code of Night, Rovac's elite secret instrument of vengeance.

Castle Vaunting could not be saved; it would have to be abandoned to the enemy. The Heenmor hunt came first.

When Prince Comedo found Alish on the battlements, and asked what they should do next, Alish answered promptly:

'I suggest we hear their terms,' said Alish.

'Agreed,' said Comedo, promptly; he was terrified of the thought of fighting.

'I'll go,' said Alish, a skilled negotiator.

'No,' said Comedo. 'You're captain of my bodyguard. You stay. We'll send . . . Andranovory.'

Alish almost groaned, but restrained himself. Fortunately, Andranovory was drunk, as usual; as he was completely legless, he had to be excluded from the diplomatic corps. Unfortunately, Comedo then insisted on sending Hearst.

'Don't,' said Alish to Hearst, 'give them any bullshit and bluster. Take what we're offered. Remember, half a cup's better than nothing. And while you're about it, see if they've got my resting woman – you know the one. She seems to be lost.'

'I'll play the perfect diplomat,' said Hearst. 'Trust me. And, while I'm down there, I'll be sure to ask after your doxy.'

By now it was late afternoon. The drawbridge was lowered, and Morgan Hearst went downhill to the enemy. He returned toward nightfall with the enemy's terms, and the news that the enemy were now enjoying the company of Volaine Persaga Haveros, who had joined Comedo's forces in the autumn, and was now revealed to be not a Collosnon fugitive but a Collosnon spy. This man Haveros had been able to tell the enemy commander everything he needed to know about Castle Vaunting. The enemy's terms were blunt and simple:

'Our lord the Emperor Khmar requires the surrender of the ruling castle of Estar, together with all horse and weapons. Those in the castle must leave, taking with them only their clothes and their children. The ruby eye of the dragon Zenphos is to be delivered to the army of

122

rightful inheritance. The prince of the castle is to be delivered up for execution. Any and all diviners, necromancers, sorcerers, witches, palmists, makers of spells and potions or other workers of magic are to be killed, and their heads presented to the commander of the battlefield. Long live the emperor!'

Prince Comedo, realising the enemy wanted him dead, screamed, and fled, wailing.

'What of my woman?' asked Alish.

'As far as anyone knows, she's dead,' said Hearst, easily.

And Alish thought:

– One more person lost to the wreckage of war.

And vowed that, in his wars, there would be no such innocent victims.

* * *

A single candle kept night's besieging darkness at bay. Gathered at a table for a council of war were Phyphor, Garash, Miphon, Morgan Hearst, Elkor Alish and a tear-stained Prince Comedo.

'Today we find we have a common cause,' said Phyphor. 'I will name it. Survival.'

'The enemy wish to drink wizard-blood,' said Alish, 'but I haven't heard them asking for my head.'

'Your oath of honour binds you to your prince,' said Phyphor.

'That's right,' said Comedo, eagerly. 'Quite right.'

'True,' said Alish. 'But it's early days to talk of dying sword in hand. An enemy army of that size can't live off the land. They can't have more than a month's provisions at most. Their bellies will soon be making certain arguments. They'll soon decide they have to let my prince go free – and I'll go with him.'

He paused. And they heard shouts of alarm, cries, a clash of steel. Despite the speech he had just made, it was Alish who came to the obvious conclusion:

'By the hell!' he said, rising. 'The enemy are in the castle! Quick!'

'Impossible,' said Garash faintly.

But Alish was already gone, plunging recklessly down darkened stairways with Hearst close behind him. The wizards got to their feet. Compared to the Rovac warriors they were like sleepwalkers, like drugged men, unable to make that instant transition from talk to action.

Alish crashed down the stairs four at a time, eight at a time. Below, echoes hammered from the walls. The clash of steel woke iron voices from the castle rock. Vivid memories woke: the sheen of steel sweeping through the sun, blood on ice, a face demolished, falling.

Torches lit the fifth level of the gatehouse keep, where a portal opened onto the battlements. The enemy were storming the portal from the battlements. The fight was going against the defenders.

'Ahyak Rovac!' screamed Alish.

Weak words they made in translation, for they meant only 'here are the Rovac', but that battlecry was feared throughout half the world. Then Alish drew his sword. Ethlite graced his hand. Hearst joined him, his battle-sword Hast in hand, and they fought together, side by side.

*   *   *

It was night.

Prince Comedo had struggled to the top of the gatehouse keep, as far from the battle as possible. Wind and rain harassed him. He stamped his feet; he wore socks of the warmest wool and boots of the softest leather, but still his feet were cold.

Far, far below, in the darkness, the battle raged. The enemy had used big crossbows to shoot hundreds of grapples with ropes attached. The grapples had hooked

124

onto the battlements, allowing the Collosnon to swarm across to attack the gatehouse keep.

The ropes had gone up in flames when the wizards had joined the battle, with Phyphor calling out the Words which had turned the flame trench into a seething inferno, shooting flames toward the sky – but by that time over a thousand Collosnon soldiers had been on the battlements. The reverberating energies of the flame trench now made the castle itself shudder and shake.

At first, Phyphor had blasted the battlements with white fire from his hand and his staff, but now Phyphor's power was exhausted, hundreds of Collosnon soldiers remained alive, and the battle raged on without benefit of magic.

The wind, bitterly cold, drove clouds across the sky. They glowed red with reflections from the flame trench; the heavens themselves were on fire. The land, in all directions, was dark as the grave and the gut of the worm. And the wind, clawing Comedo, ravaging the clouds, was like the wind the poet talks of in the Epic of Sothor:

The wind that teaches the children of death,
The wind that teaches the hero of fear,
The wind that sharpens the teeth of the mountains,
The wind that carries the cry of the skeleton,
The wind that is rasp under hammer, the claw –

Comedo clutched the retaining wall as the wind threatened to tear him from his feet.

– So they are here. In the castle. They will conquer. Yes. The gates will fall. Yes. Tapestries torn. Yes. Blood on the floor. Yes.

– No!

Fists grip, jaw tightens, pulse throbs. A scream wells in his throat and bursts out: no no no no no! The wind laughs it away; the wind sings of millstones, breaking

125

rock and grinding bones. Comedo screams again. They must not! They must not conquer! By the red hells of leprosy and rupture, they must not!

Wind, night and darkness mock him, and enjoy.

* * *

Elkor Alish, the best swordsman of Rovac – and, according to some, Rovac's greatest war leader – raised a heavy hand to wipe his long black hair from his eyes. He was uncertain on his feet, exhausted after a night of battle, but he knew this was only the beginning. After a day and a night it would be much worse: he would be asleep on his feet, living a nightmare.

There was blood on his sword.

He mouthed the words: I have killed again.

The words meant nothing.

The dawn was as grey as steel. Rain hammered on wet stones. Water and blood. The dead. Dead men on the battlements. Dead Collosnon in the central courtyard, which they had gained by abseiling down from the battlements. Dead Collosnon by the courtyard entry to the gatehouse keep, now barred by a portcullis. Dead refugees, slaughtered by the Collosnon in the courtyard.

The surviving soldiers of the enemy were on the battlements, keeping their distance from archers who could shoot from the heights of the gatehouse keep. How many were left? Two hundred? Three? Enough, for certain.

Alish knew they would attack again.

And he knew which way the battle would go.

Dough-faced men watched the hammering rain. Men who had repelled repeated fanatic charges now faced the day with eyes as blank as drowning. They moved slowly, with effort, as if their limbs had been swollen with elephantitis. Miphon, helped by Blackwood, was tending to the wounded.

126

'A good battle,' said Gorn cheerfully; his shoulder had been heavily bruised, a blow driving links of his chain mail into his flesh.

'Yes,' said Alish. 'It was a good battle.'

'They will make a song for us,' said Gorn.

'We can hope as much,' said Alish.

And said no more. He was too tired for sorrow or guilt. He was too tired even to wonder that he was still alive.

'Well,' said Phyphor. 'Do we have a common cause?'

Alish turned: he had not heard the wizard approach.

'Come,' said Phyphor. 'We have to talk. Miphon, are you finished? Then come. It's all right, Elkor Alish: talk commits you to nothing. So listen to us: you've got nothing to lose.'

*   *   *

They sat together in council: Alish and Hearst, the three wizards and Prince Comedo. Phyphor outlined their situation:

'If we fight, we die. Yet we can't surrender. That leaves us, it seems, no choice at all. Yet this castle holds a power which could destroy the enemy without another blow being struck.'

'What power?' demanded Alish. 'Why haven't you used it?'

'It's not yet mine to use.'

'Where is it then?'

'It's guarded by a desperate danger.'

'Really?' said Alish. 'You'll find us warriors take our dangers lightly.'

'Smile away,' said Phyphor, resisting the temptation to add the word 'fool'. Then, continuing: 'For your information, I fought through the Long War. I stood against the Neversh. I know what truly constitutes desperate danger.'

'So tell us,' said Alish.

127

'Only if you join with us in a common cause,' said Phyphor. 'You can start by telling us about Heenmor. I understand you were the only one who got to know him well.'

'I'll tell you nothing.'

'You will, you know. Then you'll take an oath to bind you to our quest to recover whatever magic Heenmor took from the Dry Pit – and to kill Heenmor while we're about it.'

'I won't do it.'

'Then the Collosnon will kill you.'

'And you!'

'We all have our privileges,' said Phyphor dryly.

'This is blackmail,' said Alish.

'Precisely. What do you say, Morgan Hearst?'

'Before I could join your cause,' said Hearst, 'My prince would have to free me from the words which bind my honour to his service. The same, of course, holds good for my dear friend Alish.'

They all looked at Prince Comedo.

'I want to live,' said Comedo simply.

'Then I will make a common cause with these gathered here,' said Hearst. 'And you, Alish? Come now! Dead is dead. We've seen dead. Do you want to finish here, like a rat in the trap? And if so, why? Alish – there's no shame in this.'

Alish bowed his head. His voice was low and toneless:

'I will tell what I know of Heenmor's magic. I will join Hearst in an oath to bind us to your service. I will make a common cause with those here gathered.'

So he spoke.

And so it was done.

128

CHAPTER NINETEEN

Smoking torches inflamed the fatigued darkness. Tunnels stumbled downwards. Phyphor's jawbone lagged. Spelaean echoes dogged their heels and played cat-rat to the fore. Garash and Alish jostled each other, and almost came to blows.

'This,' said the executioner, as the tunnels forked. 'This way.'

'I remember,' murmured Blackwood.

'Remember?' said the executioner. 'Remember? Yes, two can remember. Watch yourself, my child!'

Blackwood, silenced by this cryptic threat, said no more. Comedo grumbled about the toll on his legs; his night-time climb to his gatehouse keep had just about crippled him.

'How much further?' said Comedo.

'Prince,' said the executioner, 'prince, my prince, this is this. Left and right, room to stand.'

They gathered at the edge of the pit. The executioner's clay face swung to the dark.

'Hungry,' he said. 'Yes. No feeding this day or last.'

'Lower a light,' said Phyphor.

A lantern, lowered on a cord, at last illuminated a fraction of the slow-bulking monstrosity below. The vastness stirred, slowly; the ages had given it time enough to learn leisure.

'Feed,' said the executioner. 'We could feed him.'

He pointed at Blackwood.

'Yes!' said Comedo.

'No!' said Hearst.

Comedo hesitated, then:

'I concede the woodsman's life to the hero.'

Hearst did not thank him, but studied the gross, amorphous appetite below. It moved, with a noise like a boot dragged out of a sucking swamp.

'Moves,' said the executioner. 'Moves fast, when it wants to.'

'I'm sure it does,' said Hearst. Then, after the briefest of pauses: 'But I'll dare it.'

'Will you?' said Phyphor.

'I have already said as much.'

'But saying is not yet doing, mighty slayer of dragons.'

From the way Phyphor spoke, Hearst knew at once that the wizard was certain Hearst had not killed the dragon. Phyphor knew enough about dragons to know the feat Hearst boasted of was next to impossible. Let him sneer then: he could prove nothing.

'I'll prove myself to my word,' said Hearst.

'You will? Then remember: run to the far left-hand corner. You'll find stairs leading up into the tower of Seth. That's where the valuables are. Only a wizard of Seth can enter that tower, except by this one free way.'

'Why are the valuables in there?'

'Because there had been too much killing for their possession. All wanted them, so we finally had to agree that none should have them. Seth was set to guard them. No wizard truly trusts a wizard, but we counted those of Seth the ones we could trust the most.'

'Why hasn't anyone stolen them before?' said Hearst.

'Nobody's stupid enough to try,' said Garash.

'The lopsloss was made to be immune to all magic,' said Phyphor. 'So no wizard could try the venture. It needs a hero. Are you the man?'

Down below, with a sudden surge, the lopsloss thrust itself forward. The lantern went out. The cavernous space reverberated with the solid smack of bulk battering itself against the wall. Hearst hesitated.

'He'll do it,' said Alish. 'I'll hold the battlements as far as the tower of Seth till nightfall, if need be.'

130

As Phyphor had explained, only a wizard of Seth could enter Seth's tower from the battlements, but anyone could exit.

'Go now,' said Phyphor. 'Remember what you're seeking: two boxes, each made of lead, each box bearing the null sign of the dead zero, sign of the nether magic. Do you remember that sign?'

'Yes.'

'And don't open the boxes! If you do, you're dead. Oh, another thing. If there's a bottle there, that'll be worth bringing out, too.'

'A bottle?'

'You'll recognise it if you see it,' said Phyphor. 'Well, are you going? After dragon killing, this should be a picnic!'

Hearst's bootlaces felt too tight. Should he alter them? If he did, he would find his sword was not riding comfortably at his side. And with that adjusted, his boots would feel too loose.

'Yes,' said Hearst, nodding. 'Time to go.'

'Luck,' said Alish, and turned on his heel and strode away: he had to command the defence of the battlements.

'You'll do it,' said Blackwood, offering encouragement.

'Unless you don't,' said Garash.

'If don't, then dead,' said the executioner. 'The feeding isn't always quick.'

Below, the lopsloss sucked back, then rammed the wall with a blow which set the stones beneath them shaking.

'Sometimes,' said the executioner. 'Sometimes, though, it is quite quick. Quite'

'Lower another lantern,' said Phyphor. 'It's got no sight to speak of, so you might as well have the light.'

'No sight,' said Hearst. 'Has it a mind?'

He had heard the Miphon had some power over the minds of animals.

131

'None that I can hear,' said Miphon, knowing the question was for him.

'Well then,' said Hearst. 'Well . . . I'll do it.'

'We'll see,' said Phyphor.

* * *

Boots braced against wall, Hearst laboured down on a rope, descending toward the doom below. The lopsloss creaked and squelched; Hearst imagined that he heard little wavelets lapping against the walls below, but dismissed the thought. Breathing the increasing meat-rot stench, he almost gagged, but controlled himself. Off to his left, the lantern, hanging above the lopsloss, illuminated only a fraction of its glistening, alien flesh.

He was down far enough.

When he cried out, those above would throw meat to the lopsloss. When it moved away to take the meat, Hearst would have to let himself down to the bottom and sprint for the left-hand corner. He would be running through darkness.

'I'm ready!' he shouted.

He was answered, first, by ghostly echoes of his own voice. Then by an unintelligible shout from above. Then the meat – a dead sheep – splashed down into the darkness. It sounded very much as if it had hit water. The lopsloss quivered, shook, then began to move for the meat. Hearst let himself down to the bottom.

There really was water!

The dungeon floor was knee-deep in water. It would slow him down. Hearst hesitated. Imagining how Phyphor would greet his retreat:

'So . . . our mighty dragon-killer returns.'

Hearst was off: running. Water clogged his steps as he panted forward. The ground sagged away underfoot: water surged to his waist. And he could hear the lopsloss. It was coming after him. He lost his footing en-

132

tirely. He was afloat! The monster was hot behind. He would never make it. He struck out through the water. And there was a scream—

Something heavy crashed into the water.

The lopsloss paused, stopped. Hearst trod water, then eased his feet down, seeking the bottom. His boots touched stone. He stood there, trembling, shivering.

There was a squelch of bulk and suction. The lopsloss was moving. But which way? Hearst counted to one, to three, he was still alive, six to eight, alive, and nine, and ten, take breath—

He knew which way the lopsloss was moving.

Slowly, very carefully, he took a step forward. Then another. He eased himself through the water, gaining higher ground. Then his hand found the left-hand wall. He was on course.

Then he heard the lopsloss returning.

'No!' screamed Hearst.

Hobbled by flooded boots, he stumbled through knee-deep water. The lopsloss was gaining on him, driving a wave in front of it. The wave rocked past. It broke against rock. Rock! He ran slap-bang into it. Where now? Left? Right? He chose: right. He dodged: right. Rock opened for him. He ran, slipped, fell, clawed himself forward. The lopsloss slammed against the wall behind him, sucking and groping.

But he was inside. Safe.

Safe and sobbing.

He had done it.

*   *   *

Climbing stairs leading upward into the darkness, Hearst tripped over something. He poked at it with his sword, kicked it, then, when it didn't slither or squeal, felt it. A tree root? A tree root! Further up the winding stairway, the root thickened. Soon there were two, then three. Old and dead, some crumbling to dust beneath

133

his boots, releasing the faintest scent of sandalwood. When he reached the tower of Seth, the larger roots were as thick as his thigh.

In the tower, dead branches choked the daylight. Someone, abandoning the tower, had left a tree behind. Struggling to break through to the outer air, it had choked the tower with its branches; stairs led upwards, but the branches blocked them. Hearst drew Hast and laid about him. Dead, ancient wood shattered to dust and splinters before his blade.

Outside, a battle was in progress. He could hear it. He worked faster, coughing as the dust got to his lungs. He was sweating now. His skin and leathers, soaking wet from his swim, were covered in fine grey dust.

'Gen-ha! Gen-ha!'

That was a Collosnon battle-lung shouting: Forward! Forward! Hearst grunted and swung his sword again, driving himself.

'Gen-ha! Gen-ha!'

Sweeping away one last branch, Hearst gained the uppermost chamber. Through windows with panes of diamond, he saw a battle below: a confused pattern of knots of men locked in combat on the battlements between the tower of Seth and the portal giving access to the gatehouse keep.

At a glance Hearst saw the enemy were winning.

Where was the magic? The two boxes? There – above him, caught in branches which had lofted them to the ceiling. He hacked at the branches. They exploded into dust. The boxes fell. Lunging forward, he caught one. The other hit the ground. The lid came off. Dozens of red charms spilt out into the swirling dust, each charm trailing a thin gold necklace. Hearst stared at them aghast, remembering Phyphor's warning. But nothing happened.

Outside, the enemy shouted in triumph. Comedo's forces were falling back in disarray. Hearst looked at the heavy box he was holding. On the lid were

134

hellmouth jaws and the null sign of the dead zero, the sign of the nether magic. He had been warned of the dangers within. But—

'I held the breach at Enelorf,' he said, his voice a whisper.

He bit his lip, and lifted the lid.

Inside, two yellow jewels reclined on verdant velvet. Each was the size of a fist. Was this the great magic? These two baubles? And what was that light that sang and curdled inside them?

The floor canted abruptly, and Hearst found himself sliding toward the jaws of a waiting dragon. Screaming, he fell. Flame scalded him. Its jaws closed, biting him in half. He wailed in despair and—

Found himself lying on the dusty floor.

It was very quiet.

The floor was level.

There was no dragon.

His body was intact.

And the box? It lay on the floor beside him. The lid, fortunately, had fallen shut. Slowly, Hearst regained his feet. He sneezed, then wiped the dust from a window. Outside, the fighting had stopped. Some men stood as if stunned; others were picking themselves up from the ground.

'Gen-ha!' shouted the Collosnon battle-lung.

The Collosnon troops started forward again. Hearst knelt by the box. Delicately, using just one finger, he lifted the lid. And heard a dragon roar behind him, screamed as its flame engulfed him—

And dropped the lid shut on the box.

No pain, no flame, no dragon.

Outside, the enemy were wavering. Then came a shout:

'Ahyak Rovac!'

Yes, it was the voice of Elkor Alish: challenge echoing from tower to tower as it had when the tide of battle turned in their favour at Vaglazeen. And the voice of

Our Lord Despair completed the panic amongst the enemy, and they ran.

And Hearst whispered to himself, again:

'I held the breach at Enelorf.'

* * *

'Did it disturb you much?' said Hearst.

'What? When you opened the box?'

'What else?'

'No,' said Phyphor.

But, in truth, each time Hearst had opened the lead box, Phyphor had seen before his very eyes the double spikes of the Neversh, and had fallen screaming to the ground.

'I'm so glad you weren't upset,' said Hearst.

From the way he said it, Phyphor knew the warrior had been told exactly what had happened. Phyphor had screamed. And Garash had roared until his veins stood out.

'Now,' said Phyphor. 'What have you got there? Ah, I see. You managed to find the bottle as well.'

'Yes. But I can't find out what it does.'

'Of course you can't. If you could, you wouldn't hand it over.'

Phyphor caressed the small, green-glazed bottle, which was decorated with two metal bands. He said a Word. The bands loosened, tinkled to the floor, then shrank to finger-sized rings.

'What are those for?' asked Hearst.

'Never you mind,' said Phyphor.

He shook the lead boxes. One rattled: it held the dozens of small red charms on thin chains. Opening it, he ran his fingers through them with an expression close to lust. This was well worth killing for.

'What are the charms for?' said Hearst.

'Can't you guess?'

'I'm a warrior, not a . . .'

136

Pox doctor was the term he had in mind.

'Not a wizard,' said Phyphor, finishing his sentence for him.

'Well then,' said Hearst. 'The pair of yellow jewels in the other box, the ones that made everyone go strange when I lifted the lid – what do they do?'

'Can't you guess? They make men insane.'

'Insane?'

'They steal men's wits,' said Phyphor. 'The red charms on the golden chains give protection against the mad-jewels. Now we can kill off the enemy and save our lives, so let's be glad that Blackwood saved yours.'

'Blackwood?'

'Your woodsman friend. We heard you running through water. We knew you'd never reach safety on your own. So when the lopsloss went after you ... Blackwood gave the executioner a push.'

CHAPTER TWENTY

Name: Mystrel (wife to Blackwood).
Birthplace: Little Gidding (a hamlet later claimed for ashes by the dragon Zenphos).
Occupation: home executive.
Description: a face which, to Blackwood, is more familiar than his own (since he has no mirror); a voice which he hears in his dreams. Flesh in her flesh lives a life which is not yet entirely its own.

*　　*　　*

The next morning, the charms were shared out. As there weren't enough to go round, Miphon brewed a sleeping potion to be drunk by all the charmless before the mad-jewels were used against the enemy. Belatedly, Blackwood, who had drunk his share, realised his wife Mystrel had avoided taking the sleeping potion. He took her to Miphon, who still had some left in a cauldron simmering over a low fire. From the cauldron, purple flames rose wraith by wraith.

'I won't drink that,' said Mystrel.

'It only brings sleep,' said Miphon.'It's harmless.'

'For you, maybe. For me, perhaps. But I am with child.'

'This won't harm the unborn,' said Miphon. 'What we do to our bodies doesn't touch them.'

'Really? And when did you last bear a child?'

The challenge was unexpected; Miphon was not used to having his authority questioned by work-faded peasant women.

'I've researched these things,' he said, carefully.

'Yes. You've read about them in your dusty books. And I've felt the flesh kick in my belly. There's a difference. I've lost children before – I won't risk this one.'

Miphon was amazed at her vehemence.

'My mother taught me of the power that plants draw from the earth,' said Mystrel. 'She taught me sleeping and dreams, the end of pain and the death of fever. She taught me how to tell when a woman is with child – and to be very, very careful.'

'If you're so wise,' said Miphon, 'Why did you lose your other children?'

'Winter was the wolf that took them,' said Mystrel. 'Each time, the snow – we were starving!'

Miphon was shocked by her bitterness. Suddenly he had a vision of what had happened. Pale flesh on dark earth. Flesh formed perfectly, but never breathing. Last words for the dead. A burial. A small mound of earth. Silence under forest boughs. A woman on her knees in the thick wet rot of fallen leaves: weeping. Now he knew her loss. And was ashamed at how he had accused her, purely for the sake of rhetorical victory. Now what was he to do?

'Here,' said Miphon, placing his charm round her neck.

If he hadn't been arrogant enough to try to force her to accept the benefits of his medicine, he would have thought of that simple solution immediately. He had always prided himself on the fact that he was humble enough to put himself at the service of the common people. Now, he realised that he had never cured himself of the main failing of wizards: to treat knowledge as an instrument of force and an extension of power.

Oh well, he had plenty of time to learn.

After all, he had not yet reached his first century.

He dipped a ladle in his wizard brew, and drank.

*   *   *

Blackwood and Mystrel retired to their quarters. Soon Blackwood was asleep. For a while, Mystrel sat by the bed, carding wool. The castle was strangely quiet; usually it echoed with boots, doors slamming, distant shouts, half-heard snatches of song, and, sometimes, hammering from the makeshift forge where Lorford's blacksmith had set up shop to work on weapons and armour.

Suddenly, a horn sounded, brash and brazen. A half-remembered phrase stirred in Mystrel's memory: 'the horn of the victor which echoes the sun.' Yes. She knew the horn was a signal for butchery. The men of the castle were going to slaughter their enemies on the battlements.

The fodden woke from sleep at Mystrel's feet. As it was not human, it could not be affected by the mad-jewels.

'Shlunt?' slurred the fodden.

'No hunt,' said Mystrel. 'Just men, at their games as usual.'

'Oh,' said the fodden, still half-asleep, and sank back into its dreams.

It was still suffering from injuries received when some of Comedo's men had used it for a game of kick the cat. Mystrel was tending it because that was her nature: to care for weak, broken things that could not help themselves.

Blackwood turned in his sleep. Muttered something.

'Peace,' said Mystrel.

And let her hand trail over his cheek, lightly, lightly. Then she bent over him, smiled, and sealed his sleep with a kiss. Both times that Hearst had first opened the box holding the two mad-jewels, she had, to her horror, seen his dead body before her. Knowing what his death would mean to her, she treasured his life.

140

CHAPTER TWENTY-ONE

As the siege dragged on, many of the enemy dispersed. Alish estimated that a thousand of the Collosnon soldiers had died after attacking Castle Vaunting, that a thousand more had marched off elsewhere, and that perhaps three thousand remained.

When the flames of the castle's moat finally died down, allowing the drawbridge to be lowered, the mad-jewels would be used again, and Comedo's soldiers would march out to slaughter the three thousand.

Comedo, it was rumoured, was still eating in luxury. The rest of the castle was rationed, but Phyphor favoured them by releasing urns of siege dust from the tower of Arl, so nobody actually went hungry. Plenty of rain fell, replenishing dungeon cisterns which took the drainage from the vast expanse of the central courtyard, so there was no chance that they would die of thirst.

Miphon, turning his attention to public health, arranged for the water to be filtered and boiled before it was drunk. He brewed up a vermifuge, and dosed everyone in the castle, with the exception of a few pregnant women. He laid out a special poisoned rat bait, with spectacular results. He persuaded Prince Comedo to get rid of most of his corpse collection, and to have the few remaining items embalmed.

The castle's dogs and cats were slaughtered for food. Taking advantage of this opportunity, Miphon got rid of the castle's fleas by having every mat and rug burnt, and by having the stone floors swept regularly. His programme for eradicating lice was not so successful, as—

(a) few people were willing to shave their heads and

boil their clothes and bedding; and

(b) a substantial number of people believed that lack of lice meant that one was so sick that death was just round the corner.

He did much minor surgery. He also had a fair bit of major surgery to do, particularly amputating gangrenous limbs; as only half of his seriously ill patients died, his prestige rose enormously. Gangrene – a consequence of the enemy's failure to sterilise their weapons before using them on human flesh – was usually inevitably fatal, with most attempts at a cure by amputation simply leading to fresh infection.

Wary of the possible personal consequences of his local fame, Miphon diligently practiced the disciplines of humility. He discussed childbirth and healing with Mystrel, who proved exceptionally knowledgeable; despite his experience, Miphon found there was still much he had to learn.

They exchanged information about herbs, honey, garlic, leeches, bone setting, ulcers, cancers, vermifuges and all the other things that healers have to know about – including, of course, the various kinds of pox. Mystrel was particularly wise about the local plants; Miphon, on the other hand, knew more about exotic things like opium and ginseng, which came to Estar only by way of trade.

Blackwood and Hearst would usually be present at their conversations – but, instead of listening in, those two usually talked man-talk about the hunting of large, noisy animals, the trapping of the same, about Hearst's adventures in the Cold West (special emphasis on mammoth hunts) and Blackwood's foolhardy ventures (in his younger days) into the weirder reaches of the Penvash Peninsular (special emphasis on encounters with giant bears).

Hearst and Blackwood one day concluded an inconclusive debate – does the crocodile really exist, and, if so, is it possible to kill it bare handed? – to find Mystrel and Miphon still indefatigably talking medicine.

' . . . and, of course, garlic is good for wounds,' said Mystrel.

'Yes,' said Miphon, 'But what would you do for an ulcer that wouldn't heal? I don't think I'd use garlic for that.'

'No,' said Mystrel. 'I'd use bandages soaked in honey.'

'Honey!' said Hearst, taking an interest for once. 'That'd rot the wound.'

'You'd have to change the bandages four times a day,' said Mystrel. 'You wouldn't just leave it there, you know.'

'It'd still go rotten.'

'Now when did you last see rotten honey?' said Mystrel. 'It keeps in the hive through winter and beyond because the bees make it with a guarding. That's why you can use it on ulcers.'

'You'll have to teach your child, when the child's old enough,' said Miphon, impressed by her competence.

'Boys have a lot to learn besides herbs,' said Blackwood. 'Fishing, hunting, weather-lore – it's the women who've got time to sit at home talking of herbs and honey.'

'Oh yes,' said Mystrel, warmly. 'And carding the wool, and spinning, cleaning the fireplace and making the rushlights, putting the stew on to cook – and that's only the start of the day. Then there's baking bread, drawing water, doing the washing – '

'Peace!' said Blackwood.

Hearst laughed.

Mystrel, her temper up, gave no mercy:

' – and there's plucking birds and scraping hides, weaving the reed-mats, gathering water cress, gathering the big-ear fungus, and soap, in season – up to the elbows in ashes and animal fat. There'll be time enough in a boy's life for my son to learn what I've got to teach him.'

143

'It might be a girl,' said Miphon.

'No,' said Hearst. 'Blackwood will have a son.'

'It's not him who's with child!' said Mystrel. 'But you're right. It will be a boy.'

'I'll teach him how to use a sword,' said Hearst, who, while they were talking, was slowly incising a rune into the metal of his battle-sword Hast.

'No son of mine will go to the wars,' said Mystrel.

'Then we'll make him a wizard,' said Miphon.

'No,' said Blackwood. 'My son will be a hunter, like his father. When he's old enough. I'll take him north, into the wilds.'

But, for the moment, he spared them further stories of those wilds, for his curiosity was getting the better of him:

'What's that you're cutting into your sword, Morgan?'

'A rune,' said Miphon.

'It's a death-pledge,' said Hearst. 'Out there is a traitor – an oath-breaker. Volaine Persaga Haveros, a Collosnon spy. He swore an oath of loyalty to the prince – and a second oath of personal loyalty to Elkor Alish. When I meet him again, I'll kill him. The rune dedicates this sword to revenge.'

An oath-breaker could not be forgiven; nothing is worse than to betray a pledge of loyalty.

'If I had even a good kitchen knife,' said Mystrel, 'I wouldn't damage it like that.'

Women, it has sometimes been remarked – by Kash m'pie T'longa amongst others – have never been very enthusiastic about the mystique of murder and revenge.

'This is only a scratch,' said Hearst. 'I could tell you a tale of a sword – '

'What sword?' said Blackwood.

'Oh, it's a children's tale I was minded of,' said Hearst. 'I won't insult you with it.'

As Miphon was a wizard, he did not think it safe to tell the sword-story he had almost started on. The

144

sword in question was the blade Raunen Song, which, according to the Black Blood Legends of Rovac, bore the rune-written names of a thousand wizards.

A legendary hero of Rovac had sworn to take that sword, Raunen Song the ironcleaver, the stonesplitter, and kill each and every one of those thousand wizards. But the hero had disappeared, centuries ago, without a trace. And this was not the time or the place to encourage the ancient hatreds between wizards and the Rovac.

'Why did you leave the Cold West?' asked Miphon, taking advantage of Hearst's silence to ask a question which had puzzled him for some time. 'It must've offered you more than Estar can.'

'Yes,' said Hearst. 'But it was too cold.'

He did not elaborate.

'What about Alish?' said Miphon. 'Why did he come here? Some say he commanded armies in the Cold West. Why would a man like that come to Estar? They say he could've led the conquest of the whole of the Cold West, if he'd stayed.'

Ah yes. If he'd stayed. But after Larbreth . . . after Larbreth, everything had changed. Especially Alish.

'Well, he's here now,' said Hearst. 'And we've made a common cause together. So . . .'

He let his words trail away; nobody insisted that he complete them.

'It must be about noon,' said Blackwood, rising. 'I have to go to help with some butcher work.'

'What's left to kill?' said Miphon.

'Horses,' said Blackwood.

Hearst watched the way Blackwood and Mystrel looked at each other before they parted. What was in that look? Not a childish form of infatuation, not the ardent lust of the young – but a kind of empathy and trust nurtured by long years of shared and undivided loyalty.

He envied them.

CHAPTER TWENTY-TWO

Name: Valarkin (brother of Durnwold).

Birthplace: Little Hunger Farm (which is also his current residence).

Career: leaving home, he became an acolyte-priest of the temple of the Demon of Estar; survived the destruction of the temple thanks to his caution (which some would call cowardice – but then, some are dead, and he's not); returned to his father's farm to become a farm labourer.

Prospects: with no union, no continuing education programme, no pay, and little chance of promotion, his career structure currently seems non-existent.

Description: a young man who is not really as pretty as his mother thought he was at birth.

* * *

'To your left, Valarkin!' yelled the old man. 'To your left!'

Valarkin, exhausted, pretended he did not hear. Sheep stampeded toward the gap he had failed to fill, but one of the dogs got there first. The old man – Valarkin's father – cursed him roundly. A single sheep found the way into the pen; the rest mobbed in after it. Leelesh closed a leather-hinged gate on them.

The open-mouthed lambs panted, their breath steaming in the chill air. It was cold and grey, as it could be in summer in Estar, where the weather's caprice easily destroyed any brief prosperity a family might achieve. Spring snow could kill lambs. Then, if the summer was too hot and fine, sheep might fall victim to

146

fly strike – flies laying eggs in their backs to hatch to maggots which caused stinking black sores which could kill the animal. Rain forestalled fly strike, but prevented shearing, as wool stored wet would rot, and be worthless in the marketplace.

'Come on, Valarkin,' said the old man.

Valarkin shivered. His limbs were stiffening as he cooled down after the rigours of herding. One ankle hurt where he had twisted it jumping across a stream. His legs, to the knees, were filthy with bog-mud.

'Come on, Valarkin! If you just stand there eating air, then air is all you'll get to eat.'

It was no joke. They would starve him, given an excuse. He wished he could have them, one and all, strung up in the temple for a sacrifice. Yes!

The girl Leelesh, the voiceless moron his father had made Durnwold marry to get her dowry of a dozen sheep, opened the gate for Valarkin then guarded it while he caught a sheep. He wrestled it out of the gateway, dragging it by the neck. As soon as they were in the open, the sheep struggled convulsively. He lost his hold. It bolted – straight into the wooden fence of the pen. Grabbing it in a throttle, Valarkin pulled it backwards, clawing at the wool. Man and beast rolled over and over each other.

'It's not mating season yet!' yelled his cousin Buffle.

'You'd better tie its legs together,' jeered the old man. 'Like the other women, when they shear sheep.'

'Who's shearing who?' cried Buffle, as Valarkin struggled.

Valarkin, breathless, did not respond. Muddy, panting, he dragged the animal to where his shears lay waiting. One of his cousins had secured a sheep and started to shear while Valarkin had been fighting his animal to a standstill.

They expected him to shear, but did not choose to instruct him. They thought him a fool to have ever left the farm. As his father said, it might be a poor living, but they had never starved yet, and, isolated here in the south-cast of Estar, they were safe from most of the world's violence – pirate raids, bandits and Comedo's excesses – even if it was a long way to take wool to market.

They thought him a fool; worse, they hated him for his pride, so it pleased them to make him their resident fool. He knew they had expected the sheep to race him for the horizons. They would have been happy if it had. But it was not Valarkin but cousin Afeld who was first to lose a sheep.

'Whoa!' shouted Afeld, as the delinquent twisted free and ran, trailing half its fleece across the ground.

'It's not a horse,' said Buffle.

But Afeld did not hear, for he was already sprinting downhill after the sheep. Dogs and children followed. The dogs barked, the children screamed, and the old man – red-eyed and furious – bellowed abuse at Afeld. The sheep was cornered where two ditches ran together, and was sheared on the spot.

A little shearing, and Valarkin began to feel the strain in his forearm. Each snip freed only a little wool. Not knowing that wool came more easily off the larger, fatter sheep, he had chosen a small, light animal, thinking it easier to manhandle. It was giving him a hard time. He fought the four kicking limbs, lost control, grabbed the brute by the tail, hauled on its ears, and finally knelt on its neck and subdued it.

'Come on, Valarkin,' said Buffle, with a grin which showed small brown and black teeth which he was destined to lose before the age of twenty. 'I've finished mine already.'

He is only a boy, thought Valarkin. Only a boy, thin as a rabbit, a cast in his eye, a low-grade sacrifice we would have clubbed to a cripple then battered in the dark till the god drew nearer . . . till the room became cold . . . till mist formed, and the face: maw of mist, eyes of shadow . . . time for the high priest to ask for a

148

granting, then time to withdraw ... sometimes, a scream ...

'Come on Valarkin!'

He bent to his work, his back already aching.

With time, the ache got worse.

Between the shearers' raids the remaining sheep stood bleating in the pen. Their pounding hooves and guttering urine steadily mucked the ground to mud. When men entered the pen, the rearing hooves of panic-stricken sheep marked the fleeces of their sisters with mud. Any sheep not properly controlled whirled around when grabbed, threatening to send its attacker sprawling. A fall would be a disaster.

Once, as Valarkin regarded a sheep from a certain angle, the heavy head momentarily reminded him of equine grace and nobility – but the illusion was transitory. They were stupid, filthy animals. He hated them. He sheared without mercy, shaving the wool close to the pinkness of the skin, not caring if he clipped it to leave a little disc of white into which tiny bubbles of blood would flourish, swell then merge.

Once he knelt on a sheep's neck so hard for so long that, released, it lay still, convinced it was dead; he gave it a shove, and it got on its way. Sheep smells thronged his nostrils; their dung stained his knees. He was revolted by their smell, their stupidity, the way their bowels gave way in the middle of the shearing. He was repulsed by their blood-heat when he shoved a knee to belly-softness to assist with control.

Valarkin worked on, nearing collapse. He did not hear the sheep bleating, the clippers clicking, the women laughing and gossiping as they folded fleeces. His world was limited to his blurring field of vision, the straining muscles in his right arm, the ache of his back. He did not hear the arrival: he did not know who had come until he was called.

'Valarkin!'

He looked up slowly. Tall, the man was tall, tall on a

149

high horse. Valarkin had a confused impression of leather, sword, shield-boss, chain mail ... the world swayed as blood ebbed from his head, and he lowered his head to save himself from passing out, lowered his head close to the world of wool and dung-heat. When he looked up again, he saw it was Durnwold smiling down on him.

'Greetings, Valarkin. How are you, my brother?'

'Still breathing.'

He was too tired to say anything more.

Durnwold swung down from the saddle and hobbled the horse expertly – there were no trees to tie it to, and the rickety pen could scarcely withstand the assaults of the struggling sheep.

'You look tired,' said Durnwold.

'I am,' said Valarkin.

The ewe he was working on, as if sensing he was distracted, struggled suddenly. Valarkin subdued it. He wanted to smash it with his fists. He wanted to rip its guts out. He wanted to vomit.

'I want to talk to you,' said Durnwold.

'What about?'

'The future.'

'The future?'

'The temple's gone for good, isn't it? So what now? Is this what you want for the rest of your life? You hated it when we were children. Has so much changed?'

Valarkin was about to reply, but at that moment his father – who had been away getting a drink from a nearby stream – returned to greet his son:

'Durnwold! What are you doing here?'

'What am I doing? I'm standing on my own two feet, as I said I would.'

'On your own two feet, is it? That's a clever trick. You're a strong, brave lad, Durnwold, to be standing on your own two feet. You still have your head as well, I see. How long do you hope to keep it? The rumour says there's enemy raiding Estar. Collosnon foreigners. Are

150

you going to fight a whole empire with that shiny, bright sword of yours?'

'What do you know of the Collosnon empire?'

'Durnwold, lad. Do you think your da's a know-nothing? I've been to the Lorford markets, haven't I? More years than counting. I've heard the talk. They've got armies the ants themselves would envy, those ones.'

'They sent five thousand men against us,' said Durnwold.

'Now don't try shallying your da, Durnwold lad. You'd be dead if they'd done that.'

'We slaughtered them,' said Durnwold. 'We had wizards to help us.'

'Help from pox doctors?'

'I've met them. They're not like what you'd expect.'

'Pox doctors!' sneered his father, and spat.

It was now that the women and children, who had held back from Durnwold – not recognising him, or knowing him yet fearing him – tentatively began to approach. Soon they were crowding him, shouting and jabbering, clamouring for attention.

'Get back to work,' shouted the old man, waving his arms as if he was scaring away geese. 'Scram your backsides!'

He chased them away, then took Durnwold aside and spoke earnestly to him. Valarkin ground his knee a little harder into the flank of the sheep. He set to work again, cutting, thrusting, tearing, jabbing.

The last of the wool, complete with is complement of dirt, came free from the sheep. Valarkin slapped the animal to set it on its way. Durnwold broke away from his father and came over.

'What did he want?' asked Valarkin.

'Some money. He got a bit.' Durnwold broke off to yell at the children: 'Get away from that horse, you! He'll eat you!' Then, to Valarkin, quietly: 'There's plenty of money these days. Plenty of everything – we had the spoils of a whole army to divvy up between us.'

'Was it a hard battle?'

'It was easy. Wizards won it for us. Did you know there were wizards in Estar?'

'I met them myself,' said Valarkin, 'The day after the temple was burnt. But as for the Collosnon – we knew about raiding parties, but nothing about any army.'

'Oh, there was an army all right,' said Durnwold.

They talked together out of earshot of the others. Durnwold told of the enemy army's arrival, attack and destruction. Valarkin listened intently as Durnwold told of the mad-jewels and the red charms.

'And what now?' said Valarkin.

'Now we go east,' said Durnwold. 'To the land of Trest. Wizard hunting! We'll bring that thug Heenmor to bay then –'

'Chop him to bits with swords and hatchets!' said Valarkin, using a well-remembered phrase from their boyhood games.

Durnwold had always played at being the emperor across the seas, with Valarkin as his master of ceremonies.

Talking together, the brothers found time had not destroyed the empathy they had had before their careers had put leagues of distance and silence between them, as Durnwold strove to satisfy his ambitions through the sword, while Valarkin sought power and prestige in the temple.

'I thought I might find you here,' said Durnwold, 'but I wasn't sure.'

'Where else would I go?'

'It's a wide world.'

'I'm a priest,' said Valarkin. 'All Estar hates me, for that reason. After the temple, I visited Lorford – but I was lucky to escape alive. This was the only place left. Everything I hoped for is ashes.'

'So the temple really is gone for good.'

'Yes. All finished. Over. I'm the sole survivor. The temple is in ruins. The Deep Pools, choked with rubble.

152

The High Priests, dead. The powers of summoning, the farsight secrets – dead with them. The five elder books are ashes. It cost the temple generations to learn our god's desires – to learn how to praise, to sacrifice, to plead. All that knowledge is gone. It can't be replaced except by revelation – which might come to one man once in a century. We can't control the god any more. It's over.'

'Why didn't you come to me?'

'I was ashamed. I failed, so I was ashamed.'

'It was never your fault,' said Durnwold.

The old man started to yell at Valarkin. He wanted Valarkin back at work. Valarkin gave a sigh almost of despair – a short, forced sigh, as if he had been hit in the pit of the stomach.

'Sit down,' said Durnwold.

Valarkin subsided to the ground, and watched as Durnwold shed his cloak, his chain mail and his sword.

Leelesh let Durnwold into the pen – he did not so much as glance at her – and he chose a fat sheep. He grabbed it by the front legs, lifting it so it danced helplessly on its rear hooves. He walked it out of the pen to the shears. The animal, pulled back against his right leg, found all four cloven hooves helpless in the air. He set to work, first clipping away a couple of ragged patches of dirty wool clinging to the belly near the teats.

The rest of the underside was bare of wool, but for a collar of wool round the neck; there was no wool on the face, only a thin layer of short, wiry, white hairs. Durnwold cut away the collar of wool, then began to shear in earnest, slowly peeling the fleece away from the left side of neck and flank, until he reached the backbone.

In places the underside of the fleece was yellow, in places creamy white, however dirty the outside might be. Durnwold rolled the sheep onto his left leg and cut the fleece from the other side. One of the women took it as it came free. Durnwold knelt on the sheep's neck and cut away the ragged bits of wool clinging to its tail, then the dung-stained dags between its hind legs.

Durnwold made it look easy, but he could make any physical skill look easy.

Soon, the shearing was finished; they released the lambs. Set free, the lambs ran wild, sometimes springing straight into the air with four legs stiff, as kittens sometimes do. The lambs thought their mothers lost – the sheep smelt different now they were shorn – so the air filled with the bleating of distressed lambs. It would take a while for them to recognise their mothers, even though the mothers found their offspring without any trouble.

Two were not set free straight away, for, overlooked earlier in the year, they had long tails and unclipped ears. Valarkin was made to hold one. The old man clipped through one of its ears. The lamb thrashed and struggled; it was a sturdy beast now three months old. Seizing the tail, the old man twisted it in the middle till it broke.

'A knife cuts more blood,' he said. 'Now turn it loose.'

The lamb stood for a moment, fresh red blood from its mauled ear streaming through its short, tight head-wool. Then it bolted. The old man worked the second lamb the same, mumbling his satisfaction through broken yellow teeth:

'We'll have no long-tails like we did last year. No fights over who owns what, either. Those greedmouths on Tip Hill, they'd suck the spit from our mouths if we didn't stop them. Two years in a row they've snatched lambs we never marked. Now come over here, Durnwold.'

The old man spoke again with Durnwold – Valarkin guessed he was after a promise of more money – then set off after the others, who were carrying the wool sacks back to the small, smoky, dirt-floor huts where

Valarkin and Durnwold had been born and raised. The trampled earth around the pen was littered with dirty little scraps of wool.

Valarkin shivered.

'Well?' said Durnwold, putting on his chain mail. 'Are you coming with me?'

'Where?'

'To war. Wizard hunting. Swords and hatchets!'

'I'm no warrior. You know that.'

'This is the age of the warrior,' said Durnwold, arming himself with his sword again.

'It's a dark age, then.'

'All ages are dark, for those that won't make the best of them. Are you coming?'

'I need time to think about it.'

'Time is not in my gift, said Durnwold. "All I can give you is a chance.'

He sauntered over to his horse, unhobbled the animal, swung up into the saddle and rode to the pen at a trot.

'Well?' said Durnwold, looking down, reins in hand, reins falling to the bit which the bridle secured in the horse's mouth. Leather and cold metal. A tall man with a sword.

'What should I bring?'

'Everything you've got that's warm and woollen. We sleep rough tonight, and it's cold despite the summer.'

He helped Valarkin up behind him, and the horse carried them toward the huts.

*   *   *

From the door of his house, the old man, Grenberthing, watched his two sons ride away. His body ached from the day of herding and shearing; he knew it would still be aching on the morrow. He saw neither of the young men gave a backward glance at the place they were leaving.

155

– So there they go then, the strong one and the oddling. Nothing for them but a sword in the belly, but how can they know that? Kits don't know they're born blind till their eyes open. What's to open your eyes, my bravos? What's so fine in living with folks who walk on air? They may walk on it, but they don't eat it. Without us and our like, the castle would starve in less than a season.

– Durnwold. Was a life for him here. A dowry, a dozen sheep. Richness. The woman could still be bred from. She was a child bright enough, till the ice broke under her that winter, and her mother worked her body gone blue till it breathed. Strong body, meat and milk, heat in the right place. I'll have her down myself if you don't come back. Down and under . . .

– And Valarkin. What does the oddling think he'll do in the cold outside? Stay here, and we could make a man out of him, but no, he has to walk on air. I remember when he was a child. I took him up on that blea hill in the rawky weather, and he croodled down like he was scared of the sky. Stay here, and we could make him something.

– But now, they're going, the two of them. So go then, but there's nothing to gain but a sword in the guts. And the hand that drives it will turn it.

CHAPTER TWENTY-THREE

Before dawn, Morgan Hearst, and the half-dozen men who had volunteered to go with him, left the castle, riding eastward toward daybreak. They planned to go to the seaport of Skua, taking a corduroy road which the Collosnon had built across the swamps to the north of the Eastway, to give their invasion a road sufficiently wide for baggage wagons.

Hearst's mission was to gain intelligence on the strength of enemy forces at Skua; if the target proved worthy, Prince Comedo's troops would march there to dare another bloodbath under the aegis of the mad-jewels. The plan was for Hearst and his men to link up with the main body of Comedo's troops at the High Castle in Trest: that was when a decision would be made.

At Skua, Hearst would also try to discover – perhaps by kidnapping someone for interrogation – whether Volaine Persaga Haveros was still alive. If the oath-breaker was not now rotting down to earth along with the other thousands of unburied Collosnon dead near Castle Vaunting, then Hearst would try for the traitor's head.

Durnwold had wanted to come with Hearst, who had told him it was more important for him to see how Elkor Alish organised a small army for the march: that way, he would really learn something.

Riding east to the rising sun, Hearst felt light-hearted, excited. War again. What can compare with it? Nothing! Some day he would die – and maybe soon. But war was the only life he chose to live, and he would accept whatever death it gave him. He remembered other places, other times, when, facing death, he had challenged it with a roar which was half berserker rage, half exultation.

So many battles. He had fought on a frozen river that was breaking up in the spring, so that ice would suddenly tilt or break, sending men in full armour plunging into freezing water. He had fought knee-deep in surf, blood in the water bringing sharks among the fighters. He had fought in fields of clutching mud, in forests, in ravines, on mountain slopes. He had fought when wounded, matching sword with sword when he had the sun in his face and blood in his eyes.

– Death will be death, in its own good time.

But for now, a Collosnon cavalry horse under him, companions to left and to right, a shared word, a joke . . . it was enough.

Soon, the night was defeated. It was dawn. Back at Castle Vaunting, doors banged open; cursing squad leaders roused their sleeping men:

'Get up, you idle corpse-rapists. Come on! Move yourselves! Hands off cocks! On with socks!'

A rising wind, sweeping in from the Central Ocean, caught the doors, slamming them from side to side. A battle-horn sounded: rouse, rouse!

The soldiers yawned and grumbled, stumbling into clothes and armour, but the leave-time feeling was upon them. Hot porridge to fill the belly for the long day. Snort of horses: a Collosnon mount for every man. Jingle of harness. Smells of sweat, leather, horse dung. Arguments.

'Andranovory! That's my horse you're sitting on!'

Last jokes. Sleep rubbed from sore eyes. The laboured breathing of men with brewery breath. Echoes crashing through hangover heads. Men yelling and quarrelling over missing clothes, lost boots. Clatter of swords and armour. Obscenity upon obscenity.

On their mission east, they meant to destroy any Collosnon forces they found in Trest, and to find and

158

kill the wizard Heenmor. The Melski had now told Blackwood that Heenmor had not gone north, as far as they could discover; scouts had found a marshland fisherman who had survived the Collosnon invasion, and who claimed to have seen Heenmor going east at the end of winter.

Prince Comedo himself had solemnly sworn that everything possible would be done to kill Heenmor, and to secure the death-stone which Elkor Alish had described so well, so the wizard could take it south to return it to the Dry Pit.

Prince Comedo woke in his clothes. He reached for the jug by his bed and drank deeply. The door opened; Gorn peered in, then, seeing the prince was awake, withdrew. What was the matter with him? Did he think that a prince of the Favoured Blood would oversleep on this day, his day, the day he rode out at the head of his army?

He took another swig from the jug.

His bottle, where was his bottle? Here! His green beauty, safe and smooth to carry him. That was part of the bargain he had made with the wizards. The woodsman Blackwood would carry the bottle, for the prince – his judgment was not necessarily impeccable – was convinced that Blackwood lacked the will to oppose him or betray him. Certainly he was more trustworthy than any of the unprincipled cutthroats who served Comedo as soldiers.

The priest Valarkin would carry the spare ring for the bottle. Comedo congratulated himself on another brilliant choice. As a temple priest, Valarkin was automatically hated, and had failed to win favour with the prince's soldiers since arriving in the castle. If he ever wanted to steal the bottle, he would find it difficult to persuade anyone to conspire with him. Yet Comedo knew that Durnwold would protect his brother Valarkin if any soldier made a move against him. So you could have your cake and eat it – or, in Comedo's

159

idiom, keep your virgin virgin yet shag it senseless.

Comedo, cradling the bottle in his arms, imagined himself emperor of half the continent, with people falling down to worship on their knees at the very mention of his name. Hail him! Mighty warrior! Mighty conqueror! War, obviously, was the life he was made for.

Elsewhere in Castle Vaunting, Blackwood woke beside Mystrel. His eyes were gritty; he had not slept much during the night. He remembered how she had wept; how she had despaired. But he had told her their future should be safe enough.

Comedo's men would march with the mad-jewels to defeat any enemy they met, so there was no danger there. Blackwood was vague as to how the castle would be guarded while they were gone, as he had not been privy to the councils of war which had made the arrangements – but no doubt something would be done. In any case, it was not far to the High Castle. Five days' easy riding should get them there, so it was hard to see how they could be away for long.

Somewhere, not for the first time, the sound of a battle-horn roused the castle.

Blackwood dressed. He buckled on his belt; he was taking his hunting trousse, a bow and a quiver of arrows, and his canvas rain-shelter. Like every other man, he would also be taking a pack; these had back-straps so men could carry them, though horses would take the weight on the journey to the High Castle.

Every man carried in his pack the issue Alish had insisted on. There were rations for ten days (dried meat, salted fish, barley flour, rice) and an issue of siege dust which would support life for twenty days if they ever got hungry enough to start eating it. Alish had also insisted that every man carry spare boots, fishing lines, fish hooks, at least one woollen blanket and at least two leather waterbottles.

Mystrel was still sleeping; Blackwood decided it was

160

best they parted that way. They had been through enough pain already. He left, catfoot, silent. Mystrel distrusted Prince Comedo, thinking he had some terrible fate in store for his some-time huntsman, but Blackwood doubted that Comedo would dare move against him now – not when the Rovac warrior Morgan Hearst owed Blackwood his life, and would doubtless be ready to repay that debt if the occasion arose.

He could not guess what future lay ahead for Mystrel and himself – and for the child they were expecting – but he knew the future had to be better than the past.

Outside, Elkor Alish was attempting to dominate the vast expanse of the central courtyard with his voice. He was harrying his underlings, checking armour, weapons, harness, boots, packs. Despite this business, he could not avoid the thought: here he was, again, setting off to war.

War? Collosnon soldiers might die, but the true enemy was a wizard, Heenmor. It was not so much a war as a manhunt. But afterwards . . . yes, then there would be a proper war. The wizards had promised Prince Comedo that he would be given the mad-jewels once Heenmor had been killed and the death-stone recovered. Each mad-jewel was good for a year of use. With that magic to aid them, Comedo's armies would push south, killing as they went, until they reached the Far South and the Great Dyke itself.

Blood would be shed – some of it, perhaps, innocent. He would allow it for the sake of the ultimate cause: to take revenge for the ancient crimes of wizards. As a member of the Code of Night, Alish was sworn to that cause. And if he could lay hands on the death-stone as well . . .

Putting hesitation behind him, Elkor Alish faced the future with a resolute will, denying uncertainty with his voice and demeanour.

Durnwold rose early, to see how Alish got things done – but Valarkin slept in to ensure he was properly rested.

161

Chances for sleep might be scarce if they were attacked on the march.

Valarkin had, the night before, oiled every bit of metal worth oiling, greased every bit of leather, rearranged the items in his pack a dozen times till it sat comfortably on his back – even though he knew a horse would carry it to the High Castle – and before going to sleep had rehearsed every sword stroke Durnwold had taught him in the few days they had been allowed for preparation.

If intellect could conquer, then Valarkin was determined to triumph; if preparation meant success, then he would astonish a whole generation. Whatever happened, he was now Comedo's ring-bearer, guarding a ring giving access to the green bottle, which was now loaded down with provisions of luxury. Providing he survived this campaign, he would be in a position to gain power. That was what he wanted: what he needed.

Miphon woke slowly, reluctant to face the horror planned for their departure. Phyphor had warned him, on pain of death, not to interfere. This morning, his mind was a turmoil. Should he obey? Or try and warn the intended victims? Or try and kill Phyphor? The truth was, Phyphor had the authority of the whole Confederation of Wizards behind him. And Miphon could not kill Phyphor and Garash and Comedo and Alish - he would only get himself butchered.

Reluctantly, hating himself, Miphon decided to comply with Phyphor's instructions.

He checked his gear. In his pack were selected medical items, including knives, hooks, needles, thread, laudanum, honey, bandages and garlic. He felt a certain sense of futility. He could doubtless save a few lives here and there, but what was the good of that in the face of so much slaughter?

In another tower, Garash woke with a little grin on his face. He was looking forward to the fun planned for their departure. And for the chance, if their expedition succeeded, to try to grab the death-stone for himself.

One did not lightly plan to outwit and doublecross a dangerous wizard like Phyphor, but Garash was determined to do it. For power. And for revenge: he still remembered the day of horror after he had been caught by Heenmor's blast-trap, unable to see the light, and thinking himself perhaps blind forever.

Mystrel woke a little later. She thought she felt something – the child in her belly? It distracted her only momentarily. Blackwood was gone! She opened the door. The corridors were silent, empty. She ran, calling his name.

Alish, elsewhere, was handing out the small, red charms on golden chains. The men had not expected to see them again so soon: only a chosen few had been told they were leaving one of the mad-jewels to guard Castle Vaunting. Now some guessed: but all of them, even those with their favourite drabs and doxies living in the castle, put on the red charms without question.

None dared argue with Elkor Alish, the master swordsman, for after the battles against the Collosnon he was no longer known as 'the man who does not shed blood'.

Blackwood's turn came. Blackwood was last.

'What's this for?' said Blackwood, holding the little red charm on its golden chain. 'We're not using a mad-jewel today, are we?'

'Put it on,' said Alish.

* * *

It was a quiet room, empty but for a man crippled by Heenmor's magic: the man whose hands were chunks of rock, whose left leg had been turned to rock below the knee, whose face was disfigured with stone. His one good eye watched as Phyphor entered, carrying a lead box which bore the null sign of the dead zero: the sign of the nether magic.

163

At that moment, Questor entered the room. He was the nominal captain of all the soldiers, and the prince had designated him to be left in charge of the castle 'as a mark of my special favour.'

'What are you doing?' said Questor.

Phyphor made no reply, but took out one of the mad-jewels. Misty yellow light swirled and pulsed within it. Questor tried to draw his sword. He lurched, staggered. His face began to slacken. Before sanity left him completely, he screamed, realising what was happening. Then he laughed, flapped his hands like wings, and went reeling away, colliding first with one wall then the other.

Phyphor looked at the man who had been partly turned to stone. There was no intelligence now in his eye: no suffering. And soon he would be dead.

* * *

Alish shouted orders. Men began to move out, all on horseback but for Blackwood, who had yet to mount. Seeing his wife among the witless victims of the mad-jewels who were now milling aimlessly in the courtyard, Blackwood ran to Comedo to request permission to stay.

'What?' said Comedo.

His horse clattered through the long passage between the central courtyard and the drawbridge. Blackwood ran alongside the horse, shouting, darting glances backwards.

'What?' said Comedo, laughing.

They came out into the sunlight. Blackwood shouted again. They were on the drawbridge now.

'What?' said Comedo.

Blackwood screamed at him.

Comedo, riding high on his high horse, laughed again. He reached down, snagged the fine chain round Blackwood's neck, and tore it away. He threw it

164

sideways. It flashed in the sunlight then fell through dizzy depths into the fire dyke.

Blackwood swayed. The world floundered. Horses buffeted past. A vulture spread its wings in his throat and screamed. The sun clawed his back. He shouted at it. He stepped to the edge of the drawbridge. One foot stepped to the gulf.

A hand hooked into his hair and dragged him back. Blackwood twisted his head and saw Mormormorgan gar garn morgarnn, hearse, Hearst, is that your name, Hearst?

No. It was Alish, who had acted just in time to prevent the destruction of the precious green bottle Blackwood carried.

One moment of clarity:

'Mystrel!' screamed Blackwood.

Then he lost the power of speech.

The little army paused while the prince's bottle-carrier was tied onto the back of a horse: he would recover himself once they were out of range of the mad-jewel.

* * *

Alone in the castle, Murmer, thumb and fist, bent fox-fur creature, stalked, killed:

– Ha! Have you, have at you, fork-meat. Shlust shroost! Dreams now, milk-warm, dreams. Saaa!

CHAPTER TWENTY-FOUR

Valarkin woke in the night, and not because of the cold – he was already used to that. He was lying on tough swamp grass, but, after a long day in the saddle, he could have slept on a bed of nails.

He was awake because something was feeding on him.

Not lice, gnats, fleas, mosquitoes or leeches, but something bigger. It was hurting him; it almost covered his chest. Reaching out, Valarkin discovered something cold, pale and greasy. He tore it away from his flesh and hurled it into the darkness.

His body stung where the creature had been feeding. It glimmered in the starlight, sliding back for another try. Valarkin, hissing, pulled out his knife.

The creature flowed onto his leg. He slashed at it. His knife cut through its thin flesh, slicing into his own leg. The creature shot away with rapid, jerky movements. Valarkin tore a strip from his blanket, bandaged his wound, then sat on his pack, knife in hand, waiting in case the creature came back. He began to shiver uncontrollably.

The night was cloudless; the stars were hard, cold, intolerably distant. The lone star called Golem's Eye glowered with red malevolence. To the east lay the frozen starstorm of the galaxy called Maelstrom. And what awaited them in the east? Unlike some others, Valarkin doubted that Heenmor would be lingering in Trest waiting for his executioners.

By starlight, nothing betrayed their marshland camp-site except a single fire, and a horse which snorted nearby, making Valarkin start – he was a little bit afraid

166

of horses. He walked to the fire, treading cautiously lest he trample on some sleeping warrior. Blackwood was tending the fire; nearby, the wizards Phyphor, Garash and Miphon lay asleep.

As Valarkin settled himself by the fire, Blackwood put on some more wood. For a while they sat silent; the fire whispered and hissed, occasionally settling with a slight crack as charred timbers broke under their own weight. Elkor Alish had arranged for some horses to carry loads of firewood – otherwise they would have been short of fuel at this camp amid the swamps.

'You're hurt,' said Blackwood at length.

'There was a white thing – I slashed it.'

'Oh,' said Blackwood. 'A quiver.'

'Is that what it's called?'

'Yes. If you cut yourself again, come to me. I could bandage that better than you have.'

Valarkin took that in silence.

Blackwood poked the fire. Though everyone was asleep but for himself and Valarkin, the camp was safe enough; only a one-horse path led to this island of dry ground deep in the swamp, so enemies could scarcely surround them from all sides then attack.

Sitting there, Valarkin remembered the warmth of his father's hearth. He had never thought he would regret leaving the farm, but he did. He was not made for this life of hot sun, cold nights, mud, insects, rebellious horses and the company of coarse, brutish, dangerous men.

Caught in the throes of nightmare, the wizard Garash twisted in his sleep then groaned. Fire-stars glowed in the branches of a swamp-tree above him, flickered, then died away. Garash turned, settling deeper into sleep.

'What can be the matter with him?' said Valarkin.

'Pox doctors have their problems too, mister.'

'What are the wizards really like? You've been with them a lot, haven't you? Especially Miphon. Do they

167

talk of ... of power? Do they say where their power comes from?'

Blackwood remembered Miphon and Mystrel talking together about honey and garlic.

'If you're so interested, why don't you ask them?'

Valarkin did not reply, but sat thinking about the green bottle strung on Blackwood's belt. After two days in the field, Prince Comedo had had enough of the fresh air; using one of the two rings that commanded the bottle, he had retreated to the quarters prepared for him inside. Valarkin, who held the second ring, was to fetch the prince from the bottle when they reached the High Castle in Trest.

'Do you know the countryside well?' asked Valarkin.

'I know my way,' said Blackwood.

'If men were hunting you, could you escape?'

'Yes, if I ran toward danger as well as away from it. North: they'd never find me there. Not in the mountains of the Penvash Peninsular ... that's fearsome country.'

'The bottle you hold is very valuable,' said Valarkin. 'I hold the second ring which commands it.'

He waited.

Blackwood poked at the fire again. Coals gleamed dragon-hot. All around were sleeping men whose lives were in his trust. In the green bottle at his belt, Prince Comedo lay sleeping: that was another trust.

'Mister, my fate takes me east,' said Blackwood.

That was the peasant in him speaking. His forefathers had bowed to feudal masters for so many generations that rebellion was now unthinkable. Valarkin knew this; he remembered how his own father, who scorned the castle and its people, found in that scorn only pride in his own way of life, where to own two milch cows was the height of ambition.

However, in the temple, Valarkin had learnt that men can control gods – even though, if the truth be known, the temple's god had only been a creature of the third hierarchy, which is to say, a common demon. Since men could control gods, they could certainly master the leaders foisted on them by tradition.

'There's wealth in the bottle,' said Valarkin. 'Including a whole room full of books. If we could learn to read them, they'd surely teach us magic.'

'Or get us killed,' said Blackwood, dourly.

'Don't be afraid! Think . . . think of your wife.'

'There's no way for me to rescue her,' said Blackwood, who had been carried helplessly witless for a whole day till they got out of range of the mad-jewel.

'Look,' said Valarkin, holding out a thin chain. A charm gleamed on the end of it.

'Is that yours?'

'I've got another one. The prince gave me this one for safe keeping. Put it on.'

Blackwood took the charm, weighed it in his hand, then slowly put it on. Just then, one of the sleepers woke, and made his way to the edge of the swamp; returning to his bed, he disturbed half a dozen others, who cursed him sleepily. Valarkin waited for everyone to settle down before he spoke again:

'If we start now, we can outpace them to Castle Vaunting, rescue your wife and run for Penvash. They'll never catch us.'

'And the prince?'

'Settle his fate as you will. Are you with me?'

Blackwood hesitated. The common wisdom of Estar taught that each had his weird, and had to endure the doom he was fated to. He knew of only one tale in which a man of peasant stock had tried to take control of his own destiny. That was the tale of Loosehead Robert, who had gathered together a rag-tag army to make war against his prince. After a series of disasters, he had been driven into the hills.

There, in a cave, while thinking wild thoughts of triumph and revenge, Loosehead Robert had watched a spider build its web. Into the web had flown a fly. And how it had struggled! Five times it had almost broken free, but the spider had got it in the end. And Loosehead Robert, looking from the devouring spider to the mouth of the cave, had seen his prince's soldiers standing there, grinning at him. All mothers in Estar told their children the lessons Loosehead Robert learnt, first from the spider and then from his prince's shunting irons.

– But perhaps the story was not told quite right.

He had a charm to protect himself against the mad-jewel. And a companion to share his dangers. He would dare it. He would try.

'I'm with you,' said Blackwood.

Valarkin wanted to leave then and there, but Blackwood took the time to cut swatches of swamp grass and tie them round the hooves of four horses. With a change of horses and a head start, they should be able to outdistance their pursuers easily. Then he made sure that they packed all their gear and tied the packs to the horses. Only then did he agree to set out.

Leaving the dryland island on which they had been camping, they found the passage of Prince Comedo's little army had churned the one-horse track through the swamps into a quagmire. Blackwood's expertise with horses did not extend far beyond an intimate personal knowledge of what it means to be saddle-sore, but his common sense told him they would have to lead the animals till the track improved. So they went on foot, Blackwood leading, the horses roped behind them.

It was slow going, and hideously noisy in the thick mud. After only fifty paces, Valarkin swore softly.

'What is it?' said Blackwood.

'These horses. They won't move.'

Blackwood slurched back through the mud. He was starting to sweat. He had no skill with recalcitrant horses. The first horse whickered at him when he grabbed its bridle. He swore at it, softly, urgently. Then

170

listened, trying to hear any noises from the campsite that would suggest anyone had woken.

What he heard was someone moving.

But not in the campsite: in the other direction!

Someone was sneaking along the path toward the camp, guided in by the light of the campfire. And they were close.

Blackwood sliced through the ropes connecting the horses.

'Turn them around,' he whispered. 'Back to the camp.'

'But – '

Blackwood slapped a hand over Valarkin's mouth, and whispered in his ear:

'Someone out there.'

Valarkin started to turn the horses around. This was very noisy. Almost immediately they were challenged from the night in a foreign language. It was the enemy! Blackwood slapped the nearest horse on the rump and shouted:

'Rouse! Rouse!'

Men and horses plunged through the mud toward the campsite, but the enemy gained on them. Twenty paces from the dryland island, one of Valarkin's horses lost its footing and went down on its knees in the mud, blocking the path. By then, the enemy were almost upon them. Blackwood grabbed Valarkin and dragged him into the swamps. They crashed into the water, and the enemy –

Hesitated, moaned, screamed, thrashed around in the dark, sang or babbled with laughter. Blackwood realised what had happened. Someone had brought the mad-jewel out of its lead box.

'Let's go,' said Blackwood.

But at that moment Alish's voice rang out:

'Close the box!'

And suddenly the noise of madness ceased abruptly, and, after a brief pause, was replaced by sharp, angry enemy voices. At the campsite – so near, and yet so very far away – there was a lot of uninhibited swearing as various individuals crawled out of the swamp. Half of them had gone to sleep with their protective charms tucked away in their boots or their packs, so the use of the mad-jewel had been almost as disastrous for the defenders as for the enemy.

'I'm cold,' said Valarkin.

'Shut up!' hissed Blackwood.

But it was too late. One of the enemy gave an urgent command, and attackers waded into the swamp. Blackwood eased back, deeper and deeper into the cold, dark water. Valarkin started to move in the opposite direction. Toward the enemy. He had to be mad. Blackwood concentrated on moving quietly. Something underwater slithered against his legs: an eel.

An enemy soldier cried out in triumph, seeing Valarkin by starlight. Blackwood shrank back behind a clump of rushes. The next moment, he heard a slap as if someone had clapped their hands, a splash of water, then a cry of astonishment from the enemy. Blackwood realised what had happened. Valarkin had used the ring he wore to vanish himself into the green bottle at Blackwood's waist.

Now the enemy were not really sure if anyone was out there. Abandoning the chase, they started to push toward the campsite. They must have known they were grossly outnumbered, but they advanced regardless. To try what?

Blackwood heard Elkor Alish arguing with the wizards, ordering them to use fire against the enemy, and receiving an unqualified refusal. Suddenly there was a shout as the first of the Collosnon gained the dryland island. And the fight was on.

Men hacked each other in the darkness.

With his noisy progress masked by the uproar of a confused and savage battle, Blackwood forced his way through the swamp, gaining the dryland island before the fighting ended.

* * *

At dawn, Elkor Alish counted casualties. The enemy had lost fifteen men. Five of his own were dead; two others, who would have to be carried to the High Castle, could be expected to die from their wounds. One was missing, but his protective red charm was found in the top of his pack: if the Collosnon had managed to kidnap him for interrogation, it was unfortunate but not disastrous, as without a protective charm the enemy could not steal the mad-jewel which had been left behind in Castle Vaunting.

Alish realised he had been overconfident: an unpardonable failure for a professional soldier like himself. He had relied on wizard magic, believing, in any case, that any surviving Collosnon would be too demoralised to be a threat. Now he knew better.

Now he must make his men wear their protective charms at all times, so the mad-jewel could be used at a moment's notice, without fear of men mutilating themselves or drowning in the swamps. Proper sentries would have to be posted at night – which meant Alish would have to wake himself up from time to time to make sure his sentries had not gone to sleep. In this ragtag outfit, there was nobody he could delegate the duty to. Except Gorn – but Gorn, when given responsibility, was a savage disciplinarian, and Alish did not want to wake up to find someone had got their head hacked off as a consequence of falling asleep on sentry duty.

Alish also needed to lecture Blackwood and Valarkin. He could prove nothing, but he suspected they had been making off in the night when the enemy attacked. Otherwise why would he have found them unloading their packs from muddy horses after the battle?

Even without proof positive, Alish would have

punished the pair severely, except that his will to justice was disabled by his guilt over his own hand in the decision to leave a mad-jewel behind in Castle Vaunting. He was sure that setting a jewel to guard the castle was the right move – but he should have forced Comedo to agree to evacuate the castle first.

He consoled himself with the thought that taking Heenmor took precedence over everything else. Garash had casually suggested inflicting madness on the castle's surplus population and Comedo had taken the idea to heart; Alish could not afford to waste the time needed to argue Comedo out of his enthusiasms.

So . . .

. . . Blackwood and Valarkin got off with a lecture.

'We now know the enemy have got patrols following us,' said Alish. 'It's obvious what they want. A prisoner: to interrogate. To find out our numbers, our intentions, and the nature of the unthinkable powers we've used against them.

'That's what I'd want, if I was the Collosnon commander: information. And I'd happily tear a man apart with red-hot hooks to get it. You may think you can escape from me. Perhaps you're right – but you can guarantee the enemy would kill you if I didn't.'

Alish saw that Valarkin was too frightened to give him any more trouble, and that Blackwood would not try anything again because he had lapsed into a mood of profound fatalism. Alish was right. In Blackwood's case, a brief stand against authority had brought instant and absolute failure, thereby confirming the beliefs which had been bred into him.

Besides . . . he could not hope to get away for another day at the earliest, which was a long time in the lives of the helpless people left behind at Castle Vaunting . . . by now, he knew, there was probably no point in returning even if he had been allowed to.

*   *   *

They marched on without event – until, one evening, disaster befell Valarkin. At first, when his waking nightmare started, he panicked, drew a knife – then found there was nothing sensible he could do with it. He decided his only hope was to ask the wizards for help. And quickly!

First he went to Phyphor, who listened with little patience then – doubtless with malicious intent – told him to take his problem to Garash. But when Valarkin did so, he was interrupted by a roar of fury:

'I am not a pox doctor!'

Garash was so angry that sparks jumped from between the fingers of his clenched fists. His protruberant eyes bulged in fury.

That left only Miphon, who was showing Blackwood, Durnwold, Elkor Alish and a handful of interested fighting men how a poisonous yellow bladder-shaped fungus called cauchaumaur could be made safe to eat when brewed up with the petals of a red flower called summerfire.

'Miphon,' said Valarkin.

'What is it?' said Miphon.

He did not glance away from his simmering cauldron. He was watching for the instant when the brew would turn purple. Then he would have to add cold water immediately, cooling the brew, which would be safe to eat if eaten straight away. It was a very delicate operation.

'I need to talk to you.'

'I can't leave this. What's the matter?'

'I'm sick.'

'Sick?' said Miphon.

All sorts of things occurred to him: food poisoning, typhoid, dysentry. The last would be the worst: one person with dysentry could contaminate the whole army faster than anything.

'If you're busy, I'll talk to you later.'

'No,' said Miphon, 'I'd better know straight away.'

'Well – '

'Spit it out,' said Alish.

'Yes,' said Miphon, 'We have to know.'

'Well . . . a leech has crawled up the eye of my penis.'

The reaction from the fighting men was instantaneous: roars of laughter, hooting, backslapping. It was the best joke they'd heard for days.

The brew in the cauldron turned purple. Miphon poured in a helmet-full of cold water. The colour changed, quick as fingers snapping, to a deep orange.

'While it stays orange you can eat it,' said Miphon.

As the men set to, tucking into the orange mixture, Durnwold glanced at Valarkin – and Valarkin saw that he had embarrassed his brother.

'Have a piss somewhere,' said Durnwold. 'Leeches don't like salt or hot water, and there's both when you piss.'

'He's right,' said Miphon, still watching the brew in the cauldron in case it had not been completely neutralised. 'It'll come out as soon as you start making things uncomfortable for it. There's nothing to worry about.'

One of the fighting men made a low-voiced remark to his neighbour, and that set them off again, laughing. Valarkin knew that he would suffer for this for a long time: jokes, winks, ribald asides. As if life hadn't been hard enough already!

Death, death, death: death was the only cure for the laughter. Each mouth to taste ashes, each eye to see char: Valarkin muttered the words of the Bitterbane Curse, but there was no god to hear them.

CHAPTER TWENTY-FIVE

Trest: a land bounded to the east and south by hills and mountains, to the west by marshland swamps, and to the north by the sea. The port of Skua, which is a fishing village, is on the northern coast.

Ruler: Prince Jeferies, a cousin of Prince Comedo of Estar. He governs from his High Castle, a stronghold of wizard make located, roughly speaking, in the middle of Trest.

* * *

Reaching Skua, Hearst and his scouting party found an invasion fleet at anchor, and the surrounding countryside alive with enemy patrols. Wearing stolen Collosnon armour, and daring much on the basis of a little of the enemy's command language, Ordhar, which he had learnt from Volaine Persaga Haveros, Hearst infiltrated Skua.

All he collected was rumours, and the news that some very important people had gone missing, including the enemy's invasion commander, Lord Pentalon Alagrace, and the spy Volaine Persaga Haveros. After pushing his luck further than he should have, Hearst left Skua unscathed.

On his way to the High Castle, his small band of men had to avoid parties of Collosnon soldiers retreating north. Hearst guessed that the High Castle had been under siege; arriving there, Comedo's men would have attacked the besiegers, triumphing with the aid of the mad-jewel, leaving small disorganised groups of survivors to flee to Skua with news of a fresh disaster for the invaders.

Hearst was, therefore, not surprised to find the countryside around the High Castle littered with dead bodies, and Comedo's men being fêted as liberators.

A council of war was held, at which Hearst told the story of his adventures, and in return received the latest intelligence. Before the Collosnon invasion, the wizard Heenmor had called at the High Castle and had requisitioned four horses and some supplies; his visit had been attended by the death of three men, all of whom had died from snakebite.

Jeferies, lord of the High Castle, had sent trackers to shadow Heenmor; they had lost him in the Kikashi Hills, to the east. The council of war decided to pursue Heenmor east, and take a slap at the Collosnon in Skua on the way back.

Everything was going well. Morale, in particular, was sky-high. Few of Comedo's men had any fire in their bellies, but they revelled in the slaughter of armies of magic-disabled Collosnon soldiers – and looting the bodies afterwards. Only one warrior was unhappy – Hearst – but he waited until he was alone with Elkor Alish before voicing his discontent:

'Blackwood,' said Hearst.

'What about him?'

'You know what I'm talking about. His wife. The castle. The mad-jewel. Why wasn't I told?'

'Prince Comedo wanted it that way.'

'You could've –'

'What? Told the prince his rights over his own castle, over his own subjects, over a man guilty of a crime against his law? Since when did we lecture princes on the governance of their realms? Did we speak against Tan Siander when he ordered the child sacrifice at Tanokavoy? Did we snub the Bailiff of Chi'ash-lan when he wanted –'

'Alish, this is different!'

'Different? How?'

'I owe a debt to Blackwood, I thought –'

'What? That I should help you pay your debts? Believe me, I owe you nothing!'

* * *

A banquet was held, celebrating the start of the adventure east. Everyone was in high spirits, ready to do justice to the feast, but eventually, one by one, even the mightiest trenchermen met their measure. At last, only a few were left in the Great Hall of the High Castle, the rest having been dismissed by a surfeit of food and drink. Since Comedo's army had captured a small Collosnon baggage train when they raised the siege of the High Castle, there was no shortage of either.

Finally the only men in the hall not dead drunk were those at the High Table, including Jeferies, Comedo, Comedo's ring-bearer Valarkin, the Rovac warriors Elkor Alish and Morgan Hearst, the wizards Phyphor, Garash and Miphon, and a few favoured warriors, including Durnwold, Hearst's protégé. These worthies had restrained themselves earlier in the evening, but, with their social inferiors no longer present to bear witness, they were overindulging themselves with a vengeance.

Morgan Hearst, drunken, boastful, was telling how he killed the dragon Zenphos:

'Through the eye. The eye! You should have heard the bellow. Louder than thunder, hear me true. Then it thrashed like the big sea-sunder which snaps a ship's keel. Hope was just a jest then: I knew for certain its death-agony would kill me. By the singing knives, I sang my terror then. But luck – luck was with me.'

'So you lived,' said Jeferies.

'Oh, the night is young,' said Hearst. 'We've not even started living yet.'

'Of course he lived,' said Durnwold. 'And he threw down the dragon's false eye – a ruby as big as your head. I can vouch for it: I was there when the ruby fell.'

179

'I lived, yes,' said Hearst. 'But coming down again – that was another story. Worm holes, drop shafts, stones and darkness, oh, there was no end to it. I could find my way back up again easy enough, even in the dark. But to find the way down in the first place – why, it was almost as bad as the climb.'

'But he made it,' said Durnwold. 'He made it. A toast, I say, to Morgan Hearst, warrior of Rovac, dragon-killer!'

Goblets were lifted and the toast was drunk, except by the wizards, who could hardly toast a Rovac warrior – history could not be forgotten as easily as that.

'Truly,' said Jeferies, 'We are fortunate to sit together at one table, wizards and warriors, heroes and princes. There has never been a gathering like this in Trest for ten generations.'

'Twenty!'

'Thirty!'

'Ever!'

'For certain,' said Jeferies. 'Now, I wouldn't like you to leave here without some entertainment worth remembering. Fortunately, we have here something entirely unique, the magician Lemmy Blawert. Bring in the conjurer!'

In came Lemmy Blawert, a sly, greasy, dingy little man with a horse-hair wig, a forked beard, a silver earring and a tarnished lower-lip ring. He limped forward, grinning, his body shapeless under grey and greasy robes. He bowed to Phyphor.

'Who is this individual?' said Phyphor.

'One of the world's wonders,' declared Jeferies, smiling. 'I trust he'll not disappoint you.'

'He looks a regular rat-rapist,' said Phyphor, in idiomatic Estral; since reaching Estar, the wizards' close dealings with the people had given them a fair grasp of Estral, the native language of the region, besides improving their command of the Galish Trading Tongue.

'Laugh you may,' said Jeferies, 'but Lemmy Blawert will show you a thing or two.'

Lemmy Blawert took out a pack of cards and fanned them out so only their backs could be seen.

'Take a card, master, any card.'

Phyphor hesitated, then took one.

'It's the fool,' said Lemmy Blawert with a grin and a cackle.

Phyphor flicked the card over: it was the fool.

'Put it back, master, anywhere any,' said Lemmy Blawert, setting the pack down on the table. 'I'm not touching so there'll be no fiddling, no fooling.'

Again Phyphor hesitated, then he slid the fool into the middle of the pack. Lemmy Blawert produced a wand.

'Rowan this is this wand, rowan, sacred to the mysteries. You'll see a mystery now tonight.'

He passed the wand over the cards once, twice, thrice.

'No touching so no fiddling, as you see masters, see me see, no touching, no fiddling. Now pick the top card, master.'

Phyphor turned over the top card. It was the fool. There were shouts of applause. Lemmy Blawert aped a bow then tucked the cards away inside his robes.

'I'll see those cards,' said Garash, reaching into the magician's robes. Then he swore, wrenching his hand away. Bright blood flashed where one finger had been torn open.

'It's the rat, master,' said Lemmy Blawert apologetically. 'He don't like strangers much. But here's the cards for you, master.'

He reached into his clothing and with a flourish scattered cards over the table: emperors, dragons, heroes, soldiers and a single fool. He left them where they fell.

'Dice, anyone? I've two dice to roll for your money with even odds. For me, the one-eyed one, the six-eyed

181

six. A one wins for me, a six wins for me, and any roll where there's one and one or one and six or six and six. Even odds I'll give you. I win if one shows or six shows or both show. Whoever rolls against me has the numbers two, three, four and five. Even odds and fair dice.'

Lemmy Blawert retreated to a corner to roll dice with those prepared to wager with him. Miphon bandaged Garash's finger with a strip torn from a napkin.

'So you're off tomorrow,' said Jeferies.

'Heenmor has stolen a long march on us,' said Elkor Alish. 'We must travel fast.'

Perhaps they would find Heenmor hiding out in the Kikashi Hills, but Phyphor had already suggested that the renegade wizard might be running for Stronghold Handfast. That abandoned castle in the east, deserted by its last owners in days long forgotten by both the written word and the spoken, lay on the Central Plateau within the circle of the Ringwall Mountains. To get there, Heenmor would have to reach the Fleuve River, travel downstream to Ep Pass, cross the Spine Mountains by way of that pass, traverse the Dry Forages then climb the Ringwall Mountains themselves.

'Well then,' said Jeferies. 'If you must travel fast, why not travel a little way with a fast woman before you set out? But first: drink. More drink! Come on you dogs, drink! The night is still young, she may be a whore but she's young enough, so more drink – and minstrel, strike up a song!'

'Yes, master,' said the last minstrel left on his feet; he was very drunk.

He struck up a tune on an old and famous harp; unfortunately, a harp deteriorates with age, and is seldom any good after a century or so. Worse, this instrument had not been tuned; the minstrel fumbled the fingering and seemed to have forgotten half the words of his song.

Prince Jeferies threw a goblet of wine; inebriated, he missed, but wine spattered his harpist, who ceased playing.

'Well,' said Jeferies. 'It seems I can't offer you a song. Still, I can organise a flogging, if that would suit.'

'It would indeed,' said Garash.

The minstrel blanched.

'Oh my prince,' said the minstrel. 'Oh honoured born, oh child of the Favoured Blood –'

'Silence!' roared Jeferies. 'Well, who's for a flogging?'

Hearst stood.

'There's still time for a song, if you'd rather.'

Jeferies looked around and decided that none of his guards were sober enough to administer a flogging.

'A song, then! What instrument do you play, man of Rovac?'

'On Rovac we favour the drum,' said Hearst.

And Elkor Alish remembered the drums of Rovac on the night the city of Larbreth fell. He remembered Hearst striding down the halls of her palace with his fingers knotted in her hair, the weight of her head swinging free and bloody in the light of flaring torches. He remembered Hearst's face: the smile as creamy as lust. Ah yes, Alish remembered.

'We have no drums here,' said Jeferies.

'My voice will suffice then,' said Hearst.

'Yes,' said Jeferies. 'But remember your mother tongue is gibberish to us.'

'Were we on Rovac to speak in a universal language known to all the world, it would make no difference,' said Hearst. 'For few hear us without their minds being disordered by fear. But this much most men know: Ahyak Rovac!'

His shout echoed through the hall, startling some of the nodding guards.

'The song,' said Comedo impatiently.

'The song, yes,' said Hearst. 'I learnt it in Estar, so I will sing it in Estral – and let none say the Rovac are

183

slow to learn. It is the song of the Victory of the Prince of the Favoured Blood.'

Prince Comedo clapped like a child: and indeed it was in childhood that Saba Yavendar's song of the Victory of the Prince of the Favoured Blood had become his favourite.

'On Rovac we prefer to sing with a foot on a corpse still cooling,' boasted Hearst. He looked Phyphor full in the face, then Garash, then Miphon. 'Is there any here who dares challenge Rovac?'

'None,' said Alish, as nobody else cared to open their mouths with Hearst in a mood like this. So Hearst hammered his fist on the table, once twice thrice, and began the song, which was in the Alacamp manner, half-chanted, half-sung:

By moon we come riding like tide on the flood,
The stars for our guide and a prince of the Blood
To lead us and speed us while night slips away
To give us the blood-sky, the promise of day.

Valarkin knew that once these fighting men got their enthusiasm worked up, they could go on chanting and singing all night, for there was no shortage of battle songs and war epics.

– But it is all absurd, their mindless bull-roaring stupidity. Sweat curses sinew, bone butchers brawn, chopping away till a single hero stands gloating over pools of blood and piles of lopped-off testicles. What's the sense of it? They think they're powerful, but they're not: they're just mindless meat that labours with a sword instead of a spade. Power lies with those who command, not those who spend their lives strengthening their sword-arms.

Valarkin scarcely listened while Hearst went on and on, giving them the pedigree of the prince the song dealt with, the names of the most notable warriors who rode to the battle, and the reasons for the fight: a drunken argument, a broken vow, an insult, a theft, a rape and a kidnapping.

Ride with the whip,
With the spur let us ride,
With the horn to the lip
As steel draws pride.
And the scream! And the Scream!
It is one throat and all:
Blood trims the sword as the dawn trims the sky:
Wheel them, heel them, fleet them along:
It is ours! It is ours!
Raise the Banner, the Song!

And hail him, hail now, prince of the blood,
Our leader, our hero, our child of the sun,
Prince of Dominion, his glory begun.

The horn of the victor echoes the sun,
Victory gained, his Triumph begun.
Rides he with sunlight and rides he with flame,
For his is the kingdom, the power it is his,
Handmaidens his to give and bestow,
Gold is his bounty –

Hearst broke off in mid-song. He could not go on, not with Alish watching him like that. Hearst swayed, unsteady on his feet. He picked up a goblet of wine, paused, swayed again. Then drained it and flung it away. It rattled over the stones of the floor and came to rest. He grabbed the edge of the table to steady himself, then all his control over his grief broke, and the words blurted out:

'Alish, Alish, what went wrong? Once we were friends!'

*   *   *

It was long after midnight. All those at the High Table who were still conscious were drunk, even the wizards, but they seemed determined to continue until they dropped. The kitchen servants had drunk themselves legless, so it had fallen to Gorn and Valarkin to prepare further refreshments for the High Table.

Gorn had found a clutch of eggs laid in clay compartments by a wasp; breaking away the mud, he extracted half-paralysed spiders and spread them on a slice of bread and butter. They lay fat, black, helpless; motionless but for an occasional stirring in one or two limbs.

Lemmy Blawert lay with his head on the kitchen table, snoring loudly. His rat, dead drunk, lay in his lap. Valarkin had already explored the secrets of Lemmy Blawert's robes, discovering the sources of the magician's magic: a pack of cards made up of nothing but fools.

Valarkin poured drinks, and to each he added a touch of cauchaumaur. The dose was light, and should prove just enough to tip drunken men into a long, deep sleep.

'What are you doing over there?' said Gorn.

'Just putting something in the drinks,' said Valarkin.

'What is it?'

'Nutmeg.'

'Don't put any in mine,' said Gorn. 'I don't like it.'

'As you wish,' said Valarkin.

He had already dosed Gorn's drink. He was not afraid that Gorn would remember anything, thinking him rather half-witted: in truth, Gorn was just a bit slow, and, at the moment, rather drunk.

'Ready?' said Gorn.

'Ready,' said Valarkin.

They carried trays out to the High Table. By now all the guards had left the hall. Morgan Hearst, the man Valarkin feared and hated most of all, was asleep with his head on the table. They set refreshments down in front of the revellers, who began to eat and drink.

186

Prince Comedo was the last person at the table to see what was on his bread and butter: he did not notice until he had eaten half of it. His face lost colour. He staggered to a corner and disgorged everything in his stomach in a roar of vomit. The laughter from those at the table went on as if it would continue forever.

'A toast,' said the wizard Garash, steadying himself against his mirth. 'A toast to the vigorous appetites of those of the Favoured Blood.'

'I'll drink to that,' said Jeferies, tears of laughter in his eyes.

Everyone drank to it, except Prince Comedo. He turned the ring on his finger that would take him back to the silence and safety of the green bottle, but nothing happened: the bottle was too far away for the ring to work. He stalked off to find Blackwood and the green bottle: he could not bear to stay and face the laughter. Gorn picked up Comedo's goblet as if he would drain it.

'You've got an appetite like a pig,' said Valarkin.

'Me?' said Gorn, pausing.

'Yes, you,' said Valarkin.

It was dangerous to say it, but Valarkin thought a second goblet of poisoned wine might well kill Gorn – and he wanted no dead bodies to proclaim that people had been poisoned. He just wanted everyone to go to sleep.

Gorn set the goblet down with great care. He rose from the table as if to teach Valarkin a thing or two. But found he did not feel well. He sat down again, blinking.

'I don't feel well,' he said.

As Valarkin had predicted, shortly the small dose of poison put all into a deep sleep. He smiled at their comatose bodies. So much for all those proud men who flaunted their egos as if they were lords of time and space: they were fools, and he had gained the upper hand effortlessly.

Valarkin crept to Phyphor's side and slipped his hand under the wizard's cloak. He withdrew the lead

box which bore the null sign of the dead zero on its lid.
The box was heavy in his hands.

'You!'

Valarkin wheeled. Hearst was staring at him with
bloodshot eyes.

'You! A drink! A drink for a fighting man!'

'My lord,' said Valarkin, putting down the lead box
and hastening to obey. He gave Hearst the goblet which
had been intended for Prince Comedo.

'My name is Hearst and Hast is called my sword,'
said Hearst, his drunken tongue half-crippling the
Estral he was speaking. 'My name is Hearst and Avor
sire was mine, and yes my sword is Hast, and there was
a dragon, a dragon once, and I held the breach at
Enelorf.'

He drained the last of the wine. Then swayed, slipped
sideways and collapsed bonelessly on the floor.

Valarkin recovered the heavy lead box again. The
hellmouth jaws leered at him. Hearst had seen him with
the box! What now? Kill him? Every moment spent
standing there was dangerous: someone might come
into the hall and discover him. First things first: dispose
of the mad-jewel.

If Valarkin could have snaffled all the red charms
worn by the wizards and the fighting men, the castle
would have been his to control. He could have set
himself up as a prince, a monarch, a warlord. But try as
he might, Valarkin had not been able to think of any
safe way to secure all the red charms: sooner or later he
must run up against a man who was still fighting fit. He
was not prepared to run such risks. What he was doing
was dangerous enough.

Outside, he scuttled through the shadows under the
cold starlight. The Golem's Eye, burning sullen red,
reminded him of Hearst's bloodshot eyes; he shivered.

He came to the castle well, which plunged down into
darkness. Opening the lead box, he took out the mad-
jewel. Then dropped it into the well. Nobody would

ever find it there. Morning would find Prince Jeferies and all his retainers witless, helpless, their castle uninhabitable until the mad-jewel exhausted its strength.

The expedition, deprived of the magic by which it had planned to overcome Heenmor, would have no choice but to turn back. They would return to Castle Vaunting, where Valarkin would live comfortably as Prince Comedo's ring-bearer. There would be no more of this hideous life of mud, leeches, hills, swamps, constipation, diarrhoea, danger, fatigue and merciless laughter.

Valarkin threw the empty box into the well and crept back to the Great Hall. Now he would swallow a pinch of cauchaumaur, and sleep away the night with the others. But what about Hearst? Hearst had seen him with the box that held the mad-jewel! True, thanks to the cauchaumaur, he would wake from poisoned sleep with his memories blurred, confused and entangled with nightmares. But what if he remembered the crucial scene with clarity?

– Kill him!

Yes, that was the only way.

Valarkin, softfoot and trembling, stole through the shadows toward his victim. How to kill him? What weapon to use? In sleep, Hearst twisted; his face contorted; he bared his teeth then hissed:

'The lopsloss! The lopsloss! It's coming!'

Valarkin looked around wildly. But of course there was only the hall: only shadows and sleeping bodies. He knelt beside Hearst.

'Stormguard,' muttered Hearst.

Valarkin's fingers tightened round the hilt of Hast. He began to ease the weapon from its scabbard. Suddenly Hearst sat bolt upright. His eyes, blood-red, intense with fury, glared at Valarkin. He gripped Valarkin by both arms, fingers nailing themselves into the biceps.

'The Stormguard!' shouted Hearst. 'The Stormguard! They've broken! They've broken! They're running!'

Then his grip relaxed and he sank back to the floor, his eyes closing slowly. Valarkin backed away slowly on his knees, trembling, trembling. His biceps still hurt.

'Alish,' said Hearst. Then, louder: 'Alish!'

His shouting would rouse the whole castle. Kill him now? Easy to say, but what if one of Comedo's men, roused by his shouting, burst into the hall while Valarkin was driving a blade home into Hearst's body? Valarkin remembered an old battle-cry out of songs and legends: victory to the brave. From his own thoughts came the dry rejoinder: and life to the cautious.

He crept back to his place at the High Table and downed his pinch of cauchaumaur. The last thing he heard before nightmare claimed him was Hearst's anguished cry:

'Alish! Not now, not now!'

CHAPTER TWENTY-SIX

Silently, without a cheer or a shout, without a smile or a laugh, the expedition rode out across the drawbridge of the High Castle. Alish surveyed the wreckage of the Collosnon army: corpses bloated and rotting in the sun. A week had been wasted in the High Castle while he and Hearst interrogated each and every man about the mad-jewel: discovering nothing.

As the expedition went past, flies rose from dead soldiers. Doubtless the dead had thought they had an easy duty: to starve out the High Castle by siege while the invasion swept west into Estar and then, perhaps, south to Dybra, starting on the road for the rich lands of the Harvest Plains. They had not known they would meet their doom when magic made their strength and courage useless.

Alish remembered the working routines of that methodical butchery. He took no joy in the sight of rotting corpses, or in his memories of slaughter. At least the blood and bones would feed this poor soil, which could always grow enough potatoes to supply the castle with vodka, but never enough to flesh out the thin faces of the common people.

At least the challenge ahead was clean and honour-able: to hunt down a wizard of power and evil and kill him. And after that, if Alish could command the death-stone and lead armies south in conquest, any collateral casualties would be pardoned by his purpose: to right the ancient wrong and exterminate all wizards.

Alish saw Prince Comedo riding toward him. They had debated whether to bring Jeferies with them; instead, they had left him to wander witless in his castle

191

with his followers and retainers. Jeferies would never believe that the mad-jewel was lost somewhere in his castle: he would think it a plot to deprive him of his kingdom. Better that they have a dead ally rather than a live enemy.

'My lord,' said Alish, greeting Prince Comedo.

'Elkor Alish, I have been thinking.'

'Indeed,' said Alish.

'Yes,' said Prince Comedo. 'I have determined against our continued advance into danger. It's pointless, as we can't defeat Heenmor without the mad-jewel.'

Valarkin had been working on Comedo's fears, and had done his job well.

'What do you advise, my lord?' said Alish.

'I do not advise,' said Prince Comedo. 'I command. I require our return to Castle Vaunting.'

'My lord,' said Alish, 'Heenmor has gained a season on us already. We've not time to go back for the other mad-jewel. Besides, going back, we might run into the Collosnon – we might find ourselves heavily outnumbered.'

'This quest has ceased to amuse me,' said Prince Comedo. 'Do you understand?'

'I will discuss it with the wizards,' said Alish.

He knew it heartened the troops to know they were being led by a prince of the Favoured Blood. In time, he might have to cut Comedo's throat, but for now he would stall to get the maximum benefit from Comedo's presence.

'I will retire to my palace of convenience,' said the prince, meaning his green bottle. 'You will arrange what is necessary. When I emerge again, I expect to find us closing with Castle Vaunting.'

'Yes, my lord,' said Alish.

Prince Comedo rode away; Alish guessed that they would not see him again for days, if not weeks. By then, it would be too late for anything Comedo might do to matter.

The expedition continued east toward the Kikashi Hills, beyond which lay the Fleuve River and the Spine Mountains. Reaching the hill country, they came upon the ramshackle camp of a family of charcoal burners. Questioned, these people said yes, Heenmor had passed this way. A number of people lived in the hills – deer hunters, truffle hunters, a few lepers, and, more recently, a few Collosnon deserters – and news travelled. Rumour claimed that some Melski had helped Heenmor, 'the blue and ginger giant', to travel down the Fleuve River.

The expedition was on the right trail.

The hills – 'Mountains if they're molehills,' muttered Garash darkly – were rugged and densely wooded. Finding sheer cliffs ahead, and the few hill trails impassable by horse, Alish organised a horse slaughter. Easy come, easy go. They chopped up their mounts, crammed the horse-stomachs with bits of meat and plenty of water, then boiled up the meat in the stomachs and gorged themselves.

Then went on.

The soil was light and sandy, and the pine tree had dominance. Blackwood did not like this unfamiliar kind of forest, but the others were happy enough. They slept each night with the wind lulling through the branches of the pines; they made big fires out of resinous pine cones, throwing on handfuls of pine needles which would flare up like a sudden blaze of wizard magic. In the steep-climbing hills, the land was clean, with far fewer biting insects than the lowlands they had already travelled through.

Durnwold took every opportunity to train with his brother Valarkin. On long summer evenings they sparred together, bearing shields, wielding heavy sticks rather than swords. They used sticks for safety, to prevent damage to their weapons, and so no clash of metal would ring out through the evening to alert any unpredictable strangers living within earshot.

Each evening, as Valarkin picked up his stick and put his arm through the leather thong inside the shield's curve, then grasped the iron bar bridging the space made by the shield boss, he felt more confident. His attempt to steal the green bottle and escape with Blackwood had failed, as had his effort to make the expedition turn back by throwing away the mad-jewel. Since he could not escape this quest, he would do his best to cope with its rigours. But that was not to say he liked it.

Often Valarkin thought of the man his brother Durnwold admired so much – the Rovac warrior Morgan Hearst – and wondered if he would get a chance for revenge.

Since Hearst was Durnwold's friend, Valarkin had to keep his bitter knowledge to himself. He was certain that his temple's god had killed the dragon Zenphos. He was a priest, and knew the god's power: the dragon's last flight had been its death throes. A handsome sacrifice had persuaded the god to kill the dragon: he could still remember the screams of the tender boys they had dedicated during seven days of ceremony.

Valarkin knew Hearst must have found the dragon dead in its lair on the mountain of Maf. If Hearst had admitted it, Valarkin could have persuaded Prince Comedo to rebuild the temple. He could not have reconstructed the secrets that had been lost, but ... everyone would have believed. Attributing fine weather to the goodwill of the god, he would have made the sun in the sky his miracle, proclaiming storm and foul weather to be the god's wrath. One proven miracle – the dragon's death – and they would have believed for a lifetime.

There was no chance of that now: but there might still be a chance for revenge.

Climbing the unfamiliar, ever-rising cliffs and hills, their pace slowed. They moved cautiously along the pine forest trails, with scouts out ahead and a rear-

194

guard behind. At dusk, Elkor Alish sent out clearing patrols to circle their camp site and ensure no enemy was creeping up on them in the twilight; he always chose to camp on high ground, with good defensive prospects, and posted sentries to watch out the night.

He was acutely aware that, while they might be questing for Heenmor's head, a Collosnon revenge force might be questing for them.

After days of hill climbing, they reached the high, isolated uplands of the Rausch Valley. No humans lived here, for the sandy soil would support no crops, and was worthless for grazing. Isolated from the moderating influence of the sea, the valley was blanketed by snow all through the winter; when the spring melts came, the entire valley flooded as snow melted on the mountains of the Coastal Massif.

They marched to the Fleuve River which drained the valley, and followed it downstream, in a southerly direction, to a point where the valley narrowed as the hills closed in. From here, the prospect to the east showed them high mountains, some still tipped with snow. From a Melski encampment, they learnt that the Melski had indeed taken Heenmor downriver to Ep Pass, where there was a pass across the Spine Mountains.

It now seemed certain that Heenmor was making for Stronghold Handfast. And, of course, the expedition must follow – but there was a problem.

CHAPTER TWENTY-SEVEN

On the raft belonging to the Melski headman, Blackwood turned to Hearst:

'It's no use. He refuses.'

'Try again,' said Hearst.

'Mister, they'll talk us out till the river runs dry, but
they'll never changesay.'

'Tell them,' said Hearst, 'they can't hope to stop us
travelling downriver, no matter what they've promised
to Heenmor. Tell them it might come to bloodshed if
they try to stop us.'

Blackwood addressed the Melski headman, whose
language came easily to his lips. In his exile years in
Looming Forest, the Melski had been his friends and
companions. Looming Forest: Estar: Mystrel. Was
Mystrel still alive?

'Old father,' said Blackwood. 'You of the current-
cunning, of the long-song memories, know that not
everyone honours the virtue of their spawning.'

'Lor-galor,' grunted the Melski headman in assent.

'Now these of the dryhard standing by your home-
banks take no part of the Cycle; on them lies no
restraint against murder. They can be like stormwater,
destroying with as little reason. I offer no threat, but the
others lack the honour of peacemakers.'

'You do well to warn us,' said the Melski headman.
'You are one who has honour. May your days lie
downstream.'

Then the headman sat back.

'Honoured father –' began Blackwood.

'It is no use,' said the Melski headman. 'You have the
courtesy of our tongue upon your lips, but we cannot

unspeak our speaking. The river cannot flow back to the hills, or words unsay themselves. We cannot offer you way by right down the river. If necessary, we will break the Cycle to preserve our truth.'

'What does he say?' asked Hearst.

'He says no,' said Blackwood. 'They won't let us follow Heenmor, even if it means a fight.'

'What's Heenmor paid them?'

'He paid them with their lives, mister. I'm sure you've made that kind of bargain now and then yourself.'

'Try again,' said Hearst, hurt by Blackwood's bitter tone.

'Old father,' said Blackwood. 'He wishes that I fish again.'

'We have given our answer,' said the Melski headman. 'Our word binds us. Is that entirely beyond their understanding?'

'They are not entirely without reason,' said Blackwood, 'but they are fated on this journey, for they also have spoken words of binding.'

'To whom have they spoken these words?'

'To each other.'

'Then they can unspeak their words between themselves. We cannot, for our pact is with our blood and the blood of another. We sought only to save our lives – that charred pine on the further shore is the mark of the power he showed us. In this time of danger, you could choose the way of example.'

'I have tried that way. It almost cost me my life.'

'And now the one who sits beside you forces you to talk. Well then, let us talk. Tell me how the families fare in the flow of the Hollern River, for there are years and leagues between us.'

'I will speak first of Hor-hor-hurulg-murg,' said Blackwood, 'for he was closest always; he bears himself with honour.'

197

* * *

Alish watched Hearst and Blackwood leave the headman's raft and walk back along the jetty to the riverside.

'Well,' said Alish when the two drew near. 'How did it go?'

'No joy,' said Hearst.

'They'll try to stop us,' said Blackwood. 'Even if it means fighting us.'

'Then let's get it over with,' said Alish. 'We'll go through them like a knife through butter. We'll clean them out, take their rafts and be off downstream by sunset.'

'No!' said Blackwood. 'It would be murder!'

'They're only gooks,' said Alish.

'Mister, I value them as my own.'

'That's nothing to me,' said Alish. 'Come on, Morgan, let's get everyone into position. I want to start –'

'Hold a moment,' said Hearst.

'What's this hold a moment?' said Alish. 'We're sworn to this quest. We have to go downriver. If we have to kill to cut the way clear, we do. The mountains to east are impassable unless we travel by way of Ep Pass – and that lies downstream.'

'There's more than one way to scalp a scat,' said Hearst. 'We can backtrack a little, slip through the forest and join the river further downstream.'

'Blackwood?' said Alish. Then, as Blackwood hesitated: 'He knows the answer to that. His love-hearted Melski will follow us if we leave to make sure we head back home.'

'Perhaps,' said Blackwood, 'but they might miss a small group that slipped away while the rest of us stayed here.'

'No!' said Alish. 'I'm not travelling with a fist of five when I can travel with an army. We might meet more Melski downstream, so we need our numbers.'

'Alish,' said Hearst. 'Let me go and scout out the land with Blackwood and one or two others. Then we can talk possibilities.'

'As you wish,' said Alish. 'Who will you take?'

'Blackwood, Durnwold, Miphon. We'll be back by dayfail.'

'Good speed,' said Alish.

* * *

Watching Hearst's scouting party slip away into the forest, Alish thought Hearst's life-debt to Blackwood was clouding his judgment. And Alish was disturbed that Hearst had taken Miphon to help him. Miphon, sensing things unseen by ordinary men, might well be useful in the forest – but a Rovac warrior should never become dependent on a wizard.

Alish had already made his decision. He had to do his duty, no matter how painful. His duty was to the Code of Night and the destiny of Rovac; his duty was to secure the death-stone for the highest purpose, to avenge the ancient wrongs and set history to rights – and no gabble of waterway gooks could be allowed to stand in the way.

Quietly, moving from man to man to advise each individually, Alish began to give his orders.

* * *

Elkor Alish, son of Teramont the Defender, warrior of Rovac, blood of the clan of the eagle, a man born into a free people and sworn to the cause of the Code of Night, stood with his hand on the hilt of his sword Ethlite, looking at the river, the rafts, and the eastern mountains tipped with snow that shone white-bright as the sun, great world-candle, lit and warmed the entire continent of Argan.

So it was killing time again. Voice would be raised

199

against voice and blade against blade, making more corpses to rot down to maggot-filth. Well, there was no helping it. They were faced by the bare necessity. Delay would give Heenmor a better chance to escape or perfect defences against the pursuit he evidently expected.

– Mine is the highest duty, the cause which forbids doubt. Mine is the cause which overrides even an oath sworn by steel and blood. I am of the Code of Night.

Alish looked round. Were the wizards ready? Phyphor gave him a nod: Phyphor and Garash were ready to help out if they must, though they would prefer to conserve their strength to fight Heenmor. Since the loss of the mad-jewel, the wizards had spent as much time as possible deep in the Meditations, building up their powers.

Outwardly, everything seemed normal. Some men were making a pretence of cooking; others sat on the river bank watching the rafts. Alish began to walk down to the jetty. Four warriors joined him: he hoped this fist of five could reach the headman's raft without alarming the Melski. The men talked softly and joked together, but Alish walked in silence, and the wind walked with him.

A few Melski children were playing about the camp making happy whistling and grunting noises. They would die. So? They were not human. They were only gooks. The children chased each other, and the wind snatched at their cries and flung them away.

Alish walked on, and he remembered walking to other battles, ah, so many battles, and once he had sworn it would never happen again. Yes, when he had seen Hearst holding her head he had sworn that enough was enough: he had seen too much killing. But then there had been war at Castle Vaunting, fighting in the swamps, butchery at the High Castle: and now it would happen again. And who could deny that his hands remembered the skill of slaughter?

A few men gave Alish sly glances as he and his shadows walked down to the jetty. Every man had weapons within grasp or snatch. They were greedy, excited, over-eager. If all went well, the Melski headman would be first to die. They would charge the rafts before the Melski – now leaderless - had time to arm and organise. If all went well, the surviving Melski would stand and fight: they were noted for stubborn courage in battle.

But what if cowardice or good tactical sense took the Melski into the water? That was their element, where they could breathe through their gills and their green skins, and swim with their webbed hands and feet far better than any human. Things might get difficult, especially when night came and the rafts floated down the dark river with the enemy grouping silently in the water . . .

A couple of men were cleaning their helmets, needing to keep their hands busy while they waited. Those were the nervous ones. There were always nervous ones. What if the charge faltered or failed? What if the men turned and ran in panic? Could that happen? With this rabble, of course it could happen.

There was someone coming up behind. Alish stopped and turned. It was Gorn.

'What are you doing here?' said Alish, startled. 'You're supposed to be in charge of our rear party.'

'You don't need me there,' said Gorn.

It was true. Truth was, Alish did not want to see Gorn in action again: Gorn at war, battle axe amok, eyes manic, lips parted as if in the pleasure of lust. If there was a pause, a lull in the battle, Gorn would wipe his hands over his head, leaving blood in his hair. Worst of all, after the fighting, Gorn would go round finishing off the wounded. He never made a clean kill: he always used five strokes of the axe for the ending. Left foot, right foot, left hand, right hand – then the throat. And all this time he would sing a wordless moaning dirge, eyes by this time blank slaughter.

'I sent you where I wanted you,' said Alish. 'Go!'

'I want to be in at the kill,' said Gorn.

It was no time for argument. Everyone was waiting for them, and Gorn could be stubborn when he chose.

'Come on then,' said Alish, 'but do nothing until I strike the first blow.'

The first raft rocked beneath their feet. Three rafts away sat the Melski headman and the rest of the Melski elders.

Alish was tempted to look back; he was afraid the men on the shore might betray the plan by grouping for the charge. The Melski were not experienced warriors, but their natural suspicion of strangers would make them wary.

But it was too late to look back now.

The wind sang in his ears. The trees across the river spired up into the wind. Green, dark green, rising to blustery blue. There will be screams on the wind and blood in the screams. Soon. It is happening. It cannot be stopped.

A few Melski were swimming, turning lazy circles in the water. Others were dozing on the rafts in the sun; some were inside the cabins. Alish could hear Gorn panting. The sound repulsed him.

The sun: too hot. Wind brisked about him. Glare from the water. He narrowed his eyes. He could smell Gorn. Sweating. Alish blinked. He was breathing too quickly. He tried to control his breathing.

What was wrong? It was hardly his first battle. He was Elkor Alish, warrior of Rovac, veteran of the Cold West. Now he was starting to sound like Hearst when the drink was doing his talking. But it was true. He was a professional, a veteran of countless battles of blood and slaughter.

Was it going into combat without helmet and shield that made him so uneasy? To avoid arousing the suspicions of the Melski, they wore no armour but a little chain mail. Without armour, was a man more vulnerable to his memories?

202

They were almost there.

They stepped onto the headman's raft. The headman, a big muscular Melski, stared at them intently. There was a pause. Alish felt his heart pounding. His mouth, dry, tasted of metal.

The Melski headman slowly stood up, the better to protest at the intrustion of so many strangers onto his raft. His chest inflated, then sank as he delivered a belch of discontent. He was preparing himself for oratory. There was plenty of time to observe his heavy muscles, his sunken eyes, his prodigious neck.

'You've upset him,' said Gorn, grinning. 'Come on, you'd better say something. Let your sword do the speaking.'

Alish said nothing. He knew they were all waiting for him.

'Hor-hurop!' said the Melski headman.

Gorn looked at Alish.

'Hor-drup! Muur-muur. Muur hulp! Mulsk!'

Alish stood there, trembling.

And Gorn attacked.

'Yar!' screamed Gorn, hacking his axe to the headman's chest.

The headman staggered, belched blood. Gorn hacked for the neck. Alish lugged out his sword Ethlite. Around him, blades were lunging and slicing. And suddenly it was all over: they stood panting on the raft with corpses at their feet.

'Alish,' said Gorn. 'You were too slow to eat with us.'

And he laughed, and wiped his hands through his hair. With whoops and yells, the men on the shore were charging onto the carpet of rafts. There was a clamour of pain, of Melski bellows, clashing metal, whirring arrows. Shield and sword, the charge swept forward. Sleepers and sunbathers were cut down. Bewildered Melski stumbling from their cabins were killed in the doorways. A few dived for the water, but most stood their ground and fought.

Some charged Alish and his fist of warriors, isolated on the headman's raft.

'Alish!' shouted Gorn. 'Back to back!'

They stood back to back and braced themselves. The Melski came in a rush, green muscles swinging clubs, swinging sunglitter swords. They shouted as they came:

'Huur!'

'Gaar!'

'Horg-hulg!'

Alish took out the boldest: stabbed for the gut, drew free, then swung for the neck, shouting as he swung. The wind whipped away his shout. The boldest went down, then the onslaught was upon them.

Alish struck at a face. It slipped away. Ethlite swung free, slewed to slice at a leg. A falling Melski crashed against his hip. Alish went down on one knee. A Melski loomed over him. A club swept down.

Alish parried, rose to his feet. Again the club swung. His sword sliced air to meet it. His blade slid along the wood and carried away the hands that held it. Alish stepped back for room to move, then hacked at the head. He spun, and his sword met flesh. A spurt of blood. He turned again, meeting a face with the edge of his blade.

Again he wheeled, to find a Melski driving at him with a sword. Alish parried. Their blades locked hilt to hilt. Face to face they struggled, close enough to kiss. Alish slammed his forehead into his enemy's face. The Melski reeled backwards. Alish chopped sword to ribs. Again. Again. Hack through, hack through.

His blade pulled free from the bloody shatter of ribs and arced up for the throat. Something struck him on the back of the head. He fell.

Alish saw water snatch his sword. Then he embraced the cold shock of water. Chain mail jerked him down. Briefly, he glimpsed his blade, a thin thread of blood wisping away as it twirled down into the depths.

In slow motion, he struggled with the chain mail, as

204

one may struggle with a monster in dreams. Pressure hurt his ears. His struggles snapped the thin gold round his neck, which fell away, bearing the red charm down into the depths. Then the jerkin came free. Alish rose, feet kicking slow and clumsy in his waterlogged boots.

Looking up, he saw a raft just above him. Contact! Volumes of green slime broke free and filtered away as he clawed along the underside of the raft. He surfaced, gasped air. A Melski glanced down in surprise, then stamped on his face.

Alish went down. Under, under. He looked around the shadow-green underwater world. In the depths, a wounded Melski turned slow, bloody circles towards darkness as it tried to swim away from agony. Bright surface was the sun. Smudged green shadows were the rafts. Alish swam, then surfaced.

He threw back his head and engulfed an ocean of air.

A small frightened Melski, perching on the edge of a raft, threatened him with a knife. The knife was pitted with rust. There were dried fish scales on the blade.

'Muur!' said the Melski.

Alish screamed at it. The Melski dived in panic.

Alish pulled himself from the water, still gasping in buckets of air. The combs which had held his long black hair in place were lost: his hair fell free. He wiped it out of his face.

Alish snatched up the first weapon he saw – a Melski club – and stood in the sunlight, blinking and gasping. He coughed. The sun was a slash of light in the blue sky. Clouds boiled in the wind. He glanced around and was dazzled by the sunlight on the water. Men, shouting, were plunging from raft to raft, but where were the Melski? Some – little ones – sat in shock, rocking from side to side, moaning. Elsewhere there was still some fighting, but here it was over.

Many of the cabins were burning where cooking fires had been scattered from their foundations of sand and rocks. Smoke streamed across the rafts, driven by the wind, confusing everything. There was fighting some-where in the smoke. Alish could hear shouts, screams, the thump of boots, the whirr of arrows, the groans of the wounded. He heard the quick crackle of flames sprinting through bamboo cabins, occasional explo-sions as joints of bamboo heated up then burst.

The Melski club felt heavy in his hand. He dropped it. He saw a sword, but did not pick it up. Ethlite was gone, Ethlite, Ethlite, his sword, his lover, snatched by the river, drowned too deep to dive for.

The weariness that came over him then was sudden and absolute. Without looking any more at the flames and the smoke, without listening any more to the fighting, he started walking back toward the shore. Rafts rocked underfoot as he stepped from one to the other. Some water moved inside his left ear; he shook his head to try and get rid of it. His nose was bleeding. The wind knifing through his wet clothes felt cold.

Alish passed a few of the men who had already begun to plunder the dead. They had all been fighting: they were all hot, red-faced and sweating still. Most were bloodstained; a couple were wounded, but only lightly. Water squelched in Alish's boots as he walked.

On the shore, the two wizards of the order of Arl, Phyphor and Garash, stood watching the battle with detached interest.

'Alish!' said Phyphor. 'That was well done. That was very well done.'

Alish ignored him, and walked past without answer-ing. Wizards! This slaughter was all their fault. A plague on all your houses, then, if you have houses.

In the camp site were the dismembered remains of a few Melski children; one body had fallen into a fire and was charring with a foul stench. Alish threw himself to the ground, threw himself to the earth, wet though he was. He was the leader, and to collapse was not one of his privileges, but he collapsed all the same. He would have wept, except he was too proud to weep, ever.

CHAPTER TWENTY-EIGHT

In the evening, they set off down the river. That night they heard Melski in the water, exchanging recognition signals. Alish feared an attack, but none came: the Melski seemed content to drift downstream with the rafts. When dawn came, there were none to be seen in the water – but soon afterwards, the leading raft saw one asleep on a rock. It woke, and dived into the water, and the current carried it away.

Alish feared the Melski might go downstream ahead of the rafts to organise an ambush. The river banks were growing progressively steeper: soon it would be possible to drop rocks from above.

He also worried about Hearst, who sat apart, brooding. Why? Because he had failed to help Blackwood's Melski friends? Because Alish had lied to him? Or because he had missed the battle?

Whatever the problem, Alish hoped Hearst would not do anything reckless – he did not wish to have to kill the best warrior in his command. However, if it did come to a confrontation, there was no doubt who would win: they had matched blades in practice often enough to know that Elkor Alish was by far the better swordsman.

Another who worried about Hearst was Durnwold, who valued the Rovac warrior above all because he had shown that the world could dispense with the governance of the Favoured Blood. The common wisdom throughout the continent of Argan was that the world would collapse in chaos without the guidance of its traditional rulers, but Hearst had proved that a common warrior could be both wiser and stronger than a prince. When Comedo had grovelled in helpless fear as the Collosnon attacked, Morgan Hearst had dared the lopsloss, secured the mad-jewels – and had then gained victory for Alish by using his judgment and opening the lead box holding the mad-jewels.

However, one man cared nothing for Hearst, and that was Blackwood, who believed that Hearst had conspired with Alish to get him out of the way so the attack on the Melski could proceed without possibility of betrayal. As survivors of the court intrigues of Chi'ashlan, about which they sometimes told outrageous stories of treachery and deceit, the Rovac were entirely capable of such a stratagem, and Blackwood knew it.

Hearst, for his part, was brooding on the distance separating him from Alish. It had come as a shock to know that he had been excluded from the secret councils which had decided to use a mad-jewel to stand sentry at Castle Vaunting, but now Alish had deceived him, had in fact told him a direct lie – and that was something entirely different again.

Hearst had blurred memories of an argument in Castle Vaunting. He had been drunk at the time, but he thought he vaguely remembered Alish threatening to kill him. Had that really happened? And if Alish had really said that, had he really meant it? Was it possible that they might one day match steel against steel, with lethal intent?

No. That was impossible.

In the Cold West, they had been inseparable. They had shared the same tent, and sometimes the same woman . . . and then . . . and then everything had changed . . .

*　　*　　*

As the rafts drifted at leisure down the river, Alish completed a commander's rounds by trying to make peace with Blackwood. He had little success.

'Mister,' said Blackwood. 'Don't try that comrade-talk with me. I know what happened. Murder. Women and children. Killing fishermen, stealing their boats.'

'They're only gooks,' said Alish.

'Mister,' said Blackwood. 'You don't believe that.'

Alish had seen alcoholic Melski in Lorford: gross green stumbling wrecks blinded by the alcohol which, for them, was an addictive drug bringing death in two or three years. Many scorned the Melski because of the inability of their body chemistry to handle basic poisons. But Alish, no brawling boneheaded blademaster, was too widely-travelled to find such provincial sentiments satisfactory.

Unlike some other people – for instance, the Korugatu philosophers of Chi'ash-lan – the Rovac had no formal theory of war crimes. Nevertheless, the concept was not unknown to them. One did not murder an embassy come to parley during a truce, systematic genocide was considered a bit excessive, and the habit of serving prisoners with bits of grilled meat cut from their own bodies was generally frowned upon.

Moreover, Alish, having learnt a certain unforgettable lesson from personal experience, knew the human cost of what he did – and knew that, as far as ethics were concerned, the term 'human' could reasonably be extended to cover the Melski. He did not find his latest battle-memories easy to live with.

'It happened,' said Alish. 'It's done.'

He spoke as if the words were a formula for ending recriminations: and amongst the Rovac, they were.

'It was a cruel business,' insisted Blackwood.

'It was necessary.'

'Oh yes, everyone has to die, so I suppose death's necessary.'

'Listen, Heenmor is evil: evil without redemption. Ours is a just cause. We don't want to shed innocent blood, but we had to. We're trying to save the world!'

209

'The world will be much the same when Heenmor is dead,' said Blackwood. 'Only then you'll have to find another excuse to kill people.'

'You don't understand, Heenmor – '

'Oh, I understand, mister. You've thought yourself a reason to kill lots and lots of people and be proud of it. Well then, kill away. Be happy in your work.'

'I don't enjoy killing.'

'Oh, you don't? And I suppose your sword doesn't either? And does that make the dead less dead?'

'What would you do in my place?'

'I could never be in your place, mister. I could never swim through that much blood to get there. But swimming makes some happy, it seems. Your fighting men look happy enough.'

'Of course,' said Alish. 'We've won a victory.'

'It wasn't much of a victory.'

'You're right,' said Alish. Speaking, he felt that he should be glad that Blackwood seemed to have abandoned the subject of his personal sins. But he wasn't glad. It was painful to talk about it, yet worse to keep silent. And who else could he talk to? Not Hearst! 'Yes,' he said. 'You're right. It wasn't much of a victory. There was no fighting to it.'

'Just butchery.'

'Yes. But that's the sort of victory men love. They're getting the best part of their reward now. Inside that cabin.'

Since the evening of the day before, men had been taking turns to go into the cabin he indicated.

'What are they doing in there?'

'What do you think?'

'Is it always like this after a victory?' said Blackwood, looking away.

Alish studied the banks, which were steadily becoming cliffs as the rafts glided down the river.

'Men imagine victory often enough during our campaigns of mud and rain,' said Alish, slowly. 'And when victory comes, they make it everything they had imagined.'

'But not all soldiers can be like this.'

'No,' said Alish. 'Some are worse. The Rovac are worse. In the Cold West, it was policy. Our very name became another word for terror. In the Cold West, there was nowhere for our victims to run to, not during the snows. I remember . . .'

'Yes, well,' said Blackwood, who presently had no appetite for any gut-slaughter stories, 'Perhaps you could forget, too.'

'Oh no, no . . . I could hardly forget. I remember the time . . . yes, the time when we conquered the city of Morlock on the river Tenebris. We conquered it for the Emperor Yan. Yan, Yanyl – there were marching songs made about that, I can tell you.'

They were talking in Estral, and Blackwood had no hope of understanding the relevant pun in Rovac, equivalent to Ars – Arse. But Alish did not think of that. His eyes were unfocused; the sights he saw now lay far away in time and distance.

'The city fell to us on the same day that the spring thaw broke up the river of ice. That was a night . . . that was a night they talk about still. They were soft in that city . . . they screamed even before they were touched . . .'

He said no more, but he remembered. Yes. The room had been hot if you were near the blazing fire that glowed on the heaving flesh, or frigid if you were by the slit windows that looked out over the river. The ice had grated as floe clashed with floe all night in the swirling water. Toward morning one of the women had made a sound like the grating of old iron against old iron. She had made that sound deep in her throat and soon after that she had died.

And he remembered . . . yes, the room in the small village under the shadow of the Far Wall that stretched across the tundra . . . a smoky cave in the Valley of

Insects . . . the inner sanctum of the desecrated Temple of the Thousand Snowflowers . . .

'Sorrow is sweet,' said Blackwood, knowing that some people can positively enjoy the sentimental satisfactions of remorse.

'Not all sorrow, woodsman. Let me tell you a tale . . . a true tale of the wars in the Cold West. It is the tale of . . . well, listen and you will hear.

'I had been ten years fighting in the Cold West when there fell to my forces the task of capturing a small city state. It was by the coast. It was important to us: the only harbour for five hundred leagues that did not freeze in winter. Hot springs – a hot river in fact – emptied into the harbour and let ships use it all year round. We laid siege to the city.

'It was a bitter siege. The city was weak, but the people worshipped a god that was strong, and gave them aid. Led by a woman warrior-priest, they fought us, and their defence held, thanks to the powers of their god. The name of the city was Larbreth. Have you heard of that city? No? Well, I suppose you hear little of the Cold West here in Argan.

'One day, the people of the city made a sally against us. They shattered our ranks. I fought their leader, hand to hand, sword against sword. Well, I am not one for boasting, but I was the best man with a sword in all the armies of Rovac. She disarmed me. She took me prisoner. Ethlite was her name.

'She was two hundred years old. Her god kept her body young, but she was wise with the wisdom of generations. They did not hate us, do you know that? They knew who we were and what we were, but they did not hate us. She . . . she chose me. Was she in love? I think she was too wise for unthinking passion. But she chose me.

'I say they understood us, but they did not really understand. When she knew I was in love with her, she trusted me. She did not understand that the will is

212

stronger than love. Poison was the way I chose. While her body was still warm, I opened the city gates. That was a victory to remember. Oh yes, I remember . . .'

He remembered that day, and he remembered the night of that day, when the drums of Rovac had worked to a frenzy, and every man had lubricated himself with blood . . .

'So we had a victory. I took her sword, and named it after her. Ethlite, I called it. That was the best sword I ever held, but I never used it in the Cold West. I went back to Rovac. I wanted . . .'

But he could not speak of that. He could not speak of the Code of Night. That had been his choice: to renounce the mercenary campaigns which had given him fame and glory, and to dedicate himself to the tasks of righting Rovac's ancient wrongs.

'Mister,' said Blackwood. 'We have to bury our dead. Otherwise they end up living our lives for us.'

'And you're the one who was sorry for the dead Melski!'

'Mister, we mourn to free us for the future. From the sound of it, you're still trapped in the past. Is it the past, perhaps, which makes you drive so hard after wizards?'

Blackwood was only talking, in the most general terms, of the fanaticism which Alish had demonstrated in his pursuit of Heenmor, but Alish was provoked into saying:

'That's nothing to do with the past. Wizards are the final enemy. All of them!'

There. He had said it. He had touched on the hidden matters: the secrets of the Code of Night. But he needed to talk, yes, more than ever before he needed to talk.

'Wizards defeated the Swarms,' ventured Blackwood, who knew that much at least from legend.

Alish laughed.

'I've heard those stories, the same as you have,' said Alish. 'Who do you think makes them up?'

'Wizards, perhaps. They should know their own business, after all.'

'We have records on Rovac going back to the Long War – records which prove that history ... history didn't quite happen the way it's told.'

'You have long memories, mister.'

'Yes,' said Alish. 'Remember Rovac has never tried to conquer, only to serve as mercenaries. That's why we've 'scaped the cycle of rise, decline and fall that empires suffer. Our archives are intact. So let me tell you a little of the history of this continent, Argan.

'There was a time when the Swarms lived much, much further south than they do now. Way back then, the people who called themselves the Dareska Amath lived in the lands bordering the Ocean of Cambria. They were warlike, always engaged in blood feuds and clan fights.

'Then the wizards, who wanted to rule the known world, decided to capture an entity known as the Skull of the Deep South. The Skull commands the Swarms. Controlling that power, the wizards could have conquered the world.

'They persuaded the Dareska Amath to help them, and the Dareska Amath agreed. Armies marched south in support of the wizards. They suffered great losses at the hands of fearful enemies, but they persevered, for there were heroes among them. In the end, though, in a crucial battle against the Swarms, the wizards broke and ran. It was an act of cowardice which led to a terrible defeat and the end of the expedition.

'Now the wizards knew the Swarms would begin to move north. They had committed a crime against humanity by stirring up the wrath of the Skull of the Deep South: so they decided to kill all witnesses. They laid waste to the lands around the Ocean of Cambria.

'That was the time of selection. Only the best fighters and seafarers survived the destruction of our home-lands. Exiled from Argan, they sailed west till they

214

came to the islands of Rovac. Our destiny is to destroy the wizards and recapture the lands around the Ocean of Cambria.'

'I have never heard that story before,' said Blackwood.

'It is not a story lightly shared,' said Alish.

'I understand,' said Blackwood.

And Alish lay back on the raft, shut his eyes, and was quiet, as if sleeping.

*   *   *

Another short summer night passed, uneasily, but without incident, and morning found the rafts still drifting down the river. That morning, Comedo emerged from his bottle and blinked at the river, the rafts, and, not the least of his amazements, the sunlight.

'What are we doing here?' he said.

Nobody paid him any attention. The least of those fighting men now felt himself to be a questing hero; their respect for the Favoured Blood had declined with their shared experiences of marching and battle which had occured in the absence of that Blood.

'What are we doing here?' yelled Comedo.

'Look!' cried an anonymous wit, safe in the company of his fellows. 'It's the rare and famous hairy woubit!'

There was a light splatter of laughter.

Comedo stalked over to Hearst, who was trailing a fishing line off the end of a raft.

'Where are we? What are we doing here?'

'We're going down the Fleuve River on some Melski rafts,' said Hearst. 'Soon we'll reach Ep Pass. Then we'll head east across the Spine Mountains, making for Stronghold Handfast.'

'Valarkin said as much,' said Comedo, looking pale and agitated. 'But it can't be true! I said to go home! Days ago! I've had enough, do you hear me? I want to go back.'

215

'My lord,' said Hearst. 'You're surely comfortable enough in your miraculous green bottle.'

'Didn't you hear me? I want to go back.'

'You pledged yourself to pursue Heenmor to the uttermost limit and to do all in your power to destroy him,' said Hearst. 'We're to kill Heenmor and give his magic death-stone to the wizards for them to take south and return to the Dry Pit.'

'I withdraw my pledge,' said Comedo.

Hearst spat.

'A man's word is not like a snake that comes out of a hole to look at the sun. It can't run back inside.'

Comedo started to scream. Some men looked up, slow and lazy as Hearst was, and studied his face. Comedo screamed himself hoarse. It did him no good.

'I want to go home,' said Comedo.

Hearst laughed in his face.

Comedo's face twisted in anger. His mouth clutched breath, then he began to scream again. Screaming, he spun round and round, then suddenly twisted the ring on his finger and dissolved into smoke which was sucked back into the bottle.

The rafts drifted on down the river.

They enjoyed hot, lazy, sunlit weather in which a single day seemed to stretch half-way to eternity. Drifting downriver in that golden weather, the men sunbathed, gambled, tattooed each other, swam in the riverdrift, told jokes and obscene stories, exchanged confidences, caught fish and invented new ways of cooking it: with cloves and a pinch of siege dust; smoked slowly over burning pine resin; guts and flesh mixed together in a clay ball with a little barley flour, and baked. Some men, like Durnwold and Alish, practised weapon skills. Elkor Alish put on spectacular displays of shadow-fighting as he accustomed himself to the balance of an antique Melski blade which he had taken for his own use.

And Comedo did not return.

216

CHAPTER TWENTY-NINE

Alish lay half-asleep in the sun, dreaming vaguely about conquering Argan with the death-stone. Should he take Prince Comedo on his campaigns? There might be rulers in Argan who would find it easier to bow to a prince of the Favoured Blood than to a Rovac mercenary. He would think about it . . .

'Elkor Alish.'

He opened his eyes, and saw the woodsman Blackwood.

'What is it?'

'We're almost there. We're almost at Ep Pass.'

'Good,' said Alish, getting to his feet.

Throughout the flotilla, men began to rouse themselves. They heaved on sweep-oars, guiding the rafts toward a stony beach on the eastern side of the river. Beyond the beach was a gap in the cliffs about two hundred paces wide: the beginning of Ep Pass, the way through the Spine Mountains.

Downstream, the river narrowed, running swiftly between towering cliffs; perched on rocks by the racing river were a few dozen Melski, some with small fires burning. Some of the men tried the range with arrows.

'That's enough of that!' said Alish.

There was no point in going to war with the Melski, who had passed up every chance of ambush and seemed to be planning no more than the recovery of some of their rafts. It would be a long, slow journey for them to oar their way upstream, but for the task they had greater strength in their chests and arms than most humans.

On landing, Alish had the rafts dragged ashore.

217

Despite the proximity of the Melski, he did not want to march east immediately, thinking it best to scout ahead a little first, to get an idea of what the country was like. He chose Hearst and Durnwold to go with him.

As they set off, Hearst called to the wizards:

'Garash! Care to stretch your legs?'

Garash looked up, but did not favour them with a reply.

'I don't think he's exactly thrilled at the idea of mountain climbing,' said Durnwold.

'Stiff socks,' said Hearst, meaning tough cheese. 'He needs a good sweat to unblubber him.'

It was a hot, dry, bluesky day: one of those days on which it is impossible to believe that it will ever be wet or cold again. They walked uphill between scattered rocks, some many times the height of a man. Though the ground was stony, gnarled and twisted trees with dark green leaves wrested a livelihood from the soil, making little thickets between the rocks.

The cliffs closed in; it grew quieter. Soon they could no longer hear the noise of the river or the men by the river, only the sounds of their boots on rocks, the tatcheting of insects, the hush of their own breathing. Small lizards darted over the rocks, sprinting for shelter as the men approached.

'Stop,' said Alish.

'What is it?' said Durnwold.

'I see it,' said Hearst. 'Smoke! Over there!'

'It could be Melski,' said Durnwold.

'Or Heenmor,' said Alish.

'We don't know enough to start laying bets,' said Hearst, 'but we'd best go back for the wizards in case it is Heenmor.'

Alish looked at him.

'Are you afraid . . . friend dragon-killer?'

For a moment, they stared at each other.

'What do you think?' said Hearst.

'I think you know the answer better than me.'

218

'He's not afraid,' said Durnwold. 'There's no sword –'

'Enough,' said Hearst. 'We'll go on. But if it is Heenmor, how will we take him?'

'His only protection is a blast of fire or the bite of that snake of his. If we come at him from three different directions, if he hesitates for a moment – we should do it.'

'And what if we run into something altogether different?' said Hearst. 'What if it's a band of twenty head-hunting nomads? Who knows what manner of people live in this part of Argan?'

'If it's not Heenmor,' said Alish, 'we retreat, quietly. I estimate the smoke is . . . a hundred paces ahead. Let's split up. Durnwold can go right, I'll go left and you go straight ahead.'

Hearst nodded.

'Draw your sword now,' said Alish to Durnwold, 'so when you're closer you won't have to take it from its sheath.'

'It's sheathed in oiled leather,' said Durnwold. 'It won't make any noise.'

'Yes, but if you're crawling forward through vines or brambles, you might make a noise like earth's own bone-breaking if you have to jerk out your sword in a hurry.'

Durnwold drew his sword. Hearst already had Hast in his hand, and Alish was holding his Melski blade.

'Quiet now,' said Alish.

They separated. Durnwold went right, Alish went left, and Hearst went straight ahead. Hearst had the hardest job: he was making his way through a close-growth of runtling trees.

He went tenderfoot and slow. The highriding sun pooled his shadow at his feet. Everything was very bright. He saw the yellow-green veins patterning every leaf. His heart beat soft-quick thud. Stepping forward, he used the side of his boot to ease away any twigs

219

before letting his weight settle as smoothly as unguent oil easing onto a baby's backside. Finally he could see the little cooking fire that was sending up the smoke.

There was Heenmor, twice the height of any ordinary man, hair ginger, beard blue. And there, asleep on a rock at his feet, was the snake. Hearst could see a shack, a latrine, a stack of firewood. Heenmor had been there quite some time: waiting for any pursuers? Heenmor was sitting with his back to a small cliff. Hearst could see Durnwold was working his way to the top of that cliff. He could not see where Alish had got to.

Hearst started to ease forward. Suddenly, Heenmor looked up from his fire. He stared straight at the trees where Hearst was hiding. Hearst froze. He saw the snake had woken: its head was weaving this way and that, seeming to point at the trees. Heenmor got to his feet.

At the top of the cliff, Durnwold put down his sword and picked up a rock. Hearst could see him clearly. The boy was thinking! Slowly, Heenmor lifted his staff of power, and pointed it at the trees where Hearst was hiding. Durnwold stepped to the edge of the cliff, raising the rock high to cast it down.

And the lip of the cliff gave way.

Heenmor snapped his head around at the noise, saw Durnwold falling, and threw himself to one side. Durnwold crashed to the ground. The copper-strike snake lunged at him. One beat of the heart, two, three, five – and the poison had done its work.

Heenmor wheeled, raised his staff, and shouted a Word. Hearst threw himself flat. A blast of heat roared through the trees. He smelt the stench of burning leather as it singed the heels of his boots. The trees around him crackled into flame.

As Heenmor shouted, again, again, blasting the ground to right and to left, Hearst lept to his feet. Flames were roaring up around him from the burning trees. He forced his way back the way he had come, chopping away burning boughs which tried to hold him.

At last, Hearst reached bare rock, and collapsed to the ground, coughing, gasping. His eyes were streaming with smoke-tears. His knuckles, cheeks and neck stung from minor burns; his leathers were scarred by fire in a dozen places. Alish? Where was Alish? Hearst almost called out: but that would warn Heenmor.

Slowly Hearst began to advance on Heenmor's position, skirting round the burning thicket, crouching low to make himself hard to see.

Meanwhile, Elkor Alish, who had sheltered behind a rock when Heenmor scoured the surrounds with flame, now stepped out to challenge the wizard. As Alish strode forward, Heenmor raised his staff and shouted a Word.

Nothing happened.

Heenmor's power was exhausted.

The copper-strike snake slithered forward, dominating the space between Heenmor and Elkor Alish. It moved this way and that, swaying, bead-black eyes unblinking. Now was Alish's chance to kill Heenmor. If he stepped forward, the snake would bite him. Then he would die. But, before dying, he would still have time to shorten Heenmor by a head.

Heenmor took something from his khaki robes.

'With this, I can conquer the world,' said Heenmor.

Then he smiled, raising the death-stone above his head. He spoke a Word.

Elkor Alish turned and ran, crashing through the burning vegetation, bounding from stone to stone, gasping air and acrid smoke.

'Alish!'

That was Hearst.

'Run!' screamed Alish. 'The death-stone!'

They ran, and it was downhill all the way as they lept from stone to stone, taking desperate chances in their efforts to get away.

221

From behind came a harsh, aggressive grinding sound. Underfoot the rocks trembled, shifted. The two men slipped, fell, picked themselves up and ran on. Bursting into the camp site, they found men already on their feet, startled, alarmed.

'To the rafts!' shouted Hearst. 'Rafts, or you're dead! The death-stone!'

The grinding noise was getting louder. The sky above was turning grey. Men dashed for the rafts, many screaming in hysteria. Once afloat, some tried to go downstream, where the Melski were now diving into the water. Others shouted that they must try to oar upstream against the current. Blackwood, riverwise in the Melski way, and also cool enough to see the obvious – that they could never row upstream fast enough – roared out the first orders of his life:

'Downstream! Downstream! All speed away!'

Men took up the shout:

'Downstream! Downstream!'

The rocks of Ep Pass were beginning to move. One broke free from the earth and charged for the rafts, roaring huge unintelligible words. Five men were crushed in its path, pulped like newborn chickens hit with a hammer.

Phyphor, running for dear life, collided with Garash, who shoved him toward the charging rock. It struck him a glancing blow then crashed into the rafts still left on the beach. Splintered logs flew through the air. Then the rock fell into the river and was silenced by the water.

Phyphor's left leg had been snapped: the big bone in the thigh showed white through the flesh. Miphon dragged him onto a raft. He screamed all the while, for with his injury the slightest movement is agony.

'Durnwold!' yelled Valarkin. 'Durnwold, where's Durnwold?'

He grabbed hold of Hearst.

'Where is he, where is he, where's my brother?'

Hearst knocked Valarkin senseless with a single short jab to the chin, threw him onto one of the rafts, jumped on himself and pushed off. The current caught his raft, spun it round, then bore it away downstream. There were twenty rafts now on the water.

Behind, men struggled to get the remaining rafts into the water. One became river-borne, and then: the light went dim, and in that dim grey light Hearst saw the men freeze in their positions. Then the raft sank: turned to stone.

The wave of grey death swept forward, but the current of the river ran faster, and carried the survivors away from the lethal magic of the death-stone. Behind them, a skin of stone formed on the river's surface then broke under its own weight and sank; the river ran on.

Downstream they went, the rafts scattered far apart until Blackwood, on one of the leading rafts, ordered sweep-oars to be used to slow the drift and allow the others to catch up. Hearst and Alish found each other, and considered the situation.

'We'll have to stop as soon as we can,' said Alish, 'Then try to land and climb the cliffs.'

'It'll be a murderous climb,' said Hearst. 'You might be able to make it, but nobody else could.'

'We have the green bottle,' said Alish. 'Get Valarkin.'

'What do you have in mind?'

'Valarkin can use the ring he commands to take people into the bottle. When everyone's in, Valarkin can join them and I'll make the climb with the bottle at my belt.'

'What if you fall?'

'What choice do you have?'

'I'll get Valarkin.'

Hearst went and found Valarkin, who had now regained consciousness. He watched sullenly as Hearst approached.

'Durnwold?'

'Dead.'

223

'It's your fault.'

'We can talk about fault later. Right now, we need you.'

'Why should I help you?'

'Because your life is in the balance along with the lives of everyone else. Do you know where this river ends? The Fleuve River buries itself underground, and nobody knows if it ever comes up again. If you want to stay alive, hear me out.'

Valarkin heard what Hearst had to say, then he snarled, spat, and reached for the ring on his finger. Hearst was too slow to stop him turning the ring. Valarkin was gone; sucked into the green bottle Blackwood was carrying, gone to join Prince Comedo.

Hearst should have killed him straight away, yes, but Durnwold had been Hearst's friend, and Valarkin was Durnwold's brother. Another time . . . by the singing knives, he hoped they lived to see another time.

Everyone by now realised there was no going back. The rafts buffeted down the river between high cliffs. Facing up to the prospect of an underground journey into the unknown, Hearst and Alish lept from raft to raft, and ordered the men to tie down packs and sweep-oars. Patches of turbulence which sent waves sweeping across the rafts gave point to those orders.

Just after they shot some white-water rapids, a shout went up from the leading raft. Looking ahead, they saw they were being swept toward the mouth of a huge cave.

Hearst, still hoping for a way out, scanned the approaching rock face – but cliffs which had previously been sheer had now developed a pronounced overhang. There was no escape.

The rafts shot into the cave, into the darkness, and they were lost from the sight of the sun.

CHAPTER THIRTY

There was a scream in the dark.

'What was that?' said Hearst.

A reply was shouted back, but it was confused by the hollow thunder of echoing water. After much shouting, Hearst learnt that a Melski had surfaced beside one of the rafts and had stabbed at random, skewering the foot of a soldier.

Alish had the rafts drawn close together and roped to each other for security, to make it more difficult for the Melski to kill them off in the dark, one raft at a time. He conferred with Hearst; apart from ordering the men to sleep in shifts, and to move around in groups of two or three, they could think of no further defensive measures they could take.

'I only wish,' said Hearst, 'that we could send men underwater to kill the Melski.'

'That would be a battle worth making a song about,' said Alish. 'But who would dare it apart from yourself?'

Hearst made no answer, doubting that he would dare it himself.

Alish counted heads. There were two hundred and sixty-two survivors. They had, as far as he could determine in the dark, a hundred and seventy packs. This meant there was a shortage of blankets, but the system of sleeping in shifts would compensate for that. Alish had spare clothing divvied up so everyone had enough to keep warm in this cool underground air.

Now all they could do was wait.

They could hear the water racing against the rock walls, sometimes foaming against rock outcrops, but they could see nothing. There was no way to keep track of passing time. It was like being in the belly of a worm.

'Alish,' said Miphon.

'I'm here.'

'Where?'

'Here.'

'Good. Is Hearst around?'

'You're standing on him,' said Hearst.

'Sorry,' said Miphon, shifting his foot. 'What about Blackwood?'

'What do you want with me?'

'It's not me who wants you. It's Phyphor. He's dying.'

'Does he want someone to hold his hand?' said Alish. Silence. Then:

'I think you should see him,' said Miphon.

'We'll see him,' said Hearst.

'This way, then.'

'Which way is that?'

'Link hands and I'll lead you.'

They went from raft to raft, occasionally stepping on men in the dark, till Miphon brought them to a halt.

'They're here,' said Miphon.

'Let them identify themselves.'

'You know who we are,' said Alish.

'So you're here, Elkor Alish. And Morgan Hearst?'

'I'm here,' said Hearst.

'So am I,' said Blackwood.

'Then listen,' said Phyphor. 'Miphon's given me a potion. I have a short time – then pain again. But I'll be dead before the pain comes back.'

'What do you want from us?' said Alish.

'Your oath.'

'I've already sworn to go questing after Heenmor. Are you asking me to reaffirm my oath? Do you think I'm an oath-breaker? No man of Rovac ever breaks an oath – though not so much can be said for wizards.'

'Elkor Alish, I trust your oath, but now I want you to take on a further burden.'

'And what might that be?'

226

'To kill Garash!' hissed Phyphor.

'We can't,' said Alish. 'We'll need him to help us kill Heenmor.'

'I've thought of that,' said Phyphor, an edge of pain already in his voice. 'So you must swear that when Heenmor is dead, you will kill Garash.'

'Why should we do you that favour?'

'Listen,' said Phyphor, urgently. 'It's true what Miphon says. The death-stone does have the power to tamper with the very fabric of the world. If you survive to see the daylight, you must hunt Heenmor down before he has time to experiment and perfect control of that power.'

'We know that,' said Alish, irritated.

'Yes, but listen,' said Phyphor. 'By now, Garash believes Miphon's claims, too. He's had time to think through the truth of it. He'll find such temptation irresistible. So when Heenmor's dead, you must kill Garash. Otherwise he'll kill you for the death-stone.'

'I know why you want Garash dead,' said Alish. 'I'll take no vows of murder to secure a wizard's revenge.'

'Elkor Alish . . . these injuries will kill me, but I have three thousand years left to me. Three thousand years left to dispose of as I choose. I've paid for them.'

'What do you mean?'

'I earned those years in the Shackle Mountains. A bargain with powers beyond your imagining. Believe me. Take the oath, and I will give you a thousand years of life. Think on it, Rovac warrior.'

'Sorcerers can be expert liars. What proof do you offer?'

'Elkor Alish,' said Phyphor, his old man's voice pale from bloodloss. 'You will have the power to enter the tower of Arl. And you will understand the High Speech, the reading of it, the writing of it, the speaking of it.'

That meant: that meant Alish would be able to read what was written on the death-stone.

'I will take your oath.'

'Let me hear it then.'

'I, Elkor Alish, son of Teramont the Defender, warrior of Rovac, blood of the clan of the eagle, swear by my heart's blood and by the powers of the fire-flood hell that when the days of the wizard Heenmor are ended, Garash will die as soon as my sword can find him.'

'And you, Morgan Hearst?'

'I, Morgan Gestrel Hearst, son of Avor the Hawk, song-singer, sword-master, warrior of Rovac, swear by my sword Hast and the hand that holds it that I will see Garash dead as soon as Heenmor falls.'

'Good. And you, Blackwood?'

There was no answer.

'Blackwood?'

'I'm no wizard,' said Blackwood. 'I'm no warrior. Why choose me?'

'Because you have the best motive for murder,' said Phyphor. 'Because it was Garash who told Prince Comedo to leave a mad-jewel in Castle Vaunting. It was Garash who caused your wife's death. There . . . so now you know. So now you must kill him.'

'Mister,' said Blackwood, 'I'd be simple to think the truth's that simple. In any case, I don't want any part in any killing – or your thousand years of life, either.'

Phyphor sighed.

'As you wish,' said Phyphor. 'But will you . . . will you do this one thing for me . . . hold my hand before I die?'

'Mister,' said Blackwood, 'I can't refuse a dying man. Here's my hand.'

'Good,' said the dying wizard. 'Good. It's good to have a touch of life in my right hand. Miphon . . .'

And Miphon, needing no instructions more explicit than that, silently urged the others into a circle. Phyphor, Alish, Hearst and –

'What's this?' said Blackwood, as Hearst grabbed his free hand. 'Let go!'

Realising he had been tricked just as a child might have been tricked, Blackwood tried to break away. But it was too late, because –

Their bodies were locked rigid by crushing weight and pressure. He heard the sullen double-drum of a labouring heart, cried out as light seared his eyes, and then –

Darkness, and then –

Sunlight, and a young boy running along a wild open beach, laughing, his arms outstretched, rain and sunlight falling together as he raced the wind, and then –

A canyon ablaze with flame. He named it: Drangsturm. And then: a castle which probed for the sky, huge wings against the sun, a Word and a blast of power –

A small room smelling of burnt flesh and acrid smoke, voices raised in fear and anger, the harsh commands –

A ruined fortress on the border, wind, the evening light failing, surf breaking on the shore, and, as Saba Yavendar said, where wind may walk but men no longer –

Again darkness, the crushing pressure, a heart at first loud and then lisping, soft, slow, soft . . .

'Blackwood,' hissed Phyphor, dying. 'You will find your wife's corpse, and then . . .'

His voice faltered into silence. The last strength left his hands. It was over.

'He's dead,' said Miphon.

At that moment, there was a shout of triumph from the leading raft. They could see daylight ahead. Everyone cheered as they swept toward the light, but elation turned to despair when they got closer and saw the daylight was from a gap high up in the rock roof. It gave them one brief glimpse of blue sky capping a sheer rockfall shaft, then darkness claimed them again.

Soon daylight was only a memory. Now any of a thousand dooms might write them out of history. The rock roof might draw right down to the water, drowning them. An underground waterfall might shatter rafts and bodies. They might sail out onto a vast underground lake, where the river's current would become lost, allowing them to drift and starve with nothing to guide them to the outlet.

As they drifted onward, hunger came, and was fed; returned, and was fed again.

$$* \quad * \quad *$$

Downstream they floated.

The flow of the river slowed, grew sluggish, offering them less hope of early escape from the darkness. The hollow roar of running water diminished to a muttering churgling; men, no longer compelled to shout, spoke with muted voices, and as the days went by they spoke less and less.

They caught fish. They scragged wet flesh from fine-comb bones with knives that were going rusty in the darkness. The rafts knocked together in the darkness, and, as men lay dreaming, that sound translated itself into the restless trunfling of nameless monsters. Men developed sores from lying damp on damp rafts; Gorn complained that his gums were bleeding, but he could have been imagining it.

Downstream they floated.

Blackwood listened to the steady chutter-gutter of water, to the thonk-clonk of rafts knocking against each other. He felt as if they were being mumbled down a long dark throat. He imagined them being digested in the darkness, becoming first blind then toothless then hairless, sores eating through to the bones, until after weeks of hunger and damp there were only twisted bones and gristle on these waterlogged rafts going downstream through the darkness.

Gorn came to Blackwood one day.

'Have you got a tinder box?' he said.

'I have,' said Blackwood. 'And it's dry. But everything is damp. There's nothing dry to burn.'

'No,' said Gorn, 'I've been carrying things we could burn. They've been next to my skin for a long time now. Bits of bamboo, small strips of wood. They're dry now.'

'That was a good idea.'

'I thought so too,' said Gorn. 'Light the fire for me. We'll build it right here, on the raft. The logs are too thick and sodden to catch fire.'

'Then what are you scared of?'

'What?'

'Sorry,' said Blackwood, who had spoken without thinking. 'I must have been imagining things.'

'No,' said Gorn. 'You're right. I'm afraid. I'm afraid . . . I may have gone blind in the dark.'

'I'll light the fire,' said Blackwood.

The first sparks from the tinder box delighted Gorn, for he could see them. But it was hard work lighting the fire. Blackwood persisted till the moment brighter than magic when the spark caught, twisted into flame, flared, hissed, crackled, then burst into a conflagration that set light and shadow leaping in the gloom. Gorn whooped. Men stirred, woke and staggered to their feet. And what a crew they were: sunken eyes, unkempt hair, faces marked by bad dreams and despair. But now, seeing the fire, they cheered.

'Hah!' shouted Gorn. 'Light! Light!'

Then something screamed.

High overhead in the darkness it screamed. It screamed with malevolence in the bowels of the earth. It screamed with pain, with rage, with hatred.

'Out!' yelled Hearst. 'Put the fire out!'

Gorn dashed his arms into the water. With his wet arms he swept the fire over the side of the raft. Men filled their helmets with water and flung it on the burning remnants. There was the hiss of fire relapsing into char. Then everyone waited and listened to the darkness.

There was the sound of wings beating overhead. One

231

set of wings. Two sets of wings. A dozen sets of wings. They were huge. They circled. The rafts bumped and nuzzled each other. Men sat rigid as if skewered. Fingers tightened on weapons. The wings circled, circled, and then ceased to be heard.

After they had no longer heard the wings for a long time, someone ventured to speak . . .

*   *   *

In the darkness the men began to die. They did not cease breathing straight away, but they slept more than they stayed awake. They ceased to talk. Few of them bothered to fish. Those who did fish caught flesh which tasted strange; exploring fingers found these fish had no eyes. Some were reluctant to eat them, and ate only siege dust and the occasional handful of mouldy food from their packs.

'They'll all be corpses if this goes on,' said Alish. 'We've seen it before.'

'We have indeed,' said Hearst.

They had seen it happen often enough in the Cold West. There, in the snows, a man who gave up the will to live would be dead overnight. Here underground it was not really cold, but if the men did not eat they would die all the same.

Garash and Miphon stayed sane. They settled into a pattern of meditation which absorbed most of their waking moments. If asked what their mumbled chanting was for, they would say they were maintaining the Balance and building their powers. Blackwood, Hearst, Alish and Gorn moved to the raft the wizards were on; the chanting was better than the unbroken ripplerush of the water.

Every so often, Alish and Hearst would rouse themselves to make a tour of the rafts. Alish would try to encourage the men, and Hearst would curse them and kick them, and warn them the Melski would come and cut their throats. Both tried to get the men to talk, sing, move, fish, eat. When Alish and Hearst were on their rounds, Gorn and Blackwood talked to each other. The wizards hardly spoke at all, but did not seem to be disturbed by the men talking.

'Are you enjoying our holiday?' said Gorn one day, when most other subjects of conversation were exhausted.

'I'd rather work than be idle,' said Blackwood. 'And I don't like this dark wet hole.'

'I used to be a great one for dark wet holes myself,' said Gorn. 'The smaller and warmer the better. How about yourself?'

Blackwood said nothing.

'I knew a man who liked them old,' said Gorn. 'Hard to believe, isn't it? But that was his fancy. We were together the night we sacked a city in the Cold West. It was a city by a river of ice. He had an old one and I had the youngest. I'll always remember that night, you know. He got rich. He found it was always the old women who had treasure hidden in the safest place. They didn't think anyone would touch them, you see. But they were never safe with him. That's something to remember, isn't it? Look for the oldest face, if you want to get rich. Me, I just wanted to ride them.

'So my friend got rich. Then he fell into a crevasse in a glacier, a crevasse being a crack and a glacier being a river of ice, if you know what I mean. He always said he'd like to die wedged tight in a crack, but I don't think that was the sort he meant. There were those who wondered why I risked my life to climb down to his body, but I knew there was more than one set of jewels hidden in his clothing.

'So I went back to Rovac rich. But I could never settle down. I always wanted . . . the excitement. The moment just before it all starts, when the blood boils, when it sings in your ears. And afterwards . . . afterwards . . . the way their mouths gape. When there's a knife at their

233

throats. I wanted another campaign, not a dangerous one, but just something to give us some fun. So I came to Estar with Alish and Hearst.'

'As a bodyguard.'

'Yes,' said Gorn. 'But Hearst was with us, so I knew there'd be action sooner or later. Soon Hearst was planning a war for the prince. It would have been good.'

Gorn sat in silence, reflecting on how good it had been. Images swam in Blackwood's head, roused by the tales Gorn had told him. White flesh on red velvet. Blood staining satin sheets. Hands of mud fingering, mauling, repressing, while screams thrashed and floundered under smothering weight.

He made himself think of other things.

He thought of Estar. Estar in sunlight, and the blue flowers of spring that bell as bright as the sky. He thought of green grass and baked potatoes, bees and birds on the wing, leaves budding and hot roast meat. If only he could have escaped, if only he could have rescued Mystrel and led her away from the madness at Castle Vaunting into the safety of the Penvash Peninsular in the north . . .

Mystrel . . .

It was no use thinking of the past. And, his eyes hot, he told himself that revenge could not alter the past.

He wept.

Later, falling asleep on the rocking, rocking raft, he dreamt of thighs, breasts, buttocks, dugs, damp hair, a woman's heat . . .

He woke to the raft, to the sound of water, to the sound of rafts bumping against rafts; he woke to the damp of a skin of leather against his skin; he woke to a night darker than blindness.

Cold leather.

Cold metal.

What had woken him?

A wave slapped against the side of the raft and spattered his face with spray.

'What is it?' he said.

'Hush,' said Gorn.

Blackwood peered into the darkness. He felt that he had been living in darkness for a lifetime: eating and drinking and dreaming the darkness. Their stomachs were bloated with congealed shadows.

There was another wave. And a smell, a stench like the stink of black mud and rotting vegetation. There was something in the water, and it was huge.

'What is it?'

'Pray to your god if your god can hear you in this place,' said a voice, Miphon's voice. 'Otherwise be silent.'

They were silent.

They listened.

There was a surge of body bulk and a splash. A wave rocked the raft again. Listening, they heard furtive scrabblings and small splashes. They realised those Melski who still survived were coming out of the water.

The raft heaved up.

The ropes securing raft to raft burst. They were thrown up and over to the shock of cold water. Blackwood grappled current in the darkness. He swam, then realised he could as easily be swimming down as up. He was breathless, but let himself float. He began to drift up. So that way was up. He struck out for the surface. Air slapped his face. Breath burst into his lungs. A wave slopped up his nose and a raft clouted him. He grabbed for the raft. Somewhere a scream cried for mother then shrilled into agony.

There was the sound of rending timbers. Then another scream. Snapped off short and bloody. Blackwood hauled himself onto the raft, crawled towards the centre, then bumped full-face into alien skin. He realised there was a Melski on the raft. The next moment, the Melski grappled with him.

His knife was out and in faster than a scream could escape.

235

He was panting.

There was a rumbling roar from a throat that sounded big as the mouth of a small river. Blackwood lay on the raft, waiting to hear that roar closing with him. But he heard nothing more, nothing but the ripple of water and the small talk of rafts and loose logs discussing their chance encounters in the river flow.

Much later, when Blackwood asked what they had been attacked by, Garash would not say. Miphon said only: 'If there had not been enough of us to more than satisfy its gluttony, we would never have got past it.'

* * *

More men died.

Their bodies, weighted with armour to sink them, were thrown overboard. One body woke as it was being searched for valuables; Alish realised that some of his men were now so far gone it might be hard to tell the living from the dead. He checked every corpse himself after that. The last check he did was to bare the chest, make a slit with his knife, then put a finger on the heart to see if there was any movement. He never found any, but at least that way he was sure they were not throwing living men overboard.

A simple burial: a splash, and that was it. No chants, no rites, no songs of remembrance. They could not even see the faces of those who sank away into the darkness.

Finally Alish could no longer bring himself to make the rounds of the remaining rafts. He knew why they were here. They were here because, face to face with Heenmor, Alish had failed to close with the wizard and kill him. Of course, as soon as Alish had stepped forward for the kill, the copper-strike snake would have bitten him – but Heenmor would have died.

Now he was going to die anyway, and, because his courage had faltered at the critical moment, all the men in his command were going to die as well. Uselessly.

For no purpose. And Heenmor, given time to experiment with the death-stone, would doubtless one day obtain sufficient control of it to destroy the world – and of course Rovac was part of the world the wizard would destroy.

Accepting his death, accepting his failure, Alish sat silently, his mind empty, or slept, dreaming of shadows and glottal rock-swallowing boglands. Hearst talked to him, shook him, abused him, pleaded with him, threatened him, hit him, sang to him, threw water in his face: all to no avail. Alish had given up. He was certain to die before very many more days had passed.

It was about this time that Blackwood started coughing. The rafts drifted on, occasionally bumping and grating against loose logs from those rafts which had been smashed to pieces. Blackwood coughed . . . and coughed . . . and slept . . . and woke coughing. There was phlegm in his throat. When he coughed with his hand to his mouth, his hand came away greasy. He did not know what was wrong with him, but he felt sick.

Now that Alish would no longer make his rounds, Blackwood and Gorn helped Hearst. Blackwood went from raft to raft, coughing. At least he could give men something to swear at. More men died, and the bodies were rolled overboard. Each time Blackwood pushed a body into the water, he remembered the words of Saba Yavendar:

The will may require, but the night has the flesh:
To darkness, to darkness.

Darkness, yes, darkness, and the darkness went on for so long that in the end Blackwood began to dream he had been born in it. He thought it would go on forever.

CHAPTER THIRTY-ONE

It was Blackwood who saw the light first, but he took the distant glimmer for no more than another of the hallucinations that had begun to make his waking moments nightmarish. Then Hearst, who still trusted himself to tell reality when he saw it, named that far-off rumour of day.

'Light,' was all he said.

Light.

Soon they could all see it. It was faint: pallid as the belly of a dead fish. But it was daylight.

As they drew closer, things began to take on shape, then colour. Looking around, they found it hard to recognise their comrades because of their ragged beards and prison pallor.

Then the river shot the rafts down a foaming whitewater chute, swept them out into the sun, and left them drifting on the surface of a huge lake hemmed in by high cliffs. The water shimmered with heat-haze. Some cried out in pain, for the sun hurt like the blinding light after the darkness of the womb.

'There's a bird scratching my eyes,' wailed one man, waking from nightmare to nightmare.

Gorn cursed him, and he was silent.

The rafts drifted, idle, silent. The survivors lay face down under the hammer of the sun, sheltering their faces from the blinding light. Then Hearst rolled over; but he kept his hands over his eyes. Red bloodlight filtered through his fingers. Light . . .

– So we have come through. Yes. And some have said that Morgan Hearst would never lie down till death laid him out, but I'm happy enough to lie here now. Now, yes, and forever if I could . . .

The sun beat down on his corpse-flesh.

After a while, he opened a narrow slit between his fingers. Slowly he scanned the drifting rafts. He was amazed at the height of the heavens, at the intense blue of the sky, at the ferocity of the sun. His lips cracked apart in a smile.

– Yes, we have come through.

And then:

– But look at us! A meal for vultures. Or, at best, a band of half-dead runaway slaves.

Fungus sprouted from the logs in mounds and lugs, white, orange and purple. It sprawled across leather in threads of white or bile-green splashes. Hearst counted the rafts: only eight left. On one was nothing but a corpse; on others sat men in various stages of collapse. The survivors were as pale as the inner bark of trees, the white flesh of grubs, the kernels of almonds. Some had inflamed scarlet rashes, boils, and stinking ulcers.

Blackwood had cold, grey, slimy smoke drifting in coils about him. He coughed, and more smoke vomited out of his mouth. Hearst went to help him. Blackwood waved smoke away from his face.

'I wouldn't come any closer if I was you,' said Blackwood.

'He's right,' said Miphon. 'Stay away for the moment. The smoke is parasitic, but the light will weaken it. Soon it'll trouble him less, and be too weak to batten onto anything else.'

'How can I get rid of it?' said Blackwood.

'You can't,' said Miphon.

Hearst shook Alish by the shoulder.

'Time to move,' he said.

'Time ran out long ago,' muttered Alish.

Hearst again tried to rouse him to action, then gave up.

'Oars into water,' sang out Hearst, getting to his feet.

His voice drifted away over the dazzling surface of

239

the lake. Slowly men began to grub away the sodden ropes holding down the sweep-oars. Every knife was rusty and blunt; one could have wept to see those fine blades so cankered and dishonoured. With oars in the water, the men began to work the rafts toward the shore. Seven moved; the eighth, with only a corpse on board, stayed where it was. Slowly they drew away from it.

'You're lighter,' said Hearst to Gorn.

'My travelling companion has suffered,' said Gorn, looking ruefully at the remnants of his paunch. 'The wizard Garash also looks lighter than he was.'

The rafts crawled along under the sun like crippled insects. Hearst tried to strike up a rowing chant, but none would take up the song, so he let his voice trail away. On the eighth raft, the one they had left behind, the body stood up. Hearst realised it was Valarkin, who now cut free an oar and set the raft in motion.

'We mustn't lose him,' said Miphon. 'He's got the ring to the bottle. We should try and get into that bottle soon.'

'Yes,' said Gorn. 'There's food in there.'

'We'll take him when he gets to the shore,' said Garash.

'He's going the wrong way,' said Gorn.

Hearst shouted.

'Valarkin! Where are you going? Valarkin!'

'Maybe he's heading for the other side of the lake,' said Gorn. 'Shall I swim after him?'

'What's the use?' said Hearst. 'He could always throw the ring in the water if you caught him. Besides, there might still be Melski in the water.'

'There's a bow tied to my pack,' said Blackwood. 'Over there. The quiver is inside the pack. You might try that.'

Hearst found the bow. He fitted an arrow to the string and drew the bow. The string snapped.

'It's rotted through,' said Hearst. 'Garash?'

'I have enough power to kill him,' said Garash. 'I have more than enough power to kill him, but the fire would also destroy the ring.'

They had no way of catching Valarkin.

Under the sun the fungus grew brittle, curled up, became black, writhed and began to stink. Slowly, too slowly to leave more than the slightest ripple of wake, the rafts worked their way toward the shore. Those not on the oars lay for the most part as if dead, sheltering from the sun under weatherworn cloaks.

Gorn drew a helmet-full of water and peered at his reflection.

'How's your beauty?' said Hearst.

'Better than I'd expected. I'd have thought my hair would have gone grey after all we've been through.'

Garash peered at the shore with his protuberant eyes. In places the rocks were black, in places red; some were stained yellow with the sulphur-spill of hot-water springs. Steam rose in plumes from fumaroles.

'It won't be easy getting up those cliffs,' said Garash.

'We'll make it,' said Hearst. 'How do you feel now, Alish?'

'I feel like the yolk spilt from an eggshell.'

'Rest then. You'll feel better later.'

The first raft crunched against the stones of the shore. Those on the oars let them drop and sat down or lay down.

'Ashore!' yelled Hearst. 'On your feet and get ashore. Move now, move! My sword's in my hand, and it won't be the flat of it I'll be using.'

He got them moving.

It was hot; the water which fell on the stones as they splashed ashore dried swiftly. The sun had already begun to scald pallid flesh. Hearst had spindly trees cut down to make crude shelters for them to work under. He ordered the survivors – there were forty-six of them – to unpack and spread everything out to dry. The

241

packs disgorged gear white with fungus, musky with rot, dripping with slime.

'Andranovory!' yelled Hearst, seeing a man standing idle.

'I haven't got a pack,' protested Andranovory. 'Mine's missing.'

'You haven't got a cock, either,' shouted Hearst, 'but that never stopped you sucking one. There's more packs than men, so get your finger out of your arse and do something useful with it.'

Andranovory, grumbling, secured a spare pack and dumped a load of mouldy clothes and rotten food to the stones. A small bundle broke apart, scattering the glitter of jewels and golden coins. His morale improved immediately.

'That's mine!' cried a man suddenly.

'Yes, sure,' said Andranovory. 'Like your third nipple and your fourth arse,' which was a traditional insult in the parts he hailed from. 'You want to fight me for them? Well then, come on.'

And he drew a blade.

'Belay that, you mother-riding animals!' shouted Hearst.

And proceeded to castigate them severely, using terms so obscene that even Gorn was seen to blush.

Hearst had just restored order when one man suddenly doubled over and began to cough up worms. They were blood-red: the colour of the gills of a fish. They wriggled on the hot stones. Hearst squashed one with the toe of his boot: blood squirted out. Miphon knelt down beside the victim, though he suspected there was nothing he could do.

Garash lit a fire to dry out a small cache of supplies he had carried with him. Finding his maps and manuscripts reduced to pulp, he swore in a language nobody else could understand. Stones around the fire trembled: one split apart, shattering into flying fragments. His rage was impressive, but it wasted energy.

With gear spread out to dry, men set to work on knives, swords and battle axes with sharpening stones. Many fires were lit; there was no need for all of them, but it was good to see fire again and smell smoke.

Hearst knew the smoke, rising into the clear blue sky, would betray them to any observers . . . but judged that the risk was worth it. He would let the men have their friendly fires. At Hearst's orders, some men dragged one of the rafts ashore, then split the logs, using axe heads as wedges. The sun would dry the wood soon enough, giving them plenty of fuel.

Hearst examined his own gear. The stitching of his boots was rotten and they were falling apart. He would have to see what he could do about it . . .

Gorn was boiling something up in his helmet. It proved to be handfuls of pale blue water snails, some almost the size of a thumb.

'There's plenty of them on the rocks near the shore,' said Gorn, 'In water less than knee-deep.'

'Good,' said Hearst. 'Good . . .'

One man was barbering. At his feet, the colours of straw, bark, soot and flame shone in the sunlight. A bumblebee, the workaday insect common to all the world, lumbered along the shore. Hearst savoured the intense pungent smell of an aromatic herb hidden somewhere among the thin, scrubby trees. He stretched, then smiled, then laughed aloud.

– Truly, we have come through.

On the lake, Valarkin was a dot in the distance.

* * *

Evening came early to the lakeside as the sun fell away behind the cliffs and cold shadows engulfed the shore. The waters of the lake became grey. Men ceased their labours and sat by their fires, occasionally feeding sticks to the flames.

Hearst had the rafts hauled up out of the water – they might need them yet, and there might be a few Melski who had survived the journey through the darkness – then he chose his guards for the dark hours.

'There will be stars tonight. Maybe even a moon – who knows? Those on guard will have enough light to see by – if they stay alert. If not, they may wake to find the Melski cutting their throats.'

Men grumbled, but Hearst knew it would do them good to re-establish the routines of campaigning.

Blackwood was suffering as the night set in. Soon his cough worsened until it was almost as bad as it had been towards the end of the long underground journey. Miphon led him to a fire. Blackwood bent over it and gulped in hot, dry air. The cold smoke that trailed from his mouth writhed, suffered and withdrew.

'Breathe in the heat,' said Miphon. 'Breathe in the heat. Take it down into your lungs. Deep down.'

The cold smoke appeared again between Blackwood's lips, and again cringed from the heat.

'Breathe deep,' said Miphon. 'Breathe deep.'

Hearst lay back on the stones he would be sleeping on, and, looking at the night sky which he knew so well, saw something had happened which he had not thought possible: while they had been underground, a new star had made its debut in the sky. He could just hear Miphon's voice, soft, warm, encouraging:

'Breathe in,' said Miphon. 'Breathe in.'

And that gentle voice reminded Hearst of the way Alish had talked to him that time in Valley Sharator, when Hearst lay pallid with pain, clammy-skinned with shock, his shoulder dislocated by a fall from a horse. Breathe in, said Alish, passing him the opium pipe. And Hearst had breathed in. Breathed in. Taken it in. Breathed in darkness, breathed in sleep. Then Alish had taken his arm, saying, this may hurt a little . . . And he had breathed in, first pain, then darkness.

Sleep . . .

At Miphon's urging, Blackwood breathed in the heat.

'Soon you'll be able to get to sleep,' said Miphon. 'If

you can sleep through to morning, you'll feel better when the sun rises.'

'Tell me,' said Blackwood. 'What's the cure for this?'

'I've already told you,' said Miphon. 'There's no cure.'

'There must be something.'

'Well . . .'

'Tell me.'

'This is old lore, and old lore is never certain,' said Miphon. 'But the old lore says a draught of the blood of a dragon mixed with the blood of a man is certain healing for all ills.'

'Then there is a way.'

'If you can find your dragon and kill him,' said Miphon. 'Then, yes, there's a way. But there's a price for the cure.'

'What?'

'This is old lore from the dreamtime,' said Miphon. 'And the old lore says, who drinks this draught of mixed blood will never love a woman and will never hate a man, will never be able to kill – not even in self-defence – and will never call any place home.'

'Is that all it takes – blood and blood?'

'So it's said. Now breathe in. Deeper. That's right. Deep and steady. Deep.'

And Blackwood breathed in the heat. Would he ever get a chance to try the cure? And would it work? Having seen so many things he would once have thought impossible, he could scarcely answer 'no' to either question. He had seen madness at work in broad daylight, armies destroyed, castles abandoned, a prince mocked, a wizard killed, and Rovac warriors running in fear. He had been told he had the chance to live for a thousand years.

It might happen: anything might happen.

* * *

245

Hearst woke in the night. He lay there, listening, hearing a creaking snore which he knew to be Gorn's. The snore grew louder and louder then stopped. Gorn had stopped breathing. It was something he did sometimes while sleeping. Hearst waited. There was a snort as Gorn woke, a shifting of stones as he rolled over, and Hearst knew he would be asleep again already. Hearst had been a long way with Gorn; they had shared the same shadow on many roads.

Looking at the night sky, Hearst saw the red star they called the Golem's Eye was low on the horizon formed by the cliffs on the other side of the lake. Where were the guards? He could hear no murmur of conversation, and there was no fire burning. So they were probably asleep – or lying in the night with their throats cut.

Blackwood coughed in his sleep and shifted restlessly. Garash, in his dreams, murmured something:

'Again,' said Garash, 'Again . . .'

The words were in the High Speech. So Phyphor had spoken the truth. Hearst could understand the High Speech of wizards, and perhaps he would also live a thousand years.

Then he heard something else. The splash of water. Once, twice . . . thrice. Getting to his knees, Hearst peered towards the water. He could dimly make out a man standing there. The shadowy figure jerked, and there was a splash . . . a splash . . . and a third splash further out. Someone was skipping stones.

Again.

A stone kicked white splashes from the water once, twice, three times . . . then a fourth, far out and distant, so that one could not be sure whether it was the stone hitting the water one last time or a fish jumping.

The man did not throw another stone, but stood staring out across the dark water for so long that Hearst had time enough to think of other things, like the hollow hunger in his stomach. Eventually the figure returned to the camp, moving cautiously to keep down

246

noise, though he was not skilful enough to move soundlessly.

He sat down by the black ruins of a fire and raked the ashes with a stick till red embers pulsed and glowed. Hearst watched him blow on the ashes, and heard him whisper soft, loving words, as one might whisper to a favourite horse. Then the man threw a handful of dry leaves onto the embers. Flames kicked up, showing Hearst it was Comedo who sat there, fascinated, watching the fire.

Comedo fed the fire with scraps of bark, twig and leaf until it had consumed everything that had been set aside for kindling in the morning. Blackwood coughed. Comedo walked over to inspect his suffering, and Hearst thought how easily Comedo could have killed Blackwood as he lay helpless there . . . how easily Comedo could have killed any of them.

Suddenly Comedo was gone. Air slapped into the blank space left by his retreat into the bottle. Hearst stood up, feeling his joints creak, and walked without a sound to the edge of the lake. It was as black as a mouth which might with a soundless suction pull him in deeper and darker than drowning; it was as black as the underground river and the dreams which floated down that river. But there were stars reflected in that obsidian blackness. Star, white star, guiding star . . .

– The kick of the sea, yes. The stars above, waves breaking white on a dark shore, yes, and all aboard knowing which shore it was. Rovac, and journey's end. Yes. Remember that. You will see it again some day: the waves breaking on the shores of Rovac. Ah, but when?

He was sick, yes, homesick.

– Preach me no lovesongs for distant lands. We have at least this: a windless night beside fresh water. Night, and the promise of dawn. That should be enough for any warrior-man of Rovac. Hast, half-brother, blood-

247

brother, there will be another morning for us, and that is enough.

Some of the stars went out.

Hearst looked up. Something in the sky blotted out stars, extinguished whole constellations as if a giant had flung a black cape across the night sky. The shadow moved as he watched. Something was flying up there! It was huge. He remembered Maf: the dark cave, the huge beast, the folded wings . . . now the wings were in the sky above him. The dragon wheeled low. Hearst was certain they had been seen: but the wings passed above the cliffs and were gone.

Hearst – his hand on the hilt of Hast – waited for the wings to return. They did not. He was glad he had been the only one to see it: he did not want the camp to panic. He turned away from the lake and with a shock saw Comedo standing watching him. He had not heard Comedo re-emerge from the bottle. Hearst stepped towards him. Comedo turned the ring on his finger and vanished again.

Gone.

What a prize that bottle would be, if only they could get into it. There would be food in there. And wine – body of the grape, body of the sun. Hearst had seen Valarkin supervising the loading of the bottle. He had seen wine taken in by the barrel, wine and food and featherdown quilts. What else had gone into that bottle? Did Comedo have a woman in there? Body soft as bread, body warmer than the sun.

– Kill him then. Set a trap. Kill him when hc slips out to enjoy the stars again. If he ventures the sun, it will be easier still.

Hearst found the guards asleep, as he had suspected. He found the one he had appointed guard commander, and laid sharp steel across the man's throat. The man opened his eyes and stared up with a rigid, unblinking stare. Hearst held the sword there for ten or twenty heartbeats – ten of his, twenty of his victim's – then he withdrew the blade.

'You stand watch till morning.'

*   *   *

Morgan Hearst slept long and late, and woke to the sound of voices and occasional laughter. It pleased his heart to see his men working on their gear, gathering water snails, or collecting algae to boil and eat. Some were fishing, using pumice for floats for their lines; the light grey volcanic rock, full of air bubbles, floated lighter and higher than cork.

Elkor Alish was still asleep, lazy as a turtle basking in the sun. Let him sleep then. Hearst would organise things. Morgan Hearst would cope with the world of rock, sun, water, rust and steel. But he despised Alish for letting control and self-control escape him – and wondered what had gone wrong.

Hearst found Miphon turning two birds on a spit over a bright fire.

'You can cook better over a bed of hot coals,' said Hearst, squatting down by the fire.

'Yes,' said Miphon, 'but I'm hungry.'

There was grease on the flesh; Hearst could have eaten a barrel of grease. Give him an ox and he would have eaten it entire, meat, marrow and bones together.

'Did you sleep well?' said Miphon.

'Well enough.'

'I woke in the night,' said Miphon.

'And?'

'I saw you. I saw what you saw.'

'What do you suggest we do?'

Miphon shrugged.

Hearst picked up one of the feathers which had been scattered when the birds had been plucked; he twirled it between his fingers.

'How did you catch the birds?' said Hearst.

'I called them to me.'

'Magic must make life easier.'

'There's nothing easy about the Meditations,' said Miphon. 'That's how we build power. And how we preserve the Balance.'

'What is the Balance?'

'The universe was created with a will to ordained order which attempts to destroy any anomaly, particularly one as gross as a wizard. The Balance is the field of force - a sphere built of willpower – which we create to preserve ourselves. The more power a wizard accumulates, the greater an anomaly he becomes, so the more work he must do to preserve the Balance.'

'I knew a man who used to talk like that,' said Hearst, 'but only when he was drunk.'

Miphon smiled. Little rankled with him: he was difficult to upset. Warriors lived by their skill with weapons, which they valued above all else; warriors found it hard to concede that they were no match for most wizards, and disparaging wizards was a natural way for warriors to protect their delicate egos.

'But what does it mean?' said Hearst. 'What does the Balance mean? In simple terms?'

'What's the secret of leadership?' said Miphon. 'In simple terms?'

'Initiative,' said Hearst instantly.

'So that's the secret,' said Miphon. 'Give a man that word and he'll lead armies to conquest.'

'Not quite.'

No, it was not that easy. A leader needed combat skills to meet any blade-challenge from the ranks. He must know when to kick and curse, when to praise and flatter. He must become a diplomat to deal with priests and princes. On campaigns, he must make swift, sound decisions on the basis of scanty information. He must know when to advance, retreat or parley, and must be always seeking ways to keep his enemies unsettled and off balance. That was the beginning of it: but there was much more.

'Quite not quite,' said Miphon. 'A single word cannot

hold the secret. In a word, that simple word you want, the Balance is harmony. If a wizard cannot achieve it then the quest for power will kill him. What do you want now – a lecture on the applied metaphysics of self-determined intelligences, or a piece of this scrawny fowl?'

'Compared to me, the bird's positively fat,' said Hearst. 'I'd love a piece.'

As they ate, Hearst remembered – vaguely, as one may remember words spoken in dreams – why Stronghold Handfast was so important. Its makers, long dead and forgotten, had mastered the art of creating architecture which would protect its inhabitants against the force in the universe which would attempt to destroy an anomaly. Once there, Heenmor, having no need to divert any of his energy to the preservation of the Balance, would be able to devote all his powers to the study of the death-stone.

Hearst tried to remember what Stronghold Handfast looked like. He was irritated to find that he could not picture it clearly. But he could remember what it was built of: millions of blocks, variously blue, green, red, and yellow, each block as shiny as glass, and each block no larger than a man's thumb.

He stopped eating.

'What's the matter?' said Miphon. 'You look very peculiar. Have you found worms in the meat?'

'I was . . .'

'What?'

'Nothing,' said Hearst. 'Nothing.'

Miphon chewed a bit of meat in a meditative way, the sharper pangs of his hunger now appeased; he swallowed, spat out a small piece of bone, then, suspecting the source of Hearst's discomfort, spoke:

'You'll find you've inherited at least some of Phyphor's memories along with things like a knowledge of the High Speech. You won't have access to those memories at first, because they'll be completely disorganised to begin with. However . . .'

'What?' said Hearst, in alarm. 'He'll take over my mind?'

'He's dead,' said Miphon. 'The mind-masters are the wizards of Ebber, not the wizards of Arl.'

'But if I'm thinking thoughts that aren't mine –'

'Then what? Are you ever afraid your dreams will take you over? No? Then look on these memories as a new set of dreams – only it's usual to forget dreams, bit by bit. These dreams you'll recall. Slowly. Sometimes a word may help the recall – not a magic word, just one with special meaning. Consider this one: Araconch.'

Araconch.

Hearst thought about it, and smelt . . . dried ink. Remembered faded lines crawling across parchment. An inscription in a crabbed hand: Here Be Dragons. Irritation at hearing someone laugh, in, of all places, the Sourcing Room: the Map Room. Maps. Of course . . .

'These are the Araconch waters,' said Hearst, indicating the expanse of lake. 'To the north . . . difficult country . . . then . . . the Blue Lakes, yes. Then the Broken Lands. A river . . . if we can get that far, then the river will take us to Kalatanastral, the city of glass . . . from there, yes, the Ringwall Mountains themselves . . .'

Hearst fell silent, thinking of the distances they had to cover. Since he had orientated himself by sun and stars, he knew they were in the north-west quadrant of the lake; they would have to march north for about fifty leagues over broken country to reach the Blue Lakes, after which another fifty leagues or so would take them to a tributary of the Amodeo River.

If they could find or make a boat, three hundred leagues or so by river would bring them to Kalatanastral, from where it would be about seventy leagues across plains, hills and mountains to the towers of Stronghold Handfast. All in all, the better part of five hundred leagues.

'They say the winters here are harsh,' said Hearst.

'Then we should make all speed to try and reach Stronghold Handfast before the snows,' said Miphon.

'How soon can the soldiers travel?'

'The worm-sick man will be dead by tomorrow,' said Miphon, working a bird's tail feather into his faded, weatherstained hat, which, stored in his pack throughout the underground journey to this southern lake, looked almost too decrepit to withstand the sunlight.

'And the others?'

'Give them ten days or so to rest and harden their skin to the sun.'

'What about Blackwood?'

'I think . . . I think he won't survive the winter. But he should still be able to travel with us.'

'I had a dream,' said Hearst. 'I had a dream that he might be cured by a draught of the blood of a dragon and the blood of a man.'

Miphon guessed that Hearst, falling asleep, had heard Miphon telling Blackwood about the cure for his illness, and had worked the words into his dream.

'A dream is a dream,' said Miphon, dismissing it.

Miphon knew Hearst owed his life to Blackwood, thanks to the episode at the lopsloss pit; the last thing Miphon wanted was for Hearst to throw his own life away in a reckless attempt to kill a dragon for blood with which to redeem Blackwood's life.

'So there's no saving him,' said Hearst.

'He might last a little longer if we could shelter him in the green bottle. But of course Valarkin's taken the ring.'

'I'd thought of setting a trap for Comedo,' said Hearst, 'but that might be difficult since a twist of a ring can take him from us. Any ideas?'

'Grab him,' said Miphon. 'If he uses the ring you'll be pulled inside with him, where you can overpower him.'

'Good,' said Hearst.

'What will you do with him when you catch him?'

'I've nothing special in mind,' said Hearst. 'All I want is the ring. But if I could get my hands on Valarkin – I'd roast him over a slow fire till his bones blubbered.'

Valarkin, refusing them the use of the green bottle after Durnwold's death at Ep Pass, had cost many men their lives, for no good reason. Thinking of the geography of Argan, Hearst realised that once Valarkin found the outlet from the lake, he would be on the Velvet River, which would take him downstream through the Manaray Gorge and the Kingdom of Chenameg to the Harvest Plains and the city of Selzirk.

Once the expedition had recovered the death-stone, if their path to the south took them through Selzirk, then Hearst, perhaps, might get a chance to hunt Valarkin down. He wondered whether to inscribe another death-pledge on his sword, to stand alongside the rune which marked his vow to take the life of the spy, Volaine Persaga Haveros. He decided against it. Haveros, though an oath-breaker, was a warrior: Valarkin was simply vermin, unworthy of the honour of a death-pledge.

Digesting food slowly, Hearst began to plan how he would ready his men for the journey north. First, they would catch lots of fish, and smoke them; with that, plus the little remaining siege dust, they would be able to cross the broken country to the north.

Miphon, with fewer immediate worries, lay back and looked at the sky, scanning the birds. He looked as if he was at peace, but he was not. There was a problem he had not quite solved. At Ep Pass, when the rocks had started to move, one had charged for the men, killing five and injuring Phyphor before demolishing three rafts and plunging to its destruction in the waters of the river.

No rock had charged after that.

In the panic of those moments, Miphon had found the minds of the rocks wide open, and had managed to control them sufficiently to stop any further charges. If he ever again met rocks which had been liberated by the death-stone, would he be able to gain complete control over them? How many could he control at once? And for how long? Such questions might one day mean the difference between life and death.

Overhead, wheeling through the clear empyrean, was a bird. Miphon sensed its special kind of remorseless questing, and named it for what it was: vulture. If he chose, he could call it down by deluding it into thinking it saw dead men lying there. Miphon did not hesitate: vultures were edible, and he was still hungry.

CHAPTER THIRTY-TWO

Elkor Alish pioneered the climb from the lakeside, risking his life on slopes of rotten rock while the others caught fish, roasted crickets, and pounded roots to a pulp to try and make them edible. Tackling precipices which made others blanch, Alish slowly regained his confidence; perched on a high ledge amid a region of drifting steam and boiling waterfalls, he felt a sense of superiority as he looked down on those below.

They had survived. The underground journey could now be seen as a test, a necessary preliminary to greatness. A warrior should welcome such tests, for they eliminated those who were weak in body or in spirit. When he finally closed his hand round the death-stone, he would know he had earned it, and that his sufferings justified his claim to the power.

By killing Heenmor at Ep Pass – and dying in the act – he would have spared his men their underground journey. However, the wizards would have taken the death-stone south, thwarting the destiny of Rovac. Surveying the world from heights which diminished the men below to ants, Alish knew that history required and justified the sufferings of their underground journey.

Elkor Alish knew of gods darker than most men's imaginings, and feared them, but what he really worshipped was the historical process which selected and trained men like himself; he saw himself in terms of the history of his people, the purpose of his existence being to administer the justice of the dead and destroy Rovac's ancient, evil enemies.

So Elkor Alish found his confidence on those rock

walls, and found also, on a more mundane level, the one way up to the rim of the cliffs: a steep slope of scoria, where there was only the occasional rock outcrop, and no steam or boiling water.

Hearst and Alish spliced together all the bits of rope and twine they could find, ending up with enough length to link the men together, though they were dubious about its weight-bearing capacity. When the climb began, there were regular pauses as the stronger climbers took the rope higher, securing it to the next solid rock.

The climb, beginning at dawn, proved hard going. None dared throw their full weight on the rope lest it part under the strain, though the wizards seemed prepared to trust it more than the soldiers.

Soon the only sounds were stones grating under boots, the intermittent shuffle-rush of sliding scree, the panting of sweating men burdened by heavy packs, and the occasional clink of steel against rock. There was no sound of insect. No breath of wind. Labouring upwards, they saw nothing but the scree in front of their faces, the stones that slid, shifted and frustrated their strength.

As they climbed upward, any who cared to look down when they stopped to rest – and those few needed to squint against the dazzling glare – saw the rafts were growing small beneath them. But they were only a fraction of the way up the slope.

Like the others, Blackwood sweated, panted and cut his hands scrabbling for handholds in the loose scoria, but derived one consolation from his hard labour in that the exertion in the sun made the smoke parasite suffer, so it irritated him less.

Miphon, climbing just behind Blackwood, twice saved him from sliding away down the slope. Miphon was hardly panting; it irritated Blackwood to know that the wizard was finding the climb almost easy.

Hearst called a halt.

Strung out on the slope, the men rested.

'There's a strain on the rope,' said Hearst. 'Don't throw your weight on the rope. It can't hold you all.'

His voice died away.

A stone rattled down the slope, starting other stones moving far below. Then silence again.

Blackwood wiped a hand across his forehead, which was slick with sweat. His throat was dry. He turned to Miphon. 'You look like you could climb all week,' said Blackwood.

'It's your dust,' said Miphon, grinning. 'I get strong eating it.'

'You'll have more than that to eat if this climb goes on. It's killing me.'

'You're not going to die,' said Miphon. 'Not for a thousand years.'

'If you say so,' said Blackwood.

But he could tell that Miphon was just trying to keep his spirits up. Miphon grinned again, face good-humoured beneath his feathered hat.

'If it's any consolation, others are suffering more than you. Can't you hear Garash, grunting like a pig?'

Blackwood smiled; it was his first smile in a long time.

Someone was drinking from a leather bottle with a noisy gurgling of water. Blackwood, narrowing his eyes, looked up the slope to see who it was. It was Footling.

Hearst sang out the order for the climb to begin again.

Blackwood felt as if he had hardly rested at all, but even that short pause had been enough to make his muscles stiffen. He was dismayed. After all the years of hardship his body had endured without fail, would his strength abandon him here, in the wilderness? He dreaded the prospect of being left behind if he could not keep up with the others.

Suddenly the bottle hanging from Blackwood's belt began to shake and rattle.

'No!' shouted Blackwood.

Everyone stopped climbing.

'No!' he cried.

But a stream of vapours shot out and coagulated into the form of Prince Comedo. He screamed as the sunlight seared his eyes. He slipped on the scoria and fell. Blackwood made no effort to save him: it would have endangered the whole party. But Comedo grabbed Miphon's boot as he slid past. The wrench shook the rope.

It parted, breaking just above Blackwood's hands.

He grabbed for the end of it, but found himself off balance and sliding. So was Miphon. Soon the thirty people below the breaking point were sliding. Some managed to brake themselves with their boots before they had picked up too much momentum. Others grabbed outcroppings of rock. But the rest were swept away down the slippery sliding slope.

Hearst, safe above the rope-break, screamed at his men, ordering them to roll onto their backs. Blackwood already had, to let the stones grind and rip at his leather pack instead of his belly, while he tried to brake with his feet. Comedo, still clinging to Miphon's boot and still screaming, lacked the self-possession to do anything to slow his fall. Miphon booted him in the face. Comedo let go and slid to the bottom of the slope.

Blackwood and Miphon came bumping down after him with half a dozen others. The rest were still clinging to the rope far above them, or were scattered through all the points in between. Comedo was screaming like a bayoneted baby, his face torn, his clothes ripped, his body gouged and scraped.

'See what you've done?' snarled Blackwood, picking himself up.

Comedo cringed like a dog that knows it is about to get kicked, and blubbered through a mask of blood:

'It was so hot, so hot, so stuffy. It was so sway and jolty, voices so cruel. I was sick, sick, oh I was so sick and suffering, and nobody comforts, I scream and nobody comes, nobody, oh I suffer, poor me suffering, poor me.'

Miphon, ever the healer, stepped forward to see what he could do. Comedo smelt of neglect, defeat and musty self-abuse. His hair was dirty and unkempt; he was half-shaven; his skin had erupted into boils. His wounds and welts, half-disguised by dust and blood, looked terrible, but Miphon suspected most of them were superficial.

'Kill him, Miphon,' said Blackwood. 'Kill – '

A spasm of coughing racked his body. He doubled over, then was forced to his knees. He clutched at his belly. Cold smoke dribbled out through his twisted lips.

'I don't like this place,' moaned Comedo. 'I don't like it.'

'Kill him,' said Blackwood, raising his head high enough to look at Comedo. 'He's good for nothing else now.'

But Miphon was examining the prince with skilled hands, satisfying himself that the damage was all superficial. Blackwood forced himself to his feet. His last fit of coughing had felt as if it was tearing his innards out; he held his gut with all his strength to reinforce it against the pain.

The others had picked themselves up by now and were dusting themselves off. None were seriously hurt, which was a minor miracle. One of those graced by the miracle was Gorn, who stalked toward Comedo, axe in hand. There was no doubting his intentions. Comedo reached for the ring.

'Miphon!' shouted Blackwood. 'Stop him!'

Miphon grabbed Comedo. But Comedo twisted the ring – and the two of them dissolved into a fog which was sucked into the bottle so fast that there was a rush of wind as air swept into the place where they had been standing.

'Give me the bottle,' said Gorn.

The bottle was hanging from Blackwood's belt by a

thread; the slide down the slope had almost torn it away. Blackwood pulled it free and passed it to Gorn, who shook it.

'Come out, you scag!' shouted Gorn. 'Out!'

Nothing happened.

Gorn hurled the bottle against a rock. Chips scattered from the rock. The bottle was unharmed. Gorn marched toward it.

Blackwood grabbed his arm.

'Gorn, it's no use – '

Another fit of coughing interrupted what Blackwood had to say. Gorn shook himself free and attacked the bottle with his axe. Men stood round watching till Gorn had exhausted his anger.

'We'll wait,' said Gorn. 'The wizard must be able to overpower that little scag. Then we'll do him. We'll do him dead.'

Gorn sat down on a rock to wait.

Blackwood coughed again. The dust he had breathed in while sliding down the slope was combining with the parasitic smoke to cause him agony. He had to have water to wash the dust out of his throat. There was dust on his boots, in his hair, in his eyes and on his lips; up on the slope, the dust kicked up by the slide was still settling measure by measure through the hot dry air. They could hear Hearst shouting something at them, but what he was saying they could not tell over the distance.

Blackwood walked to the water and stooped down. A Melski lept from the water and threw him backwards. His pack absorbed the shock of the fall, but the creature got its hands on his throat. He clawed for its eyes. His fingernails scraped across tough skin. Then the creature thrashed and screamed: Gorn had axed it open. Blackwood threw it off. He unshipped his knife.

More Melski came plunging out of the water. There was a brief and furious fight. The Melski outnumbered the men two to one, but they fled when reinforcements came crashing down the scree slope.

The odds had given the Melski the better fight: there was one dead Melski, there was a spare Melski arm twitching on the stones, and there were three dead men. Blackwood watched the amputated arm with fascination. It shed little drops of water in its spasms. Stones clinked as the fingers flexed and contracted. Slowly the sun dried it and it ceased to move.

Hearst was in a filthy mood when he got down to the water's edge. He spat in disgust at what he saw.

'We were outnumbered,' protested Gorn.

'Outnumbered! By animals!'

'They had weapons,' said Gorn.

'Yes, and a rabbit has teeth. Where's Miphon?'

'In Comedo's bottle,' said Gorn. 'Comedo grabbed him and pulled him in with him.'

'Then why hasn't he come out?'

'We're waiting,' said Gorn.

'You're waiting! What kind of answer is that? A Rovac warrior and you let this happen. Don't speak to me, I don't need your excuses. Who's dead?'

'Trother, Onger and Ilchard.'

'Let's have their packs off then,' said Hearst. 'Move, man, move! And you! And you!'

The packs were rifled for food and clothing. They had plenty enough weapons already, so Hearst broke the blades the dead men had carried. He studied the three bodies. Ilchard had a nice pair of boots, and they looked about the right size . . . Hearst whipped them off and got his feet into them.

'Now we wait,' said Hearst. 'We wait until Miphon comes out with Comedo's head in his hands.'

But they waited in vain, and Hearst, growing tired of watching the sun shifting shadows over the rocks, gave the order for the climb to be resumed.

* * *

In the afternoon, long after resuming their climb,

they saw the surviving Melski come out of the water and haul one of the rafts onto the lake. From the height Hearst's men had reached, the Melski looked like insects setting sail on a bit of twig. When the Melski were well clear of the shore, they stopped; perhaps they were fishing.

The expedition was still climbing at nightfall; they finished their climb by starlight. Before they reached the top, one man slipped and went rattling away down the slope. He shouted as he slid away, but they did not hear him cry out again. Perhaps he hit his head on a rock. When morning came, they saw his body lying lifeless far below.

The sun, rising in the east, glittered on the vast expanse of the Araconch Waters, and illuminated snow which capped the higher peaks of the mountains to the west. The men, still somewhat weak from the underground raft journey and the consequent underfeeding, could have done with more sleep and rest, but Hearst got them moving.

They set off in a northerly direction, beginning a trek through a land of barren hills, steep bluffs and overhanging cliffs, gorges and waterless riverbeds. This shattered landscape would make for slow going.

Some twenty leagues to the north, clearly visible from the higher ground, rose the cone of a volcano, from which a little smoke ascended. From memories of an old and faded map never seen by his own eyes – the wizard Phyphor had consulted it once, in Castle Margus – Hearst named that volcano: Barg. The name was a contraction of the name of the sometime ruler of the Empire of Wizards, Barglan Stanash Alkiway.

And Hearst remembered the inscription mapped over the countryside around the volcano: Here Be Dragons.

CHAPTER THIRTY-THREE

'No closer,' said Comedo. 'No closer, or I swallow it.'

He kissed the ring.

Miphon took another step forward. Comedo grinned and parted his lips, stretching a thread of saliva to breaking point. His tongue lolled out to accept the glistening gold. Suddenly he snapped his mouth shut and gulped. Miphon swore. Comedo plucked the ring from his mouth and capered up and down: a grotesque figure of dust and blood, blood and tatters. He was, Miphon was sure, quite mad.

'I fooled you then, didn't I? Your heart squeaked nicely, nay? A mouse, and I stepped on it. I fancy that, for Miphon's fancy's fool, the mute word's moron. Nay?'

Then suddenly the pretense of humour was gone:

'Now down on your knees and grovel! Or I'll swallow it.'

Miphon shook his head, and said, as he might say to a dog or a horse:

'Soft now, soft, I'm no harm to you, soft now, easy.'

Slowly, carefully, as if easing out over thin ice, he began to close the distance. Comedo lept away, and shouted:

'Belly down to the dust or I'll swallow the ring.'

'Swallow it then,' said Miphon, suddenly angry. He drew a knife. 'Swallow it, and I'll rip you from vent to gills.'

'That blade may kill, but hardly the hand that holds it.'

'You're still walking, but that doesn't make you immortal.'

'I'm mad,' said Comedo. 'You mustn't hurt me. I'm mad, I can't help it.'

An extravagant cringing fear had replaced Comedo's arrogance. He was like . . . like what? Like a patch of sky in which any sort of weather might manifest itself. Princes have the opportunity to create the kind of reality that suits them.

'I won't hurt you,' said Miphon, regretting his outburst of anger.

'You couldn't anyway,' said Comedo, suddenly fierce, drawing a blade and snarling. 'Magic doesn't work in the bottle, does it? Blade against blade, I can take you. No contest. Now what will you tell your toenails if I go outside with the ring and leave you counting days to years – forever!'

'Try it,' said Miphon.

'Not today,' said Comedo. 'I'm a prince, not a prince's fool, my princely fool. But the swords won't be waiting outside forever. The dragon will munch them down, soon if not later. I saw the dragon from the shores of the lake. It flew from my dreams: practising. Wonderful! Bones crunch slowly. I wish I could watch.'

Miphon watched Comedo as one might watch a scorpion. The subdued green light from the walls of the bottle allowed him to see everything clearly here, for they were in the neck of the bottle. Downstairs the rooms would be gloomier. How many rooms were there? How many chambers? Miphon had no idea. He had never studied the magic of enchantment of bottles: it was old lore, now commanded, to the best of his knowledge, only by the order of Varkailor.

Suddenly Comedo ran for the spiral staircase that led downwards. Miphon chased him down the stairs, and found himself in a storeroom a hundred times the size of the room above. Firestones studded the ceiling, shedding light on massive barrels of water, ale and wine, on sacks bulging with potatoes and onions, on fish smoked and salted, dried meat, pickles, hams, bunches of herbs and dried figs.

'Come and get me,' said Comedo, with a giggle. 'Come and get me.'

'I will,' said Miphon grimly.

This was getting too dangerous. He should have knifed Comedo in the room above. Would Hearst have hesitated, or Gorn, or Alish? Even Blackwood would not have hesitated under the circumstances. Comedo dangled the ring over a drop-hole.

'Don't drop it down there!' said Miphon.

'Why not?'

'We'll never see it again.'

Miphon knew all about the drop-holes. They would have a common opening located beneath the overhang of a tower at one of the wizard castles – in the case of this bottle, most probably Castle Vaunting. Anything thrown into one would finish up in the flame trench which circled the castle.

'We don't need to see it again,' said Comedo. 'We already know what it looks like.'

Miphon lunged at Comedo, who skipped back, snatched something from a shelf and hurled it at Miphon. It shattered at Miphon's feet: a jar of pickled pigs' trotters. Comedo threw another one. Miphon ducked. The jar clipped a barrel and burst in a shower of ceramic shards.

'Come on then,' said Comedo.

Miphon threw a jar at him.

'Missed,' said Comedo.

The prince danced away down another flight of stairs. The chase ended in a totally bare room. It was much larger than the one above, but was split in two by a massive stone wall which was fantastically carved with figures of wizards, warriors, dragons, and creatures of the Swarms. In the wall was a single doorway, flanked by twisting stone pillars.

There were no firestones here, but the bare floor was

patterned with a filigree tracery of green light which supplemented the dull glow from the outer walls.

'You can't run much further,' said Miphon. 'Give it to me.'

Comedo backed toward the doorway. Miphon followed him cautiously. The other half of the room was also bare and featureless, apart from a stairway leading downwards. Miphon tried to circle round Comedo to cut off his escape down that stairway.

'Don't hurt me,' said Comedo. 'Oh don't hurt me.'

'Give me the ring,' said Miphon. 'Now!'

Comedo's fingers opened, and the ring fell to the stone floor. It rolled round and round in ever-diminishing circles, then fell, shivered and was still. Comedo backed away. Miphon stalked toward the ring, now ready to kill Comedo if he tried to grab it back. But Comedo kept retreating, with fear, despair and terror written on his torn and bloodstained face. Miphon scooped up the ring.

Comedo skipped back through the doorway and threw a lever hidden in the decorative carvings on the other side of the wall. A huge portcullis crashed down between him and Miphon, blocking the doorway. Miphon stood there unbelieving. Comedo had tricked him. Just like that. He had managed it so easily, so easily.

Comedo laughed.

'Now you'll grovel,' said Comedo. 'Now you'll grovel, now, down on your slime on your belly, because it's mine now. Mine!'

For a moment Miphon was dismayed, then he smiled. Of course! One turn of the ring would dissolve his body into mist, which would reassemble outside the bottle.

'You forget,' said Miphon. 'I've got the ring.'

'Have you now?' said Comedo. 'Have you now? Take a closer look, Mr Wizard. Take a closer look.'

Miphon held up the ring to study it by the dim green

underseas light. But one ring looks much like another. He jammed it on a finger and turned it. Nothing happened.

'Do you want the magic ring?' said Comedo. 'Do you want it?'

Miphon walked to the portcullis. On the other side, Comedo grinned at him. Comedo opened his mouth, and fingered a ring out of the dark wet shadows within.

'You're my prisoner now,' said Comedo.

Miphon put his hands to the cold metal bars of the portcullis. He tried to shift it. He might as well have tried to move a mountain.

'You need me,' said Miphon, thinking quickly now. 'You could die from your injuries. They're starting to rot already. I can tell. You're going to die if you don't get my help.'

'Pox doctor!'

'I tell you, if you don't get my help –"

Comedo shouted Miphon down, screamed at him, alternating rage with sarcasm, bitterness and spite. Miphon's bluff had failed. Turning, he walked away toward the staircase that led downwards deeper into the bottle.

'Run then,' said Comedo. 'Run then. You'll be back, when you get tired of drinking your own piss. You have to eat, you know. I'll feed you – once you've eaten. I've got you now. I'll have you licking out the inside of my nostrils before I'm finished with you.'

At the head of the stairs there was a hatch which Miphon could close and bolt after him. He did so, shutting out the sound of Comedo's ranting. Water, yes, he would need water: he was already thirsty, his throat dusty from that long slide down the scree slope.

But did he really dare venture downwards in search of it?

The stairs were dark. The steps, hollowed by many feet, reminded him of the bottle's great antiquity. It dated back to the Long War against the Swarms, thousands of years before his birth. It might well contain dangers unknown to the age he had been born into.

He did not hesitate. He had no choice.

He descended the darkened stairs.

On reaching the bottom, Miphon found himself in a huge room bigger than any of the chambers above. The dim light from floor and walls showed him the room was empty.

Prince Comedo had been indulging in histrionics when he had sobbed that inside the bottle it was 'so jolty sway'. There was no trace of motion inside the bottle. The horizons were always the same. The fluids within the inner ear were as quiet and steady as the silent waters of a landlocked underground sea. The bottle was a self-contained world where the air felt dead and lifeless, as if nothing had stirred in it for centuries. The dull green glow from the walls, like the eye-vein patterns sprawled across the floor, had nothing to do with the world outside; the illumination was a property of the bottle itself, giving no hint of night or day. The temperature was constant, cool but not chill; neither sun nor frost in the world outside could alter it.

Miphon tried to remember his days in the sunlight – which already seemed a long time ago. He tried to remember the bottle swinging from Blackwood's belt. It widened from the neck for a third of its height, then for the next two-thirds it tapered very slightly to a flat base. Since the rooms were still getting larger, he could not have descended more than a third of the way to the bottom, if that.

Someone's tracks showed in the sparse scattering of dust on the floor. Miphon followed them to the next stairway and descended. He guessed Valarkin had left the tracks, as he doubted that Comedo would have cared to explore this bottle on his own – and the tracks had all been made by one person.

Reaching the bottom of the stairs, Miphon entered a

room where the walls were almost lost in the misty green distance. He followed dusty footprints till he was close enough to the walls to see the chairs, desks and shelves of books that were arrayed there. Valarkin, judging by the tracks, had lost his nerve and turned back at this point. And no wonder.

The silence was enormous.

– This is what it will be like after the death-stone kills everything.

Miphon shivered, and went on.

Had this place been a library? A prison? A holding pen for hostages? Or a refuge in times of fire, flood, war? It could have been used for conferences, allowing wizards of different orders to meet, safe in the knowledge that none could use magic on the others. Perhaps Miphon might be able to find a ring that would let him leave the bottle.

Otherwise, the only way out was by a drop-hole, which was suicidal. Anything thrown into a drop-hole was subjected to tremendous acceleration; climbing down, one would be torn from the walls by that acceleration and spat out at the other end at a considerable velocity. Even if Miphon could, by a miracle, have got safely to a drop-hole's exit under the overhang of one of the wizard towers, he would have needed a second miracle to survive the difficult climb to the top of the battlements. If the fates denied him a double miracle, the drop-hole promised only a death in the flames of the fire-dyke.

So: no ring, no escape.

On a table was a chess game, which had been abandoned at a difficult stage. Miphon puzzled over it for a while, then placed a wizard aboard a dragon to be ready for flight or attack. He walked around the board to look at it from the other side. Now the counter to that move . . .

Miphon shook himself.

A Rovac warrior caught in this trap would have been

270

tearing the room apart to find some ring or key or tool or clue that would secure release. No Rovac warrior would have given up without – at least! – ransacking this vast room. Could a wizard do any less?

Part of the problem was that Miphon, like any wizard of Nin, had always had that comforting thought at the back of his mind: if the worst comes to the worst, if there is no other way, then I will begin the rites of recall. I will recall the powers too terrible for a human being to be trusted to live with: I will open the book of Nariq.

But here in the green bottle, his magic would not work. He had no more resources here than any mortal man. Nevertheless: he had the room to search. He began.

Much later, he found the ring, which lay on a page of an open book. He put it on the ring finger of his left hand, then twisted it experimentally. It was only as he twisted it that he noticed the red bottle that stood on a nearby bookshelf. The ring turned full circle and Miphon was sucked into the red bottle.

CHAPTER THIRTY-FOUR

Fear is the mind-sharpener.

A shadow wheeled over rock and sand. The men scattered. They dived for cover, and lay still. They could hear the creak of wings labouring through the sky. The shadow lurched over the rocks, once, then again. The dragon was circling overhead. Then they heard it alight on a bluff overlooking the ground where they were hiding.

It was hot. Hot and quiet. Morgan Hearst lay in an anorexic shadow in the lee of a rock. The desire to look up almost overwhelmed him, but to move could be death. Instead, he concentrated on his hand. He flexed the fingers: they were his own. But he saw the hand in all its strangeness, as though taking his first look at the paw of an alien species.

'I've got cramp,' said Erhed, a young man who had the weakest brain of any of Comedo's soldiers.

'Shut up, Erhed,' said Hearst.

'But I've got cramp!'

'Shut up!' hissed Hearst.

'I've got – '

Alish closed the distance in a convulsive leap. Smashed Erhed with a chunk of rock. Silenced him. Hearst lay still as death. Would that movement attract the dragon's attention? Would this be the end? He waited. And waited. And the dragon: did not swoop.

So Alish had saved them. Alish, hearing Erhed so close to panic, had acted. And Hearst had not: had been afraid to move, even though he had seen that Erhed was about to panic and run, bringing disaster to all of them.

In the Cold West, men had rightly called Hearst fearless: he did not remember being afraid in those days, not even at Enelorf when the troops of the Stormguard broke and ran in panic. Morgan Hearst, son of Avor the Hawk, had been bold to the point of recklessness, scorning fear and doubt.

However, when the chill of the Cold West had begun to get to his bones, Hearst had lost the absolute certainty which had previously characterised his every action. He remembered how they had been skirmishing outside the walls of Larbreth when the joints of his right arm had begun to seize up. He had wielded his sword left-handed while he made his escape. He had known fear then; and many times since.

And knew it now.

Where was the dragon? Was it still high on that bluff, or was it moving softfoot down to the killing ground where the men lay hiding? Could a dragon move softfoot? Was it playing a game with them, as a cat will play with a mouse? How long could the men lie there in the shadow of fear? Sooner or later one was sure to panic and run.

Hearst heard the dragon take to the air. The wings creaked. The shadow plunged overhead. Where was it headed? Was it gaining height, ready to dive down to attack them?

'It's gone,' said Alish, in a voice Hearst remembered from the Cold West: the voice of Bloodsword, He Who Walks, Our Lord Despair. 'On your feet,' said Alish. 'It's gone. Come on. Up! You, and you: carry Erhed. He's stunned.'

As the men slowly got to their feet, Hearst consulted with Garash.

'I thought dragons only flew by night,' said Hearst.

'No law tells them to,' said Garash. 'They may choose otherwise here.'

'What do you suggest we do then?' said Hearst.

'There is nothing to do,' said Garash. 'Except hope.'

'What's this?' said Alish. 'Taking advice from wizards, are we?'

'There's nobody else to ask,' said Hearst.

'Then we can keep our own counsel,' said Alish.

'Many value the advice of wizards, manroot,' said Garash.

'When fear speaks to fear, courage sees no reason to listen,' said Alish. 'We march.'

* * *

The challenge came the next evening. The Rovac warriors had heard not so much as a rumour of trouble, but then, they had been busy – Alish scouting ahead for the easiest route, Hearst helping Garash and Blackwood over the more difficult parts of the trail, and Gorn bringing up the rear to make sure no stragglers lagged behind. Those who wished to conspire had been given all the opportunities they could have wished for.

The mutiny was planned and led by Atsimo Andranovory, an experienced, dangerous man. Born in Lorp, a poverty-stricken land on the west coast north of Estar, he had spent part of his early life as a fisherman in the Lesser Teeth, before joining the Orfus pirates. Boozing and brawling had destroyed any prospects he might have had there: after quarrelling with a pirate captain, he had been put ashore at Iglis, in Estar, and had put his sword at Prince Comedo's command.

In Castle Vaunting, Andranovory had never amounted to much – he had just been a drunken bully boy. Even after they had left the High Castle, the thought highest in his mind had been the proper care and rationing of the two skins of hard liquor which he had carried in his pack.

However, it was now a long time since Andranovory had put alcohol to his lips – or, for that matter, to any less conventional part of his anatomy – and he was clear-minded and ready to assert himself. He knew full well that it would be easy enough to gain the Velvet River and retreat to the Harvest Plains in the south, whereas the journey north was taking them into danger, with every chance that winter would catch them on the desolate uplands of the Central Plateau.

Andranovory soon found he was not the only one who thought it was better to sing about heroes than to try to emulate them. After all, in this desolate wasteland there was no chance of any pillage, plunder or rape – unless, as Erhed said, one was to find a very young and tender dragon. All that was needed was the right moment to strike.

At the camp they made that evening, the right opportunity arose, for Elkor Alish unbuckled his sword to give him complete freedom of movement for a difficult climb up a cliff face to raid a bird's nest. Andranovory let him make the climb – he fancied an egg as much as anyone – but moved his men into position with a nod or a wink.

When Alish descended, he noticed nothing odd, for his concentration was devoted to treasuring down the half-dozen bird's eggs he was carrying in a string bag, gripping the draw-strings in his teeth.

When Alish jumped the last little bit to the ground, he found a half-circle of men confronting him, and Andranovory holding his sword-belt.

'Good evening,' said Andranovory.

And smiled.

As adrenalin armed him for action, Alish glanced around, noting men standing guard over Garash, Gorn and Hearst. How easily they had been taken! They must have been half-asleep. The wizard Garash, despite his power, was helpless when someone was holding a knife at his back – as Alish had proved during their first confrontation at Castle Vaunting.

Beside Hearst stood a man who held the battle-sword Hast, and was gloating over the firelight steel. Hearst gave Alish a little nod, and Alish, giving no answering signal, waited just long enough for Andranovory to begin to speak.

'The boys and me,' said Andranovory, drawing the Melski blade, 'Have been thinking, and – '

Alish smashed the eggs into his face and butted him in the stomach. Then pushed him, sending him reeling back into the crowd. And Gorn and Hearst were moving, smashing fists and elbows into the nearest faces. Hearst tossed a weapon through the air. Alish grabbed for the hilt, snatched the sword from the air, and screamed:

'Ahyak Rovac!'

Gorn and Hearst, both now armed with weapons not their own, broke free from the mutineers and danced into position, moving with an effortless grace in which there was not the slightest hint of a swaggering boast or bluster – only the perfect economy of absolute professionalism.

'Three against forty,' said Alish. 'The odds are even!'

And some of the mutineers fell back, as if believing him. The more clear-sighted saw that Alish was simply making war on them with words, but, all the same, none wanted to be the first to die. And nobody, watching Our Lord Despair flanked by Gorn and Hearst, could for a moment have believed that those three warriors would surrender, whatever happened from now on.

Andranovory, pushed forward by the others, hesitated, then picked up the Melski blade which he had dropped when Alish had butted him.

Alish moved.

Light blurred through the air. Steel halted a fraction from Andranovory's throat. Then Alish withdrew the blade.

'What have you got to say to me now?' said Alish.

Andranovory looked around.

'Come on, boys,' he said.

Nobody moved.

'I think you'll find they're suddenly hard of hearing,' said Alish.

'Then it seems I must surrender to your . . . justice!'

And with the last word, Andranovory swung at Alish, putting all his strength into the blow. The Melski sword slashed through the air.

Elkor Alish moved like a dancer. One hand gripped the hilt of Hast. The other slid along the flat of the blade so that his arms were widespread, bracing the sword. Andranovory's full-strength swing sent the Melski blade slamming into this barrier, cutting edge impacting with flat steel.

The Melski blade shattered.

And Elkor Alish was moving again, sidestepping, pirouetting, outflanking Andranovory with nimble steps which suggested that he could have made a spectacular career for himself as a dancing master in one of the courtly cities of the Cold West.

The mutineer, still holding the Melski sword with its jagged stump of blade, tried to turn to meet him. Alish tripped him expertly. Andranovory went sprawling. The battle-sword Hast sliced down – and sheared away part of his scalp.

Alish dug the point of the sword into the bloody piece of skin and hair, flicked it into the air and fielded it. The piece he had cut away was half the size of the palm of his hand. Andranovory lay on the ground, dazed, half-persuaded he was dead. Alish gave a small bow, and offered him the trophy, saying:

'Madam, you seem to have mislaid your wig.'

The joke allowed the tension in the air to dissipate with a roar of raucous laughter, leaving the chief mutineer hurt, bloody, humiliated, discredited – but alive.

After a certain amount of swearing and threatening, meant mostly to flatter the rebellious fighting men by making them think he took them seriously, Alish had the camp settle down for the night, and returned the battle-sword Hast to its rightful owner. To replace the broken Melski sword, he claimed Andranovory's blade: a cutlass, the kind of weapon favoured by the Orfus pirates.

Alish went to sleep that night on a piece of high ground at the most northerly point of the campsite, so that anyone who chose to walk south during the night would not have to step over him. Gathered together on that high ground were, apart from himself, Gorn, Hearst, Garash and Blackwood.

Those last two did not suspect what was going to happen, but both Gorn and Hearst knew, though Alish had not said so much as a word to them. The Rovac warriors knew that, if Alish had seriously meant to quell the mutiny, he would have killed Andranovory, roasted the corpse, extracted oaths of loyalty from all present, then made them eat dead flesh in a ceremony that would have marked their minds with unforgettable horror.

As it was, Alish had clearly decided that, on this trek north, the fighting men, in their present mood, would be more trouble than they were worth.

When they had left the High Castle, the presence of a Collosnon army in Trest had made it wise to take as many armed men with them as possible. And when they had encountered the Melski on the Fleuve River, armed force had allowed them to speed their journey by seizing rafts to use the waterway which would otherwise have been barred to them.

But now, their main challenge was distance. Numbers would not make their journey any faster – and the foraging would be better for a small party. And Comedo's men, easy enough to intimidate and bring to heel on the early stages of the journey, were a different proposition now that they had been hardened by the nightmare underground river journey.

Hearst woke in the night, and heard small mutterings, a faint clinking of steel against rock, sounds of searching and finding, a grunt, a hiss . . . Blackwood coughed heavily in his sleep. Silence. And then again the noise started, the muttering, the scrape of boots on stone, the sound of steel.

In the night, men were gathering up their possessions and slipping away. Now, if ever, was the time for Hearst to challenge Alish's judgment. But he did not. For, quite apart from anything else, with so few travelling companions left, Hearst would have a better chance to renew that friendship which had once flourished so: and which had then failed, suddenly, after the siege of Larbreth.

* * *

Come morning, Garash was dismayed to find that the soldiers had deserted: he went so far as to order Alish to bring them back, only to find his orders were dismissed with scornful laughter.

Gorn and Blackwood did not care one way or the other; Alish declared that a small group could travel more safely than a large one, at least in this dragon country, and they trusted his judgment.

Their march north took them past the heights of the volcano known as Barg, and from then on the volcanic nature of the terrain grew more pronounced.

They passed hot springs, with water which was still drinkable, although heavily contaminated with chemicals from the bowels of the earth. They encountered more of the smoking fumaroles which they had seen at the Araconch Waters, and also things which were new to them: pools of boiling mud, land where the ground shook and rumbled incessantly, places where smoke and sulphur made the air almost too foul to breathe, and huge pits plunging down to depths where the earth seethed and muttered.

Alish estimated their progress north at roughly five leagues a day; if they had tried to make better time, they would have risked losing someone. In places, ground which looked solid proved to be just a thin crust roofing a pool of gently-boiling liquid death; they had to advance carefully, scouting out the way and probing dubious spots to see if they were solid.

On the morning of the second day after they passed Barg, they found a scratching rock. A heap of scales lay beneath it, some dull and cracked, others new and shiny. The scales crunched underfoot; one or two of the older ones cracked, but none shattered into fragments.

'Can these scales be worked?' said Hearst.

'No,' said Garash. 'Cut them or drill them, and they fall apart.'

'It might be possible to glue them onto a foundation of leather,' said Hearst.

And he began to talk of craftsmen he had seen in Chi'ash-lan, in the Cold West, and mentioned the various glues they had used.

Later in the day, they found dragon dung. It was hard – almost like rock – and there was not much of it. Why hard? Water conservation, explained Garash. No liquid wasted.

'I didn't see any in the dragon's lair at Maf,' said Hearst.

'Dragons don't foul their own lairs,' said Garash.

'I roamed all over Estar in the years the dragon Zenphos lived there,' said Blackwood, 'and I've never seen anything like this.'

'It's water-soluble,' said Garash. 'The droppings would always dissolve in the first rain.'

And that prompted Hearst to make a joke about the impressive size and smell of mammoth droppings he had seen in the Cold West.

It seemed to Alish that Hearst was taking every opportunity to launch into reminiscences about the Cold West; worst still, he tried to encourage Alish to tell his own stories about campaigning in that land of ice and snow. That evening, Hearst actually talked about

280

Larbreth itself, and the treasure gained in the sack of that city; he went so far as to sing a lewd song the Rovac had made about the siege of that seaport stronghold, a song which began:

Their legs were closed as tight as their gates
But we broke the both of them open.

For Alish, the very mention of Larbreth again awakened appalling memories: Hearst striding down a hallway, smiling, fingers knotted in the hair of a woman's head, which he had held casually, as if it had been a hunting trophy.

Furthermore, Alish was angered at how lighthearted Hearst had become, full of levity and enthusiasm. For Alish, the quest for the death-stone was assuming the nature of a sacred pilgrimage, undertaken as a rite of atonement to make amends for his thoughtless indulgence in battle-lust and war-glory in the Cold West; he welcomed this barren land of shattered rock, foul air and poisoned water, for it allowed him to perfect his mood of suffering and repentance; Hearst's high spirits, at moments infecting the others with an access of positively rollicking good humour, seemed a gross affront to the spiritual aspirations which Alish had made the centre of his being.

Alish did not know how much more of Hearst's joking and boasting he could take.

*   *   *

The next day they passed right beside a dragon's lair. They could not avoid it: in this land of cliffs, pits and quaking earth, they were lucky to find a way forward at all. They crossed the danger zone one by one, ducking from rock to rock, quick as rabbits. Even a man laden with a pack could move fast when fear inspired him. They were all hot, flushed and panting by the time they reached the comparative shelter of a clutch of tall rocks

281

out of sight of the dragon's lair. They shrugged off their packs and sat on them to rest.

'By the tit that mothered me,' said Gorn, 'I've never moved so fast before. Not in all my days.'

'Me neither,' said Hearst.

'Yes,' said Garash. 'It's one thing to enter the lair of a dead dragon, quite another to walk past the lair of a live one, isn't it?'

'Watch your tongue, pox doctor,' said Hearst.

'But he has a point, doesn't he?' said Alish.

Hearst turned to Alish.

'What do you mean by that?'

'It's true, isn't it?' said Alish.

'What do you mean?'

'The dragon on Maf was dead, wasn't it? When you entered its lair, it was dead, isn't that so?'

And Alish was on his feet, his eyes alive and blazing.

'Do you think it's a secret, Morgan? How many people do you think you've fooled? Who could listen to your drunken boasting and think you told the truth? We've shared the same shadow down many roads: do you think I didn't know you for a liar the first time I heard your story from your lips? Do you think I don't remember the night before you made the climb? You stank of fear.

'Why so silent, dragon-killer? I know what you are. A coward and a liar. A coward not once – but twice. Remember Ep Pass? Heenmor set the trees alight. Did I run? No: I stepped forward to meet him. Where were you, Morgan? Where was your sword? What happened to our plan: one to manage the snake, the other to kill the wizard? You were off and running, Morgan. You cost us the death-stone. We could have had it, then and there. We could have had Heenmor's head. You cost us the death-stone, and you know what happened afterwards.

'Speak up, Morgan. Come on. What's the matter? It's true, isn't it? Do you care to dispute it? You've got a

282

sword at your side. You know how to use it.'

Hearst stood there, shaking, speechless in the face of this tirade.

'Come on, Morgan. Where's your blade? Will you match me, steel for steel?'

Morgan Hearst abruptly turned on his heel and walked back the way they had come.

'Hearst!' cried Blackwood. 'Hearst, come back!'

'Let him go,' said Gorn, not caring whether Alish or Hearst was in the right, but knowing that their dispute had to be settled now.

'If he wakes the dragon, it's death for all of us,' said Garash. 'Hearst, stop!'

Hearst did not look back. Garash raised his right hand.

'Watch yourself, or my knife will taste your kidneys,' said Gorn, standing behind Garash. The wizard stood quite still. He knew Gorn would have no hesitation in killing him if he harmed Hearst.

'Blackwood!' said Garash. 'Blackwood! Alish! Get him back! Bring him back!'

'No,' said Alish.

'I'll get him,' said Blackwood.

'Don't move, as you value your life,' said Alish.

And so they stood there and watched Hearst retreat out of sight. Then they waited.

CHAPTER THIRTY-FIVE

Rock was underfoot; overhead, the sky.

Morgan Hearst stood at the bottom of the steep slope leading to the dragon's lair. Now was the moment of decision. Hearst knew he could not simply creep back to the others and confess that his fears had defeated him, for Alish had clearly given him a choice between facing the dragon or his sword.

Shadows crowded the mouth off the dragon's lair. Death waited inside. If life was the most important thing for him, then his choice was simple: if he wanted above all else to live, then he should turn and sneak away, slipping away to the south and abandoning this quest.

But from his earliest days, Hearst had learnt that life is worth living only for the things that give it significance: the honour and the glory that a warrior wins by resolute action matched to high resolve.

Life is a mere matter of calories, hydration and defecation; if that was all Hearst valued, then on many occasions in the past he would have turned and run from overwhelming danger. And now, above all else, he wanted to redeem himself in Alish's eyes. They had been battle-comrades before, close as blood-brothers; if it was a lie that had poisoned the words that passed between them, then there must be a truth to redeem the lie.

Carefully, he studied the slope and the entrance to the dragon's lair; his studies told him nothing. He could not pretend that further hesitation would add to his knowledge. He drew his sword Hast, though he knew that, face to face with a dragon, it would be about as much use as a toothpick.

He began to climb.

His shadow flickered over the broken ground, dodging from rock to rock. Stones shifted underfoot, slipped, and clattered down the slope. At Hearst's feet there was a flash of movement as a snake struck at one of his boots. He kicked it away. Its fangs had left marks deep in the leather.

Hearst paused, watching the entrance to the dragon's lair. His shadow crouched against a rock, silent, waiting. There were many talon marks on the rocks outside the entrance; stray scales were scattered in the cave mouth, where the rock had been rubbed smooth by the dragon forcing its body in and out. Half a dozen men could have walked arm in arm through the mouth of that cave.

Inside, it was gloomy. The air stank, but the cave was empty. Empty: but it opened onto another chamber, from which came a dull ochre glow.

– Strength, man of Rovac, strength.

Step by step, balance by strength, Hearst dared his way toward that glow. His breathing was the breathing of a ghost, a ghost with no shadows: dead men have no shadows. But balance is balance and poise is poise, and:

– We have a chance.

He found himself looking into a vast chamber lit by firestones which had been stolen from some place of wizard-work. By that light, he saw loose scales, heaps of treasure – and the dragon.

The dragon!

It was alive, it could not be doubted that it was alive: the fires that showed between its parted jaws hissed and pulsed with its breathing, and in sleep its entire body moved with a slow, regular rhythm, as if it was forever stretching and relaxing.

– Strength now, strength!

The ground was slippery. Hearst glanced down, and by the combined light of firestones and dragon-fire he saw he was walking on glass, in which were embedded rings, swords, crowns, goblets, sceptres. Generations of treasure were buried in this cave, but more still lay about in loose heaps.

– Forward, warrior, battle-song hero!

And one pace, then one pace more. And in the heat his body was greased with sweat, his thighs trembling, hot sweat, eyes red, legs wet, forward, one step, a spear –

He sheathed Hast, and chose a pair of spears from the heap of treasure. They were ornamental weapons, chased with silver and gold, but the killing blades were steel, and the balance was right. No hesitation now, but:

– Aim and throw!

The first spear struck home. And Hearst, snatching up the remaining spear, was running even as the steel lanced home. He slipped on the glass, went down, scrabbled for balance and was off again. As the dragon roared. The walls of the cave flushed red with reflected fire as the dragon blasted flame at random.

Hearst, spear in hand, made it to the gloom of the outer chamber. He stood gasping, panting, chest heaving. Hearing the dragon lumbering forward, Hearst opened his mouth and screamed, at the last moment shaping the scream to words:

'Ahyak Rovac!'

And, calmed by that incantation of courage, he counselled himself quickly. He had taken out the right eye: now for the left. He waited. The massive head came thrusting through the entrance. Hearst threw the second spear. Then ran: fleeing to the furthest corner of the outer chamber as the dragon raged forward, spouting flame and bellowing in agony.

With both eyes gone, only memory guided the dragon as it hauled itself towards the cave mouth and the open air. It was moving slowly now: crawling, dragging itself along. It stopped, half-way out of the cave, its body jamming the exit. Spasm after spasm shook its body.

And what if it died now, its massive corpse jamming the entrance?

– Forward, Morgan, forward now, darkness, a night attack, one foot, two, strength, warrior of Rovac, steel and strength, balance, by the hell, by the fourth hell, you have a chance, sweet blood and vodka, a chance, Hearst, Hast, brother, blood-brother, hold my hand my blood my brother, hold me tight, hold for chance, one chance.

– Sword to be strength, strength to be sword:

'Hah!'

Shouting, Hearst thrust Hast between the over-lapping scales armouring the dragon. The blade drove no more than a handspan into the dragon's flesh: but now in its dying rage it knew its enemy was in the cave behind it.

The dragon's body convulsed. Hearst clung to his sword, his lips locked back in a snarl which was half a scream. The dragon's tail coiled and thrashed, snapping this way and that, sweeping bone-crunching death through the darkness. But it could not reach Hearst. Rock screamed as talons tore it open. The darkness belched as wings endeavoured to unfold, as leather-tough membranes battered against restraining rock.

Hearst grunted, trying to force his sword in deeper. There were no decisions left: his only hope lay in brute strength and endurance. His hands were slippery. He could not tell whether they were wet with sweat or blood.

Then the dragon started to back into the cave. Those massive limbs, with all the dragon's dying strength behind them, forced its weight backwards into the cave. Hearst braced himself, knowing the dragon had just one reason to get its head back into the cave: to ravage the forked creature now tormenting it.

Forcing itself backwards, the dragon, by its own efforts, drove Hearst's sword-blade deep into its body. Hast was that sword, firelight steel forged on Stokos. It cut through sinew and tendon, sliced through blood vessels and nerves, probing bctwccn thc monster's ribs.

Pain convulsed to agony. The dragon lurched forward, jerking Hast from Hearst's hands. Hearst jumped backwards. Then ran, fleeing from the sweep of the tail which sought him as the dragon plunged forward.

The rock walls of the cave found him, and mothered him, and he clung there, clung to the rock, exhausted, half-weeping, his heart kicking like a baby. He heard a bellow from the dragon, then a hint of daylight diminished the darkness.

Gripping his head with both hands, Hearst forced his head to move to face the cave mouth. His eyes closed against the daylight. He set fingers to his eyes, and was about to force them open, when, in a sudden moment of clarity, he appreciated what a grotesque spectacle his own fear was making of his limp wet rag-doll body.

He was going to die anyway. Here, fear would not permit escape: he was trapped. The dragon would come back, and he would die. So die with pride, then. Die like a warrior.

– On your feet, manroot.

He rose, his feet braced for balance as if he stood on the heaving deck of a ship plunging through heavy seas. He threw back his head, mustered his pride, then gave all his strength to his challenge:

'Ahyak Rovac!'

Echoes pumped back from the rocks of the cave. Quietly, his mind echoed the echoes:

– Ahyak Rovac.

He saw his bloodstained sword lying on the floor of the cave near the cave mouth. Boldly, he strode forward and picked it up. He was ready now. This was his fate, and he knew it: to die in battle. And when all is said and done, a death in battle is no worse than any other.

But where was the dragon?

The cave mouth yawned open, empty.

Slowly, uncertainly, Hearst stepped forward. As he gained the cave mouth, loose scales slithered underfoot. Down below, at the bottom of the steep slope, the dragon lay helpless, racked by the pain of its death-agony. A little sparse vegetation, set ablaze by dragon-fire, burnt with quick, pale flames in the bright sunshine.

Hearst stumbled forward. His boot caught a loose scale, which flicked up into the air, glittering in the sunlight. Then loose stones gave way underfoot, the ground slid from under him, and he sat down suddenly. He stood up, and sheathed his sword in the interests of safety.

The sun was hot. Hearst glanced up at the sky, at the blazing disc of the sun. Then he turned his gaze back to the dragon. Stones clinked as it moved, weakly now, in its last efforts to escape from its pain.

So he had killed it.

He noticed there was blood on his hands. His own? Remembering Hast's bloodstained blade, he unsheathed his sword. He should clean it before sheathing it. Of course. So stupid of him to forget. Go forward, then. Down to the dragon.

He went down the slope to claim his kill.

And there he stood, Morgan Gestrel Hearst, son of Avor the Hawk, warrior of Rovac, song-singer, sword-master, leader of men. His sword Hast was in his hand, with the blood of a dragon-kill on the blade. It should have been his moment of triumph, sweet as his first conquest, sweet as his first kill. But instead he felt numb: empty.

– I would not even care to make a song of it.

*   *   *

'We should leave,' said Garash.

'No,' said Gorn.

'You heard those bellows,' said Garash.

289

'I heard them,' said Gorn. 'He was killing the dragon.'

'Impossible,' said Garash. 'The dragon must have been killing him. If it's quiet now, doubtless that's only because it's gargling with his blood.'

'He's a warrior of Rovac,' said Gorn.

'A warrior's ego might be a match for a dragon, but never his sword,' said Garash.

He glanced at Elkor Alish, who said nothing.

'I'm going to see what's happened,' said Blackwood.

'No,' said Garash.

'Someone has to go and see,' said Alish.

Leaving his pack by the rocks, Blackwood went softfoot through the sunlight. Soon he saw the dragon. And Morgan Hearst. The Rovac warrior was picking his way toward him with the uncertain steps of a convalescent invalid. As for the dragon: an occasional twitch indicated there was a little life left in its body, but it was fading fast. Sunlight glittered on its scales, which glistened with a trace of iridescence.

'You're bleeding,' said Blackwood.

'Am I?' said Hearst.

'Here,' said Blackwood, touching.

A scalp wound at the back of Hearst's head had soaked the hair with blood. Blackwood's hand was bloody when he removed it.

'It's just starting to hurt now,' said Hearst.

Who was beginning to feel the pain of other cuts and bruises he had suffered in the struggle with the dragon.

Blackwood walked towards the monster's head.

'Careful,' said Hearst, 'I wouldn't call it dead yet.'

Blackwood turned.

'Miphon told me the blood of a dragon, mixed with the blood of a man, cures all ills.'

'I heard that,' said Hearst. 'I heard that, but I thought it was part of my dreams.'

'No, he said it,' said Blackwood, advancing.

'All right then – but I doubt that the best blood in the world is much of a cure for incineration.'

While they argued it out, the dragon quietly expired, and made not a murmur of protest when Blackwood, gingerly, touched a sluggish trickle of blood slowly weeping from an eye socket.

'That may not be enough,' said Hearst. 'And the blood you got from me may be too dry already.'

'Sure,' said Blackwood. 'And the dragon may have to be a virgin born by a harvest moon, for all we know. I'll try it and see.'

In his hand, the blood of a dragon mixed with traces of the blood of a man. He remembered Miphon's words: the old lore says who drinks this draught of mixed blood will never love a woman and will never hate a man, will never be able to kill – not even in self-defence – and will never call any place home.

'Why do you wait?' said Hearst.

'Because this may be a mistake,' said Blackwood.

'Miphon told me you wouldn't survive the winter,' said Hearst.

Hearing the words spoken, Blackwood knew they were true: he had felt his strength weakening as the long march and the smoke parasite made their demands on his body. His choice was to live or to die. He chose to live, and licked a little of the mixed blood from the palm of his hand.

And swallowed.

He cried out as the blood scalded his throat. Then he felt heat glow in his stomach, as if he had just drunk a flagon of hot mulled wine. Then he felt the heat sweeping through his blood vessels. His heart pumped faster. He felt a thousand pulses beating in his body. The blood pounded in his skull. His femoral artery throbbed painfully. He swayed.

'What is it?' said Hearst. 'What's wrong?'

The sun slipped sideways. Hearst caught Blackwood as he fell, and lowered him to the ground.

291

Blackwood lay there, dazed by the power of the sun. All his life he had thought of the sun according to the conventions of his people, who named it as the eye which allows the world to see. But now he knew the true nature of the sun, which is not to see but to give.

The sun gave without stinting, gave with a passion which was neither love nor hate, but which was a profoundly self-involved rapture. And Blackwood saw that, while the nature of the sun is to give, it is profoundly selfish, for it does not care whether its gift helps or harms.

The sun, then – lording the heavens with a passion which would not care if the world entire were to be destroyed by the glory of its own joy in the creation of its gift.

Dizzy with revelation, Blackwood gaped.

'What's wrong?' said Hearst.

Blackwood closed his eyes, then opened them. Morgan Hearst loomed over him. Skin stretched across skull. Mirthless gash of teeth and tongue. A killer. And the eyes – concerned now, but, apart from concern, revealing a bitter loss and loneliness. Grief consoling itself with the –

'Blackwood? What's wrong?'

'Nothing,' said Blackwood, struggling to his feet. Hearst helped him. A dribble of smoke spilt from Blackwood's lips, fell to the ground, coiled, writhed, dispersed in the sunlight.

'Can you walk?' said Hearst.

'I think so,' said Blackwood.

The throbbing in his blood vessels was diminishing; the beat of his heart was slowing from its frenzy.

'Here are the others,' said Hearst.

They were approaching, moving quickly now they saw the dragon was dead. When they drew closer, Alish said to Hearst:

'I salute you.'

His voice was stiff and formal.

292

'Thank you,' said Hearst. 'Now let's be moving. There's carrion birds gathering overhead, showing our position to everything and everyone for leagues in every direction.'

'Are you sure you're fit to travel? You're bleeding.'

'A scratch, no more,' said Hearst. 'I've got legs, still, and I can use them.'

And Blackwood, listening, knew this brusque warrior-style efficiency of speech was being used to repress a passionate outcry. He could not say whether the words left unspoken were words of love or hate, but he did know that this Rovac warrior, Morgan Hearst, was not the simple unsplicer of flesh that he pretended to be.

'We can't go yet,' cried Gorn. 'There may be treasure in the cave. We have to explore!'

'It's the truth,' said Garash, unwisely. 'There may well be treasure.'

And, after that, nothing would do but for Gorn to venture into the cave, where he glutted his greed with gold and diamonds.

* * *

Onwards, then. Fumaroles. Bubbling mud. Crinkled rock left by old lava flows. Once, tiers of pink and white terraces, ten times the height of a man, which had been built up by hot springs depositing chemicals for years lengthening to generations.

Gorn staggered along with enough loot to buy out an empire. However, after a day, he conceded defeat, and abandoned all but a king's ransom. After another day, Alish and Hearst managed to bully him out of half of that, which was then flung into a pool of boiling mud. But his pack was still overloaded.

Blackwood had no lust for dragon gold. He had other things to think about. He realised the cure for his illness had indeed . . . changed him.

293

To Blackwood, each new vista, the moment after he had first glimpsed it, seemed as familiar as if he had known it all his life. It seemed to him that he knew this shattered landscape as well as he knew the lands of Estar: given this instant empathy with every landscape, he would now call no particular place home, for he would be at home in all places.

Some sheltered city dweller might have been terrified by this change, but to Blackwood it did not seem unnatural. Living for years in the wild, he had developed his powers of observation so he could interpret the weather-signs by a single glance at the sky; after a moment's consideration, he could judge the age of track-signs and much of the nature of the animal which had made them; navigating without maps and sleeping in the open had taught him a keen appreciation of the landscape he moved through.

In the days when he had dared the unfamiliar territory of the Penvash Peninsular, he had been able, without conscious effort, to look at a range of hills and identify the slopes that would give the easiest approach to the main ridge line, and those gullies and ravines where water was most likely to be found.

Heightened powers of empathy with the landscape did not trouble Blackwood, but he was disturbed by similarly heightened perceptions of people – particularly when he saw the hackiron hatred with which Elkor Alish regarded Morgan Hearst.

Yet if Alish was disfigured by hatred, he was nevertheless amazing to watch for he brought such physical grace to everything he did. Training with a sword in the evening, an ardent spirit matching total concentration and total commitment to perfect economy of effort, he revealed a matchless capacity for joy in performance.

Watching him, Blackwood sensed how Alish felt in those moments of perfection: like a god, buoyed up by limitless possibilities. Yet dedication was not matched by wisdom, for this mastery of the potentials of flesh and steel was entirely self-involved; the discipline served to preserve the warrior's inner being, denying change, allowing a fanatic hatred to survive for years without nourishment.

This was a man who denied himself change. Matchless energies, essentially joyful and godlike, were warped to the service of narrow disciplines which preserved an earthbound hatred. Blackwood saw this, and also saw that there was no way for an outsider to change the man without destroying him, for his hatred was not an expendable excrescence like a wart – it was part of the complexities of the inner fabric of the man.

Yet if, one day, Elkor Alish were to find a way to choose to change, then perhaps he might become a perfect manifestation of something which Blackwood soon came to think of as the flame of life. To varying degrees, he saw this flame in each of them: Hearst, Alish, Gorn and Garash. What he saw was the beauty of the vitality which graces every human life.

Blackwood was no mystic; he had no desire to see visions. He repeatedly told himself that it was all delusion, that the dragon's blood was working on him as liquor works on a drunkard, distorting the way in which the world is seen.

Yet in the end he had to admit that he saw something which was really there to be seen. For he could remember a day – long ago now – when he and Mystrel had walked together in Looming Forest, in spring:

Sky, blue sky, the colour of my lover's eyes;
Leaf, young leaf, her hands no softer.

Blackwood had been in love that day, not only with Mystrel but with all the world. It had only been for a day, or perhaps only for a single morning, but in that time he had seen the flame of life which is in all things. Now he saw it from moment to moment, day after day.

One may survive occasional visions. From old memories inherited from the wizard Phyphor, Blackwood knew the poet Saba Yavendar had spoken of such visions. But Saba Yavendar had seen them only now and then: he had been able to make his peace with the world in which he lived, as evidenced by his ability to write a paean of praise for bloody slaughter, the song of the Victory of the Prince of the Favoured Blood, which Hearst had recited in the High Castle in Trest.

How could Blackwood live constantly with such visions? He knew that if he ever had to raise his hand against another man, he would be unable to do it. How could he bear to take a blade and destroy that flame of life? Yet if he could not defend himself when the need arose, sooner or later he would meet his death, and probably sooner rather than later.

A saint might, perhaps, have welcomed such visions – but Blackwood was no saint. In a hard and often bitter life, Blackwood had, by suffering, learnt to live with the realities of the world. Now, for him, the realities had changed, and it seemed he must go through all that suffering again.

* * *

After marching across leagues of monotonous flat lava country, in which there was no drinkable water, they passed between the blue lakes. The water, heavily contaminated with sulphuric acid, was a deep, unnatural blue, and Blackwood cautioned against drinking it.

North of the blue lakes, the volcanic nature of the terrain was less pronounced; the going became easier. They thought they might be clear of the dragon country – then they came upon a clutch of dragon eggs. Gorn attacked one of the eggs, smashing and battering at it until he was gory with yolk and white. Hearst stopped him from damaging the others.

Nearby was a pool of boiling water, seething with steam and fury. It bubbled and tumbled, never still, never silent. Hearst had one of the man-high eggs rolled into the pool. Then another. Then a third. The eggs bobbed up and down in the boiling water. One cracked; white stuff forced its way out, hardening in the water into fantastic forms like mould and fungus.

The eggs, when cooked, were good eating, though between them the humans could not consume a single egg entire. Gorn dipped his helmet into the boiling water, and when the contents cooled he washed himself as well as he could. But they could not spare the time for Gorn to cool enough water to wash himself properly, and so he stank of dragon's egg for the next two days, until their march took them to one of the tributaries of the Amodeo River.

The tributary offered them a route north through the Broken Lands and then through the Dry Forages to the city of Kalatanastral. They had no boat, and there was no timber in that country, but reeds grew by the riverbanks, and, at this end of summer, the low water level made it easy to gather the reeds.

An expert can fashion a one-man reed canoe in a single day, but these amateurs were three days making their little flotilla. Then they set forth on the slow-flowing muddy waters; the windings of the river meant that their first day's journey took them toward the west, although ultimately the waterflow would swing to the east, bearing them toward the eastern coast of the continent of Argan.

Their journey took them through lands which legend held to be uninhabited and uninhabitable, but clearly the legends were wrong. On some days, they saw signal fires burning to east or to west. Once, they passed half a dozen lean-to shelters, primitive windbreaks built for a transient camp then abandoned.

The country downriver was flat and monotonous, with sparse grazing, yet they saw, once, in the distance, the dust of a herd of animals on the move; the distance was too great for them to determine what the animals were, and the Rovac warriors resisted the temptation to trek inland for some hunting – they could not afford such frivolities.

They had no need to leave the river to search for food, because it afforded them a sufficiency in the form of eel and water-rat, frog, carp and heron. Their evening hunting was done with sharp skewering stakes, fire-hardened spears or stones flung from improvised slings; the fishing was good.

Yet they saw no human beings until, one day, they saw a stranger some distance downriver, riding an animal of some description.

'I hope the natives are friendly,' said Hearst.

'If not,' said Garash, only half in jest, 'I claim the kidneys. I could do with a change in diet.'

'I'll fight you for them,' said Gorn, not joking at all; he liked kidneys.

'No,' said Garash. 'You have the brains. You could do with a little extra.'

'Peace, children,' said Alish.

Soon they could see the stranger was a hunter, mounted on a kind of shaggy, heavy-bodied ox. He observed them from the river bank without any sign of curiosity. He was an old man with dirty blond hair now fading white, that hair being plaited into a heavy rope which hung down his back.

'Hey,' yelled Gorn. 'If that animal's female, she can earn herself some money.'

No answer.

'Well, if it's male, we can still do business,' shouted Gorn. 'It's been a long time. My friends are a bunch of prudes, no fun at all after sunset.'

No answer.

'How about yourself, then? You don't want to die a virgin, do you?'

Even this sally raised not a flicker of interest in the

298

old man's timebeaten face. The ox snorted, stamped one hoof, then wheeled away from the river and set off toward the west.

'The locals seem rather snobbish,' said Garash.

'I don't know,' said Hearst. 'He might come back with friends to invite us to a feast – with our livers and lights as the main course.'

'No,' said Blackwood.

From the behaviour he had seen, Blackwood knew that the old man had no interest in strangers, being content with his own universe, with the dull flat plains which he roamed, with his clothes the shades of earth and dung, his spear ornamented with irregular strips of free-hanging cloth, and the conversation of the wind-chimes which hung from his stirrups and tinkled as the ox lumbered westwards.

They argued it out as they drifted downriver, with Gorn boasting vigorously about what he could do with a brace of native women or even – and it was hard to tell if he was joking – the native cattle.

But no invitations came to feast – or be feasted on.

*   *   *

Autumn rains were swelling the waters by the time the travellers reached the Lanmarthen Marshes, where the river lost itself in a wilderness of swampgrass and water-rooted trees. Here, however, lived Melski families, and Blackwood was able to enlist their help for guidance through the marshes; the Melski confirmed that it was indeed, despite the continuing fine weather, autumn.

Once free of the marshes, they followed the Amodeo River through a barren land where no grass grew, and thus came to the city of Kalatanastral, the city of glass. It was built on a rectangular pattern, three leagues by three, with a grid of streets running north-south and east-west. The buildings were, as the legends said, of glass, but, as the travellers discovered, there were no ghosts in that city; they did not hear a single note of the fabled Dawn Songs.

Kalatanastral was a dead place in a dead land. Most of its glass buildings were sealed against the light; others were guarded by oblate spheroids of steel mounted on delicate thin-stemmed legs, half-sentient machineries from the Days of Wrath. The intruders knew better than to challenge those guardians.

If they followed the Amodeo River further, it would take them some hundred leagues or so north-east to the little fishing town of Brine and the ocean that washed against the eastern shores of Argan. However, their way now led north-west, over the barrens to the Ringwall Mountains, and across those mountains to the Central Plateau and Stronghold Handfast, where they would have to challenge the wizard Heenmor for possession of the death-stone.

Garash, as ever, spent much time in meditation; when he dreamed, the death-stone always figured in his dreams, and he knew the task of taking it for his own use would be safer and easier now that he no longer had to contend with Phyphor – or, for that matter, with Miphon.

CHAPTER THIRTY-SIX

How fares the sun?

Miphon wondered about that as he mumbled down another mouthful of siege dust. He also wondered if iron filings might make a pleasant change from a diet of siege dust: he rather suspected they might.

The red bottle held stone urns packed with enough siege dust to feed him for centuries. There was water, too. He would not starve, or die of thirst. Prince Comedo would die before Miphon did: age would kill the man before it killed the wizard.

With Comedo dead, Miphon would be left with no way of escape, unless he cared to choose the quick death offered by a drop-shaft. He would have no chance to get his hands on the ring commanding the green bottle. He would live on, mumbling siege dust, sipping water and dreaming of the sun. In time, no doubt he would forget what the sun looked like. Perhaps one day someone entering the bottle with another magic ring would find him, and then the story would be told:

– In a red bottle in a green bottle in a country where I, my children, have never been, sat a greybeard wizard who was four thousand years old . . .

Four thousand years! Yes, he could rot here that long – or longer. This was worse than the journey underground, for their river journey had promised them that before too long they would meet with death or deliverance. And there had at least been other people, other voices.

Miphon finished his meal, such as it was, and picked up his bow, which was one of many – the red bottle, packed with siege dust, water and weapons, must have been built to house an army. Comedo had sometimes visited Miphon at the portcullis, but Miphon's most strenuous diplomacies – pleas, threats, cajoleries – had achieved nothing. Now he was going to try murder.

The bowstring was slightly sticky with preservative grease that had protected it . . . for how long? It was difficult to bend the bow to string it.

There: it was done.

He was on the third level of the red bottle, with all the room he needed for target practice. He nocked an arrow, drew the bow and aimed at one of the faceless helmets that hung around the walls. He loosed the arrow.

The bowstring vibrated, stinging his thumb. The arrow clattered into a rack of throwing spears. The next one went wide, and the third caroomed off the ceiling. Miphon swore.

He had always thought of himself as a practical person, particularly since the months on the Salt Road when he had dealt with tasks of tending fires, finding food for the donkey and cooking. But those were routine tasks which he had learnt – however painfully – years ago. Archery was a new skill which he would have to master, and no amount of intellectual analysis would make the labour shorter.

To be trapped in the bottle where magic was useless was like being crippled. He had not realised he had relied so heavily on magic.

He fired another arrow. It slammed into a helmet – the wrong helmet.

*   *   *

– In a green bottle.

– In a green bottle . . .

– In a green bottle in a country where I, my children, have never been, sat a greybeard wizard. The wizard

302

had a red bottle but he was trapped in a greenbottle, greenbottle redbottle, no sun no wind no rain and never never never so much as to hear or see a bluebottle . . .

– In a green bottle . . .

Miphon had for years thought of himself as a hunter because of his love of the chase, of the moment of mastery when the wing high in flight hesitates, circles, then dips. However, he lacked the hunter's patience. Now, waiting in the shadows behind the portcullis, with arrow nocked, he suffered.

He knew Hearst or Gorn or Alish would have been patient as death, despite creaking knees, aching backs, stiff necks and rumbling stomachs. They would have waited. Could a wizard do less?

This wizard, lulled by the unvarying green glow of the bottle, caught himself falling asleep. That would never do. If Comedo came sniffing down those stairs and saw Miphon asleep behind the portcullis with bow and arrow at the ready, he would never come back.

Miphon would only have one chance. He would have to kill with the first shot. Then drag Comedo's body to the portcullis so he could take the ring from Comedo's finger. That would be easy enough to do: tie a rope to a spear then hurl the spear into the corpse.

But what if Comedo was not wearing the ring?

Of course he would be wearing the ring. He always brought it with him to gloat. Miphon would kill him. And get the ring. But what if, escaping from the green bottle, he found himself – well, he might find himself anywhere. Even, perhaps, in a dungeon in Stronghold Handfast, a prisoner of the wizard Heenmor. There was no way to say it was impossible.

Footsteps!

Miphon started. Trembling with excitement, he readied the bow and arrow. The footsteps came closer: and there was Comedo, in full view. Comedo saw him! He screamed in panic, and turned to run – too late! Miphon's arrow slammed home. Slammed into Comedo's shoulder. Comedo fell face-first to the stones. Miphon nocked another arrow, but by then Comedo had made it to safety.

'You'll pay for this!' he screamed. 'You'll pay. I'll have you eating glass before I'm through!'

'My prince,' said Miphon in desperation, dragging a little package from beneath his jerkin. 'Look what I've found! A surgeon's kit! Needles, thread, knives, bandages! I can heal you! You need me now!'

Miphon had indeed found a very beautiful surgeon's kit in the red bottle. But Comedo, unimpressed, was only provoked into showing further disrespect for the medical profession:

'You slime-licking pox doctor!' he howled. 'By the syphillis sore you were suckled on, I'll see you pay for this. I'll have you, by the balls of the tenth demon, I'll tear your head from your shoulders and shit on it. What a coward's trick. By the knives, the lice in the slit between your legs have got more courage that you have. Don't think you'll catch me again. If you want to speak to me, yes, if you want an audience – '

Miphon would listen no more. He retreated down the stairs, back to the lower levels, and then into the red bottle. Water and siege dust, siege dust and water: it could keep him alive forever.

– In a red bottle in a green bottle in a country far, far away, where I, my children, have never been, sat a greybeard wizard who was four thousand years old . . .

It could keep him alive forever.

CHAPTER THIRTY-SEVEN

'There it is,' said Garash.

From a high ridge, they had a view across bleak and broken country. Far off, about seven leagues distant, loomed the uprearing vertigo of Stronghold Handfast.

'Impressive, yes?' said Garash.

'Some think so,' said Hearst. 'Saba Yavendar always used to think it was ugly.'

'Really,' said Garash.

'Yes,' said Hearst.

And saw Garash looking at him oddly. Of course, the memory was not Hearst's, but a stray recollection inherited from the wizard Phyphor.

'What do you know of Saba Yavendar?' said Garash.

'His poems are famous.'

'Yes, but the man – '

'Don't you recognise a joke when you hear it?' said Hearst.

'A joke, hey? Does that count as humour where you come from? Don't bother me with any more of your jokes.'

'As you wish,' said Hearst.

Garash again looked at him suspiciously: that was not the way Rovac warriors talked. As you wish. As you please. If it suits your convenience. . . .

'We're on the skyline,' said Blackwood.

'No matter,' said Elkor Alish, buoyed up by excitement at the sight of Stronghold Handfast.

'Blackwood's right,' said Hearst. 'We'd better get off the ridge.'

Hearst did not share Alish's excitement.

As they scrambled down the other side of the ridge,

Hearst thought about Saba Yavendar. He remembered him quite clearly: a short man with a big ugly nose, a quick grin, and broken blood vessels mottling his face where years of drinking had done their damage. Phyphor had known him well.

Blackwood halted amidst jagged uprisings of rock and clutches of boulders which would shelter them from scrutiny but still allow them a clear view of the landscape ahead.

'What do you think?' said Blackwood. 'Shall we camp here?'

'It's not far now,' said Alish.

'We won't get there today,' said Hearst. 'It would be foolish to try. Let's just go down into the valley and camp for the night.'

'We can go further than that,' said Alish.

'The sky looks like snow,' said Hearst. 'I want to make camp early. I don't want night to catch us unprepared.'

'A little snow won't hurt us.'

'If there's snow, I'll want fire. Remember why I left the Cold West.'

'I remember,' said Alish 'I remember . . .'

And was silent while Hearst scanned the torn landscape confronting them.

'To the left looks easier,' said Hearst.

'I prefer the right,' said Gorn. 'It's steeper but shorter.'

The two Rovac warriors argued it out. Blackwood did not take sides, though he was sure which was the easier, and was relieved when Hearst won the dispute.

'Let's move out.' said Hearst.

They shouldered their packs and continued their descent. With plenty of time remaining till dayfail, Hearst called a halt in a small valley where tall rocks provided a little shelter. Spindly trees grew here and there; without any chitchat, they felled trees, made a rough lean-to and built a pile of firewood. There would be no cooking: they now had enough food for only one meal each day, which was breakfast. At this rate, their rations would be exhausted in a week.

Some time before darkness, it began to snow. The air seemed to warm a fraction, then, white by white, flake by flake, the snow descended. The first flakes, landing on the dark rocks, puffed out to nothing. But light, white, air-light, more snow fell, settling white on black, white on white on black, then white on white on white.

Blackwood coughed.

'You're not sick, are you?' said Gorn.

'I thought you'd recovered,' said Hearst.

'I have recovered,' said Blackwood, and it was true: the parasitic smoke was long dead. 'I coughed, that's all.'

But he was touched by the concern in their voices. Shared hardships had made them allies against the dangers of the world.

Hearst flexed his hands, which were going numb in the cold, took his tinder box, and, with the skill which comes from long experience, he lit the fire.

* * *

Dark, and . . . Stars!

And how cold!

'Who – '

'What?'

'Ahyak Rovac!'

'Hold!'

'Who's that?'

'Blackwood?'

'I'm here . . . '

'Miphon!'

'Who else?'

'Miphon, how did you – what took you so long?'

'Here I am.'

'Is it warm in the bottle?'

307

'It's freezing cold out here. For certain it's warmer inside. Hold my arm. Blackwood.'

'Here. I'm here.'

'Hearst. Alish. Gorn. Garash, come on, Garash. Where are the others?'

'Dragons ate them.'

'Oh. I'm sorry about that.'

'So was the dragon. Their armour gave it indigestion. Come on now!'

And Miphon twisted the ring on his finger, and the whole party was sucked into the green bottle.

'Here we are,' said Miphon.

'The bottle's gone from my belt,' said Blackwood.

'Of course,' said Miphon. 'You're inside it now.'

'Food,' said Gorn. 'I can smell food.'

'Down here,' said Miphon. 'Down these stairs.'

'Where's Comedo?' said Alish.

'Ah,' said Miphon. 'Thereby hangs a tale . . .'

* * *

For hungry men, stomachs demanded satisfaction before curiosity had its turn. When appetites were satisfied, Miphon told his story.

' . . . so there I was, trapped behind the portcullis,' said Miphon. 'I must admit, I felt foolish to have been caught so easily.'

'You should have ripped his guts out right at the start,' said Gorn.

'So you were caught behind the portcullis,' said Alish. 'Did you try to raise it?'

'Yes, but that proved impossible. However, I went deeper down in this green bottle. After a while I found a red bottle, together with a ring which I could use to enter it.'

'I see,' said Hearst. 'Given that, you could easily escape. I can guess what you did. You reached through the bars of the portcullis to put the red bottle down on the other side. Then used the ring to transport yourself into the red bottle. Then used the ring again – and came out of the red bottle on Comedo's side of the portcullis. Then you found Comedo and overpowered him.'

'Exactly,' said Miphon.

'But what took you so long?'

'Well . . . how long do you think it took me to find the red bottle?'

'I see,' said Hearst. 'The green bottle's bigger than it looks from the outside.'

'Of course,' said Miphon, 'Or how could we be inside it?'

'How can something small outside be large inside?' said Blackwood.

'All enchantment is an anomaly,' said Miphon.

'Words are words,' said Blackwood. 'Facts are facts.'

Miphon laughed at his bewilderment. It was the first time in a long time that he had laughed. It felt good.

'So where's Comedo?' said Alish.

'The red bottle's sitting right there,' said Miphon, 'See? Beside it is the ring which commands the red bottle. Comedo's in there for safekeeping.'

'Bring him out,' said Alish.

'Time for that later,' said Hearst, 'When we've finished our business with Heenmor.'

'How far is there to go?' said Miphon. 'How far are we from Stronghold Handfast?'

'We can get there tomorrow,' said Hearst. 'It's rough country, but we're all fit enough to tackle it.'

Miphon glanced at Blackwood.

'You look much better,' said Miphon.

'I'm cured,'said Blackwood.

'How?'

'The old lore tells how.'

'Really,' said Miphon. 'I have got a lot to hear about.'

'Yes,' said Hearst. 'And it'll give you something to chew on, as Andranovory said when the dragon bit him in half.'

'Which dragon was that?' said Miphon. 'The one which killed all the others?'

'Oh, there were five dragons actually,' said Hearst, 'But one was just a baby. It was chasing mice when we found it.'

At which point Miphon began to suspect that he was being kidded, because his reference books said – and he believed them, though such tomes were not always entirely accurate – that:

(a) the immature form of the common or land dragon lives primarily on sulphur; and

(b) dragons are afraid of mice.

Nevertheless, he did not interrupt. It was Elkor Alish, in the end, who told the truth. Alish wanted the Rovac to be credited with Hearst's dragon-kill. He wanted the wizards, Garash and Miphon, to understand the superiority of the Rovac. Even though he suspected that he would shortly have to kill both wizards.

And, perhaps, Morgan Hearst as well.

CHAPTER THIRTY-EIGHT

Stronghold Handfast.

At ground level, fifty-seven arches giving entrance. Walls rising abruptly, then bulging out in bubble-smooth curves. High above ground level, as if designed to permit entrance and egress by air, three dozen randomly-spaced vents twisting inwards into darkness – entering one of those vents, a dragon or even one of the Neversh would have looked like a gnat flying into a mammoth's mouth.

Higher still, a delicate tracery of arches and linkways patterned the sky; rising through this spiderweb fantasy, seventy-six towers soared skywards, each swelling suddenly toward zenith. Stronghold Handfast, then: made by masters so long forgotten that it was no longer possible even to say whether they had been human.

This entire structure was made of building blocks no larger than a man's thumb, and, in their millions, they changed colour with a slow, crawling rhythm, so that at any one time some were blue, some green, some red, some yellow. This gave the impression that the structure was, in some ominous way, alive.

'It looks deserted,' said Blackwood.

'Maybe,' said Hearst.

They had spent a long time concealed amid rocks near one of the entrances to Stronghold Handfast, but their scrutiny had told them nothing more about what they might be faced with.

'Let's charge,' said Alish, rising, 'and see how far we get.'

'We could wait for darkness,' said Garash.

311

'Wait if you wish,' said Alish.

'All right then, I'll come. But maybe we should go in through the back door.'

'For all we know, this is the back door.'

'Oh.'

'Wait a moment,' said Hearst. 'What's the hind legs?'

By which he meant: what's plan B?

This Rovac idiom sounded very peculiar in the Galish Trading Tongue, which they were using out of courtesy to the wizards, who spoke no Rovac.

'If we don't get in through the nearest entrance,' said Alish, 'it'll be because we're dead, so we don't need any hind legs.'

'That's just as well,' said Garash, 'because I was born without them in any case.'

'Yes,' said Alish. 'Like the rest of the chickens. Now run!'

They sprinted across the open ground to the nearest entrance, boots crunching in the crisp snow. Garash, whose sprint was rather leisurely as there was no dragon or similar to inspire him – in the traditional story about the tortoise and the old, old wizard, there is no mystery at all about why the tortoise won the race – was last to gain the entrance. It was doorless.

'Which way now?' said Blackwood, finding he had no empathy whatever with the utterly alien maze confronting them.

'Silence,' said Hearst. 'Listen.'

They waited: listening, watching. Hearst, Alish, Gorn, Garash, Blackwood, Miphon: they were all tense, apprehensive, on edge.

Hearst drew Hast, but the balance of the blade gave him no confidence. He was unnerved by Stronghold Handfast. Unlike any architecture he had seen before, it had no symmetry. From where they stood they could see into a great hall where in some places the roof dipped low but where in other places it soared upward into dizzying heights. Pillars rose at random to support

312

the weight of the roof: some square, some arched, some twisting upwards in spirals.

– A pile of rocks, but. Who are we to be frightened of a pile of rocks? But what hands? What feet? Strength, man of Rovac, strength. Are you not a hero?

Hearst failed to draw comfort from his own thoughts.

Somewhere along their long journey – perhaps when he had inspected the corpse of his first dragon-kill – he had begun to have his doubts about the merits of the ethos of the kind of ruthless, sword-slaughtering heroism celebrated by the songs of Rovac.

Still . . . he had sworn his oath, so he could hardly turn back now. Whatever his thoughts about heroism, he had no doubts whatsoever about the sacred nature of an oath.

So, sword in hand, he followed when Alish advanced. The others also followed, glancing back from time to time at the daylit entrance, which steadily receded behind them. Suddenly a coil of liquid black light flickered to life in the air in front of Alish. His sword outpaced his scream:

'Ahyak Rovac!'

Trembling, blade in hand, heart sprinting, Alish confronted the twisting coil of black light. His challenge echoed from wall to wall, repeating itself time and time again, growing louder with each repetition, until it sounded as if a giant was bellowing out the traditional challenge of Rovac. Then the echoing scream began to diminish, at last falling away to a whisper, then to nothing.

Slowly, the twisting coil of black light began to slide away, hissing softly. It hesitated when it was twenty paces away: waiting for them? Alish glanced round at the others: none dared to speak, lest that place amplify their merest whisper to a shout. Hearst shrugged, and gestured to indicate they should proceed.

And what else could they do?

Not knowing the nature of that softly hissing entity of

black light, they could not hope to outwit it and enter
Stronghold Handfast unseen. And it was already too
late to enter unheard!

Alish darted forward. The others followed.

The black light led them through halls and corridors
to a region of Stronghold Handfast where the air felt
dead and cold, and where the writhing colour-shifts
shaping their way across the walls seemed slow and
lethargic. Here Garash, losing his nerve, hesitated.

'Come on,' said Alish.

His voice seemed muffled. Irritated, he spoke louder:
'Come on!'

His voice had no echo in that dead place. So cold. No
smell of living thing. No life-sign: no husk of insect, no
feather of bird, no leaf of tree.

The black light – spirit? ghost? messenger? servant of
the stronghold's long-dead masters? – led them onward.
Finally they reached a hall where they could breathe
more easily, and where their footsteps no longer
sounded muted and muffled.

They looked down the length of the hall. And saw:
Heenmor.

He sat far away at the end of the hall, seated on a
throne of sorts. He had not seen them.

Garash raised his hand.

'Forward now,' said Garash, his voice hardly more
than a whisper. 'If he moves to raise his hand, I'll kill
him. Miphon: watch for the snake.'

As they walked forward, the coil of black light did not
accompany them. Instead, it: disappeared. Uneasily,
Hearst looked back to see if it was following them – but
it was nowhere to be seen.

As they drew nearer to Heenmor, still the immensely
tall wizard did not move.

'Is he dead?' said Gorn.

'Forward,' said Garash.

They advanced with a rush. Hesitation could not
save them now. Closing with Heenmor, they saw that

his body had been turned to stone. Near him lay the stone egg, the death-stone. Experimenting with its powers, he had risked too much, bringing about his own death.

'Hold!' said Blackwood.

They halted abruptly. The copper-strike snake still guarded Heenmor's body. It moved: menacing them: supple, lithe, quick and flexible, swaying this way and that.

'Miphon,' said Garash. 'Draw it away from us.'

"I . . . I can't!'

'What's wrong?'

'I don't know,' said Miphon. 'Perhaps this hall's built to stop my kind of power. I can't make contact with the mind of the snake.'

Garash swore.

'I'll kill it myself,' he said.

And said a Word.

Fire blazed from his hand.

But the snake survived: it was faster than any fat wizard. Garash spoke again: a Word. And again. And again. Stone cracked and splintered. Fire blazed in fury. Waves of heat swept through the hall. But the snake dodged, ducked, twisted: and survived.

Garash raised his hand again and said a Word.

Nothing happened.

The snake moved to the left, menacing Gorn and Blackwood. They fell back, and it moved to the right, menacing Hearst and Alish. They in turn retreated. It threatened Miphon and Garash, who also drew back.

'Blackwood,' said Alish.

'Yes?'

'Draw it off. I'll snatch up the death-stone. Then we can be gone from this place.'

'All right,' said Blackwood.

'I'm with you,' said Gorn.

'Are you ready?' said Blackwood.

'Ready,' said Alish.

Blackwood and Gorn stepped forward, slowly, slowly. The snake menaced them. They dared another step. The snake slid closer. Alish darted in, snatched up the death-stone, glanced at the writing on it: then raised it in his right hand and shouted a Word.

'Alish!' screamed Hearst.

And threw himself forward. The snake twisted, lunged forward, and struck at his sword-hand. Hearst glanced at the bloody red puncture marks in his hand where the fangs had gone home, then at Elkor Alish, exultant, holding aloft the death-stone. He heard the grinding sound as that power began to manifest itself.

Hearst strode forward, switching his sword to his left hand as he moved, and the sword rose:

– Strength, man of Rovac! Strength!

And the right hand was gone, falling away. And Hearst closed the distance: one step, two.

Alish saw Hearst coming with Hast swinging bloody in his left hand. Alish threw himself to one side, rolling out of reach. He switched the death-stone to his left hand, and all time the grinding sound was growing louder. Alish drew his blade and faced Hearst.

But Miphon took Alish from behind, roping an arm round his neck and twisting the ring on his finger. Miphon, Alish and the death-stone disappeared: sucked into the green bottle.

Silence.

Hearst glanced around and saw Gorn watching, hardly believing what he had seen, his mouth gaping. Blackwood, having succeeded in distracting the snake, was leading it away down the hall, enticing it with a complicated dance of taunt and dare.

'I don't believe it,' said Garash.

Hearst glanced at the stump of his right wrist. It was white: bloodless. Every blood vessel had clamped tight in shock, as blood vessels sometimes will in the moments after amputation.

So there stood Morgan Hearst, and in his hand was

Hast, blade of firelight steel, poised and balanced. And Hearst could not help but remember an oath freely given and well rewarded:

'I, Morgan Gestrel Hearst, son of Avor the Hawk, song-singer, sword-master, warrior of Rovac, swear by my sword Hast and the hand that holds it that I will see Garash dead as soon as Heenmor falls.'

Heenmor was dead, and there stood Garash. And there stood Hearst. His right hand was gone, cut free with a lethal dose of poison in the flesh, but he could still wield Hast left-handed - as he had once in a desperate skirmish outside the walls of a city known as Larbreth.

Hearst stepped forward.

He was moving in a daze: moving in a state of shock. Men had sometimes said it was hard to tell his thoughts, but his intentions were clear enough now. Garash saw him coming, and pulled free the shrivelled twist of wood that he wore hung round his neck.

'That's enough,' said Garash, stepping back.

And Hearst thought:

– I'll never reach him.

But he stepped forward to close the distance. Alish, Elkor Alish, traitor, oathbreaker, had tried to kill him, had betrayed him, and if there was a time for Morgan Hearst to die then this was it.

Garash said a Word. The twist of wood extended, grew, and became a staff. Yet Hearst strode forward, Hast in hand. So Garash said a Word –

And Gorn, throwing himself forward on the attack, was caught by the full force of the blast of flame from the staff. The twisted wreckage of his body fell to the ground: he had died too fast for even a scream.

Garash said a Word.

Nothing happened: the power of his staff was exhausted.

Garash turned and ran.

Hearst moved to follow him, but at that moment the

317

blood vessels in his right wrist relaxed, and suddenly he had to clutch at the stump with his left hand to try to staunch the pulse of arterial blood, to try and stop himself bleeding to death.

Miphon, materialising in the great hall, saw Hearst clutching the stump of his wrist. He saw the charred remains of Gorn's body, identifiable by his boots and his battle-axe. He saw Garash retreating at speed; there was no sign of Blackwood, who had led the copper-strike snake out of the hall.

Hearst turned to look at Miphon. Blood was forcing its way between his fingers from the stump of his right wrist.

'I think I'm finished,' said Hearst.

'Not yet,' said Miphon, pulling his surgeon's kit from beneath his jerkin.

And he went to work.

At the hands of any common quack or chirurgeon, Hearst would have stood a good chance of dying, but in his time Miphon had dealt successfully with many appalling injuries sustained by Southsearchers and members of the Landguard in their battles against the swarms – and, sometimes, against each other. Miphon had all the experience he needed.

Working in a welter of blood, hissing, sometimes swearing softly, he managed to strangle the major arteries, tying them off with loops of thread. He worked quickly, doing what he had to, knowing that he had only limited time before shock was succeeded by pain.

Already he was reviewing the practical difficulties of keeping an amputee alive in that hostile environment. If they could find food, it would be best to stay in Stronghold Handfast for some days to allow the wound time to start to heal; after losing a lot of blood, Hearst would need time to recover his strength, and an immediate trek across the Central Plateau would increase his chances of dying of gangrene, as it would be harder to keep the wound clean when they were living rough in the open.

Miphon wished he could take Hearst into the comparative safety of the green bottle, but that would be impossible. Inside the green bottle, Elkor Alish had almost managed to kill him, but Miphon had jumped down a drop-hole. As he fell down the drop-hole he had turned the ring on his finger and had been transported back to the hall in Stronghold Handfast.

Alish was now trapped in the green bottle, together with the death-stone, which was useless to him in that place where no magic had any power. But while Alish was in the green bottle, Miphon dared not return there.

'It'll be all right,' said Miphon, finishing bandaging the arm-stump. 'It'll be all right.'

But Morgan Hearst, warrior of Rovac, hero of the era, broke down and wept, tears burning hot from his eyes, body racked with grief. So Miphon held him and rocked him and soothed him as shadows and darkness settled in the halls and corridors of the ancient fortress on the Central Plateau, Stronghold Handfast.

CHAPTER THIRTY-NINE

There was snow on the ground when Blackwood, Miphon and Morgan Hearst left Stronghold Handfast. They presumed Garash had gone south to the Amodeo River, which would afford him a passage to Brine. So, to avoid all possibility of confrontation, they trekked north across the Central Plateau then over the mountains to the Scourside Coast.

Blackwood, weather-wise sky-reader, was their route finder. Miphon, mind-tracker, found their food: rodents in winter burrows and earthworms in the richer pockets of soil. Under Miphon's care, Hearst's wound had healed by the time they reached the sea.

They found a fishing village crouching in the marginal shelter of a razorback ridge: huddling smokestone cottages lit by guttering whaleoil lamps. The villagers were unsure what to make of these winter-weather visitors. Some were frightened by the cold, bitter grey eyes of the man with only one hand. Asking his name, they were told 'Hast': the Rovac warrior had taken the name of his sword, for there was little difference between them now, as one was a death-dealer and one a death-seeker, wishing only for an ending.

As for Miphon, although at first he seemed young, vigorous and cheerful, his eyes betrayed a desperate anxiety. Nightly, he dreamt of Elkor Alish exploring the depths of the green bottle, seeking and searching in the silent gloom, sword at the ready in case anything menaced him. In his dreams, Alish escaped; armies marched at his command; entire cities and civilizations were laid waste by the death-stone.

Miphon told himself that Alish had scant chance of

320

finding a ring to set himself free from the green bottle. But what if he escaped down a drop-shaft? In theory, that was impossible. Morgan Hearst said Elkor Alish was the best climber he knew, but if Alish tried to descend a drop-shaft, then intolerable forces of acceleration would pry him loose from the walls and send him hurtling down into the waiting fire trench. It seemed there was no escape that way – but Miphon had to remind himself that, trapped behind the portcullis, he had spent days without seeing the obvious way to set himself free.

The wizard puzzled the villagers, as did the third visitor. At first sight, he seemed the oldest, yet his face was as puzzled as if he had only just been born: odd things moved him to laughter or to tears. Many thought him simple, a moon-child: yet his talk was always sensible.

The visitors arrived as bad weather was setting in; a fishing smack, with a crew including a man who had fallen in heavy seas and dislocated his shoulder, struggled to haven through a mounting storm. The casualty had been half a day with his injury by the time the boat came to safety; someone skilled in manipulation can put a shoulder into place with ease if it has only just slipped out, but by the time Miphon saw the man, the muscles had long since locked rigid.

Miphon hated to be ruthless, but their need was great; he promised to put the shoulder back if he could have the boat. Even though the crewman was white-faced with shock and agony, he was in two minds about it; in a village such as this, a boat was wealth. Pain forced his choice. There was a hurried consultation with his family, for he did not own the boat, and would need others to guarantee the price to the owner, and share the debt-burden.

The agreement was made; now Miphon had only to remedy the injury. Opium would have been the drug of choice, to dull pain and put the victim into a stupor, but there was none to be had; this Scourside village lacked even a name for the substance. That being so, Miphon had water put on to boil, to produce steam. He saturated a length of cloth with alcohol, then wrapped it round the injured joint and associated muscles. Despite his tenderness, his patient cried out, as well he might in the face of such pain.

With the help of a steady flow of steam, the alcohol slowly penetrated the muscles, dulling the pain sufficiently for Miphon to try and put the joint back. He took the arm and pulled it outwards from the body – steadily and slowly – then bent the arm at the elbow and moved it in an arc, bringing the hand toward the chest.

Miphon knew exactly what he was doing; he had a name for every muscle and every bone, and knew how they worked together. He had done this often enough before: there were few injuries he had not seen and treated at some stage in the years gone by. The joint slipped home with an audible clunk.

It was done.

*　　*　　*

Given a break in the weather, Hearst decided to put to sea without further delay, despite the danger of renewed bad weather; he found the only resolution for his sorrows was constant action. The renascent storm caught them at sea at dusk; soon they were in desperate trouble. They could not set a sea anchor and ride out the storm with a barc mast, because the wind would have swept them onto the rocks of the shore.

Then Blackwood took the helm and began to give orders. With a precise reading of wind and wave, with immaculate timing in his orders, with an exact estimate of how much strain the rigging and timbers of his cockleshell command could endure, he saw them through grim hours of light and darkness in seas that could have sunk the best ships of the fleet of Rovac.

For Blackwood, the night in the raging weather

brought divine release and giddy exultation.

Cursed by an empathy with all living things, he endured the terror of a rabbit seen ravaged by the talons of a hunting hawk, even as he thrilled to the beauty of the killing creature which was, after all, being true to the heart of its own nature. As for the conflict of human wills, such as he had seen in the bargaining for the boat – he found that almost unbearable.

But, guiding the boat through the storm, matching his new powers of empathy and heightened perception against the inanimate, he was free to rejoice in his abilities.

The long struggle with the sea took them clear of the shore, then, when the wind veered from north-west to west, they ran before it, and were driven far out to the east. Blackwood began to fear they would be swept far out into the Eastern Ocean, there doubtless to sink, for their boat was now taking in water.

However, eventually, when the wind slackened, they found themselves in sight of a cold granite island. There Blackwood brought their leaking boat to harbour. He was exhausted by then, and faltering; he almost wrecked the boat when crossing the bar at the harbour mouth. But they survived.

The island, they found, was Ork, the home base for a pirate fleet.

*   *   *

The leader of the pirates of Ork was Ohio. He claimed that a brother of his, Menator, commanded pirate ships on the west coast of Argan; they had gone their separate ways because of a quarrel, but now Ohio was thinking of rejoining his brother.

Ork had lately been blockaded for weeks by Collosnon warships. The Collosnon navy was determined to destroy the pirates, and Ohio's men – mostly recruited from Scourside villages – had no belly for a fight. Storms had scattered the blockade, but Ohio could not leave until ships damaged in an earlier attempt to break the blockade had been repaired. While they delayed, the navy returned.

The travellers sweetened Ohio with a gift of that fraction of Gorn's dragon treasure which they had brought with them from Stronghold Handfast. Taking this gift in secret, he did not have to divide it with his men. In exchange for the visitors' gift and their silence about the same, Ohio offered to take them with him when he left Ork; they accepted the offer.

It was on the island of Ork that Hearst acquired a steel hook. It curved out from a short, rounded length of wood, the hollow end of which, padded with leather, fitted over the stump of Hearst's right hand. Iron bars ran from the wooden block all the way to a cunning piece of jointed flexible plate armour at the elbow, which would take the strain if Hearst lifted weights with the hook. He chose to file the end of the hook to a point and sharpen one side to a cutting edge; Miphon warned that this would diminish the overall utility of the hook, but Hearst snarled that he was a warrior, not a washerwoman.

The day came when it was time to leave Ork. Hearst, Miphon and Blackwood travelled in Ohio's lean clean-lined flagship, the *Skua*, and it was Blackwood who took that ship out to sea across the bar at the harbour mouth.

They had chosen a wild day on which to set sail. One ship was wrecked on the bar, but the others got clear of Ork, and the blockading Collosnon ships found it impossible to close and board in the heaving seas.

Both pirates and naval ships ran before an easterly wind, till the weather settled enough for the navy flagship to close and grapple with Ohio's *Skua*. A boarding party crossed and combat began. Then the weather took a turn for the worse, some of the grapples were hacked away, some tore loose, and the Collosnon boarding party was isolated on the *Skua*.

It was a fight to the finish.

CHAPTER FORTY

To the south, a lee shore raised prow-cleaving cliffs. Those wave-breakers slewed as the ship plumbed the sea's hollows. Morgan Hearst braced for balance as the *Skua* heaved up again, breaking free from the weight of the waters. He challenged the shrill scream of wind through rigging:

'Ahyak Rovac!'

Lightning forked across the sky. Bone-breaking thunder followed. His enemy menaced him. Hearst grunted, striking:

'Huhn!'

Swords swung: metal to metal.

One blade shattered.

'Huhn!' said Hearst.

Driving his blade home.

His enemy gaped, pain too wide to scream. Hearst drew free his sword as the ship plunged down, then turned to face another challenge. He felt no fear: he was more than ready for death.

'Huhn!' said Hearst, as the ship recovered the sky.

It was a threat: but his enemy closed. Sword, cuirass, helmet. Cold steel with the sea-sting beaded upon it, grey upon grey. Eyes, sea-red, mad with fear and anger. Hearst swung left-handed, a cripple in combat. His enemy parried, almost took him with a quick thrust.

– So it's death then.

– This death as good as any.

– Hastsword, my hero.

– My brother in blood.

Hearst struck one desperate blow, sword wide-slicing for the hope of death with glory. Then he was open, whore-wide open, off balance and falling. Metal thrust for his belly. Falling, he twisted to one side, evading the thrust.

His enemy shouted, raising his sword for a killing blow. Then a rip-rent squall struck, hit so fast that all went down as the ship heeled. The wet-wood deck canted, sliding to the sea's yawn. Hearst clawed his steel hook-hand deep into the wood as he started to slip. The mast gave with a sick greenstick snap.

Slowly the ship lumbered up toward level. Hearst worked his hook-hand free from the deck. Getting to his feet, he stood with his sword Hast in his left hand, looking for his enemy. Gone. Overboard. Sea's spray drenched the deck as a wave struck. A moment later came rain with the sting of ice in it. A buffalo-shouldered brawner came lumbering through the sleet toward Morgan Hearst.

'Huhn!' said Hearst.

Swords clashed.

The brawner knocked his blade to the sky.

So there he was, Hearst disarmed and his enemy chopping for the kill. Then the ship heaved up as a wave went whale-under. The brawner staggered, sliding. Hearst closed, for to close the distance was the only chance he had.

Hearst's hook-hand, right hand, dextrous, sliced through the side of the brawner's neck. The big artery gave with a spurt of blood that shot three paces, and would have gone a dozen but for the wind feathering it to a red mist soon lost in the sleet. Hearst saw his sword Hast caught in a raggage of rope and canvas. He grabbed it. He braced as another wave struck the ship.

The wave surged over the deck, sliding the brawner to the scuppers and gone, overboard: vanishing into grey waves with one flash of colour where sealight glanced from a ceramic tile slung round the dead man's neck. With quick-blink despatch, the body sundered under for once and for all.

Gone.

'Ahyak Rovac!' screamed Hearst.

And turned: steel seeking steel, challenge seeking challenge. But no swordsman faced him. He glanced right, glanced left. The Collosnon were cleared from the deck: the pirates had victory. Ohio's voice rose against the wind, thundering orders. The deck was a shambles of blood, canvas, spars and rigging; the lee shore was closing; it would be a near thing. Morgan Gestrel Hastsword Hearst sheathed his blade and set his hand and his hook to the work.

* * *

The *Skua* almost came to grief on the coast, but managed to find haven in a narrow strait between the coast and an island which lay only a little way offshore. A Collosnon vessel that tried to follow it was wrecked: the pirate blades were ready, and the few survivors failed to survive their survival.

For ten days the *Skua* lay at anchor while storm weather swept the seas; when it ventured out again, there was no sign of the Collosnon fleet or of the other pirate ships.

Riding the winter weather along the northern coast of Argan, the *Skua* headed westward. They struck once at a fishing village, a place of low houses and narrow graves which sheltered in a bay called Edge by a mountain called Scarp; they gained a haul of heavy-armoured lobster, glissando fish, broad-wing depth-ray and red-veined whiplash-eel. They sailed away leaving the sky behind them smudged with smoke.

Hearst worked words in his head, marking the monotony of their progress:

Cold is the cold sea,
Grey is the grey sky,
Wet is the wet wave,
Dry is the clear eye.

And what would Saba Yavendar have thought of those lines? Hearst remembered the poet so clearly: a squat little man, not much bigger than a dwarf, who used to drink so he was buoyed up by alcohol when he stood up to recite in his battlesword voice:

Down from the mountains the open veins
Run blood-red to the sea-coast plains.
Sing Talaman-ho!
Tala is a he-ro!

There had been a sneer in the word "hero". And Talaman's face had darkened with anger as Saba Yavendar went on to detail Talaman's heroism: the celebrated rape of his sister's son, the slaughter in the city of Hunganeil which had surrendered without resistance, the week of feasting on 'small pig' at the mountain called Quinneroom, and the murder of the oracle of Ellamura.

Oh yes, if ever true heroes walked the earth then Saba Yavendar was one of them. But in truth Hearst had never met the poet; he recalled only the memories of the wizard Phyphor. He lacked the curiosity to explore those memories further: he lived only to seek his death in battle.

He almost found it when the *Skua* encountered another Collosnon warship. In a desperate fight, the Collosnon ship was set ablaze and the *Skua* went aground on a shoal close to shore. The pirates had victory, but they had to wait until the incoming tide floated their ship off the rocks before they could go anywhere; meanwhile, the smoke from the burning enemy ship slowly drifted up into the sky.

* * *

Morgan Hearst sat on the canted deck of the *Skua*,

watching the smoke of the burning Collosnon ship and brooding on his fate.

His closest friend, Elkor Alish, had become his enemy. He had lost his right hand, becoming a cripple. And he had lost his faith in the warrior ethos of Rovac, and had nothing with which to replace that faith.

So he wished to die – but in battle the habits of a lifetime did not allow him to do anything less than his best. He had fought well: something which other people had noticed.

'You did well,' said Ohio, coming up to Hearst, who was cleaning the last blood from his sword Hast.

'If you say so,' said Hearst.

'It's the act which makes it so, not the saying. One day you must tell me where you learnt to fight.'

'It's a long story,' said Hearst, sheathing his sword.

'So is life,' said Ohio. 'There's time enough for all the stories. You could tell me now: we'll have time enough before the tide floats us off these rocks.'

'I doubt it,' said Hearst.

'Try,' said Ohio.

'Death is my story, and the carrion crow will tell it.'

'There's no crows in this country,' said Ohio. 'Just skua gulls. Why so sour, friend Hearst? You fought well, but from the look on your face a guess would have to say you'd lost the battle.'

'If you say so,' said Hearst.

'You're a strange one, you are,' said Ohio.

He scanned the sea, looking in case any other ships had come in sight. But there was only the burning hulk of the Collosnon warship. The sky was clear; the light wind aired the smoke toward the shore. The tide was slowly rising.

'How are you?' said Miphon, coming along the deck toward the two men.

'No injuries here,' said Ohio.

'Not unless you want to count this,' said Hearst.

'Oh, your hand,' said Ohio, seeing the ugly blood-

329

bruise under Hearst's left thumbnail. 'You'll lose that nail for sure.'

'No,' said Miphon. 'I'll fix that. Wait.'

Miphon picked his way along the canted deck of the ship to where a group of pirates were heating up a brew of red wine and spices over a fire built on a bed of sand. He scraped some hot coals into a small pannikin and returned to Hearst. Miphon blew softly on the coals; they glowed cherry-red; he heated the blunt end of a needle.

'No,' said Hearst.

'It won't hurt.'

'That's not the point.'

'Then what is the point? You'll lose that nail unless you let me work on it.'

'The point . . .'

'Tell me,' said Miphon.

'I'm tired of . . .'

'Of what? Being attended to by a pox doctor? Do you think they'll get to hear about it on Rovac? Come on, give me your hand.'

Hearst extended his hand. Miphon heated the needle again and touched it to the thumbnail. He did it several times, slowly burning a hole through the nail.

'Does it hurt?' said Ohio.

'No,' said Hearst.

'But then, if you're a Rovac warrior, you wouldn't admit to the pain.'

'It shouldn't hurt,' said Miphon.

'I knew you were something special,' said Ohio. 'I always knew you weren't just the wandering swordsman you claimed to be. But I never guessed you were from Rovac.'

Miphon touched needle to nail again.

'Is that a Rovac sword?' said Ohio. 'How much is it worth?'

'The sword is from Stokes, where all the best steel comes from,' said Hearst. 'As to what it's worth, well, there's no price that would buy it.'

330

And he looked hard at Ohio.

'I've no designs on your property,' said Ohio. 'I was just curious.'

Miphon touched needle to nail one last time. Blood welled up from the hole he had made.

'That should take the pressure off,' said Miphon. 'There's no reason now why you should lose the nail, so long as you're careful with it.'

'Good,' said Hearst.

'Tell me about Rovac,' said Ohio.

'About Rovac?' said Hearst.

'Yes.'

'It's a place where the ground's the ground and the sky's the sky,' said Hearst. 'The people there are born of women, some nine months after their parents couple. To live they eat and drink; at the end of living they find they die.'

'But seriously,' said Ohio. 'Tell me –'

There was a shout as a pirate cried out in alarm. Looking to sea, they saw a Collosnon warship rounding a point of land. It was about five hundred paces away. Some of the crew cried out in panic.

'Stand fast!' shouted Ohio. 'We'll be afloat before long! Stand fast, you – we can outfight that ship. Stand fast!'

There were murmurs of protest still among the crew. With their ship stuck fast they were in a bad position, unable to manoeuvre. They had taken heavy casualties in their last battle. Under the circumstances, they had little stomach for facing up to the Collosnon yet again.

On the enemy ship a battle-banner was run up high. Marines on the deck could be seen arming and armouring. Then four harpoon-head arrows slammed into the deck of the *Skua*. Each was armspan-long; they had been hurled by arbalests, winch-cranked crossbows used most commonly in siege warfare.

The *Skua*'s crew began to take to the water. Ohio

shouted at them, but four more outsize bolts hit the deck. This time each was wrapped around with fiercely burning rags saturated with whale oil. Fires started. A few men tried to put them out. Then one was cut down by a crossbow bolt. The enemy ship was three hundred paces away and closing.

The death completed the rout of the pirates. Ohio was left standing on deck, bellowing obscenities at those who were fleeing. They were clumsy swimmers, most using dog-paddle; their labouring efforts disturbed the dog-brown seals which lay on rocks near the shore. The fire on the ship was now out of control.

'I could swear this ship is afloat,' said Ohio.

'It is,' said Hearst.

A small wave rocked the ship, scraping it against the rocks beneath. Only Miphon, Hearst, Blackwood and Ohio were left on deck. Four men could scarcely hope to put out the fire, let alone sail the ship.

'I'm going,' said Hearst, with a glance at the enemy craft. It was approaching slowly, with a man at the bows dropping a lead line to make sure the warship did not run aground on a shoal; it was too close for comfort.

Hearst, Miphon and Blackwood took the plunge to the cold shock of the sea. Burdened by clothes, boots and swords, they floundered through the bitter chill of the sea.

Ohio swore, then, drawing a knife, cut his thigh-high seaboots down to ankle length, then jumped. And was dragged straight down, for he wore a heavy treasure-belt at his waist. Ohio cut the belt free and bobbed up to the surface, a pauper. Trying to breathe, swear and spit out water at the same time, he almost drowned himself.

In the end, Ohio gained the shore, and, shivering uncontrollably, followed the other three up the tidal rocks, finding graspholds and footholds amidst slippery seaweed. Limpets and chitons clung to the rocks, armoured against the sea. Crabs retreated, some sidling into pools of water, others clattering into deep crevices.

Then the climbers reached the higher rocks, bare but for barnacles.

Ohio, gasping, sat down to catch his breath.

'You'd better hurry,' said Miphon to Ohio, 'or you'll never catch your crew.'

'What?' said Ohio. 'That cut-throat mob of Scourside eagermouths? What good's a crew without a ship? And where do they think they're running to? There's no fireside to the east for a hundred leagues. Would you run that way?'

'No,' said Hearst, getting the words out with difficulty because his teeth were chattering so hard. 'We'll go west.'

'Then I'll come with you, unless you object.'

'I don't mind,' said Miphon.

'The more swords the better,' said Hearst.

From the Collosnon ship came a shout:

'Sagresh!'

'I wish I knew what they were saying,' said Ohio.

'They're calling on us to surrender,' said Hearst. 'But they'll never catch us in the hills. Come on, let's go.'

They set off quickly to try to generate enough heat to warm themselves. Ahead lay a steep, rocky climb leading toward a high ridge. Mosses, lichens and stubborn salt-wind grasses grew amongst the rocks, but there was not a scrap of vegetation that could reasonably be considered as cover. The four knew they could be seen by the Collosnon, and that their progress would be followed closely; gaining the heights, they did not immediately try and hide, but instead turned to survey the shore.

The incoming tide had allowed the Collosnon warship to come right in beside the rocks of the shore.

'There's nobody ashore yet,' said Miphon.

'They won't follow us,' said Hearst. 'We've got too much of a start: they'd never catch us.'

But even as they watched, the ship started to disembark large white animals.

'Horses!' said Ohio.

'They must be dreaming,' said Miphon. 'They'll never get horses up that slope.'

'I don't think they're horses,' said Blackwood.

'I know a horse when I see one,' said Miphon. 'Even at this distance.'

Riders mounted up; a party of twenty turned east to follow the pirate crew, while eight started to make their way up the slope toward Hearst, Miphon, Ohio and Blackwood.

'Those aren't horses,' said Ohio.

'What did I tell you?' said Blackwood.

'They're the size of horses,' said Hearst, 'but they climb like goats. Miphon, what do they look like to you?'

Miphon listened, trying to catch the thoughts of the animals, but they were still far away. Besides, his powers were at a low ebb. He had been forever seasick on their voyaging, and had scarcely been able to practice the meditations at all.

'I don't know what they are,' said Miphon.

'Who cares?' said Ohio. 'Let's run!'

Inland, a few leagues south, mountains rose abruptly from a landscape of peat bogs, lakes, pools and tarns; the broken country in between, with its skull-smooth outcrops of grey rock, offered no vegetation of any height.

'If we can make it to the mountains,' said Blackwood, 'we'll be safe.'

'You go then,' said Hearst. 'I'll make my stand here. With luck I can hold them up long enough to give you a chance.'

'Don't be a fool,' said Ohio. 'For all we know, they'll turn back rather than chase us inland. Come on.'

And they began to run. There was only a light wind; there was no sound of bird or insect. Their feet went soft over grass and the worn-down nubs of rock outcroppings. Jogging south, they wasted no breath on talk.

Arriving at the top of a small bluff overlooking a tarn, they disturbed two gulls, which rose from the dark waters, leaving silent circles spreading ripple by ripple across the surface. The gulls wheeled silently overhead, grey feathers in flight in a grey sky, and then were gone.

The four scrambled down the rock face of the bluff and skirted round the edge of the tarn; underneath grass, mud quaked beneath their weight. Another slope confronted them; up they went.

The hunted men began to feel they were moving in a dream, where there was no end to the cool, odourless air, the black pools, the salt-wind grasses, the silent grey rocks and the grey sky reaching away to the horizon.

Then they heard the white riders hallooing behind them:

'Yo-dar! Yo-dar!'

'Sa-say!'

Then it was no dream any more: it was sweat, heat, strain and gut-wrenching effort as they tried to force themselves along faster. Finally they paused on a high point, panting, faces flushed, limbs shaking with fatigue.

'We can't outrun them,' said Miphon.

Hearst drew his sword.

'So it ends, then,' he said.

– So make a stand, song-singer, sword-master, leader of men. Make a stand, Hast, my hero, my brother in blood.

'Let's split up,' said Ohio. 'If we separate, one of us might get away, if we run quick enough.'

'You run,' said Hearst. 'I'll take my chances here.'

'If you take odds like that, I'll gamble against you any time,' said Ohio. 'Don't be a fool: run.'

The riders were having difficulty getting their animals down a slope that was almost sheer, but soon they would be past that obstacle.

'They will remember me as a brave man, at least,' said Hearst.

'I'd rather be remembered as an old man,' said Ohio.

'No chance of that,' said Hearst.

'Yes,' said Blackwood. 'There's still one chance.'

He held up the green bottle which they had been carrying with them, and which they had avoided entering for all these days, believing Elkor Alish to be waiting inside.

'If we go in there, we'll have to face Alish,' said Hearst.

'He's one man, we're four,' said Miphon. 'It's a good idea – the only idea. Come on.'

'What's this about?' said Ohio.

'Follow,' said Blackwood.

They left the high point and plunged down a slope, so they were out of sight of the pursuers. Blackwood threw the green bottle so it fell into the dark waters of a tarn.

'Ohio,' said Blackwood, 'Hold my shoulder.'

'Why?' said Ohio.

'Do as you're told.'

When they were all in contact, Miphon, who was wearing the ring commanding the green bottle, turned the ring.

Green went the world.

CHAPTER FORTY-ONE

'The man who rules this rules the world,' said Elkor Alish.

He held the death-stone in his hand; in the green bottle, it could do no harm.

'It's a greater thing for a man to learn to rule himself,' said Blackwood.

'So our woodsman plays philosopher,' said Alish. 'How did he come by such pretensions?'

They could talk freely and without fear: they were in separate halves of a room divided by a wall that was covered with carvings of wizards, warriors, dragons and creatures of the Swarms; a portcullis blocked the only way through that wall.

'Do you think me ignorant?' said Blackwood. 'I remember the council of war in Castle Diktat on the island of Ebonair, the battle of the Bluesky Waters, the wreck of the Dalmanasturn. I remember the Long War, the Empire of Wizards, the court of Talaman. You know what I know.'

Ohio hung back, watching. Miphon stood beside him, letting Hearst and Blackwood do the talking.

'What's this nonsense?' said Ohio. 'There's no castle on Ebonair. The Dalmanasturn is only a children's story. And what and where are the Bluesky Waters? And who was –'

'Listen,' said Miphon. 'We'll explain later.'

Elkor Alish was pacing backwards and forwards on the other side of the portcullis, declaiming in a loud voice:

'. . . then south to conquer. Ancient wrongs will be righted. The battle-banners of Rovac will fly from the towers of the Castle of Controlling Power. The Confederation of Wizards will be broken, destroyed.'

'You're mad,' said Hearst, and meant it.

'Mad?' said Elkor Alish. He laughed. 'No, Morgan, this isn't madness. It's destiny! In me you see the manifest destiny of Rovac. I have proof.'

'Proof?' said Hearst. 'And how did you come by it? From eating the moon and drinking salt water? Or –'

'Ahyak Rovac!' screamed Alish, drawing his sword.

Keen steel glittered in the gloom.

'I see,' said Hearst, 'that you've not yet lost your voice along with your sanity.'

'I found this sword,' said Alish, his voice hissing, 'deep in the red bottle.'

'It's a wonder that you can find anything,' said Hearst, 'seeing that you're navigating with your head stuck half way up your backside.'

Alish screamed at him:

'Ahyak Rovac!'

Echoes woke in the gloom of the green bottle. The sword swept toward the portcullis. Metal met metal with a rending scream. Fire blazed white and blue. Five bars of the portcullis, each as thick as a man's thumb, were cut through by that single sword-blow.

'Now bite off your prattling tongue,' said Alish, his voice intense. 'Or use it to name this blade.'

'Raunen Song,' said Hearst, unwillingly.

The sword figured in the Black Blood Legends, the song cycle telling of wrongs suffered by the people of Rovac, and past attempts to right them.

'That is one of its names,' said Alish. 'Arbiter is another – and it has others. But, yes, Raunen Song names it well. Look. See? Rune-writing on the blade. A death-pledge from our yesterdays.'

'Alish,' said Hearst, not knowing whether to laugh or cry. 'We're talking of ancient history. That was a different world. We're born into the daylight, not into the shadowland of memory.'

338

'You talk treason!'

'Treason?' cried Hearst, outraged. 'You talk of treason? You? An oath-breaker? You cost me my hand!'

'Yes! And you would have cost us a continent,' said Alish. 'You were too weak for our purposes. But now is your chance to serve your people. I've waited here for weeks, sleeping safe from assassins behind this portcullis – if it can be raised, I've not yet found the method – and I'm not disposed to wait any longer. Take the ring from the wizard so we can leave here.'

Slowly Hearst raised his right arm, bringing his steel hook up to the level of his face. The metal was green in the green light.

'First explain this.'

'I already have,' said Alish. 'A hand is a small price for a continent.'

'You broke your oath!'

'I was not born to serve my own words,' said Alish, his voice strong and clear, 'but to keep the oath sworn by my ancestors on this blade: Raunen Song. We have a dispensation for those times when we treat with the ancient enemy.'

'Oh yes? And to try to kill me along with the rest by using the death-stone?'

'You made an alliance with the enemy.'

'I took the same vows that you took. We walked in the same shadow: then you betrayed all of us. The only way for you to make amends is to yield up the death-stone. Now!'

Elkor Alish screamed:

'Ahyak Rovac!'

Tortured metal screamed as Raunen Song cut through another half-dozen bars of the portcullis.

'Cut your way through if you wish,' said Hearst. 'There's four of us and one of you.'

'Yes,' said Ohio, stepping forward. 'And whoever you are, my blade will be happy enough to bargain for your head.'

339

'Bargain,' said Alish, slowly, tasting the word. 'We could bargain, you know. Morgan, I can be gone from here any time I want.'

'He's lying!' said Miphon. 'There's no way out. If he starts down a drop-hole, the forces at work in the shaft will tear him from the walls and spit him out at the other end.'

Alish picked up the red bottle that was lying at his feet.

'I can do it, Morgan. I've found ropes and chains. I can lower this bottle down a drop-shaft. Then use this ring on my finger here to get inside the red bottle. Then use the ring again – and I'll be outside the red bottle, at the bottom of the drop-shaft.'

'Can he do it?' said Hearst, turning to Miphon.

'What do you think?' said Miphon.

'From there I'll have to climb,' said Alish. 'I'll be under the overhang of one of the wizard towers that rise from the walls of Castle Vaunting. It won't be easy, but I can do it.'

'You'd have done it already if you could,' said Hearst.

'No, Morgan. It would be death. The mad-jewel still commands Castle Vaunting; I lost the red charm that wards against it. When summer comes, a full year will have gone by. Then I can leave safely.'

'You'll never know when it's summer,' said Miphon.

'I count my sleeps,' said Alish. 'There may be an error, small or large, but if I err on the side of safety I'll survive. So you see, Morgan, I can leave before many months have passed. It's best that you give me the ring. Kill the wizard. Take it!'

'No,' said Hearst.

'Then give me the red charm from around your neck. Throw it to me. Then I can leave, now.'

'No,' said Hearst. 'We're going to Castle Vaunting. We'll set the flame trench ablaze so you'd burn if you tried to climb the castle walls. We'll keep it burning for

340

a thousand years if we have to. There'll be no way out of the bottle for you.'

'So you are a traitor,' said Alish. 'Argan is Rovac's rightful heritage – yet you deny your own people. What about you, stranger? Once I get out of here I can rule the world. Take your sword. Kill Hearst, and I can offer you – anything!'

'You're raving,' said Ohio.

'So rot you then,' said Alish. 'I'll get out of here, whether you help me or not. You'll see.'

Turning on his heel, Elkor Alish strode away. He went to the stairs that led downwards, closing the hatch after him.

The travellers searched for the mechanism that would raise the portcullis. At last Ohio found it, but even once the portcullis had been lifted, they still had to cut their way through a hatchway bolted against them. They went down the stairs cautiously in case Alish was waiting to ambush them.

In the big green room that had furniture set against the walls, they found one drop-hole with ropes and chains descending into it. Below, hanging in the open air, was a man-sized rope basket. They saw how Alish had escaped: the ring to get him into the red bottle, the ring again to get him out of it, the rope basket to catch him. He could have commanded the death-stone in the few moments before the mad-jewel overwhelmed him. The death-stone would soon destroy the mad-jewel, returning Alish to sanity.

'He had it all ready,' said Miphon.

'He must have been waiting for me,' said Hearst, his voice sombre. 'He wanted to win the green bottle too, if he could. He must have thought I would betray you.'

'What? After what he did in Stronghold Handfast?'

'His dreams are living his life for him,' said Hearst.

They hauled up the basket, with some difficulty, for the forces operating in the drop-shaft made it very heavy. Once it was inside the bottle, however, it proved to be very light; the ropes, woven together close enough to trap a stone egg, were grey and incredibly strong.

'It's stronger than woven steel,' said Miphon. 'It's from Ashmolea. It's arachnid silk.'

'What do you need to make that?' said Hearst.

'Patience,' said Ohio. 'And a lot of spiders.'

Ohio, examining the rope basket, found a few nodules of stone.

'Stone,' he said.

'Yes,' said Blackwood. 'When Alish used the death-stone, parts of the basket must have been just outside the protected circle.'

'So what's this death-stone?' said Ohio. 'And who is Alish?'

'Later,' said Hearst. 'Let's find some food first.'

* * *

'I wonder where Prince Comedo is,' said Miphon.

'Probably in the red bottle,' said Hearst. 'That's where I'd have kept him. He couldn't be trusted on the loose – he'd catch you asleep and open a smile in your throat.'

'Who's Prince Comedo?' said Ohio.

'A minor corpse-rapist of no particular importance,' said Hearst carelessly.

The legends of Argan held that it was the Noble Families of the Favoured Blood who had ended the tyranny of the Empire of Wizards, and that only these benefactors of humanity and their descendants were fit to rule in Argan; disaster would devastate any kingdom not governed by the Favoured Blood. Elkor Alish might well find Comedo a useful figurehead, if he was seriously bent on conquest.

'Look,' said Hearst, opening a jar. 'Pickles! They're still good.'

342

'So they should be,' said Miphon. 'They've not yet been here a year.'

Hearst took a pickle then offered the jar to Miphon, to Blackwood, then to Ohio.

'Thanks,' said Ohio. 'This place is amazing. I've heard of nothing like it, not in all my wanderings. It must be worth . . . well . . ."

'Do you want to buy it?' said Hearst.

'What will you sell it for?'

'What can you offer? It's worth at least a small kingdom.'

'I had a small kingdom once,' said Ohio.

'Did you now?' said Hearst, opening a jar of jam. He scooped it out with his fingers. Strawberry jam. Sweet, sweet.

'Yes,' said Ohio. 'A nice little kingdom.'

'Where was it?' said Hearst. 'East of Ork? South of Brine?'

'No,' said Ohio. 'It was in the west. It was the kingdom of Talajar which lies in the Ravlish Lands.'

'I've heard of it,' said Hearst. 'There's a trading route by sea from there to Chi-ash-lan, in the Cold West.'

'You know it well,' said Ohio, greeding into another pickle.

'Yes,' said Hearst, 'I've done my own share of wandering.'

'This kingdom,' said Miphon. 'Were you born to it or did you acquire it?'

'Truth is, I acquired it,' said Ohio. 'Not alone – my brother Menator helped me, first to gain it, then to rule it. But we had a falling out. A quarrel over a woman. It ended with war.'

'And?'

'Our battles were interrupted by an invasion from the north, which pushed us both to the sea. Taking what ships we could, we sailed east to Argan. Menator sailed on down the coast, going south, while I chose the Eastern Ocean.'

343

'Where's Menator now?' said Hearst.

'I can't say,' said Ohio. 'But it's a small enough world. I'll find him.'

'When you lost your kingdom, did you ever think of going back to your own people?' said Miphon.

'What kind of woman's talk is that?' said Hearst.

Ohio laughed.

'Not so fierce, friend Hearst, not so fierce. Our own people? No, we couldn't have gone back. They were Galish merchants, so they could be anywhere on the Salt Road between Chi'ash-lan and the Castle of Controlling Power. But even if I could find them, that's no life for me. Always dickering-bartering with narrow-eyed sharpers, the rain wet, the hail cold, then the souther you get the hotter – dust, sweat, stink and muddy water-holes.'

'A pirate's life is hard,' said Miphon.

'You're fierce for the truth,' said Ohio. 'Well, it's a simple story: some of us were born for battle, and I'm one of them. That's my story told – but yours, I warrant, is rather more fancy.'

'Yes,' said Miphon. 'But it would take some telling.'

'We've got time,' said Ohio. 'The Collosnon know we must be hiding somewhere. They'll wait. A day, perhaps – or longer.'

'Settle yourself then,' said Hearst, 'and I'll begin.'

CHAPTER FORTY-TWO

Miphon, Hearst, Blackwood and Ohio went west on foot toward Skua, going as fast as they could over the broken country, retreating to the green bottle only when the weather became atrocious; they knew that every delay favoured Elkor Alish.

Eventually they arrived at Skua, the only harbour on the coast of Trest. The Collosnon had raised a small fort to house a token garrison, and had planted thickets of cold-climate sprite bamboo, notable for its grey leaves. Otherwise, they had made little mark on the place, except by building a breakwater to protect the minimal harbour.

The travellers, eager for news and for fresh food, ventured into town and asked their way to an inn. The locals spoke their own dialect, a degenerate version of Estral; Ohio could not follow it at all, but the other three could make themselves understood.

The inn was a dark place with a low ceiling; it stank of raw spirit. On the floor were the tattered ruins of what had once been a master-work tapestry, a story of courage and heroism done in fifty colours, but now torn and sea-stained: pirate booty, no doubt. Half a dozen tough, scar-faced men sat in the shadows watching the newcomers. Hung on one wall was the silvery coiled shell of a nautilus, a thing of grace and beauty completely unexpected in such a place.

'What hassing you?' said the innkeeper.

'Have you a room?' said Hearst.

'A room we have, but have you the wherefore? The dreamstay dark is free, so they say, but they roof costs here as they ever.'

345

'We have money,' said Hearst.

He displayed a fist-full of bronze triners, part of a coin-hoard found in the green bottle. The innkeeper took one and turned it over, peering at it dubiously.

'This is the brayoz, as we call he, but has you mynt?'

'Mynt?' said Hearst.

'Yes, mynt, mynt!'

'How about this?' said Miphon, displaying a silver ilavale.

'No, no,' said the innkeeper impatiently. 'Not yoller, it's not yoller we're wanting: have you mynt?'

'Is it gold you're wanting?' said Hearst.

'God, god, yes, that's a name for it.'

'We have no gold,' said Hearst.

In fact, they had gold sanarands by the dozen: but Hearst did not think it wise to display such wealth here in Skua.

'What's the problem?' said Ohio.

'Silver's not good enough for them,' said Hearst.

'Come on then, let's get out of here.'

'I don't want to spend another night in that bottle,' said Hearst.

'Neither do I,' said Blackwood, who hated being shut inside those glowing green walls, where there was never a breath of wind and never a sound of the living world.

'Come on,' said Ohio. 'There's no point in staying here. Come on, do what I say.'

Ohio hustled the others out of the inn and onto the street; before they had gone a dozen paces the innkeeper was calling them back.

'Don't listen to him,' said Ohio. 'Don't turn back.'

Ohio did not relent until the innkeeper had followed them a hundred paces down the road, and had agreed that a single piece of silver would cover food, drink and lodging for the night for the four of them.

*   *   *

The four sat round a fire in the inn that evening, listening to the local gossip. They learnt that the Collosnon, having lost thousands of men on their first attempt to conquer Trest and Estar, had abandoned their attempt to invade Argan, and, for the time being, were content to maintain their little garrison in Skua.

Of the rest of the world, there was little news; few travellers came to Skua, so the town made its own entertainment. Drinking proved a popular sport. After supper, which was a local dish known as widow's memory – it was comprised chiefly of sausages – the travellers managed, after some argument, to extract a ration of beer from the landlord.

About then, a storyteller announced a recital of one of the more popular stories told in Skua, the legend of Morgan Hearst, the Dragonslayer from Rovac.

'Dragonslayer?' said Ohio, turning to stare at Hearst; though Ohio had been told much, he had been fed no stories of dragons and the killing of the same.

'Quiet,' said Hearst, 'and listen to what they have to say.'

The storyteller, well primed with drink, stood on a table, looked around, burped, swayed, grabbed a roof-beam for balance, then in a loud voice began to declaim his story:

Now stay your pratling chete, I say,
And soft to listen long,
A gentry cofe I mayn't be,
But truth is in me gan:
Yes, truth is in me gan, me lads,
And in me gan a tale.
Now stow you, stow you, hark and hear:
It starts upon a night, I say,
I starts upon a night.
The darkmans is for some to stew,
For some it is to nygle,
For some the dice, for some the cup,

347

To bouse till lightmans come,
But Morgan Hearst rode out that night,
Through dewse a vyle rode he,
Along the hygh pad to the mount:
Maf he called it he.

He girt no shield, he girt no sword,
But strength walked strong with he,
For strong his teeth and wide his smile:
A grin he made it he.
A man of men, a menner man,
No fear he had it he.

No pannam had he none, no none of pek,
As climbed he height on height
Till he was from the ground too tall to towre.

Hearst took a pull on his drink and swallowed it
down. There was a strange taste to it, but one could
hardly expect the best brewing in Skua. He remembered
the fear of the climb, and his own drunken boasting
afterwards. Once, he had longed to be worshipped as
the world's hero. That seemed, now, like something
which had happened in another lifetime.

He drank some more.

'Pour that away,' said Blackwood. 'There's something wrong with it.'

'What?' said Hearst, taking another mouthful.

'There's some kind of scum in it. Maybe a fungus.'

'A little mould never hurt anyone,' said Hearst, and
swallowed down some more.

What were they saying now?

He listened:

Draugon glymmar lit the cave:
A draugon lay it there.
Now beast of beasts a draugon is,
A scream would tell him well,

348

For long on sharp his crashing chetes,
And strong his stampes are.
But Morgan Hearst he had no fear,
No fear he had it he.

He had sought fame, and this was what it came to: a
drunken story roared out by the local talent to a pack of
inebriated thieves and fishermen in a stagnant garrison
town on the edge of the world.

What should Morgan Hearst rightly be famous for?

For leading men to their death at the hands of the
wizard Heenmor; for being fooled by the spy Haveros,
then failing to bring that oath-breaker to justice; for
failing to prevent the slaughter of the Melski in Rausch
Valley; for running from Heenmor at Ep Pass. And,
since the betrayal at Stronghold Handfast: for failing to
do his duty, which was to mark his sword with a death-
pledge demanding the death of Elkor Alish.

Hearst drank, and listened:

Now Hearst, his fambles held a spear,
And stepped he forward he;
He strove his arm to forward throw
To pierce the draugon ee.
A bellow did the draugon make,
A roar he made it he,
And glymmar from his gan outforth
As threshed and struggled he.

Morgan Hearst was on his feet. The shadows roared
around him, red, purple, black. Knives sang inside his
skull. Faces split to white alarm as steel flared in his
hand.

'Lies!' he shouted. 'It's all lies!'

Bones moved in the shadows. A cold moon shaped
itself to a skull. He saw Gorn, blood on his lips, death in
the sockets of his eyes.

'Lies!' he shouted.

349

Chips of wood flew as his sword splintered something that was thrusting for his face. He wheeled. The fire billowed up, out, open: he stood on the top of a cliff looking out across a thousand years of flame. Knives sang inside the fire. Men were swarming out of the flames toward his strongpoint. They were the legions of the dead.

'Come for me then,' whispered Hearst. 'Come for me.'

And he lept to meet the first, steel making steel scream, and there was blood in the scream. The blood darkened the world. There was a door in the darkness. Hearst plunged through the door. He was in a street, with buildings towering up around him, limitless pinnacles reaching for the sky.

He knew where he was: in the city of Chi'ash-lan. The night watch was making for him. In the darkness, their honour-pennants flared orange. His sword cut free in a wild arc. Blood opened green to the darkness.

Clouds underfoot as he ran, flight foot feathering the ground away. Thunder crashed underground. He screamed, answering a challenge with the echo of a forgotten voice:

'Ahyak Rovac!'

Then the visions were gone, and he was down on his face in the mud, down in the cold, with something huge murnering and slurping as it ludged toward him, lopsloss, yes, it had to be a lopsloss –

But it was only a sow in a pig-pen.

*   *   *

Shortly before sunrise, the others found Hearst in a farmyard on the outskirts of Skua. They bundled him into the green bottle and were off and away, as fast as they could go.

Whatever drug, poison or ergot had been in the drink that had been served to them in Skua, it had turned

Morgan Hearst wild and mad for half the night: all of Skua was sheltering behind barred doors after seventeen men had been wounded trying to disarm him.

By the time Skua recovered its courage and ventured outdoors, the travellers had gone, leaving no tracks behind them. Shortly a new song joined the local repertoire: 'The Ballad of the Four Mad Ghosts from the Desolate East'.

CHAPTER FORTY-THREE

Ohio, Hearst and Miphon sat on the banks of the Hollern River while Blackwood talked with half a dozen Melski on a solitary raft.

Since reaching Estar, they had already met with a leper, a bedraggled deserter, and a one-legged man on crutches who had refused to give an account of himself. It seemed that Estar lay desolate, its people dead or dispersed.

Already they knew that there was no hope of Blackwood finding Mystrel in Lorford – the ruins were abandoned – and little chance of them encountering anyone elsewhere who might know if she had survived. If the Melski could not say where she might be, then Blackwood had no hope of finding her.

The talk went this way and that for a long time. Eventually, Blackwood, looking heavy-hearted, rejoined the others. Miphon and Ohio were asleep in the weak spring sunlight.

'What do they say?' said Hearst.

Ohio and Miphon woke easily, without surprise. Only those who live safe within four walls can indulge in the deep unresponsive sleep which mimics opium stupor; those who follow the trails of the wild learn to be responsive even when dreaming, making the transition of wakeful alertness instantly, without so much as a yawn or a murmur.

'They say all through last summer none could venture within leagues of Castle Vaunting, for there was madness there.'

'And now?'

'They cannot say. No Melski will chance going

further downriver than this. They have lost too many people to the madness.'

'I always understood,' said Miphon, 'that the madness only affected humans.'

'Then you, perhaps, will have to broaden your notions of humanity,' said Blackwood.

'Have there been any convoys on the Salt Road?' said Hearst.

'The Melski have seen none, which means certainly none have travelled down the Hollern River.'

'What else did they say?' said Hearst.

'Nothing.'

'You were talking a long time to say very little,' said Hearst.

'They are a formal people,' said Blackwood. 'Besides, I had some . . . some history to narrate to them.'

'Was that wise?' said Hearst.

'They had a right to know.'

'Yes, but was it wise to tell them?'

'There is a wisdom which concerns survival of the self,' said Blackwood. 'And there is a greater wisdom which is concerned with survival of things greater than the self.'

Hearst and Ohio exchanged glances. Hearst shrugged; Ohio grimaced.

'Come on then,' said Hearst. 'Let's be moving. There's not much daylight left.'

*   *   *

Walking through riverside forest, Blackwood remembered coming this way on other days in other years. Overhead the sky was blue:

Sky, blue sky, the colour of my lover's eyes;
Leaf, young leaf, her hands no softer.

He remembered leading wizards and Rovac warriors

353

through the forest to where Heenmor had worked his magic. At the time, thinking these affairs had nothing to do with him, he had agreed to do the job simply to secure his release from Prince Comedo's dungeons.

But now, he, too, was committed to this quest. Blackwood remembered the butchery on the Fleuve River: Elkor Alish had done that. Now Alish was loose in the world with the death-stone. He must not be allowed to use it!

Many battlefields commanded by a hero's sword had seen carnage the stars might weep at, but the death-stone was a weapon more terrible than any forged from steel because it killed everything. After such violence, only silence and desolation remained: no voice of bird, no blade of grass, no spinneret spider to span space with instinctive architecture, no earth-sure badger, no mesh-wing honey bee.

It could not be allowed.

Blackwood, cursed with double knowledge, with an acute empathy for both the hunter and the prey, suffered more than any of the others at the thought of what the death-stone could do.

* * *

Five leagues from Castle Vaunting, they stopped for the night. Miphon, taking off his red charm, found no mad-jewel overpowered his mind. That confirmed what they already knew: Alish had used the death-stone, destroying the mad-jewel. Hearst sent Ohio off on a twilight scouting mission, to make sure there were no lepers, deserters or other riff-raff within threatening distance of their camp site.

With Ohio gone, the others gathered firewood and built a rough lean-to shelter for the night. Ohio returned by starshine; he had a prisoner with him, a young and frightened man who sat silent and sullen when Ohio turned him loose.

'Don't make any sudden movements,' said Ohio, 'or you'll excite friend Blackwood here. I've lost his leash, so I'll have the devil of a job restraining him if he tries to eat you.'

The young man cringed.

'What's your name, boy?' said Hearst, with raw-nerve violence in his voice.

Ohio chuckled.

'Peace, friend Hearst. We've no need to beat him to his bones for information. I've seen his friends – five hunters, camped downstream just a little. This rabbit here was strutting round the countryside with a sling-shot. His rope-soled shoes and the splicing on the belt holding up his pantaloons betray him as a sailor-boy, probably a cabin boy.'

'I'm no cabin boy,' said the young man, suddenly recovering his voice and his nerve. Mine is an Orfus blade. I'm a blooded blade of the free marauders.'

'Really,' said Ohio. 'I wonder if his captain knows his cabin boy thinks himself a full-fledged reaver.'

'My captain's Abousir Belench,' said their captive. 'He's captain three-five prime under our sealord Menator.'

'Menator?' said Ohio. 'I've heard of a famous pimp by that name, and a famous thief – but never a sealord.'

'You'll know him well enough when he has the skin flayed off your backs. We've five ships anchored at Lorford to do Menator's work. He's the sword from the north, you know. You must have heard of him.'

'Is he a bald man with a broken nose and a blue rose tattooed on his left cheek?' said Ohio.

'Yes,' said their captive. 'You know him, then?'

'He's my brother,' said Ohio.

'Sure,' said the young man, 'and the skua gull shits gold and silver. Tell me another one.'

'Believe what you like,' said Ohio. 'I don't care. So this Menator rules the Orfus pirates now, does he?'

'Yes,' said the young man, now getting positively

stroppy. 'He's lord of the Greater Teeth. He'll have you torn to bits. Nobody can stand against him. He's made us conquerors. This winter we took Stokos. Next, Runcorn: then there'll be no power in all of Argan strong enough to hold us.'

'Bold words, my sprig,' said Ohio.

'True words,' said the young man. 'You made a mistake taking me prisoner.'

'You gave me no chance to hide,' said Ohio. 'If I hadn't taken you prisoner, your fellows might be hunting me by now.'

'They'll hunt you anyway, come the morning. They'll know I'm missing.'

Hearst got to his feet.

'Blackwood. Ohio. Miphon. And you, boy – on your feet. Gather wood. Lay fires, each fire twenty paces apart. I want each of us to lay ten fires.'

Blackwood began to protest:

'But that's ridiculous, we should –'

'No, Blackwood,' said Ohio sharply, 'We're not going to let you eat the boy. Not unless he tries to run away.'

Ohio saw Hearst's plan – and so, as they set to work, did Blackwood. After a lot of labour, the fires were laid. They lit them. Then, with burning brands, they set fire to half a dozen trees as well. From a distance, there would be so much light in the forest that one would have to guess that an army was camping there.

* * *

Morning dawned grey and cold, with a light rain falling; the sunlight of the day before was just a memory. They broke camp and moved cautiously west, until they could see Lorford in the distance. There were no ships there. The pirates had left.

'They've gone!' said their captive.

'What did you expect?' said Hearst. 'Did you think

they'd worry about you when they had the safety of five ships to think about?'

'You see?' said Ohio. 'A cabin boy isn't that important.'

'I'm not a cabin boy!'

'Maybe not,' said Ohio, 'But in any case it doesn't matter. Blackwood, I've changed my mind. We'll let you eat him after all.'

At that, their captive bolted and ran. Ohio laughed to see him sprinting away; the last they saw, he was jogging along beside the river in the direction of the sea.

'That wasn't very kind,' said Blackwood quietly.

'Kind!' roared Ohio. 'Other pirates would have raped him then cut him up for fish bait.'

Blackwood – briefly – contemplated the idea of delivering an extended lecture on ethics, then – wisely – abandoned the notion.

* * *

When they reached the first stonemade ground, Hearst started to count out paces. He wanted to know how much ground the death-stone commanded; that knowledge might one day mean the difference between life and death.

They climbed Melross Hill and crossed the drawbridge: wooden beams, iron nails and steel chains now rendered in stone. Inside the castle, the wealth of gold, weapons, tapestries and precious stones had been similarly affected; they found the mad-jewel itself, a useless chunk of rock lying near a stonemade skeleton.

There was no sign of Elkor Alish.

'Perhaps he slipped when he tried to climb the castle walls,' said Miphon. 'Perhaps he fell.'

'I doubt it,' said Hearst.

They spent two days searching the castle for a sign, a clue or a message – finding nothing. Ohio was awed by the size of this wizard fortress; Argan had always been the place for wizards, and there were no such castles in the Ravlish Lands. But Miphon told him that Castle Vaunting was nothing compared to the Castle of Controlling Power by the flame trench Drangsturm, on the border between the Far South and the Deep South – to which they must now make their way, to alert the Confederation of Wizards to the disasters which had befallen them.

CHAPTER FORTY-FOUR

South, then.

Spring rains and wasting winds; the everlast road outlasting daylight. Gaunt ruins of a fallen temple. The mountain of Maf looming in the east. In the hamlet of Delve, sour-faced peasants with stories of marauding Collosnon deserters, bandits and inland-seeking pirate bands. Further south, the Rohm Mountains rearing abrupt battlements against the horizon. The sea, and a tricky hot-mud crossing of a gently respiring flame trench.

From the coast of Dybra, a view of the cliffbuilt islands of the Greater Teeth; Ohio talked of seeking passage to the pirate islands, but there was no boat to take them there. Besides, the closer he got to his brother Menator, the more he seemed to doubt the wisdom of trusting to his brother's mercy.

In Nerja, capital city of Dybra – in truth, a small town of a thousand souls – a dying king wasting away in a deserted castle spoke of a hero who had stolen away his men, inflaming their hearts with rhetoric which promised power, glory, women and wealth. In Chorst, the hero had recruited all the able men in Guntagona.

Nearing Runcorn, the travellers heard that the city had surrendered to a rag-tag army led by the reaver from the west, the Rovac warrior Elkor Alish. Closer to Runcorn, they came upon a battlefield littered with the stonemade bodies of men and horses: Elkor Alish had used the death-stone, doubtless sheltering his own men in the red bottle while he commanded that power against his enemies.

The travellers did not approach Runcorn directly,

but camped in hills outside the city. Ohio, guising himself as a Galish merchant, travelled into Runcorn on his own, bearing as trade goods quantities of siege dust and arachnid silk recovered from the depths of the green bottle.

He returned to bring them a detailed account of the activities of the conqueror of Runcorn, Elkor Alish. After defeating that city's army with the death-stone, Alish had installed his motley army of peasants and fishermen in the city. He was now busy recruiting cavalry and infantry from the Lezconcarnau Plains, otherwise known as the Plains of the Wild Horses, rich grazing lands between the Rohm Mountains and the Spine Mountains, occupying the hinterland of Runcorn.

Once Alish had gathered together an army sufficient to garrison the cities of the Harvest Plains, he would doubtless march south: he had already sent envoys to demand the surrender of those southern lands.

CHAPTER FORTY-FIVE

The sleeping man stirred, and muttered something unintelligible. Then he cried out as pain lanced home. Opened his eyes, spoke:

'You!'

And could say no more.

His eyes widened in something resembling panic.

'Don't worry,' said Hearst, holding up a blood-tipped needle. 'The point was poisoned, but it won't kill you. Miphon prepared it for me. He knows what he's doing.'

Hearst looked around the room, which was lit by a single beeswax candle. Flame melted time, silently, remorselessly.

'You've made yourself comfortable,' said Hearst.

He drew aside a curtain. The window beyond was open to the night. He saw lights in the streets spread out below this high tower, and lights on ships anchored in the harbour of Runcorn. He closed the shutters against the night.

'You know,' said Hearst, turning back to his victim, 'I still don't know why you did it. I've thought about it many times, but I still don't understand. So why did you do it, Alish?'

Elkor Alish, paralysed, made no answer.

Hearst fingered the death-stone. It was cool beneath his touch. He picked it up.

'Was it this that tempted you? Power? But you could have had that in the Cold West.'

The death-stone kicked in his hand like a living heart. Hearst set it down.

'Or was it more than mere power that tempted you? Did you think to make yourself a god?'

Alish closed his eyes.

'If that's what tempted you, it's probably impossible anyway. You know as well as I do about Words of Enhancement, Guiding, Command and Reversal. Remember Stronghold Handfast? We found Heenmor, turned to stone. Why? How? Perhaps he was trying to use those Words to perfect his command of the death-stone. Whatever experiments he tried, one of them killed him.'

If Hearst could have been assured that his words were having some effect, he might have stopped then. But Alish, paralysed by poison, could not say or betray what he felt. Hearst's only hope was to go on and on, hoping that his words would be sufficient to enlighten the man he had once counted as his friend.

'Miphon says the death-stone may, perhaps, kill anyone who uses it in any but the simplest ways. Possibly there's no way for a man to use it to become a god. So don't let the prospect tempt you – and don't have me followed when I leave here, for I'll use the death-stone if I have to.

'Not that I want to. Look at our lives. Blood and slaughter. What good has it done us? Once I thought the warrior's road led to glory, but now . . . betrayed by my best friend. My right hand gone. In my dreams, the faces of dead men. A legend in my own time – but I get no pleasure from hearing the songs they sing of me.

'Men call me a hero but what good's that when I see the dead in my dreams? Men who died because my leadership failed. And now? Enough. I go south with the death-stone, and you . . . best you return to Rovac. And as for the old stories, old legends, ancient wrongs . . . forget about them.

'Because if you really live to remedy history, then you really are mad. Every man, sometimes, in a battle or after it, may hesitate and wonder if what he does is right. And then: it's good to know our people have suffered. Thinking of ourselves as victims of an unforgivable wrong, we're free to follow the way of the sword with clear minds. We can blame the wizards, who forced our ancestors off their land – forgetting that we've made our own choices since then.

'Alish, those old tales are just excuses for murder. Nobody on Rovac gives half a shit for the lands round the Ocean of Cambria. Rovac's been our home for thousands of years. Rovac! That's home! Not some place in the south of Argan that we've never seen in our lives.

'I know there are others who think as you do. I know you're a member of the Code of Night – and we both know that on Rovac the Code of Night is something of a joke, and for good reason. Even if we did destroy the wizards, to take back our ancestral lands we'd have to kill all the people who have settled there over the last four thousand years.'

Hearst paused, sighting a handsome document drafted in black ink on vellum. He picked it up, and read it through. It was addressed to the Ruling Council of Rovac, and it commanded the armies of Rovac to battle. It spoke of Raunen Song, the death-stone and the red bottle; it spoke of the conquest of Runcorn and also of the conquest of the Greater Teeth and the Harvest Plains.

'Interesting,' said Hearst. 'You boast of conquests you've yet to make – still, no doubt, given the chance, you'd have conquered all by the time this ink reached Rovac. Given the promises you make, perhaps the fleets of Rovac would have sailed here. But the plunder of cities would be what drew them, not any thoughts of ancient wrongs and the justice of history.'

Hearst tore the document apart. Alish opened his eyes, gazed on the torn vellum, then closed his eyes again.

'As you know, I'm taking the death-stone south. And the red bottle. As for Raunen Song . . . I can't trust you with even that much power.'

363

Hearst remembered the sword cutting apart the steel bars of the portcullis in the green bottle. He took it and held it high. He spoke Words of Unbinding which Miphon had taught him. The room was flooded with violet light as energies flared from the blade.

'There,' said Hearst, laying the sword down beside Alish. 'Strength has gone out of the world. It's a better place without it. Keep the blade. And remember my mercy: I let you live.'

Alish, opening his eyes again, tried to speak – but failed.

'What do you want to tell me?' said Hearst. 'What went wrong? I wish I knew. There's a breach between us now: yet once it was as if we were of the same flesh.

'I don't know what went wrong, but I know when it happened. It was at Larbreth, wasn't it? Yes. I remember. You were held captive. None of us knew your fate. Day followed day: a long siege. Then you opened the city gates to give us our chance. We pressed home the attack.

'I found that woman, Ethlite. Yes. She lay on her bed; she was very weak. She'd been sick for some reason. She said she couldn't see properly: I think she thought I was you. Anyway, she tried to command me. She spoke as if she owned you. She spoke . . . not in a tone of command . . . but as one speaks to a person trusted to obey to the point of death and a little bit beyond. She spoke as if you were her creature.

'She asked for help. I drew my sword – I helped her, you can count on that. I took her head. Remember that, Alish. Think about that when I'm gone. My thoughts were all for you: I myself took revenge against her.

'I don't know what terror, what torture she used to break you to your knees. But we all know that anyone can be broken. Still, you gave us the city. If there was any way . . . Alish, I wake by night, in the darkness, and I'm alone. Every person I've ever valued is dead . . .

some by my sword. I could kill you now, but too many are dead already.

'Think about what I've said, Alish. You'll have plenty of time to think. It'll be daylight before that poison wears off. Apart from anything else, think about how easily I got to you. Of course, the green bottle gave me an easy way over walls and through bars. And Miphon made poisoned needles for me – three of your guards are in the same state as yourself.

'Not everyone has my advantages – but think about all the things that were in this room. Raunen Song, the death-stone, the red bottle – all worth killing for. Sooner or later, your own earth-scum guards would have cut your throat to claim them.

'And if you planned to use Prince Comedo as a figurehead for your conquests, even he would have plotted against you sooner or later. You must realise that. I've taken what would have tempted others, but at least I've left you alive. Others wouldn't have been so kind. Think on that when I'm gone, Alish.'

Hearst put the death-stone into a small leather bag. He picked up the leather bag and the red bottle, turned the ring that he wore on one finger – turned it with his teeth, since he could not turn it with his hook hand – and was inside the green bottle. Hearst left the death-stone and the red bottle there, then returned to Alish's chambers.

'I'll leave you now,' said Hearst. 'Don't try and follow us. We've got fast horses – we've stolen your best. And there's death waiting for anyone who follows us.'

*   *   *

Hearst rejoined Miphon, Blackwood and Ohio outside the walls of Runcorn.

'How did it go?' said Ohio.

'It went just as we planned.'

'You took a long time.'

'I was being careful.'

'We were worried.'

'No need to be. Come on, let's go. The more distance we've covered by daylight, the better.'

They set off in darkness, heading south along the Salt Road toward the distant city of Selzirk, capital of the Harvest Plains. Hearst decided that, on reaching Selzirk, he would leave Miphon and travel back to Rovac. He had fulfilled his oath: he had delivered the death-stone to Miphon for Miphon to take south.

He was free.

CHAPTER FORTY-SIX

They travelled south through the flatlands of the Harvest Plains, sheltering in mud-dirt villages which, as they neared Selzirk, slowly became towns. As the prospect of pursuit became increasingly remote, they relaxed. They bought new boots, new clothes, and more food than was good for them. They risked their gold in taverns and elsewhere; Ohio and Hearst were almost killed in a brothel-brawl in a place called Kelebes, but other than that the country proved hospitable.

Miphon, who had been this way before, lectured them at length about the dams and irrigation canals that drew water from the Velvet River. All dams were upstream of Selzirk, leaving the river between Selzirk and the port of Androlmarphos free for navigation by shallow-bottomed trading galleys.

Miphon went on to discuss local law, labour tax, art, poetry, song, industry and agriculture – at length. Hearst retaliated with infinitely detailed stories of the birdlife of Rovac and the combat cults of Chi'ash-lan, but Miphon, though he became irritated at Hearst's prolixity, failed to take the hint.

In the end, Ohio spoke bluntly, and silenced the pair of them. But, after that, there were arguments about stupid things such as when to stop for lunch. Without hardship and danger to unify them, they were, really, a disparate bunch of people.

For Ohio, everything lay in the future. He'd decided not to go to his brother Menator as a beggar; instead, he'd south to the great trading city of Narba, and set up in business. For Hearst, everything lay in the past: he was a ruined, crippled veteran, a man who had lost his hope, his friends, and all sense of purpose.

Blackwood, who had realised by now that the everyday savagery of human society was too much for his heightened sensitivity to bear, thought to follow Miphon to the Castle of Controlling Power, there to see if he could find a wizard to tell him how to blunt his perceptions of the pain and suffering of the world. Now that he knew Mystrel was dead, his only responsibility was to himself.

Of the four, only Miphon still carried the burdens of heavy responsibility. Though Hearst had not announced his plans, Miphon realised, none the less, that the Rovac warrior did not intend to go south with him beyond Selzirk. Yet, from that city, it would be five hundred leagues to the Castle of Controlling Power – and that was as the crow flies, it would be longer by road.

And, once Miphon actually delivered the death-stone to the Confederation of Wizards at the Castle of Controlling Power, it would still have to be returned to the Dry Pit. Which would be a dangerous journey all on its own. And then some way would have to be found to ensure that no wizard ever again followed Heenmor's footsteps into the Dry Pit.

How?

For that question, he had no answer.

*　　*　　*

They closed with Selzirk on an afternoon when the spring weather was hinting at the heat of the summer to come.

'That's a big city,' said Hearst, studying the prospect of walls and soaring towers. 'Some of the towers look like they were built by wizards.'

'They were,' said Miphon. 'In the Long War, wizards raised a castle here, on the northern side of the river.

Now the gatehouse keep of that castle is part of the palace of the king-maker, Farfalla. Many bridges span the fire dyke, and as you can see the wizard castle is only a small part of the city.'

'I hope we don't run into trouble there.'

'We won't,' said Miphon. 'The people of the Harvest Plains are very hospitable.'

'At Kelebes – ' began Hearst.

'You were drunk,' said Miphon. Then: 'And not for the first time, either. I have to tell you that neither your brain nor your liver benefit from – '

'Oh, nara zabara jok,' said Hearst, which, in the Trading Tongue, was obscene in the extreme.

'Should I bash your heads together till your brains splinter?' said Ohio. 'Or just cut your tongues out?'

'Peace,' said Blackwood, pained by this exchange. 'Let's plan out what we'll do if we do meet danger.'

'We won't,' said Miphon, demonstrating – not for the first time – a wizard's need to be seen as an expert. 'I've been this way before. I know this place.'

'There's been a lot of fish in the net since then,' said Hearst. 'With Alish holding Runcorn and threatening invasion, they're bound to be suspicious.'

'Then we'd better not try to avoid the city,' said Ohio, 'or they'll think us spies for sure.'

'Well then,' said Hearst. 'Let's do what we can – which means stay alert and take precautions. I'll carry the death-stone. Miphon, you take the green bottle and the ring commanding it. And Blackwood – the red bottle and the ring for that.'

'I'd rather not,' said Blackwood.

'No?' said Hearst. 'Then Ohio can carry it. Let's arrange that now.'

They did so, then went on toward the city. On either side of the road, bentbacked peasants were working in a leisurely rhythm in fields of rape and panic.

Hearst watched a barefoot boy shooting at small birds in a fallow field. The boy had a stave bow; he shot arrows into the air so they climbed high then plunged down, skewering their targets and pinning them to the ground. Hearst noted that the range was extreme and the archer's accuracy was excellent.

* * *

The travellers were entering Selzirk by the northern gate when the challenge rang out:

'Azat!'

A moment later, soldiers grabbed the reins of their horses. Then the gate commander stepped forward. Lurking behind him was a furtive, anxious individual, a man Hearst knew he should recognise from somewhere.

He cast about for a name.

Erhed! Yes, that was it. Erhed, one of Prince Comedo's soldiers who had deserted in dragon country deep in the interior of Argan.

'You,' said the gate commander, in the Galish Trading Tongue. 'Come with me.'

Hearst glanced around. The gate commander had numbers on his side, but it might be possible to intimidate him. Hearst put his hand to the hilt of his sword:

'Who are you to command me?'

'My name is Watashi,' said the gate commander. 'I'm eldest son of the kingmaker, Farfalla, highest power in the Harvest Plains. Mark me well: I'm the best swordsman in Selzirk, and my blade is faster than yours.'

Hearst judged the boast to be true. Clearly Watashi was a young man, about twenty-five years of age, but there were battle-scars on his face; his voice and stance indicated that he had the habit of command. He looked tough, capable, relaxed and dangerous.

'I've been here before,' said Miphon. 'Then, Farfalla's eldest son was Sarazin Sky.'

'So men have called me,' said the gate commander.

'But names may change with the times. Watashi is my name now, as I have told you. Come.'

Hearst hesitated.

'Let's go with him,' said Ohio. 'He's not polite, but at least nobody's drawn a weapon. And think of it – the ruler's son doesn't stand watch on the gate unless for something the ruler wants badly.'

'We'll come with you,' said Hearst. 'We'll let you take us to Farfalla.'

'Dismount, then,' said Watashi, who, Hearst saw, was unimpressed by the ease at which the travellers had divined his immediate intentions.

As they followed Watashi on foot, with a squad of guards behind them, Hearst murmured to Miphon:

'What does Watashi mean?'

Miphon sorted through the few dozen words of the language of the Harvest Plains which he knew:

'It means blood,' said Miphon. 'It means fear. It means death.'

* * *

Watashi led the travellers through the noisy, crowded streets of Selzirk, a city which – according to Miphon's lectures – was a centre for trade in grain, silks, pottery, and also tin and copper mined in the Chenameg Kingdom in mountainous country to the east. It was also, of course, the capital of the Harvest Plains.

'I wish we could stop,' said Ohio. 'I see some Galish merchants. We could learn a lot from talking to them.'

'We'll have a chance later,' said Hearst.

'You hope.'

'Why shouldn't I hope? Remember this word: intelligence.'

'Intelligence?'

'Yes. If I say that word, use the ring.'

Hearst's last words were drowned out by the racket of a group of men with shaven heads and saffron robes,

371

who stood on a street corner banging drums, beating tambourines and chanting over and over again the Mantra of the Sun.

'You've got the word?' said Hearst.

'Intelligence,' said Ohio.

'Right. If I say it, use the ring.'

'As you wish,' said Ohio.

They stopped then, for the way ahead was blocked by a funeral procession, and Watashi showed no desire to force a way through the mourners. Horns and trumpets blared discord to the skies: to scare away evil spirits, said Miphon. Hearst, who could hardly make himself heard over the uproar, gave his instructions to Miphon. Then the way was clear again, and Watashi led them onwards.

* * *

Farfalla's High Court was housed in one of the buildings crowding what had once been the central courtyard of a wizard castle. Her throne room was a vast chamber with a vaulted roof arching high over-head; it was open on every side to the sun and the wind. Watashi introduced the travellers, speaking for their benefit in the Trading Tongue:

'To the kingmaker, mother of all the peoples, ruler of the See of the Sun, greetings. Here before you stands the Rovac warrior Morgan Hearst, and here, the wizard from the south, Miphon. This one here we believe to be a peasant from Estar, Blackwood. And this one, perhaps with truth and perhaps not, tells me he is a Galish merchant by the name of Ohio.'

Watashi took up a position by the side of the throne, and Farfalla studied the travellers. Her silence did not intimidate them: they met her scrutiny with bold stares of their own.

Farfalla was a woman of middle years, her hair red, and her skin – thanks to a dye – the same colour. She

372

wore earrings of twisted copper; broad copper bracelets adorned her bare forearms. Her light woollen robes were the colours of blood, iron, earth and clay. Her throne, raised on a small dais, was made of white marble padded with white satin. She looked like a blaze of fire on pure white snow.

Unlike some courts Hearst had seen, overpopulated by lacquered flunkeys and ceremonial attendants, Farfalla's throne room held only a couple of scribes, some guards in grey livery, and a few serving women who stood to one side ready to obey any command that might come from the throne.

'So you're Morgan Hearst,' said Farfalla.

'Yes,' said Hearst, taking a step forward, watching out of the corner of his eye to see how Farfalla's guards would react. The guards held their positions.

'We've heard much of you,' said Farfalla.

'Then you have the advantage over me,' said Hearst.

He studied the woman. Her forearms were strong, muscular; her hands large, fingers broad, knuckles big. Her neck was thick, like that of a wrestler. The features of her face were coarse and generous: heavy bones, large eyes, large nose, large mouth, strong line to the jaw.

'You know much about me, if you care to think about it,' said Farfalla. 'I hold power over an empire. I am told the Rovac have a good understanding of imperial power.'

'Certainly we understand the limitations of such power,' said Hearst.

Watashi said something in the language of the Harvest Plains; Farfalla silenced him with a word.

'Power, for example,' said Hearst, 'gives no protection against lies. At the city gate I saw one of the world's scavengers, a deserter from a defeated army. I hope his tongue has not been allowed to guide your councils.'

'You speak boldly for a man with only one hand,' said Farfalla. 'In some places, you'd lose the other for speaking like that to the throne.'

'If murder is today's entertainment,' said Hearst, recklessly, 'then proceed.'

'You tempt me,' said Farfalla, who did not look tempted at all. 'Even so, I'll give you a chance to outgrow your adolescence. I have brought you here because you can be of service to me.'

'Says who? The man Erhed, whom I saw at the gate? That weak-minded gallowed and gutless coward? A runaway? A deserter?'

'Whatever his defects,' said Farfalla, 'I regret to say that his manners are better than yours.'

'On Rovac,' said Hearst, 'we believe in the diplomacy of steel.'

'My son, I'm sure,' said Farfalla, 'would be happy to join such negotiations. However – fortunately for you, my hero – I prefer to exercise my own intelligence rather than my son's sword-arm. Hear me out, for I have a tale to tell.'

'Then tell away,' said Hearst.

Farfalla, without protesting at his abruptness, began:

'When your men deserted you far inland, they made their way down the Velvet River, through the Chenameg Kingdom and all the way to Selzirk.

'Rumours came to me of wild tales being told in the taverns: fantastic stories of ring-magic, dragon-killing, battles between wizards, the destruction of armies. You know the truth of what you've been through; as you can imagine, a little strong liquor soon set some weird and wonderful tales afloat in the stews of Selzirk.

'I didn't quite believe the story of how Morgan Hearst, riding on a dragon, led armies against the Red Emperor of Tameran. Nor the tale of the Temple of Eternal Love by the shores of the Araconch Waters, with its trees of gold and its gardens of diamonds. Still, it was clear that something had happened that I should know about.

'I gave my orders. As you can imagine, rumours take more than a day from a riverside bar to my throne

374

room. Some of the men had left with Galish convoys, others on ships sailing from Adrolmarphos. A few had joined the criminal fraternities of Selzirk and proved impossible to locate.

'But my men arrested twelve. We interviewed them in isolation, giving them no chance to rehearse lies; once all twelve stories matched, I knew I had the truth.

'So I know you marched from Estar to pursue the wizard Heenmor, who had a power-source known as the death-stone, capable of turning men to stone and bringing rocks to life. I know all about your expedition to the point where the soldiers deserted you.

'It was midwinter when I extracted these truths from your soldiers. I knew that if you succeeded in capturing this . . . this death-stone, it would probably come south by way of Selzirk. For months my three sons have taken turns to command the guard at the northern gate: I wanted no errors, no mistakes. We've a great need for a weapons such as this, for our entire coastline is menaced by the pirates of the Greater Teeth, now grown strong enough to seize Stokos – a conquest of which you, no doubt, have yet to hear.

'More recently, from Runcorn, we have received an ugly little embassy demanding our surrender in the name of Elkor Alish and the death-stone. Knowing this Alish to be sworn to the service of wizards, and lacking any evidence of a death-stone slaughter said to have taken place near Runcorn, I have chosen to disregard this threat. Yet I see this Alish is not of your party. So is he dead? And if not, does he indeed command the death-stone?'

'On that point,' said Hearst, 'I am not sure whether I should furnish you with any . . . intelligence.'

He heard Blackwood protest as Ohio grabbed him, then there was the noise behind him of the red and green bottles hitting the stone floor. Hearst pulled the death-stone from where he had hidden it inside his leathers. He whipped away a bit of cloth that had been wrapped around it, and held it aloft.

375

'The death-stone,' he said, wheeling to survey the room. 'Move and you die.'

'Die yourself!' snarled Watashi, drawing his sword.

In Hearst's hand, the death-stone kicked like a living heart. To use it would mean death, for when the stones of the throne room came alive, the building would collapse. But Miphon, Blackwood and Ohio were safe in the bottles: they would have time to search for the death-stone when they emerged into the ruins where once the city of Selzirk had stood.

And then again –

As Watashi raised his sword to strike, Hearst threw the death-stone. It took Watashi on the forehead. Hearst was drawing his sword even as Watashi fell. Sword to throat, he straddled the unconscious body of Farfalla's son, and challenged her:

'The right words now, madam, or your son is dead.'

Farfalla got to her feet and clapped her hands:

'Leave us. Everybody.'

The throne room emptied, and Farfalla resumed her seat. She was confident – and why not? No kingmaker of the Harvest Plains reached maturity without becoming quick-witted and resourceful. And now what?

Whatever Hearst had expected, he was surprised at what Farfalla did next, which was to recite, in a Trading Tongue translation, two lines of Saba Yavendar's 'Albatross Odyssey':

'Wind to horizon making;
Birds match their wings to its shaping.'

Then Farfalla gestured at the wind-wide open view across the city and out to the open plains, across which the wide waters of the Velvet River snaked from east to west, glittering in the sunshine. It was easy enough to make out the north-south line of the Salt Road, reaching away to far distant horizons.

'It's a hundred and seventy leagues downriver to

376

Androlmarphos,' said Farfalla. 'But on a fast ship, you can make the downriver journey in comfort in two or three days.'

'My journey lies south,' said Hearst. 'Along the Salt Road. My destination is Drangsturm, and the Castle of Controlling Power. I thought you'd know at least that much.'

'I do,' said Farfalla. 'And I know the highway's windings make for a long journey. Another seventy marches, at least. On the other hand, from Androlmarphos there's just five hundred leagues of southing by sea; they tell me even a slow ship can make that journey in ten days.'

She was not exaggerating. A ship of any speed could manage fifty leagues a day – at least on the Central Ocean, where there was seldom any shortage of wind.

'Make me no offers,' said Hearst. 'I'd not trust my life to one of your pretty river boats. Not on the Central Ocean.'

'We don't take galleys to sea,' said Farfalla, 'but there are stout ships in plenty that sail from Androlmarphos. That is what I'd offer you – not just a passage to the south, but a ship entire, with the men to crew it.'

Hearst was tempted, but kept his wits about him, and stepped clear of Watashi, who was starting to recover. Watashi groaned and sat up. Hearst recovered the death-stone.

'What would you demand in return?' said Hearst.

'I'd have you organise the defence of the Harvest Plains against pirates – and against your friend to the north.'

'Alish has been disarmed,' said Hearst. 'I hold the death-stone. We need not worry about him.'

And with these words, they began bargaining.

CHAPTER FORTY-SEVEN

Miphon emerged from the green bottle after three days; Ohio and Blackwood, more cautious, waited for five. All were relieved to find Selzirk had not been destroyed, but more than a little annoyed to find that they would now be delayed while Hearst masterminded the defences of the Harvest Plains.

Nevertheless, they soon found compensations. For Miphon, it was a relief to be no longer travelling; he was able to resume a wizard's true life of study and meditation. For Blackwood, Farfalla's palace offered the solace of solitude, which, in a bustling city like Selzirk, was a considerable privilege indeed.

The rewards for Ohio were rich, as Hearst made him responsible for buying in stone and shipbuilding timber from the Chenameg Kingdom. While Ohio was not exactly corrupt, he found that a certain fraction of the money which passed through his fingers stuck to them – a process which happened so easily that he was almost able to persuade himself it was accidental.

For Hearst, there was an unexpected reward in that Farfalla, a master of Sunoya Dance – a mind/body training system perfected in Selzirk, and unknown to the world at large – was able to teach him physical and mental disciplines which slowly began to give his left hand the bladeskills which had once been possessed by the right.

And so the days passed, with spring becoming summer – and disaster fast approaching.

Hearst's plans for the defence of the Harvest Plains included new military roads, new castles, new ships, a guild of assassins, a courier service, and chains of watchtowers able to signal with windmill-style vanes during the day and with fire by night. All this cost money, but the Harvest Plains were rich.

Combined with the formation of a militia, the construction of new armouries, and, if necessary, the recruitment of a few legions of mercenaries from the Chenameg Kingdom, Hearst's plan would give the Harvest Plains a strong defence against both the Orfus pirates and more traditional enemies, namely the Rice Empire which lay to the south.

The only thing wrong was that Hearst would never have time to put these plans into effect, because the enemies of the Harvest Plains fully intended to strike before the stone and timber from the east was assembled into castles and ships.

Hearst had spoken of Elkor Alish as being disarmed, but this, of course, was far from the truth. Hearst had spent too long in the company of wizards, and had spent too much time exploring the memories left to him by the wizard Phyphor; he had acquired something of a wizard's contempt for the weapons of men.

Alish was no stranger to the ways of war; his experiences in the Cold West had given him mastery of the mixture of bribery, flattery, fear, diplomacy, brutality and generosity needed to hold together a mercenary army.

The seaport city of Runcorn, complete with its armoury, its treasury and its ships of war, was under his command. Using Prince Comedo as a figurehead, he could pretend when necessary to be a servant of the Favoured Blood. Under his leadership were men from Dybra, Chorst and the Lezconcarnau Plains, eager for a share of the wealth of the Harvest Plains.

Alish was persuaded by necessity, that most unrelenting motivator of men, to make the best use of these resources. During his confrontation with Hearst, Alish had seen Hearst destroy a document summoning the Rovac fleet to Argan. Unfortunately, what Hearst had destroyed was only a copy – the original ink had been despatched by ship to Rovac the day before Hearst manifested himself in Runcorn.

Alish had no doubt that the Rovac fleet would arrive in due course. Accordingly, it was vital that, as a minimum, he obtained control of the Greater Teeth and the Harvest Plains, as he had boasted of these conquests as if they had already been made.

The Greater Teeth, those cliff-built islands where the Orfus pirates had their lairs, were too strong for Alish to take without help from a death-stone. So he tried diplomacy.

The chief pirate, Menator, proved ready to negotiate. The capture and control of the island of Stokos had stretched his fleet and his manpower to the limit; an alliance would give him a better chance of making the conquests which his own followers, in turn, had already been promised.

And so it was that an alliance was made between these two warlords who, between them, commanded lands, harbours, northern strongholds, infantry, a substantial body of cavalry from the Lezconcarnau Plains, and a strong fleet.

Menator and Alish, two sagacious and experienced warriors who had both on occasion been bruised by overconfidence, did not simply launch an onslaught against the enemy. Spies told them Hearst was still in Selzirk, which suggested their best move was to capture a city intact and hold its population hostage.

The city which fell to them was Androlmarphos; the garrison commander and other key officials were bribed, the garrison itself incapacitated by poisoned food, and the city walls commanded by marauders from the sea before the general population had time to realise they were under attack.

Following the capture of the city, an orgy of rape, looting and torture might reasonably have been expected, but nothing of the sort took place. Alish and

Menator restrained their men. Apart from their desire not to compromise the hostage-value of the city, they did not want to see it casually destroyed as they were now empire builders in their own right.

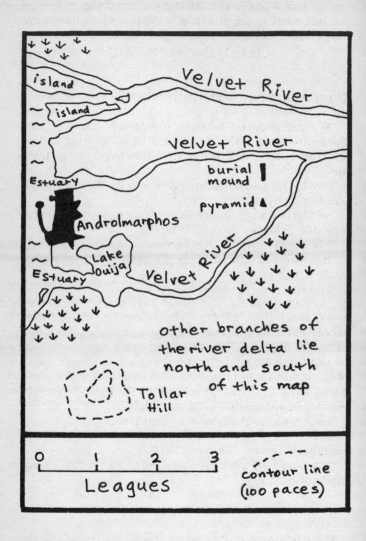

Velvet River

island

~ island

~

~

~

Estuary

Velvet River

burial mound

pyramid ▲

Androlmarphos

Lake Ouija

~

Estuary

Velvet River

other branches of the river delta lie north and south of this map

Tollar Hill

0   1   2   3

Leagues

contour line (100 paces)

CHAPTER FORTY-EIGHT

Those in the kingmaker's party reined in their horses by the riverbank.

'We can ride no further, unless we care to make the animals swim the river,' said Farfalla. 'But, as you see, there are small boats that will take us on from here.'

'My lady,' said Watashi. 'It would be dangerous for you to go any further.'

'We're in danger every time we step outdoors,' said Farfalla. 'The sky might fall on us.'

'My lady – '

'But you can run ahead of us and hold it up with a stick, if you're worried,' said Farfalla.

And that was the end of that.

They crossed the river in coracles, each of which could hold four people. They dragged the coracles ashore in the narrow end of a 'V' made by two diverging branches of the river. A thousand paces to the west was an impressive burial mound; five hundred paces south of the mound was a pyramid, and another five hundred paces south of the pyramid ran the southern branch of the 'V', beyond which was marshland.

'Let's walk to that mound,' said Hearst.

'It's a long way,' said Watashi, with a glance at Farfalla.

'It's only half a league,' said Farfalla. 'And I'm not made of butter.'

*   *   *

A battle-line requires, in its front rank, one man for

383

each pace of the frontage. This is one of the unalterable rules of warfare; men placed closer together will not have sufficient room to move, while if they are spaced further apart they will be unable to cover each other's flanks. 'Warfare' in this case, of course, refers to the conflict between the disciplined armies of high civilizations; irregular forces and barbarians tend to be less scientific in their methods.

In the 'V' formed by the diverging branches of the river, a north-south battle frontage placed just forward of the pyramid and the burial mound would measure 2500 paces; the burial mound itself, 600 paces long, offered an excellent view of the countryside.

'It's very flat,' said Ohio.

'Yes,' said Farfalla, scrutinising the dusty plains where the network of swamp and river glittered under the sun. 'The highest bit of ground is Tollar Hill, south of Androlmarphos, which rises scarcely two hundred and fifty paces skywards. The pyramid over there is higher than that.'

'Let's sit down,' said Hearst.

'Why?' said Watashi.

'We'll do what he says,' said Farfalla.

They sat. Hearst carefully studied the way the rivers fanned out to the blue immensity of the sea. Three leagues west lay lake Ouija and the city of Androlmarphos. Ships were afloat on Lake Ouija, ready to challenge any of Selzirk's craft which came down the southern branch of the river.

Irrigation ditches lay west of the burial mound, but all were dry, because they needed pumps to feed them; the pumps, worked by people or by animals, were idle; thanks to the invasion, the land was deserted.

'Would those ditches hinder cavalry?' said Hearst.

'Not much,' said one of the cavalrymen. 'They're too narrow, too shallow.'

'Usually you hardly notice them if you're out riding,' said Farfalla.

384

A group of horsemen was moving over the plains in the distance; dust could be seen rising into the air.

'It's dry,' said Ohio, licking his lips.

'Yes,' said one of the young cavalrymen. 'When it's like this it's iron-hard. I wouldn't like to take a fall from a horse when the land's like that.'

'Of course it's different in winter,' said Farfalla. 'The river floods. It's all mud then. In winter they couldn't ride the fields like that. Even in spring the mud can be knee-deep.'

One irrigation ditch ran just in front of the mound. Hearst studied the ground in silence. Thinking.

'I will command the battle from here,' said Hearst.

'This is no good,' said Watashi.

'Why not?' said Hearst.

'We need plenty of room for the cavalry to manoeuvre,' said Watashi. 'Here, what happens if we have to retreat? Behind us there's less and less room as we move back into the V-shape made by the rivers. I can imagine a disaster if too many horses were forced back into the waiting waters.'

'The pyramid and the mound provide us with two strongpoints,' said Hearst. 'The rest of the countryside is too flat.'

'Strongpoints don't have all that much relevance in a cavalry battle,' said Watashi. 'With a limited frontage like this, how can we manoeuvre? How are we supposed to outflank the enemy? They can spread from one river to the other.'

'What would you do?' said Hearst.

'I'd move forward,' said Watashi. 'I'd advance three thousand paces to the west, half-way to Androlmarphos. That's where I'd do battle. There's more room to manoeuvre when you get out there.'

'I understand what you say,' said Hearst.

For some time Hearst sat there in the sun, watching, listening, thinking. High in the sky overhead, some bird of prey wheeled over the dusty landscape. Hot. Dry.

Hard. The rivers, though wide, ran slow and sluggish under the sun.

'Is there any way to get a lot of cavalry across any branch of these rivers in a hurry?' said Hearst.

'It's a slow business,' said Watashi. 'Anybody will tell you that. You have to swim them across.'

'I see,' said Hearst.

He sat in the sun some more, then he said:

'I will command the battle from here. From this mound. Now as for that pyramid . . . what is it, exactly?'

'It's a tomb,' said Farfalla. 'We once had an emperor, a wizard of the order of Ebber, who built that tomb to his own glory. That was two thousand years ago, but we still remember the thousands who died building it. We are sitting on their burial mound. Our people paid a bitter price to raise that monument.'

'Let's go and have a closer look at it,' said Hearst.

*   *   *

Ten days after Hearst had scouted out the land, his troops began to move into position. Fleets of bamboo rafts brought them downriver; they disembarked in hot, dusty afternoon sunlight and took up their positions.

On the burial mound, a marquee was raised. Beside the marquee, two standards flew: one a dragon-banner that Farfalla had ordered her servants to make for Morgan Hearst; the other, Farfalla's own green and gold flag.

'You should not have come,' said Hearst, as he stood with Farfalla in front of the marquee.

'If we fail here, there is no hope for me or for my people,' said Farfalla. 'Things would be otherwise if you were prepared to use the death-stone against the enemy. As it is, if we lose this battle, then here is as good a place to die as any.'

Slowly, ten thousand troops moved into position,

forming up in four ranks along the north-south battle frontage Hearst had chosen. The bamboo rafts were dismantled and their poles hacked into shape to provide each man in the first rank with a sharpened stake which he drove into the ground in front of his position; holes were dug further forward of these positions. A cavalry commander might have been reckless enough to assault such defences – cavalrymen are notorious for their infatuation with the romance of the charge – but Hearst doubted that a sober infantry commander like Alish would commit horse against a line of leg-breaking holes and sharpened stakes.

Those in the first three ranks were armed with long pikes; in the rear rank were bowmen and also lightly armed skirmishers who, armed with weapons such as cudgels and sickles, would have their best opportunities if – and Hearst hoped it would be when – the enemy broke and ran.

On top of the burial mound itself was an honour guard of three hundred swordsmen and axemen; all these warriors were heavily armoured and carried shields. Hearst himself wore no armour and went bareheaded under the sun.

Toward evening, some horsemen from Androlmarphos scouted out Hearst's defences, riding just out of bowshot.

'That's good,' said Hearst. 'I want Alish to attack quickly. He'll feel more confident if his reconnaissance patrols can bring him a thorough account of the disposition of our forces.'

'What if he doesn't attack?' said Farfalla.

'He wants a quick victory,' said Hearst. 'He needs success to keep together his army of pirates and fortune seekers. Besides, Alish knows many of his men will be terrified by the thought that I might use the deathstone. If he waits, he gives such people the chance to betray his army to me. All things considered, he should attack at dawn.'

'Yes,' said Watashi. 'Particularly when he's got thirty or forty thousand men to bring against us. What did his last embassy threaten us with? Rice Empire mercenaries, armoured cavalry from Galgasoon, Sung bowmen, slingshot heroes from Breenmower, a legion of Collosnon deserters, skirmishers from Provincial Endergeneer – half the vultures in creation must be under his command.'

'We'll have more men by morning,' said Hearst. 'Ohio's taking care of that.'

'It's late in the day to be moving any more men into position,' said Watashi. 'When are they coming?'

'Some time,' said Hearst, who, tired of listening to unwanted advice, had made his battle-plan without reference to Watashi.

'Go out now and give the evening orders,' said Hearst. 'I want listening posts set up forward of our lines, and patrols to go out even further to the west. I don't want to take any chance of our being caught by a night attack.'

'I'll see that gets done,' said Watashi.

'There's also an order every officer is to give the men at dawn,' said Hearst. 'Not before, mind, in case we lose a patrol or a few sentries to a raiding party from Androlmarphos. I don't want Alish to get advance warning of what I'm going to do.'

'The order will be given at dawn,' said Watashi. 'What is it?'

'When blue smoke rises from the burial mound, fall back on the pyramid,' said Hearst. 'When red smoke rises, attack. Blue to retreat, red to attack.'

'Ten thousand men falling back on the pyramid!' said Watashi, outraged. 'We'd crush each other to death. There's not nearly enough room.'

'The effect of that order will be to have the army move south when I want,' said Hearst. 'They can all see the pyramid wherever they are, so that will give them the direction to move in.'

388

'What's the purpose of these orders?' said Watashi.

'To baffle the moon and confuse the sun,' said Hearst.

'I hope you know what you're doing,' said Watashi.

'He knows,' said Farfalla.

'Does he?' said Watashi. 'I know more about tactics than your – '

'He's good,' said Farfalla. 'Good at everything he does.'

'But no cavalry! The greatest strength of our army, just thrown away! Unless there's horses hidden in one of those magic bottles.'

'There aren't,' said Hearst.

Experiments had shown that only fifty men or ten horses could be taken into one of the bottles as a group; furthermore, horses could not negotiate the stairwells inside the bottle, and a dozen at most could fit inside the bottleneck.

'What have you got in the bottle then?'

'Provisions to supply our army for a month or more,' said Hearst, 'In case we have to lay siege to Androlmarphos.'

'So we've no cavalry.'

'Oh, we could always ride each other to war, at a pinch,' said Hearst casily.

'This is no joke!'

'So what do you want me to do about it?'

'There's nothing we can do now,' said Watashi. 'It would be a nightmare trying to bring a large force of cavalry across that river under cover of darkness. Your friend Alish will know that. Somebody will tell him if he doesn't realise it himself.'

'I had thought of that,' said Hearst. 'It will encourage him to attack at dawn, before we have another day in which to bolster our force here.'

'You sound enthusiastic,' said Watashi.

'Of course,' said Hearst. 'I now know of a certainty when my enemy will be launching his attack. That's a

389

substantial advantage in a battle like that. Now: the orders.'

Watashi recited Hearst's orders, word perfect, then went to distribute them.

And Hearst was left standing on the mound, gazing to the west where the blood-red sun was sinking. The sunset made the plains a field of blood; the distant battlements of Androlmarphos were black against the blood-red sun, and the waters of the Central Ocean were a sea of fire.

*   *   *

In the darkness, Hearst and Farfalla sat together on the burial mound outside the marquee. Hearst named the stars, and told Farfalla long stories about their loves and hatreds, their politics and alliances, and the roles they had played in the battle of the sun and the moon.

Through the quiet night came the undertones of the voices of many men sitting talking round camp fires. Some had grumbled at the loads of firewood Hearst had ordered brought to their positions: it had meant a lot of hard work for everyone. But they would be glad of that wood now: glad of their small fires and the talk that went on around the fire.

Hearst had issued orders forbidding anyone to burn bamboo, for he did not want explosions keeping people awake. However, he knew that for some, there would be little sleep – and, for a few, none. Meanwhile, there would be long, lazy conversations, ranging over everything under the heavens; far better to sit talking by fireside than to lie alone in the dark, wrapped in a blanket against the cold, trying to sleep but only occasionally managing a few moments of dreamtime, which inevitably end in nightmare.

For a moment, looking out at the campfires, Hearst wished he was once more an ordinary fighting man, without the responsibilities of command.

"What's that star?' said Farfalla.

'Which one?'

'The green one to the south of the Centipede.'

'That is Elamazure. She is a very tall lady, very beautiful, but terrible to behold, for she is one of the great judges. A jade sword rides at her side. Above all else, she judges battle: the shades of incompetent commanders have reason to fear her.'

'Why?'

'She does not judge the rights or wrongs of the wars of the world, but she passes judgment on their conduct. To her, incompetence in battle is the greatest sin, for it extends the agony, so that a conflict that could be settled with a single battle ends up lasting five years or fifty.'

'What are you afraid of?'

'I do not say that I fear anything, but . . . well, it is a heavy responsibility.'

Falling silent, Hearst heard a creaking begin in the night: that was an irrigation pump. It would drudge away till dawn, at his orders. Then he heard voices, then a sentry approached:

'Commander Hearst?'

'Here.'

'My lord, the cavalry commander presents himself.'

'Good,' said Hearst.

The sentry led him through the darkness to the cavalry commander, a big man smelling of horses and sweat.

'How is it going?' said Hearst.

'Like silk,' said the commander. 'As smooth as a dream.'

'I hope you have better dreams than me,' said Hearst.

'It's going very well. We should all be here long before dawn.'

'Have your officers received their orders?'

'Everything has been done as you wanted it to be done,' said the cavalry commander.

'Good,' said Hearst. 'Good.'

Under Ohio's command, ships had been anchored next to each other and planks laid across their decks to form a bridge across the river. Under cover of darkness, cavalry was being brought dry-shod to Hearst's army. By morning, he would have two thousand horses at his disposal.

After a conversation with the cavalry commander, Hearst rejoined Farfalla. They sat together, saying nothing now, and listened to the night. Some of the camp fires had gone out: at least some men found themselves able to sleep. For many, it would be their first battle. The creaking of an irrigation pump went on and on; the water was soaking the ground in front of the burial mound, turning it to a quagmire.

Reports came in from some of the patrols. Troops were moving forward from Androlmarphos to take up positions on the plain. Alish was moving his army onto the field of battle under cover of darkness.

'These are my orders,' said Hearst. 'Just before dawn, our trumpets will sound the attack. However, nobody is to move forward. When the trumpets sound the attack, everyone is to shout, to scream, to hammer weapons against shields. But nobody is to attack, nobody is to attack. Make that very clear.'

Men dispersed into the night to see that the orders were given, and Hearst and Farfalla were alone again.

'You should rest,' said Farfalla.

'I can't rest,' said Hearst.

'I can help you rest.'

'Not tonight,' said Hearst.

'I'll be waiting for you if you change your mind,' said Farfalla.

She retired to the marquee. Morgan Hearst sat alone, watching the stars, the campfires, and listening to the creak of the irrigation pump. He heard sounds of cavalry moving into position, heard distant curses, distant laughter. It was hard to wait, alone: hard to wait

392

for the dawn, knowing that if his judgment was wrong, thousands of his troops would be slaughtered on the field of battle, his army broken and his name shamed.

But he had a chance: and if he succeeded, he would have saved the Harvest Plains from the marauders from the north. If Hearst won this battle, he would have at least one worthy success to his name. Yet again he reviewed his failures.

Somewhere out in the darkness, Elkor Alish, once his friend, was waiting to lead an army against him. Hearst counted that as his biggest failure: but despite all his thinking about it, he could not see what he had done wrong.

* * *

Morning approached. The last camp fires burnt down to ashes. Men waited in the darkness, shivering. Then trumpets blared, announcing the attack. There was a storm-sea clamour of shouting and banging as Hearst's men chorused their rage. In the darkness, it sounded as if an attack was being launched in earnest, but Hearst knew – hoped! – that every man was holding his position.

From the lines of Alish's army, battle-horns sounded, calling men to action. There was the roar of hundreds of voices chanting defiance. The noise quietened slowly as Alish's men began to realise there was no attack, that it was a false alarm.

Hearst knew how Alish would see things. His army had been roused to battle: his men were on their feet, armed and ready, blood racing still from the shock of thinking they were being attacked. What now? He could tell them to stand down, then try to mobilise them for battle again when the sun rose. Or: he could order the advance, knowing that by the time they reached Hearst's lines there would be enough light for battle to commence.

Morgan Hearst stood on the burial mound, waiting. There was a movement in the darkness: there was just enough light for him to see that it was Farfalla.

'What's happening?' said Farfalla.

'Wait,' said Hearst.

Out to the west, the rumbling thunder of battle-drums began to boom. It was joined by the blast of battle-horns, then by thousands of voices screaming a battle-chant, then by the clash of spears beating against shields. It sounded as if all the armies of the deepest hell were advancing through the night.

'They are coming,' said Hearst.

His voice was flat, dull, dead. There was no point in worrying now. He had thought through his battle-plan, he had briefed his officers, he had given his orders. If he had made any mistakes, it was too late to correct them now.

'They sound so . . . so . . .'

'Hush,' said Hearst. 'Hush . . .'

She was standing on his right side. He wished he could have reached out and taken her hand, but he had no hand on his right side, only a cold steel hook. And in his left hand was a sword. Why had he drawn that sword? This was no battle that he could win by the dare of nerve and sinew. This was no battle where he could surrender himself to a berserker battle-trance. This was a battle that required that he stand and watch, waiting for the right moment.

Hearst knew that in the darkness, his cavalry troopers were leading their horses forward through the defensive lines of stakes and potholes, and assembling on the flat land to the west.

'The sky's lighter,' said Farfalla.

It was true. There was light enough for one to begin to make out shadowy figures: wraiths, ghosts, shapings of smoke. The heart-hammering uproar of the onslaught of Alish's forces was closer, louder, and for a moment it seemed to Hearst that he had only an army of ghosts to confront an army of raging flesh and blood.

Out to the west, lights suddenly glowed as the men of a listening post whipped away cloaks which had covered lanterns which had been kept burning through the night. The signal told Hearst the enemy were now only four hundred paces away.

'Sound attack!' shouted Hearst.

Trumpets flared. Loud and clear they rang, challenging the fading stars. Hearst's cavalry started moving at a walk, then a trot, then a canter, a gallop. As the horses thundered forward, a battle cry was raised by the thousands of lancers:

'Wa – wa – Watashi! Wa – wa – Watashi!

Watashi. Blood. Fear. Death.

Advancing in darkness, Alish's forces had become disordered as the more eager adventurers had surged ahead far in advance of the others. They had not expected to face cavalry. They had no chance to organise themselves into a wall of spears and swords which would have deterred the horses.

Out of the shadows swept shadows, thunder bearing steel, spear-blades driving home, scimitars following through, and ever the cry was raised:

'Wa – wa – Watashi! Wa – wa – Watashi!'

There were screams of pain, fear, panic. Those closest to the horses began to run; their panic spread; soon all of Alish's army was in retreat.

A sudden outbreak of shouting from Hearst's army signalled a spontaneous infantry charge. Sensing victory, they were mounting an assault. Hearst swore. This was no part of his plan! The battle had just started, and already he was losing control.

'Sound retreat!' he shouted.

The trumpets sounded retreat, but to no avail. If any men bothered to listen, none bothered to obey.

Hearst strained to see. The darkness was easing away; he began to make out parts of a confused grappling-groping battle on the plains, a hideous, brawling gang-fight from which came the screams of murder, the clash of weapons, the monstrous noise of badly injured horses.

Then the enemy trumpets sounded retreat.

'Sound retreat!' shouted Hearst.

'But the enemy's running away!' yelled a trumpeter.

Hearst cursed him; belatedly, retreat was sounded. But nobody obeyed. As light began to conjure colours on the plain, Hearst, from his vantage point, saw, all too clearly, exactly what was happening.

Alish had kept his cavalry in the rear. The cavalry was holding firm as the infantry retreated through their ranks. Very shortly, Hearst's disorganised infantry, attacking as a formless, anarchic rabble intermixed with cavalry, would be confronted by the massed, waiting discipline of Alish's horse.

It happened.

As Hearst watched, the last of Alish's infantry retreated to safety behind the cavalry screen. The attack wavered, faltered, broke. Alish's cavalry charged. Dismayed, Hearst saw his own horse and footsoldiers flung back. Alish's infantry, without any orders, began to charge.

As the battlefield disintegrated into a chaotic free-for-all, Hearst abandoned his original battle-plan: to brunt the enemy's attack, then break through on the flanks, encircle the enemy and crush them. He was a fool to have thought he could try anything so complicated with this mostly raw and virgin army. His only consolation was that Alish seemed to have no more control than he did.

But, inexorably, weight of numbers was beginning to tell; Hearst's army was – he thought – slowly being forced back into the 'V' made by two diverging rivers.

It was time to try the hind legs. He would try and lure Alish's army in between the pyramid and the burial mound, then crush it between those two strongpoints. He had massed archers lurking out of sight behind the burial mound which would give him a fist to use against infantry; wet ground in front of the mound would protect against a cavalry charge.

'Smoke!' yelled Hearst, to the men manning blazing bonfires. 'Blue – '

But someone had already thrown a bag of chemicals onto a fire. Red smoke billowed up.

'Blue smoke!' yelled Hearst. 'And – trumpets! – sound the retreat!'

A bag of chemicals was thrown onto the fire – this time for blue smoke. A pillar of green and yellow flames shot up into the sky as chemicals mixed. Some of the trumpets sounded the advance, and some the retreat. Wind blew the smoke this way and that, obscuring the battlefield completely.

Then someone threw on black smoke.

'Who threw black smoke!' screamed Hearst. 'I'll kill the man responsible!'

Black smoke was the signal which would summon ships Hearst had waiting upriver. The ships were his reserve force, and this, to his mind, was hardly the time to employ them. He was well aware of the fact that the general who wins a battle is often the one who has the last reserves to commit to the fight; the black smoke, calling in the ships prematurely, might have cost him victory.

Still, it would be a little while yet before the ships got here.

As the smoke cleared, Hearst was able to see that his men were retreating. A few came scrambling up the burial mound; most fell back toward the pyramid, or went mobbing back through the gap between the pyramid and the mound. They were retreating, obviously, not because of the totally incoherent signals, but because they were losing.

Alish managed to stop his men from following.

Hearst saw Alish's battle-standard, the blood-red banner of Rovac, moving to the northern flank. Alish's cavalry began to mass on that flank. Hearst's plan, to lure Alish's men in between two strongpoints then crush them, had failed. Alish was obviously going to attack the burial mound, the strongpoint guarding Hearst's right flank, hoping, by seizing it, to win the battle.

'Well then,' muttered Hearst, 'Come on!'

Then, in a loud clear voice, he shouted orders. On his command, a scattering of soldiers down in front of the burial mound retreated to its heights, their legs boggy with mud.

There were dead bodies on the ground between the two armies – dead men, dead horses, broken spears, fallen banners. As dust settled through sunlight, both sweating, panting armies were silent but for the screams and groans of the wounded.

'What happens now?' said Farfalla.

'Alish is gathering his cavalry for a charge,' said Hearst.

He could hear the unintelligible tail-end of shouted orders from the enemy army. Riders were galloping up and down the ranks, distributing orders. Alish was planning something. What?

'Are we winning?' said Farfalla.

'We're alive,' said Hearst.

He could not look at her: he could not take his eyes off the battlefield. His gut was knotted up. His muscles were trembling with tension. He had felt like this in other battles, but had always been able to release the tension by expending it in the fury of a battle-rage, his sword sweeping to slaughter, a shout in his throat as he gave himself to combat. Now he could only stand and wait.

'What does the enemy hope to do?'

'To storm this mound,' said Hearst.

And took his eyes off the field of battle just for a moment to glance behind him. There, sheltering out of sight of Alish's army, hidden by the rise of the burial mound that was six hundred paces long, were his archers, ten ranks of old men, children, women, servants, slaves and cripples. They had moved into position during the night; they waited patiently, gazing at the banners on the burial mound.

Hearst knew that if Alish's army gained the mound, there would be fearful slaughter amongst those rag-tag ranks. There were five thousand people there; perhaps all would die. He had been forced to argue long and hard with Farfalla to get her permission to bring them here; if they died, the responsibility would be all his.

Hearst turned back to the field of battle. Alish's blood-red banner advanced to the head of the cavalry. So Alish would lead the attack himself.

Hearst waited.

Farfalla's green and gold banner rippled in the wind. Hearst's battle-standard snapped this way and that with a crisp, clean sound. The wind stirred dust from the dry, trampled ground; Hearst smelt the dust. The sun, shining into the eyes of Alish's army, was warm on his back.

Alish's cavalry advanced at a trot on a front six hundred paces wide, facing the burial mound. The horses slowed their pace as the men walked them through the lines of potholes and sharpened stakes that were a hundred paces in front of the mound, then they formed up again for a charge to send them sweeping up to the top of the burial mound.

Hearst glanced anxiously at the ground in front of the mound. Part had been trampled into mud by stray soldiers, but most was covered with dead brown grass. However, a little water still remained at the bottom of the shallow irrigation ditch. Would the riders notice? He hoped not. Their charge, after all, would take them into the sun.

The cavalry were moving forward. At a trot. At a canter. Sunlight glittered on the sharp points of spears. They gained to a gallop. Thunder. Thunder of hooves.

The honour guard and the other soldiers on the mound wavered.

'Stand fast!' shouted Hearst.

And they answered his shout:

'Wa – wa – Watashi! Wa – wa – Watashi!'

Blood. Fear. Death.

The first riders hit the waterlogged ground. It was soft as a knee-deep bog, the same as it would be after the winter rains. Horses went down, legs breaking, riders thrown. The cavalry behind crashed into the wreckage of flesh at full gallop. The ground shook: flesh screamed. The blood-red banner of Rovac went down. Hearst wheeled, faced the sun:

'Fire!'

The nearest archers in the waiting ranks unleashed their missiles. Others saw them, and followed suit. The air hummed and sang as if vast energies had set the sky itself vibrating. High soared the arrows, then fell, a lethal, hissing rain, bringing death to those struggling in the mud, death to those few who had managed to rein in their horses short of disaster.

Against that death, courage was useless, skill no protection. Those horsemen who could escape did so, turning their mounts and fleeing. A shout of dismay rose from the ranks of Alish's army. Many of Alish's soldiers, too distant to see the mud and arrows, had seen the cavalry charge broken as if by magic, and there were shouts of 'death-stone! death-stone!' loud within their ranks.

'Red smoke!' shouted Hearst.

He would attack, and see what happened.

Red smoke whirled up into the air. The flights of arrows ceased: the honour guard charged down the mound, attacking the survivors of the cavalry charge. The rest of Hearst's army began, tentatively, to advance.

Then, Hearst's men raised a great shout. He heard the sullen thump of oar-timing drums, and, looking to left

400

and to right, saw Ohio's galleys sweeping down the rivers flanking the battlefield, crammed with warriors and archers.

The enemy wavered.

Now was the moment!

Hearst turned to face the thousands of bowmen hiding behind the mound. Their missiles exhausted, they stood silent, fearful, waiting. He waved them forward:

'Charge!' shouted Hearst.

They wavered, unsure, uncertain.

He waved them forward again:

'Charge! Charge!'

Slowly, they began to move. Up the burial mound they came. Then, reaching the top, they saw the enemy army starting to break up as men began to flee before the remorselessly advancing infantry, spurred by rumours of the death-stone and the unknown terrors of the ships now outflanking them.

With a great shout, Hearst's archers surged forward:

'Wa – wa – Watashi! Wa – wa – Watashi!'

Watashi.

Blood. Fear. Death.

That shout was the loudest thing on the battlefield. To the men in Alish's army, it seemed as if Hearst had suddenly found another five thousand troops to commit to the battle. At the distance, they could not see the shouting was from a mob of civilians who did not even have arrows left for their bows. That shock turned hesitant retreat into all-out rout.

The five thousand began to move forward.

'Hold fast!' shouted Hearst. 'Hold fast!'

But it was useless. They were out of control. They surged down the mound, floundered through the mud, and pillaged the dead, seizing swords, spears and knives, and retrieving their own arrows. Then, screaming – their voices hoarse by now – they went on the attack:

'Wa – wa – Watashi!'

Hearst turned to Farfalla.

'I can't stop them!' he said.

'Let them go,' said Farfalla. 'I think they're safe enough; I think the pirates can run faster than they can.'

And Hearst, scanning the battlefield once more, saw that Farfalla was right. Alish's army would never stop until it was inside Androlmarphos.

He had won victory.

He still held his sword in his left hand. Now, he sheathed it.

CHAPTER FORTY-NINE

With the battle over, Farfalla's historians began the task of extracting, from the day's shambling slaughter, an elegant tale of military genius suitable for the edification of posterity.

Meanwhile, Miphon took over the marquee on the burial mound, and there he worked with his saws and knives, probes and pliars, needles and bandages – stitching, padding, splinting and amputating, helped by a team of assistants and juniors.

Arms and legs were carried out by the bucketful.

Later, when the most serious wounds had been attended to, they would treat lesser injuries such as bruises, using leeches to draw out the blood from swollen knees and so forth.

Remote from this activity, Hearst searched amongst the dead and wounded for Elkor Alish. He had seen Alish's banner go down, and had presumed Alish to be dead or injured – but was coming to believe that Alish must have been amongst those who had escaped.

The last place Hearst searched was the growing pile of corpses on the burial mound – men who had died while waiting for treatment, or had expired as a shattered limb was being amputated. From the marquee itself came piteous screams as some poor wretch was attended to by Miphon or one of his helpers.

His search completed, Hearst walked amongst the wounded. Sometimes a hand would reach for his, and he would grasp it: sometimes realising he was holding the hand of one soon to die. Some bravos, grinning through masks of blood, congratulated him on leading them to victory. Some sat silent, white-faced, hardly moving, blank eyes staring at nothing.

Others were noisy.

Hearst had seen all this before, in the Cold West and elsewhere: was familiar with the wet sheen of intestines, the massive blue-black crush injuries caused by weapons battering armour, found no novelty in a horse-trampled man spitting blood or the sight of bone and tooth visible through a sword-sliced cheek.

Yet this time, the sight of the wounded affected him oddly. He had never before had supreme command of a battle – he had always been somewhere in the midst of the fighting, hacking out a reputation for himself with a bloodstained sword. Afterwards, he had never felt guilty about the wounded because he had taken the same risks and shared the same dangers.

But now he suffered an unavoidable guilt which he could not free himself from. As supreme commander of the army of the Harvest Plains, he had sent people to their deaths without risking as much as a cat-scratch himself. And, as so much had been decided by chance, error and luck, he could not even console himself with the thought that his generalship had secured the victory.

So this was what it meant to be supreme commander!

Hearst thought he began to understand why Alish had ceased campaigning in the Cold West. To stand apart and order brave men to their deaths made demands few could find easy to bear.

He saw a rider coming from the west: it was Watashi. Hearst met him, and received his report.

'The enemy is now confined within the walls of Androlmarphos,' said Watashi. 'We are raising walls and building strongpoints to protect our siege lines in case they try a sally, but I do not think they will.'

'With Elkor Alish in command, I wouldn't put any money on it,' said Hearst. 'Tell those in the siege lines I believe Alish may well try a sally – possibly tonight.'

'The enemy have taken heavy losses, my lord.'

'So have we! To win, we have to destroy the enemy's fist. That's the ruling law of warfare. Today, we bruised their knuckles – but their fist can still strike back.'

'Yes, my lord,' said Watashi.

And bowed, and left.

'So we're not finished yet,' said Farfalla, watching her son go. 'There's to be more fighting, more killing.'

'We didn't choose this war,' said Hearst.

'But we could choose to end it. With the death-stone.'

'We cannot! War with such weapons would wreck the entire world. Others can venture the Dry Pit to get such weapons.'

'Then perhaps others will,' said Farfalla. 'That does not alter our need.'

'I've seen what the death-stone does,' said Hearst. 'You haven't. You don't understand. If we started that kind of warfare, it wouldn't stop before . . . before . . .'

Hearst shook his head. It was unthinkable.

'Surely a commander errs if he wastes flesh and blood in battles a stone egg could win . . . surely that's a matter of . . . competence.'

'The death-stone would wipe out the whole city,' said Hearst. 'Do you want to save the city by destroying it?'

'Use the death-stone against the walls.'

'The stones would come alive. People would die.'

'People will die anyway. Why are you so . . . so afraid of this death-stone?'

Hearst pointed at the sea.

'Out there, the Central Ocean. Out to the west, Rovac. Beyond that, the Cold West. For thousands of years Rovac has concerned itself with the history of the lands bordering the Central Ocean, inasmuch as we've fought in the armies of those lands. But if I was to use the death-stone . . . everything would change.'

'To live is to change,' said Farfalla. 'Birth to death. That's the cycle.'

'The death-stone would end all cycles,' said Hearst, and turned on his heel and walked away.

Knowing full well that he had another reason not to use the death-stone: Elkor Alish was in Androlmarphos, and might well become a victim of the power of the death-stone, whether it was used against the city as a whole or just against the battlements where, no doubt, the fighting men would be concentrated.

* * *

Elkor Alish led a sortie from Androlmarphos that night. There was bitter fighting under cover of darkness: confused struggles in which knots of men fought to the death with no quarter given on either side. The earth works of the siege lines gave the defenders an advantage, but they were hard pressed to hold those lines.

Then, at the height of the fighting, Hearst brought fire ships down the river. They advanced under cover of darkness – galleys with oars muffled. In Lake Ouija, they were set afire – the crews only had to swim to the eastern shore of the lake to gain the safety of their own lines. Morning revealed that half of Alish's ships in Lake Ouija had been destroyed.

At a council of war, Hearst listened to battle reports in silence.

'Will they try another sortie tonight?' said Watashi.

'They'll try something,' said Hearst. 'You can count on that.'

'So there'll be more dead,' said Farfalla. 'More maimed and mutilated war victims, crippled for the rest of their lives.'

Hearst winced.

'If we can't accept casualties, then we'd better surrender now,' said Hearst.

'Morale is good,' said Watashi, 'We're ready for a long siege, if that's what's necessary. But it won't be easy.'

'You don't have to tell me that,' said Hearst.

It was then that their council of war was interrupted as a messenger was brought into their presence by armed guards. He was exhausted, his clothing blood-stained; it was clear he had been wounded in the chest. He tried to stand up straight before them, but staggered. A guard supported him. He tried to speak, but no words came.

'What's this about?' said Hearst.

'He brings a message,' said a guard. 'He passed it to me.'

'Let me read it,' said Hearst. 'Sit him down. Bring him some water. Here. Now.'

And Hearst took a piece of parchment from the guard. On one side was the original draft, written in the language of the Harvest Plains, which he could not understand; it was adorned by an elaborate signature and a wax seal. On the other side, someone had scrawled a translation in the Galish Trading Tongue.

'Who translated this?' said Hearst.

'Patrol,' said the messenger, getting the word out with difficulty. 'Thought me a spy. Questioned me, long time. Translation by patrol leader, your attention. Believe me.'

'Maybe he is a spy,' said Hearst. 'However, the message purports to be from a fortress commander on the border between the Rice Empire and the Harvest Plains. He says his castle is besieged by part of an army from the Rice Empire, and the rest of that army marches for Selzirk. He is sending this message with a sortie party.'

Hearst passed the parchment to Watashi.

'It's authentic,' said Watashi. 'I know the seal. I know the commander, too – the original message bears his signature, and has been drafted by his hand.'

The messenger spoke again. His voice was weak:

'Only one. Me. Only one alive. All the rest . . .'

'We understand,' said Farfalla. 'Lie back. Rest. Don't do yourself further injury by trying to talk.'

'So the Rice Empire hopes to profit from our troubles,' said Watashi, 'If they reach Selzirk . . .'

'Well,' said Farfalla, looking at Hearst. 'Do you still think you have time to break Androlmarphos by siege?'

Hearst met her gaze in silence. Then spoke:

'I am not going to use the death-stone.'

'You could threaten to use it.'

'Elkor Alish knows the population of Androlmarphos is his guarantee against attack by the death-stone,' said Hearst. 'He also knows that sooner or later we'll have to take the death-stone south — or else a party from the Castle of Controlling Power will come north to take it from us. Time is on his side: he won't listen to threats.'

'Then what about that pirate creature, Ohio?' said Farfalla. 'Isn't his brother the commander of the pirates? Isn't that what you told me?'

'I can't use a friend as a hostage,' said Hearst, regretting now that he had, in an intimate moment, revealed Ohio's secrets.

'Pretend, then,' said Farfalla. 'Ohio would surely consent to being tied up and led out on a horse in front of the battlements of Androlmarphos. If we made his brother believe we had murder in mind, perhaps he'd parley with us. We could come to an arrangement.'

'Alish won't surrender no matter what Menator says,' said Hearst.

'Then we can surely persuade Menator to murder Elkor Alish,' said Farfalla. 'He gets Ohio's life – and money, if he wants. And a treaty to guarantee his hold over Runcorn.'

'That's a foul way to work,' said Hearst.

'I've seen the dead,' said Farfalla. 'I've seen the wounded. All war is foul.'

Hearst thought it through, then said, his voice heavy:

'Go and bring Ohio to me.'

Watashi moved to obey.

CHAPTER FIFTY

Hearst and Miphon stood on the plains two leagues east of Androlmarphos and a league west of the burial mound and the pyramid. In the green bottle, they had two horses and four hundred soldiers. There was nobody between them and the city; the siege lines had been evacuated the day before.

Miphon was looking inland, to the east, waiting for a signal to come from the fleet anchored upriver. Hearst, on the other hand, watched the walls of Androlmarphos, and remembered what had happened outside those walls.

Ohio had agreed readily enough that they could use him as a hostage to try and get his brother Menator to negotiate with them. Ohio had been tied up and put on a horse which had been led out onto some open ground in front of Lake Ouija.

A small party, including Hearst and Watashi, had waited to receive an equally small delegation from Androlmarphos, which had included Menator. The pirate commander had refused to make any bargain with the people from the Harvest Plains, but, thinking the threat to Ohio's life was real, had tried to rescue him, even though there had been bad blood between them in the past.

In a short fight, Menator and most of his party had been killed; Ohio had died when the horse he was seated on had reared, throwing him to the ground. With his hands tied, he had landed heavily, breaking his neck.

Hearst was now forced to use the death-stone. He did not have time to recapture Androlmarphos by siege: he had to march Farfalla's army east to defend Selzirk against the invaders from the Rice Empire. As it was, he calculated they would barely reach Selzirk in time.

'Any smoke yet?' said Hearst.

'Nothing,' said Miphon.

Hearst wondered where Alish was at that moment – and what he was thinking. Did Alish suspect the death-stone was about to be used against him?

'How is the messenger?' said Hearst.

'The messenger?'

'The one from the south who brought the message about the army from the Rice Empire. I wanted you to have a look at his wound.'

'He died before I could see him.'

'Oh,' said Hearst.

So that was another death to take into account. One amongst many. Now Hearst was going to use the death-stone: but that in itself should not produce too many casualties, for he had calculated that, from where he stood, its effects should extend just far enough to destroy part of the city walls.

'Green smoke,' said Miphon.

There was indeed green smoke rising in the east. Ships anchored upriver would soon attack, expecting to find the walls of Androlmarphos breached. Hearst could have sheltered thousands of men in the green and red bottles, but, as no more than fifty men could be taken in or out of one of the bottles at a time, the fastest way to launch a mass assault on the city was by ship.

'Take your position,' said Hearst.

Miphon sat cross-legged on the hard dry ground at Hearst's feet.

Hearst took the death-stone from a leather bag. The stone egg was cool. Heavy. He raised it above his head. The shadow of a buzzard flickered over the ground. The death-stone kicked in his hand like a human heart. He cried out, his battle-hoarse voice naming the Words. The death-stone warmed in his hand. His heart faltered, trembled, kicked three times in an odd, irregular rhythm.

There was a grinding sound in the sky, which grew steadily stronger.

As Hearst watched, the few pebbles he could see on the dry earth began to tremble as the grinding sound grew louder. In a moment of hallucinatory clarity, he remembered the desperate moments at Ep Pass – rocks shifting underfoot as he fled from Heenmor, his hands and face stinging from burns, his nostrils filled with the stench of burnt leather, his eyes watering from smoke.

Now, as he watched – the death-stone heavy in his hand, his arm trembling – the little pebbles, shape-shifting, began to move. Like insects. The air was turning grey. The ground . . . the ground, outside a small circle he could have spanned with outstretched arms, was turning grey. As the ground turned to stone, the mobilised pebbles skittered across its surface like raindrops wind-driven across a pane of glass.

The air was turning grey.

And the death-stone –

'The death-stone's getting cold,' said Hearst.

His voice sounded hollow, echoed back to him as if they were standing in a cave.

'Hold it,' said Miphon.

Hearst tried to look out across the countryside to see what was happening. He saw a buzzard in the sky, saw it suddenly stall – as if hit by an arrow. Then fall. Crashing down to earth with no flap of feathers: a stonemade bird falling like a rock. Beyond that, everything was blurred and obscured, like a landscape seen through heavy rain.

The death-stone was now frost-cold in his hand.

Hearst knew the grey death was now sweeping outwards almost as fast as a man can run. He remembered Looming Forest, remembered the wizard Garash treading on a stonemade face, breaking the stone curve of an eye to reveal an eyesocket empty but for a bit of stone the size of a pea. He remembered Prince Comedo's toy – a survivor living on with

411

stonemade hands and mutilating injuries to the legs and face.

And he remembered, again, Ep Pass – a raft and its crew freezing to stone then sinking. The wizard Phyphor, the big bone in his thigh shattered by a rock. A skin of stone forming on the river's surface, then breaking under its own weight and sinking. And later, months later . . . stonemade bodies of a defeated army that had tried to defend Runcorn against Elkor Alish.

'Rest,' said Miphon.

Hearst lowered the death-stone.

His arm was shaking.

The air was clearing now, sunlight sharpening to shadows, and he could see across a grey stonemade plain to Androlmarphos. As he watched, the walls appeared to dissolve as the stones they were made of took advantage of their freedom.

'The pyramid!' said Miphon.

And Hearst saw the pyramid to the east was similarly dissolving. He heard a strange sound, reminiscent of shattering ice. Was it from the pyramid? No – it was the skimrock surface of the rivers breaking up. The air was absolutely dry, like the freeze-dried air of winter in the Cold West, and sounds carried with precision for great distances. He heard a distant, inarticulate roar, like the far-off sound of surf beating against a beach or ice-cliffs breaking away from a glacier undermined by the sea.

'What's that noise?' said Hearst.

'The rocks,' said Miphon. 'Shouting.'

The death-stone still felt cold in Hearst's hand. So much power – which any coward or criminal could use, given the chance. Appalling wars could be fought by men who would never be faced with the necessity of meeting their enemies face to face. Given such weapons, war could become, for the victors, an abstraction, a game – they would be like gods, removed from the realities of hand-to-hand combat. They would never have to make the true warrior's commitment to death, but

412

they, standing at the centre of a circle of sanitary destruction, would wreck entire civilizations.

'I'm going to get the first batch of soldiers,' said Miphon. 'Stand clear.'

He turned the ring on his finger, disappearing into the green bottle. Hearst walked out of the circle of soil onto the plain of stone, leaving the green bottle behind, so the ground was clear for the first batch of soldiers Miphon would bring out.

Abruptly, the stonemade ground in front of him began to crack and split, like ice breaking up when a heavy man steps on it. But the centre of this disruption was twenty paces in front of him, and there was nobody in sight. For a moment he imagined that something gigantic yet invisible was standing on the plain of stone, some avenging hell-fiend or star-giant.

Then the ground erupted upwards.

A rock lurched free of the clutching earth. It was large as a ship. And it roared. A funnelling vortex shape-shifted to a thunder-black mouth, lipless gash grinding as it moved. Hearst staggered backwards, stumbled, fell.

And the monster lurched toward him.

Hearst held up the death-stone, his last resort. And the monster stalled, flinched, shied away, then fled, bellowing, running like a cockroach from flame.

Elsewhere, more rocks were breaking free from the earth. Suddenly fifty men materialised around the green bottle – Miphon and the first batch of soldiers.

'Miphon, no more soldiers!' shouted Hearst. 'Stay! We need you to command the rocks!'

They advanced, Miphon driving rocks before them.

As they approached Androlmarphos, ships that had come down the river began to disembark Farfalla's army. Organising the rocks into an arrow-head formation, Miphon urged them forward, and, as the monsters smashed into the city, Hearst knew that Alish's army was doomed.

CHAPTER FIFTY-ONE

Morgan Hearst opened his eyes and saw a dragon watching him.

'Hello,' said Hearst.

The dragon said nothing, but watched him, eyes unblinking. He could not outstare it. His head hurt too much. Hoping for a few mouthfuls of wine, he reached for the leather bottle that lay beside the bed – but it was empty.

'By the balls of hell,' muttered Hearst.

The woman in bed beside him moved, and murmured something as she dreamed away the last of her sleep. Hearst eased back the coverlet, exposing bum and back. Could he rouse himself to desire again? No: he had debauched himself so thoroughly by now that all his appetites were satiated.

And he had a headache. A bad one.

His mouth, which was dry, tasted foul, as if a stale sock full of dead blowflies had been sitting in it for a couple of weeks.

And his eyes winced from the light.

He had, in short, a hangover. Not the worst one of his life – he did, after all, finally manage to drag himself out of bed – but a pretty bad one.

He dressed, slowly.

The dragon, cunning as a cat, watched him, its eyes unblinking. The stare irritated Hearst: he reached up and tore the banner down from the wall, bunched it up and threw it into one corner of the room. Then he opened the shutters, letting in dazzling morning sunlight. A mistake! He flinched as the light chiseled into his eyes.

414

'Ahyak Rovac,' croaked Hearst.

Any expert on frogs would, from that croak, have diagnosed him as being rather sick.

He found a big stone jar full of water, dunked his head in it, then, without bothering to surface, drank in big, labouring gulps. Then threw up his head and gasped for air.

He felt a little better.

He felt, to be precise, like a man of seventy who has been dead for a day and a half, which was an improvement on feeling like a man of a thousand and three years who has been dead for the better part of a century.

'I'll never drink again, not ever,' muttered Hearst. Then, yielding to the promptings of a certain innate caution: 'Or not without provocation.'

He found that, by now, he could just about endure the light coming in through the window.

From this room, high in Farfalla's palace, Hearst could look out over the city of Selzirk. The streets were as quiet as the mouse the cat played with yesterday, which did not surprise him. Overjoyed by the defeat of the invaders, by the liberation of Androlmarphos and by the news that the army from the Rice Empire had turned back rather than contend against Morgan Hearst and the death-stone, the people of Selzirk had held a festival.

Hearst had thought that, after his years of war and travel, nothing could have surprised him – but never before had he seen an entire city participate in a six-day orgy. He thought it was probably over by now: for one thing, there was hardly a barrel of wine left in the whole city.

On a big table by the window were heaps of assorted rubbish: books, charts, battle-plans, orange peel, dirty clothes, weapons, faded garlands, wilted flowers, a torn silk dress – did he really remember what he remembered, or was he only imagining it? – remnants of

415

Alish's blood-red battle-standard, a copper bracelet, a silver bangle, a scattering of walnuts.

Hearst scooped up the nuts then rummaged the rubbish till he had recovered some cold chicken and half an apple, brown from exposure to the air but still edible.

As Hearst ate, he fingered a multi-faceted black gem inside which a red flame twisted, continually moving and changing shape as if trying to escape. He had found it the day after the defeat of Alish's army which, unable to defend Androlmarphos against walking rocks, had fled the city.

During bitter confused fighting on the quays of Androlmarphos, many rocks, escaping Miphon's control, had gone reeling into the water. There had been blood on Hearst's sword then: he had been in the thick of the fighting. It had seemed, once, that he would meet Alish face to face – then Alish had been wounded by an arrow, and dragged to safety by his comrades.

The pirates had succeeded in getting only five ships to sea. Hearst had wanted to let them go, but seven of the ships captured in the battle on the quays had set out before he could gain control of the confusion. In an eighth ship, Hearst had followed.

At sea, it had seemed the better seamanship of the pirates must take them to safety. Then they had passed a pod of whales. Miphon had used his powers of control to make the whales attack Elkor Alish's ships, with devastating results.

With three ships sunk, Hearst had tried to persuade Miphon to let the others escape. But Miphon, intoxicated by success – and well Hearst knew that enthusiasm – had refused. Hearst had broken Miphon's concentration by throwing a bucket of seawater over him, and had then signalled the ships under his command to withdraw toward Androlmarphos, leaving Alish's surviving ships to pick up the men from the craft sunk by whales.

416

So Alish, as far as Hearst knew, had escaped. Hearst had let him go. And why not? Alish could do little damage now. Under Alish's leadership, his troops had lost the city of Androlmarphos and the fleet they had used to attack it; most of the men of his command were dead or had been taken prisoner. It was not the kind of record that would attract many enthusiastic followers.

All things considered, nobody had gained anything from the struggle for Androlmarphos. Men, ships and horses had been destroyed, together with the greater part of the city's eastern walls, and much good arable land outside the city was now sheeted over with stone. However, Hearst had obtained this trophy – the multi-faceted black gem with flame dancing inside it.

He had found it when inspecting the ruins of the pyramid east of Androlmarphos; it had been lying beside the golden coffin of the wizard emperor who had been buried there. Miphon had named the gem for what it was: a key to the tower of Ebber. Farfalla had insisted that it be thrown away, saying it was known that the tower was haunted by fearful danger; Hearst had kept the gem, mostly because his pride told him he had yielded to Farfalla's judgment too many times already.

He finished his meagre meal and left his quarters. In the rooms and corridors of Farfalla's palace, servants were cleaning up, repairing the damage done by the festivities. He was right: the holiday was over. And Hearst knew that soon he must go south, bearing the death-stone to the Castle of Controlling power. Having used it himself, he felt personally responsible for seeing that it was decently laid to rest.

He decided that today his first job would be to see how the wounded were faring. All had been transported to Selzirk in the red bottle or the green, and Miphon was supervising their welfare. Miphon would not have been distracted by the festivities, as Hearst knew – but he had allowed himself to neglect every single one of his responsibilities.

He still had a headache; his mind was limping along on crutches. He resisted the temptation to go and seek out a drink, suspecting that one would lead to another; Miphon had given him a severe lecture on drink recently, and Hearst, grudgingly, was beginning to think the wizard might have a point.

*　*　*

Late in the afternoon, Hearst approached the private apartments of the kingmaker Farfalla. A solitary guard stood aside to let him enter; no doorway in all of Selzirk was barred to the city's hero, Morgan Hearst.

Farfalla was sitting reading a pile of reports when Hearst found her. She looked up, smiled. He did not return her smile.

'Morgan,' said Farfalla. 'How good to see you.'

Hearst said nothing.

'Our interrogators have been at work while the city indulged itself. Look – we've charts which show the Greater Teeth in detail, and all the defences of the largest harbour on Stokos.'

Farfalla held out the charts for Hearst's inspection. He did not move, but stared at her, his grey eyes cold and hard.

'All right,' said Farfalla. 'Say what you have to.'

'You know what I've got to say,' said Hearst.

'Then it won't hurt me to hear it, will it?'

'No,' said Hearst, 'I suppose it won't.'

And suddenly he felt tired, very tired, and sat down.

'Would you like some wine?' said Farfalla.

'It might help,' said Hearst, despite his earlier resolutions.

Farfalla poured amber-coloured wine into glasses of cut crystal. The wine had a strange, penetrating, flowery smell.

'This comes from Vasserway, far to the north, in the Ravlish Lands,' said Farfalla.

'The wine or the crystal?' said Hearst.

'Both,' said Farfalla. 'You know we trade with the world.'

That, it must be said, was an exaggeration. Nevertheless, Hearst said:

'I know it.'

He watched Farfalla sip her wine, then reached out and took her glass from her hand.

'Are you afraid of poison?' said Farfalla, picking up the glass she had prepared for Hearst, and draining it. 'There. Safe, see? What kind of person do you think I am?'

'A liar!' said Hearst. 'I know that much, at least. I found the messenger, you see. The wounded man who brought the message saying the Rice Empire was invading the Harvest Plains.'

'How did you recognise him?'

'Nobody commands soldiers without developing a good head for faces. I recognised him. You know I told Miphon to make a special point of seeing to him, but Miphon was told he was dead.'

'Of course. He would have seen straight away that the man had only been recently wounded. You'd have known the same if you'd been the one to clean and dress his wound. For our story to work –'

'I had to believe he'd spent days on horseback riding all the way from the border. So you told your lie. But why, Farfalla?'

'You were talking of a siege,' said Farfalla. 'How long would that have lasted? Androlmarphos could have been resupplied from the sea. To take the city, you'd have had to storm the walls and fight for possession street by street, house by house. The city would have been destroyed, its people with it. I did what I had to.'

'You lied to me,' said Hearst.

'Considered as an instrument of state, a lie, unlike a sword, draws no blood.'

419

'Ohio died because of your lies.'

'So he died. Someone had to die.'

'He was my friend!'

'And does that make you think you have a monopoly on suffering?' said Farfalla. 'Do you know what I suffer? Do you know what I have to go through?

'I didn't want this. I never wanted this. I grew up in Kelebes, a potter's daughter. Do you know once I was chosen, I could never see my family again? That's the law. To secure the equitable government of the Harvest Plains. To protect against nepotism. Fine phrases, aren't they? Just think for one moment what that law means to the kingmaker.

'My sons are soldiers. Do you think that's what I would have chosen for them? The law decided their destiny, Morgan. I'm the ruler of the greatest nation in Argan, but I'm a prisoner of the law. You've told me how you've suffered, Morgan, but you're not the only one who's suffered.

'You can't imagine the burdens of power – being responsible for the life or death of an entire empire. You can't imagine the difficulties of government when there's so many ready to take advantage of the slightest weakness, the slightest failing. I think –'

'Don't talk to me of the burdens of power,' said Hearst. 'Power is its own reward – the greatest reward known. There's not a single person in your empire who doesn't envy you, not one who doesn't wish they could be you.'

'Do you really believe that?' said Farfalla.

'Yes,' said Hearst.

'So you'd take that power if I offered it to you.'

'Sure, sure,' said Hearst. 'On a slice of the moon garnished with stardust.'

'I'm serious!'

'Then you're seriously ill. Is it that time of month?'

She slapped him. Hard. Three times.

'You dogshit barbarian!' she said.

'I won't deny my nature,' said Hearst, wiping a trickle of blood from his nose. 'I'm clearly not the person to be offered a throne – not even in jest.'

'Morgan, I wasn't joking. And I don't joke now. My land needs a hero. To the north, Runcorn. To the south, Stokos. The enemy's strength is broken. Now is the time to strike. And, while we're about it, to clean up the Rice Empire.'

Hearst, trying to stop the bleeding from his nose, did not answer. So Farfalla continued:

'The people are ready for you, Morgan. We can teach you what you need to know – language, law, manners. Especially manners! I can abdicate in your favour. That would make difficulties, but those difficulties would yield to necessity and popular demand. Will yield! We need a conqueror.'

'I've fought enough wars already.'

'Have you? Aren't you tempted? Morgan, you could conquer all of Argan!'

He was, for a moment, tempted. He had, for a moment, a vision of a future in which he conquered all, and united the nation of Rovac with his empire of conquest. Despite everything he had said to Alish, Hearst was not entirely immune to the appeal of the old dreams, the old stories. But . . .

'Even if that's what I wanted,' said Hearst, 'I still don't believe that your people would accept me. Not as their ruler.'

'I,' said Farfalla, 'will organise a banquet in your honour. All our most powerful people will be there. You'll see then who will accept you. I won't announce you as ruler unless you decide that's what you want. You'll meet the people. You'll see what they think of you.'

'I'll come to your banquet,' said Hearst.

And, again, he was sorely tempted by the prospect of power. But he reminded himself that he had not really been formally offered anything, yet. And reminded himself, too, that Farfalla had lied to him before – and might do so again.

He was already regretting the coarse, unpardonable joke he had made about her biology. In a royal court, people could be burnt alive for less. He also had the death-stone to worry about. He thought he had convinced Farfalla that seizing the death-stone would eventually lead to her empire being destroyed in a confrontation with the Confederation of Wizards – but what if he was wrong, and she dared regardless?

He began to seriously consider the possibility that this banquet might prove to be the occasion of his murder rather than his coronation.

*　　*　　*

Blackwood entered the Hall of Wine, the largest hall in Farfalla's palace. It was fragrant with flowers: an overflow of lilies, an explosion of roses, and tender bouquets of modest flowers such as larkspur, sea lavender and sweet alyssum.

On the walls were tapestries showing work both urban and rural. At every setting at every table, plain bread and river water were set out for the guests: a ceremonial first course to be consumed before the real feasting began.

Thanks to Miphon's intervention, there had been a break with tradition: the river water had been secretly boiled, thus minimising the risk it posed to the health of aristocrats who usually only drank wine.

No guests had yet arrived; they were attending an opera which was scheduled to end about the middle of the afternoon, after which the feast would begin.

Light for the hall came through stained glass windows showing placid countryside scenes. Nothing anywhere in the hall hinted at violence, warfare or suffering.

'Ah, Blackwood,' said Hearst, emerging from behind one of the ivy-covered trellises concealing doorways through which servants would enter and leave when the feast was underway.

'Where have you been?' said Blackwood.

'Where you haven't, obviously,' said Hearst, with impeccable logic.

'No, seriously.'

'Why seriously? You have an objection to the comical? Eh? You've got a face about as cheery as a pig's backside. What's the problem, friend?'

'Miphon says . . .'

'And is that all he says? The sun says the same, so it's hardly original.'

'I haven't yet told you what he says!' said Blackwood, missing the joke entirely.

'You're worried, friend. Why?'

'Miphon says you've got men on call, armed for combat.'

'And so I have,' said Hearst, turning suddenly serious. 'And, if you really must know, I've been checking the kitchen for poisoners.'

'What are you planning?'

'I,' said Hearst, with energy, 'Am planning to stay alive. As we all have cause to know, that's hardly the easiest of enterprises.'

'Do you suspect Farfalla of something?'

'I suspect her of many things,' said Hearst. 'Of having two breasts, two hips, and heat between her thighs. Nay, I have proof positive of certain – but no, as a gentleman I must stay my tongue, even if I must not necessarily stay my stallion.'

'You seem,' said Blackwood slowly, 'to be drunk.'

'That's what they said to the dog-sodomist after the blacksmith hit him with a sledgehammer,' said Hearst. 'No, I'm not drunk. I'm just a little giddy from standing on a sword-blade.'

'You mean that you expect someone to try and kill you today?'

'I mean,' said Hearst, 'I expect the sky to either stand or fall.'

That was a standard nonsense answer which children on Rovac used on occasion to irritate each other, but to Blackwood it sounded like a random piece of gibberish.

'You,' said Blackwood, slowly, 'are not as bright and cheerful as you seem to be. You are under enormous strain. There are two tides running within you. You are not . . . you are not at all happy.'

'Happy!' roared Hearst. 'Why should I be happy? This damnable death-stone grinding my nerves to the quick and raw. Dead men underfoot in my dreams. That oh so so formidable – unpredictable! inscrutable! – woman Farfalla, who might even now be measuring cloth for my coronation robes or my shroud. I should be happy?!'

Blackwood did not risk an answer.

Hearst paced up and down, as if burning off excess energy. He had dressed so as to intimidate anyone who might be thinking of foul play. Although he did not usually favour ostentation, today he wore a cloak embroidered with dragons. Beneath the cloak, chain mail. At his side, the sword Hast. At his throat, the multi-faceted black gem which was the key to the tower of Ebber, which had been placed in a setting of shining gold which reflected the glow of the dancing flame within.

'Would you be happy if you were in my place?' said Hearst, turning on Blackwood.

The question reminded Blackwood of one Elkor Alish had once asked him: What would you do in my place? If he remembered correctly, his answer on that occasion had been rather impolite. With Hearst, he tried a milder approach.

'You,' said Blackwood, 'are free to be as happy as you like. But there's no need to be so fierce. I've studied Farfalla carefully. I don't think she means murder. I think she really does mean for you to be the ruling power of the Harvest Plains.'

'Perhaps,' said Hearst. 'But there's something mighty

strange going on here. Someone's keeping a secret from me! I can tell it by the way they look at me, the way my footsteps kill their conversations.'

'I think,' said Blackwood, 'that today they plan to consecrate you as a member of the family of the Favoured Blood. Haven't you heard of that ceremony?'

'Oh, I've heard that it happens,' said Hearst. 'But Farfalla has said nothing about performing the ritual for me. Least of all today.'

'You know it has to be done if you want to rule the Harvest Plains,' said Blackwood. 'It's only a ritual to appease the ignorant and the superstitious so they can say their ruler is of the Favoured Blood, but you shouldn't underestimate the importance of it. Most of the people of the Harvest Plains are ignorant and superstitious.'

'But,' said Hearst, 'why didn't Farfalla tell me if I have to go through with this ritual today?'

'The ritual,' said Blackwood, 'consists of an invocation in the language of the Harvest Plains. Not the vernacular, which you've started to learn, but the formal language which they call the Tongue of the Teeth of the Oldest Stone. You wouldn't understand what was being said. At the end of the invocation, they offer you wine. You have to drink. Farfalla might be hoping to get through the ceremony without you understanding what's going on.'

'I'd do what's necessary,' said Hearst. 'Doesn't she understand that?'

'Does anyone understand anyone?' said Blackwood.

In Blackwood's judgment, Farfalla truly did want Hearst as a leader for her people, and feared he might take offence if told he first had to be consecrated as one of the Favoured Blood – after all, he was a hero and a conqueror in his own right.

'I think,' said Hearst, 'you know a little more than you're telling me.'

'Do you really want to know all I've learnt since

coming to Selzirk?' said Blackwood innocently. 'For a start, I've read an old book of poetry –'

'Spare us,' said Hearst. 'Tell me, when they bring me this wine – do I have to drink it all? Does it say yes or no in those old books and parchments you've become addicted to?'

'I don't know,' said Blackwood. 'I'll try and find out, quickly. But if it's poison you're worried about –'

'It is.'

'– then I'll see if Miphon knows of anything which could protect you.'

'Do that,' said Hearst. 'And I'll be grateful.'

'Then,' said Blackwood, 'perhaps you'd give me an advance on your gratitude and reward me by letting me know the real reason why you're so badly upset.'

'I'm not upset!' roared Hearst.

And, such was the violence in his voice that Blackwood precipitated himself from the room, thinking it unwise to stay longer.

In truth, the reason for Hearst's strange mood probably had something to do with a letter he had received from a secret embassy from Runcorn. The letter, a bitter epistle from Elkor Alish, accused Hearst of being a coward, a traitor, and other terrible things.

Hearst had burnt the letter, but its words were branded indelibly on his mind.

CHAPTER FIFTY-TWO

Sunlight through stained glass splayed colours across Hearst's hands: orange, green, red. A goblet in front of him still held wine; blood-red wine. He had taken only a sip; Blackwood had told him a sip was enough.

It was done: he was now, for the purposes of the Harvest Plains, one of those of the Favoured Blood. Farfalla's intentions must now be clear to everyone.

The guests laughed, smiled, joked, pleased that the Rovac warrior Morgan Hearst had consented to sample that blood-red wine, that his destiny was settled. Yet the mood in the hall was far from light-hearted. There was something over-eager in the laughter, a hint of savage anticipation in the smiles, a touch of greed in the eyes.

Hearst knew that these people, having tasted victory, had acquired an appetite for more of the same. Perhaps that was why Farfalla now chose to yield leadership to him: because the people, desiring a war-leader, would find one if they were not given one.

Hearst watched.

He was stone-cold sober; apart from that one sip of wine, he had drunk nothing. He toyed with some cold chicken, but had little appetite for it; he had already indulged heavily in an oily, greasy concoction of milk, cream, liver, olive oil, eggs and charcoal which Miphon had prepared for him; this would line Hearst's stomach for the duration of the feast, delaying the absorption of any poisons, and afterwards he could vomit his stomach clean in private.

Hearst bit off some chicken, chewed it and swallowed it down. He felt distinctly queasy, thanks to the oily burden in his stomach, but he suspected if he complained to Miphon he would get no sympathy from the wizard. Hearst took another sip of wine. Just a small sip. Then dared a little more chicken.

A harpist was getting to his feet. He called for silence:

'Peace, I beg you, peace. Silence! Not to honour my song, but to honour the one my song praises. Peace, now!'

Farfalla herself stood:

'Silence! You know who we honour. Silence should be our duty, our pleasure.'

There was silence in the hall then, although eating did not stop, and many refilled their glasses. The minstrel struck a chord on his harp, and began. He sang in the Galish Trading Tongue, as a courtesy to Morgan Hearst; most in the Hall of Wine knew that language:

> The moon it was riding, but still we had light,
> The stars for our guide and our fortune foretold,
> For strength we were gathering in the depths of the night
> For attack at the daybreak – all strength to the bold!

With the first verse sung, Hearst knew the song was hardly original. It was a pastiche of the song of the Victory of the Prince of the Favoured Blood, which was declaimed in different languages in every kingdom of Argan. Hearst himself had roused out the words of that song, long ago in the High Castle in the land of Trest.

The minstrel told of reinforcements joining Hearst's army under cover of darkness, of Alish's army attacking as day was breaking, of the cavalry of the Harvest Plains shattering that attack, and of Alish's own cavalry meeting destruction when charging the burial mound. And then – distorting history slightly – the minstrel told of the rout of Alish's army:

And the scream! And the Scream!
It is one throat and all,
Blood greeting sword as the sun greets the sky.
Wheel them, heel them, fleet them along:
It is ours! It is ours!
Raise the Banner, the Song!

There was more: much more. At the end, everyone in the Hall of Wine cheered. Cheered? They screamed: screamed in a blood-heat frenzy. And every voice that was raised was calling for war.

Hearst remembered, vividly, the aftermath of the battle that was rousing such enthusiasm amongst the banquet guests. He recalled the wounded, the crush injuries, the amputations, shocked faces, a brave smile from a mask of blood and bone, the last words of a dying man. He felt a sudden surge of nausea, and stumbled from the hall, leaving by an exit reserved for the most important people.

Outside, he vomited into a capacious vase, bringing up every bit of the noxious mixture which had burdened his stomach. Then he returned.

'Are you sick?' said Farfalla, seeing his pallor.

'I'm fighting fit,' said Hearst, draining his goblet. The wine made him feel better. 'Give me more wine.'

'Of course,' said Farfalla. 'There's going to be another song now.'

Hearst drank deeply. Wine warm as the sun: a healing heat in his belly. A minstrel stood and began to tell of the struggle for control of Androlmarphos. Hearst remembered. Wild rocks in the streets. A man trapped against a wall then mashed. Swords in the sun. A scream hoisted on the point of a spear.

He recharged his cup. He drank.

The minstrel told of the sea battle. And Hearst remembered. Timbers heaved up in the surge of the sea's swell. The grey whales lofted up from the waters: huge humps death-heavy. They drove forward. Rend-

429

ing timbers: a mast falling: a man jumping to the drowning sea.

As he drank, wine favoured him with its intimate warmth. Song followed wine; wine followed song. Then a new minstrel rose, and called for silence:

Now silence, silence, for my song
Is more than worth the hearing:
A hero's deeds, a hero's tale
The subject of its praising.

And the minstrel began his version of the legend of how the Rovac warrior Morgan Hearst killed the dragon Zenphos in the lair on the mountain of Maf. Hearst remembered hearing that legend in Skua, the squalid port on the coast of Trest that bore the same name as Ohio's fine ship. Ohio! Dead now, killed by a fall from a horse, killed by Morgan Hearst, killed by Farfalla's treachery, by a lie about an army from the Rice Empire.

Hearst got to his feet. Looked around. Mouths opened, closed. Blood within mouths. Shadows within eyes. Bright-bone teeth glistening with laughter.

Hearst remembered the vision he had seen at Skua: an ocean of fire a thousand years wide. He remembered another vision: Gorn's head, blood on Gorn's lips, death in the sockets of his eyes. At Skua, he had run amok, sword slicing at any and every, his voice raging to madness.

'What are you standing for?' said Farfalla. 'Sit down.'

Hearst turned, stared at her. Death was on her hands. And there must be a death to pay for a death.

He drew his sword.

He remembered what happened at Larbreth. The woman Ethlite! He had taken her head: his sword slicing away the voice which had dared to speak to Elkor Alish as if to a slave. Now, here was another woman: and this one had much more to answer for.

430

'What do you want?' said Farfalla.

She was afraid.

'What do you think I want?' said Hearst.

He looked out over the Hall of Wine. Everyone was watching him. Reckless, he roared:

'What do you think I want?'

And the answer came back:

'Watashi! Wa – wa – watashi!'

Watashi. Blood. Fear. Death.

They thought he meant to kill Farfalla. And more: they wanted it. They were ready for it. In Morgan Hearst, they saw the promise of power, glory, wealth, an empire that would control all of Argan. They knew it would demand killing: they were ready for the slaughter to begin. Now.

Hearst raked his sword over the table, scattering dishes, plates, bowls, cups, bottles. He threw back his head and screamed. The crowd responded with another roar:

'Wa – wa – Watashi! Wa – wa – Watashi!'

They were as drunk as he was. And as mad. Whatever he commanded, they would do. His word would be law. They were ready to worship him. Yet what was he? Who and what was Morgan Hearst? He was a man who had been the death of those who followed him most faithfully. Who had been fooled by a woman's lies. Who had sickened of slaughter, yet, when tempted, was ready to accept command of an empire which lusted for war and conquest.

Morgan Hearst turned on his heel and stumbled from the room. Farfalla sat at the table, shock on her face, clearly realising how close she had come to losing her head. Blackwood and Miphon rose and followed Hearst at a discreet distance, knowing there was no telling what he might do when he was drunk like this.

* * *

Farfalla sat alone in the Hall of Wine, isolated

amongst her people. A drunken cavalry officer stood on a table to propose a toast to Morgan Hearst; the toast was taken up with a roar of approval. Since power is based on consent, Hearst now had absolute power: these people would do whatever he said. Farfalla, kingmaker of the Harvest Plains, was ruler now in name only.

This was what she had wanted: to place Morgan Hearst on the throne of the Harvest Plains. To free herself from the burdens of power. What she had not wanted, and had not anticipated, was the enthusiasm she saw in the hall, where people she had once thought rational now raised their voices in an uproar like ghouls baying for blood. She knew the name of this madness: war fever.

She wondered what she had done.

*   *   *

Hearst found his way to the battlements of the original wizard castle round which Selzirk had been built. At first he lurched and staggered a little, but soon his gait steadied to the regular rhythm that would defeat league after league on a long march.

Marching along, he remembered, with a terrible drink-sodden nostalgia, the wars of his youth. He sang, tunelessly, drunken snatches of songs he had learnt by campfires on foreign shores, mountains, tundras. Those early days had been the best: he had been just another soldier in the armies of Rovac, then, with no responsibility except to listen and obey.

He remembered, in particular, the Cold West. Yes! He remembered a battlefield by sunlight, rank upon rank of gleaming armour and glittering weapons. A sudden surge of pride and ego, rising to adrenalin heights. Battle-drums booming, a battle-chant roaring:

Who are we? We are the Rovac!

432

What do we do? We kill!
We kill! We kill! We kill!

Kill! Yes. That was the chant. Those were the days.
Battles in the shadow of the Far Wall. The struggle for
control of the pass commanding the Valley of Insects.
The sack of the Temple of the Thousand Snowflowers.
Grand simplicities.

And what now? Questions and confusions. And what
was the source of those questions, those confusions?
Hearst knew. In the beginning was a lie. After he had
crawled down from the mountain of Maf, he had
allowed people to believe he had killed the dragon; he
had boasted himself to a hero, and all the problems had
started.

Alish had known him to be a liar: and their friendship
had begun to fail.

So what was he to do?

There was only one way out. The trouble had begun
with a lie. The trouble had begun when he had
pretended to be a hero. Well then, the simple answer
was to become a hero. A real hero. Then there would be
no lie.

But –

Muddled with drink, he remembered, in a blurred,
half-hearted way, having doubts about the very ethos of
heroism itself. Well, no doubt those doubts were part of
the package that went with being a coward. He tried to
kick himself for his cowardice, and, as a consequence,
fell over.

'Doubt is for women,' muttered Hearst, hauling
himself to his feet. 'A hero knows!'

The battlements stretched clear and empty ahead to a
tower. The tower of the order of Ebber.

Hearst drew his sword.

He was drunk, but he drew with the grace of a dancer.
The blade leapt clean and clear from the scabbard,
slicing into the sunlight.

That was fast.

Farfalla had taught him that: had taught him how to be better and faster with his left hand than he had ever been with his right. For Hearst, that was a great gift. A gift of friendship. Yet she had lied, had betrayed him, had caused Ohio's death. What should he do with her?

– A hero will know the answer to that. Strength, man of Rovac, strength. Hastsword, my brother, my brother in blood, destiny waits for us. Strength, Hearst, hero, song-singer, sword-master, leader of men.

Leader of men. Yes. He remembered leading men to their deaths. In Looming Forest, when Heenmor – no, he would not think about it. He would concentrate on the task at hand. The man who pretended to be a hero must become a hero for real.

He had killed a dragon in the wild country deep in the heart of Argan. Wasn't that enough? No: he had been faced with a choice between the dragon or a duel with Elkor Alish. Either might have killed him. Many men go into battle for fear that if they run, their commanders will slay them; we do not call them heroes because one fear overbalances another.

The tower of the order of Ebber was closer now. This was what they were all afraid of. Farfalla was afraid of it. The people of the Harvest Plains were afraid of it. From memories he had inherited from the wizard Phyphor, Hearst knew that even the wizards of the order of Arl feared the order of Ebber.

– But we, Hastsword, my hero, we have no fear. Are you with me, my brother? Are you with me? Who are we? We are the Rovac! The heroes! Strength, man of Rovac, strength.

Hearst glanced round for one last look at the sunlight. He saw Blackwood and Miphon on the battlements. They started to run forward, shouting. At the distance, he could not hear what it was they were trying to tell him. But he was pleased to see them there.

They would witness his deed.

434

– And now. Now! Do it!

Hearst reached out and touched the substance of the tower of Ebber. It parted before his hand. With the flame of the black-faceted jewel burning at his throat, he walked into the tower of Ebber. The way closed behind him, and he stood in darkness, sword in hand.

Slowly, pale lights like wan and wasted captive stars came to life and illuminated the interior of the tower. Strange devices loomed out of the gloom: towering configurations of burnished metal in which the features of man, bird and insect were blended as if in a nightmare. They were, for the moment, silent. Quiescent. Waiting.

Hearst, bewildered, gaped at them.

The wan starlight grew no stronger. No threat came from the silent metal. Slowly, he dared a footfall forward. Then another. Gaining confidence, he walked forward, stirring up a little dust. He sneezed, vigorously, three times. Nothing and nobody challenged in response.

Ahead, he saw a stairway.

Hearst climbed the stairs. Sword poised to strike, he sidled into the chamber above. It was bare but for a series of stone tubs in which water, lit from below, glittered with an uncanny light. Looking into one, Hearst saw the water seemed to descend for leagues, clear as an ice-bright winter sky. Far below, out of reach, globes spun in that clear water, some white, some orange, some red; one globe – how beautiful! – was all browns and blues, capped top and bottom with irregular markings of winter white.

Hearst watched. Waited. Listened. Nothing moved. No challenge came. He went up the next set of stairs – then the next.

By the time Hearst reached the uppermost storey of the tower of the order of Ebber, he had only scorn for those who were afraid of it. It contained a great many strange things, to be sure – but there was nothing to be

435

afraid of. Nothing that was malignant: nothing that was even alive.

He was glad of that.

He had sobered up enough by now to see what a terrible risk he had taken. It was one thing to risk his own life: any man was free to do that. It was quite another thing to risk the entire city of Selzirk by daring to stir up whatever evil might have been lurking in the tower. As the effects of the wine wore off, Hearst saw, too, that no feat of heroism, however bold and outrageous, was going to resolve his problems, his questions. Still, in a way, he was disappointed that he had found no challenge worthy of his courage.

The uppermost storey of the tower of Ebber was almost empty. The only thing in it was a wooden staff, which looked much like the staff of power that the wizard Phyphor used to carry. Hearst sheathed his sword, deciding to take the staff as a souvenir. Blackwood, with all the reading he had done since they arrived in Selzirk, might even know how to get some use out of the staff.

Hearst took hold of the staff: and was overcome. He had no defences whatsoever against what he had encountered. He lacked even the time in which to register his protest, it was done so quickly.

And afterwards, once it was done, Hearst found that he could observe everything: but could alter nothing.

*   *   *

The wizard Ebonair – he called himself by the name of the island on which he had been born, many thousands of years before – held his staff in the only hand available to him. He looked down at the hook which had been substituted for the right hand. Clumsy. How did that happen? He scanned the available memories, saw how the copper-strike snake injected its venom into the hand, how the sword rose and fell,

436

sweeping the hand away. Truly the action of a ruthless man!

Then, scanning other memories, Ebonair changed his mind. Not ruthless at all. Weak. Confused. Sentimental. Ebonair had not tasted such agonising since the time he invaded the mind of an adolescent student priest of the Temple of the Ultimate Ethic. Weak, yes: yet successful. Such opportunities! Reclaiming the Harvest Plains would take only a word.

The wizard Ebonair had known it would take a hero to seize the key to the tower of Ebber from the pyramid tomb, and then to invade the tower itself, but he had been successful beyond his wildest dreams. Instead of using the hero's body and reputation to fight to reclaim his kingdom, he had only to step outside the tower and all would be on their knees before him.

Another memory.

Interesting.

Underground darkness. The noise of the river, rushing, rushing. A voice. Pain in the voice: weakness. Fear. 'You will have the power to enter the tower of Arl. And you will understand the High Speech, the reading of it, the writing of it, the speaking of it.' Darkness and the beat of a heart. Darkness, and then –

Interesting indeed. Ebonair had never known that a wizard of Arl could, as he died, transfer his memories to the living. A pretty trick. A pretty trick indeed. But it is one thing to pass on a few disorganised memories: quite another to preserve one's identity within an artefact while spending centuries engaged in the Meditations, building the power needed to take possession of another body.

Such long centuries! Dust. Madness. The taste of ambition sustaining the will when eroding silence seems beyond endurance. And now the time has come.

He yawned.

Grinned like a skull.

Then laughed.

He was young, free, alive, with all the world supine beneath his trampling feet!

Time to go . . .

The wizard Ebonair descended to the lowest level of the tower of Ebber, in which were gathered many metal devices from the Days of Wrath. In his last incarnation, the secrets of those devices had escaped him. In this incarnation, he hoped to do better. Ebonair commanded the tower:

'Open!'

A doorway opened to a flood of afternoon sunlight, revealing the two who stood on the battlements.

'Hearst,' said Blackwood. 'Are you all right?'

'What happened?' said Miphon. 'Morgan, you look strange. Are you hurt?'

As Blackwood and Miphon stepped forward, the wizard Ebonair let the Hearst-body sag toward the floor. Miphon ran forward and caught it, brushing against the staff of power; the wizard Ebonair took him with . . . a little difficulty. That was not as easy as he had expected!

'Miphon,' said Blackwood. 'Help me. Hearst's unconscious. Why are you standing there like that?'

Ebonair scanned Miphon's memories. Pox. Pox doctor. Scabs. Boils. Poultices. Leaking wombs. Bad backs. Leeches, application of. Bruises. Solicitous words to a man . . . what? Dying? If dying, why bother with him? Hands greasy, slimy, blood, blood, tender hands easing a cord free from the neck, taking the weight, eliciting the first birthcry – and smiling! Spare us from biology.

'Miphon,' said Blackwood, shaking him.

'Take this,' said Ebonair, getting the Miphon-voice all wrong, but the note of command was right, the peasant took the staff of power even as the wizard let the Miphon-body sag toward the floor.

'No!' screamed Blackwood, as it happened.

But for Ebonair, it was easy. Easier than taking over

438

the Miphon-body. Almost as easy as seizing the Hearst-body. Memories now. A quick scan – nothing, after all, to be gained from the mind of a peasant. Sky. Blue sky. Sky? Is that all?

Sky, blue sky, the colour of my lover's eyes;
Leaf, young leaf, her hands no softer.

The transfiguring vision. A trick, surely. A trick of perception. An illusion. Like a drug-trance. Like a mystic's starvation delusion. Not true. Not real. No!

And Ebonair screamed:

'No!'

Locked in the Blackwood-body, Ebonair collapsed.

A poet may, on occasion, see the world transfigured by visionary perception yet still come to terms with the world. A man such as Blackwood may see the world that way constantly, day by day, and survive by isolating himself as much as possible from human society, evading the pains of the world by immersing himself in scholarship and study.

But Ebonair, viewing himself through the lens of visionary revelation, saw how his entire life had been devoted to killing, distorting, maiming or repressing the flame of life which persists in every entity; worse still he saw the damage he had done to himself.

A saint may live with such visions; an ordinary man, with some effort, may survive them. For Ebonair, they threatened madness. He had to escape. He thrust the staff of power out to touch the supine Hearst-body. The next moment, Ebonair occupied that body: but in such a panic that the body was thrown into spasm.

The head of the Hearst-body slammed against one of the inert metal machines from the Days of Wrath, and was knocked unconscious.

*   *   *

Miphon came to slowly. He was groggy, dizzy. His head hurt. He blinked at the sunlight streaming into the tower of Ebber. He half-expected to see spectators crowding the entrance: surely many people in Selzirk must be able to see the doorway to the tower of Ebber was open. But there was nobody. Of course. They were afraid of it. And clearly there were good reasons to support their superstitious dread of the place.

Quickly Miphon checked both Blackwood and Hearst. Both were unconscious. So where was the wizard? Ebonair: yes, that was his name. Miphon had learnt a little from his enemy even as his enemy was learning from him: he knew to look for the staff of power. Which was on the floor of the tower. By Hearst. Which implied that Ebonair was trapped for the time being in the unconscious Hearst-body. Which meant there was a simple way of getting rid of Ebonair: kill Hearst, then burn the staff of power for good measure. But no, he could not do that! Or could he? Hearst would not have hesitated, in his place. It was the only way.

To delay the decision, Miphon sat back and tried to remember what Ebonair had discovered when rummaging through Miphon's memory. Mostly images of sickness and healing. Discovering Miphon to be a member of the order of Nin, an animal-caller and a pox-doctor, Ebonair had not looked very deeply.

There was certainly something he had overlooked.

The sleeping secrets: occult strength of the order of Nin.

The sleeping secrets: power too terrible for any human being to be trusted to live with, power sufficient to overwhelm the established order of the world. In the depths of the Shackle Mountains, in the shadow of thunder, in the place between darkness and light, they were taught by the book of Nariq, and then they were taught to forget.

Was this the time to recall the sleeping secrets? To open, as the saying went, the Book of Nariq?

No.

First, because the problem could be resolved by a simple act of murder. And second, because the sleeping secrets, whatever they were, might not be suitable for overcoming Ebonair without killing Morgan Hearst.

Miphon stood over Hearst's body. It would take only a moment: he knew where to put the blade. He could say afterwards that an evil spirit killed Hearst: the story would be true enough in its way. Hearst would have killed, if necessary.

But Hearst . . . yes, Miphon remembered how he himself, on a ship at sea, drunk with battle, had sent whales again and again to batter Alish's ships. Hearst had thrown a bucket of water over Miphon, to save the life of a man he had once counted as a friend. Yes, in Miphon's situation, Hearst would have killed if necessary – but if there was another way, he would have tried that first. Could a wizard do less than a Rovac warrior?

Yet it was an improper way to use the sleeping secrets. They were meant for the occasion of greatest danger. And what would Morgan Hearst have said to that? Miphon could imagine the answer: 'I dare!'

And, if Hearst died, there would be no chance for Miphon to present him to the Confederation of Wizards at the Castle of Controlling Power in a bid to resolve the age-old enmity between the wizards and the Rovac.

Miphon, consoling himself with the thought that he worked in the interests of the greatest good, began the Rites of Recall, and was soon lost in a trance of remembrance.

CHAPTER FIFTY-THREE

Miphon opened his eyes and saw the Hearst-body studying him intently. It held a leather bag which, Miphon knew, contained the death-stone.

'Hearst?'

'What do you think?'

Everything about Hearst-body was subtly wrong: the carriage of the shoulders, the angle the head was held at, the way the feet were together instead of shoulder-width apart.

'Ebonair,' said Miphon.

'Precisely,' said the wizard of Ebber, gloating. 'You know what I hold here?'

'The death-stone,' said Miphon. 'Careful how you use it. It brings stones to life.'

'But not the stones of a wizard castle: they've no minds left to animate. I saw that much when I scanned your memories. From here, I could destroy Selzirk without the slightest risk to myself.'

'But a mad rock might charge the battlements!'

'Ah,' said Ebonair. 'But from this warrior's memories, I see the death-stone repels the rocks it animates. I also see . . . that with this death-stone, I might become a god.'

'Heenmor killed himself experimenting with the death-stone.'

'I'm not Heenmor,' said Ebonair. 'Besides, I have an advantage he never had: your mind. You can read the thoughts of rock and stone. Isn't that right? A fascinating ability. It may help me much in my research.'

And Miphon thought:

– This has gone on long enough.

442

– So do it!

And he did.

The order of Nin cultivated the ability to read and influence the minds of things that live wild. The powers of the sleeping secrets were the powers to read, understand and control both the minds and bodies of humans, and to change the same. This power could operate at a distance of up to ten leagues.

Miphon closed his eyes. When he closed his eyes, he saw the world around him in terms of life-energies. The stones of the castle were dead, inert. Monstrous powers glowered in the silent machines from the Days of Wrath. Blackwood's mind was a dull red glow, still unconscious. Hearst's mind was another dull glow, but in that glow was a web of green energy, which could be unravelled by . . . yes, Miphon saw how it could be done.

Miphon stood up. Wrong: his ghost stood up. He looked down on the bodies of flesh and blood. With hands that had no substance, he grasped part of that web of green energy and pulled. The green web started to unravel.

The wizard Ebonair felt his mind disintegrating into the nightmarish turmoil of a bad drug-dream. But in his agony he realised this was no dream: this was his own destruction. He used the last resource available to him. He used the Ultimate Injunction.

'Segenarith!' shouted Ebonair.

Miphon's view of a world of life-energies disappeared. His sensation of inhabiting a ghost-body was gone. He was back in his own flesh. He stared at the swaying Hearst-body. The echo of that shout still rang in his mind: Segenarith. The word had been sufficient to overcome the powers of the sleeping secrets.

'A pity to kill you,' said Ebonair, his voice slow and slurred. 'Such power! But there's no other way, is there?'

Ebonair dropped the bag containing the death-stone.

443

He drew the sword Hast. Miphon tried to conjure up that vision of a world of life-energies: tried to work his way back into the ghost-body. He failed.

'Die,' slurred Ebonair.

The sword Hast ripped through the air. A wild swing. The wizard was un-coordinated, brain-damaged. He had almost been too late using the Ultimate Injunction.

Miphon leapt back out of reach of the sword. Ebonair slashed at him again. Miphon was forced back, out toward the entrance. If he turned to run, if he took his eyes off that blade, he would be killed.

The sword swung again.

Miphon jumped back – too slow!

He screamed as the blade knifed across his flesh. He fell to the stones of the battlements, clutching his pain. The Hearst-body loomed over him. A voice cried:

'Hold!'

Through eyes that were slits of pain, Miphon saw Blackwood taking the death-stone from its bag. He saw Ebonair wheel, advance on Blackwood, then hesitate. Miphon heard Ebonair begin to speak. It was hard to hear because of the pain. But then the pain was –

– less.

– Pox doctor, heal yourself.

– Bone to be bone. Flesh to be flesh. Skin to be skin.

And Ebonair was saying:

'Be reasonable. It's a generous offer. To rule the Harvest Plains is no small thing. You can't do it by yourself.'

'Tell me more,' said Blackwood.

Though Ebonair could not see how Miphon was healing, Blackwood could – and was having a hard job to keep his amazement from his face.

'You could become a wizard if you wished,' said Ebonair. 'You already know the High Speech. That makes it much easier. Have you any idea what it means to become a wizard?'

Miphon was ready.

He struck.

This time he had no sense of the world as life-energies, no sense of himself as a ghost. He had only needed such tricks of perception while he was first coming to terms with the powers of the sleeping secrets. Now Miphon used his strength swiftly, intuitively, doing exactly what he had to.

One moment Ebonair was talking. The next instant his mind had been torn to pieces. The Hearst-body collapsed again. Miphon looked at Blackwood, who stood flipping the death-stone from one hand to the other.

'You can let it go now,' said Miphon.

Blackwood dropped the death-stone as if it was poison.

'Is Hearst dead?' said Blackwood.

'I hope not,' said Miphon.

He examined Hearst's mind. The sensation was almost like listening to the mind of some wild thing – but sharper, clearer, more painful. Painful because Miphon felt Hearst's agony, his indecision, the suffering of a man trying to cope with the complexities of a world which the heroic simplicities of his upbringing had not equipped him to deal with.

And Miphon realised he could cure that pain, deleting certain memories, closing down certain lines of thought. He could instill, where necessary, an ordered doctrine of etiquette and ethics, shaping Morgan Hearst into the precise tool he needed to perform that highest function: bringing about a peace between wizards and warriors. What greater glory than to serve as a peacemaker?

Hearst groaned, sitting up.

'Are you all right?' said Blackwood, kneeling by him.

'It's all over now,' said Miphon. 'The wizard's dead.'

'What about that staff?' said Hearst.

'That's just a piece of wood now,' said Miphon.

445

'There's no power left in it any more.'

It was hard to talk in a normal tone: he felt drunk with exultation. Such power! He would use it to reform the world.

Miphon knew what had to be done to Hearst. Would he also have to reshape Blackwood? He examined Blackwood's memories, let himself see the world through Blackwood's eyes. By the time Miphon was finished, he was very quiet; he had been first shocked then humbled by what he had learnt.

In Blackwood's memories, Miphon had discovered visions. He had seen the flame of life; he had seen the beauty of the vitality which graces every life. He had seen the way in which each thing is true to its own nature: nothing can be changed by an application of cleverness without destroying its essential nature. He had learnt how much he lacked in wisdom: what he had been about to do to Morgan Hearst would have been as evil as anything ever done by Ebonair.

'What's the matter with you?' said Blackwood, seeing how quiet Miphon had become. 'You look shocked.'

'You see visions,' said Miphon quietly.

'Yes,' said Blackwood. 'It's hard. I see . . . tragedy everywhere. I see people who never satisfy more than a tiny part of their potential, who are not what they wish to be, yet could be so easily if they only knew how. I see women dancing for men they hate, slaves honouring masters unworthy to rule the life of a rat. I see . . . so much that I can hardly bear to walk through the streets of Selzirk.'

'You have a choice,' said Miphon. 'You've no need to see such visions.'

'No man was made to,' said Blackwood.

'I can take away your visions – but I can never give them back,' said Miphon. 'You will see the world only through your seven senses.'

'Do it,' said Blackwood.

And Miphon did.

Selzirk lay in darkness, yet Morgan Hearst knew the dawn was approaching. He dressed quietly and armed himself with his sword Hast. He ran his hand over his head: the hair had been cropped to the stubble he favoured for a campaign. The death-stone, couched in leather, lay next to his skin.

So he was off again. He must go south to the flame trench Drangsturm and the Castle of Controlling Power dominating the western end of that flame trench. The encounter with the wizard Ebonair had brought home to him the perils of delaying any longer in disposing of the death-stone. He was still shocked at what a disaster his drunken bravado had almost brought upon Selzirk and the Harvest Plains.

Hearst paused to look down on the kingmaker Farfalla. Had she loved him? Or had she just sought to use him? She had not protested when he took other women – so surely she could hardly have loved him. Or could she?

The night before, she had wept; in the end, Hearst had slipped her a sleeping potion. Even now, toward morning, she was in the grips of that potion. Or was she? As Hearst watched, Farfalla rolled over and opened her eyes.

She reached for him, spoke, her voice drugged, weak:
'Morgan . . . ?'

Hearst said nothing.

Fighting the drug, half-conscious, Farfalla spoke, to say:
'Don't leave me . . .'

It was a kind of love that spoke to him: a kind of need.

And to his horror, Hearst found that the way Farfalla spoke brought to his mind the way the woman Ethlite

447

had spoken in the city of Larbreth in the Cold West, when he had been standing in the shadows and she had thought he was Elkor Alish.

Hearst remembered striding through the city with his fingers knotted in her hair and her head dangling. Alish had seen him. And in Runcorn, when Alish lay paralysed by poison, Hearst had boasted of that killing, as if the murder gave him title to a kind of glory.

He knew, now, exactly what he had done. And he knew, now, that Alish would never forgive him.

He turned on his heel and walked away.

CHAPTER FIFTY-FOUR

The trio were supposed to leave Selzirk at noon, travelling by ship down the Velvet River to Androlmarphos, and from there by sea to the Castle of Controlling Power. However, Hearst doubted that they would survive such a journey. Even if Farfalla did not plot against them, their wealth – the red and green bottles and the death-stone – would tempt their guides and escorts beyond endurance.

Accordingly, Blackwood, Hearst and Miphon left Selzirk before dawn, setting out along the Salt Road on fast horses. Hearst had decided that, if they were pursued, he would not hesitate to use the death-stone; he hoped he would not be put to that necessity.

Hearst was deeply troubled by his new insights into the past; Miphon, for his part, was already beginning to worry about the delicate task of diplomacy that would face him at the Castle of Controlling Power, when he would have to introduce a Rovac warrior to the Confederation of Wizards.

But Blackwood travelled with a light heart, for, thanks to Miphon, he no longer saw visions. He had been released from the weight of an intolerable burden: he was free. Free for what? He had not yet decided: for the moment he was content to travel the Salt Road under the summer sun. Occasionally he thought of other places, other times: but it was over a year since they had first marched from Castle Vaunting, leaving it in the grip of a mad-jewel; the memories of the past were fading, and Blackwood faced the future.

Blackwood carried a fine Selzirk bow and a quiver of arrows; when they camped at evening, he set up a target and practised, sending the arrows singing home. If they sheltered in a village, Blackwood negotiated to secure food and lodgings; if they met travellers on the road, he hailed them, and passed the time of day with them for a while, exchanging information about conditions on the road.

Miphon and Hearst, busy with their own thoughts, were happy to let Blackwood handle these responsibilities. They had every confidence in him. For Blackwood, much had changed since he first left Estar: the greatest change was that he could now inspire confidence in a wizard of the order of Nin and a warrior of Rovac.

And so they travelled south, through the Harvest Plains to Veda.

* * *

Veda's battlements, blood red, towered into the sky, suggesting a monument to evil. But inside, all was peace: windowless corridors of luminous milky white, curving away in smooth arcs, led to libraries, sleeping quarters, meditation chambers and study rooms. The corridors were warm; asking about the warmth, the travellers were told that Veda fed upon heat from deep underground.

The varied wonders of Veda made little impression on the travellers, who were by now prepared to take anything in their stride; Veda would only have surprised them if it had turned out to be commonplace. Besides, Veda's greatest treasures were works of art, which none of the three had much of an eye for.

Morgan Hearst could appraise the approximate value of a piece of gold or jewellery, or tell a fine weapon at a glance, but hardly noticed Veda's artworks. Blackwood liked tapestries showing people and animals, and Miphon liked landscape paintings, but there was nothing like that in Veda. There was Aromsky's sculpture in bronze: The Ethical Structure of the

Universe. There was the anonymous ivory called The Seven Spheres of Space and Time. There was Keremansky's Temptation of Zero by Infinity. The travellers, when they noticed these masterpieces at all, thought them cold, alien, ugly, uninviting.

Life in Veda itself was strange. All work was done by the Secular Arm, an organisation dominated by military and mercantile considerations. The Secular Arm would recruit anyone and anything that could stand on two legs; for administrative convenience it used the Galish Trading Tongue.

The sages of Veda, who spoke a language almost identical to the High Speech of wizards, lived lives of meditation, prayer and study. The travellers, regarding Veda only as a waystation, did not attempt to study the sages, but did try and bargain with them for a bodyguard. Hearst, remembering how they had been picked out by Erhed on first entering Selzirk, wanted armed protection for the journey through the Rice Empire.

Miphon, negotiating with the head of the Secular Arm, took the trouble of reading the man's mind. He had given up doing this without excellent cause: he had swiftly grown profoundly tired of the murky hatred, jealousy, lust, envy, deceit, self-pity, cowardice, greed, treachery and self-delusion dominating so many human minds. He was pleased to find that the head of the Secular Arm was an honourable man who would keep to the bargain they had made.

The bargain was that Miphon would heal all illnesses that were brought to him within the next ten days – Miphon demonstrated his skills by healing the headman's haemorrhoids – then the Secular Arm would provide a bodyguard of two hundred troops to see the expedition through the Rice Empire, plus papers certifying that they constituted an embassy from Veda travelling to Provincial Endergeneer.

Day after day, while Miphon saw long lines of people,

451

Hearst practised with his sword, continuing the training Farfalla had started him on. Meanwhile Blackwood went hunting in the surrounding countryside, riding out each day with horse and falcon.

Miphon found his labours exhausting yet exhilarating. Nothing defeated the sleeping secrets. He destroyed the most stubborn infections; he made limbs regenerate; he healed injuries to the brain. Often before, working with needle and thread, sulphur and mercury, cloves and laudanum, he had found himself helpless in the face of trauma or disease. But not now!

The day they were to leave, they were invited to an audience with the Grand Master of Veda – an unusual honour, to say the least, as many of the sages themselves never got to see that worthy. They went with some trepidation; ushered into the Presence, Miphon immediately scanned the Grand Master's mind for evil intent. He was reassured by what he found.

'Greetings,' said the Grand Master.

His tone was grave and formal. That, together with the man's tranquility in repose, reminded Blackwood very much of the Melski. He remembered the day – it seemed very long ago – when he had last met with Hor-hor-hurulg-murg. Being reminded of the Melski brought back painful memories.

'Greetings,' said Miphon, using the High Speech.

Following custom, they then drank mint tea and talked at length about nothing in particular (falconry, the herbal teas of the Ravlish Lands, the comparative merits of the stave bow and the composite bow, rumours about the politics of the Chenameg Kingdom, the trade in sponges and keflo shells, the possible extent of the domination of dragons in the heartland of Argan), and then the Grand Master broached the subject which really interested him:

'Often people become legends in their own time,' said the Grand Master, 'but usually because of a trick of perspective which conjures a mortal man to the stature

452

of a giant. I've met several living legends, but none have impressed me – till now.'

'Many songs praise us, up and down the Salt Road,' said Hearst, 'but a song sings for pleasure, not for truth.'

'One is always wary of rumour,' said the Grand Master, 'but these last ten days have seen miracles happening under my own roof. By miracle, of course, I mean an anomaly for which I have no explanation.'

'All magic is anomalous,' said Miphon. 'Wizards work by producing and controlling an anomaly in the natural order of things.'

'I know that,' said the Grand Master. 'As does the least of my students. However, I had thought I knew the limits of this power to . . . to generate anomaly.'

'So your horizons now widen,' said Miphon.

'Indeed. We've always thought only limited power could be achieved by generating anomalies, so we've strived instead to exploit the natural lines of force which support the universe.'

'So I've heard,' said Miphon. 'But your mysteries are beyond me.'

'I won't try and explain then,' said the Grand Master. 'Suffice it to say that in our days of glory, before the destruction caused by the Long War, we had begun to control both the animate and the inanimate. The legends telling of sages mastering dragons are true. And as for the inanimate, investigation into the force-lines of the universe had shown us that even the air itself holds a potential for power. Before the Long War, we attempted to extract and control that potential: our efforts generated tremendous thunderstorms, killing many of the experimenters, but we thought our chances of ultimate success were good.'

'So?' said Miphon.

'So here we are, four thousand years after the Long War, only just beginning to recover the power of ages past. It occurs to me that an alliance between the two kinds of power, that to exploit anomalies and that to exploit the natural structure of the universe, would open up possibilities that we can only guess at.'

'I will give it my consideration,' said Miphon politely.

Everyone in the room knew that was tantamount to a refusal.

'Don't let the old, old legends about the Days of Wrath influence your thinking. Some say wizards give credence to those legends, but I think of them more as fables than as history.'

'I will most certainly give the matter my earnest consideration,' said Miphon. 'My way lies south, as you know; mature reflection may, perhaps, convince me to return.'

'As you will,' said the Grand Master.

Again Miphon checked to see no evil was being plotted against the travellers; again he was satisfied. The travellers bowed and left the Presence, returning to their quarters to complete their packing. Shortly after they were finished, a messenger boy called to lead them to the southern gate of Veda, where their convoy had assembled.

Miphon, still unsettled by the meeting with the Grand Master, scanned the messenger boy's mind to reassure himself that, again, everything was in order. As they followed the boy through the luminous tunnel-maze of curving corridors, Miphon pleased himself with the thought that his ability to mind-read, and to alter minds where appropriate, gave him perfect protection against attack.

He was just thinking this when the ambush was sprung.

* * *

Miphon woke. He heard footsteps. But that was ridiculous. He was in the green bottle, wasn't he? He glanced at the green glowing walls. Yes, he was

454

definitely in the green bottle. In the confusion of the ambush, finding no magic of his would work, Miphon had turned the ring on his finger to take him into the green bottle. Nobody could have followed him.

Yet he was certain he had heard footsteps.

What could it be then?

Darkly, Miphon imagined hideous evil slouching out from the murky depths of the bottle which he had never dared explore. He clawed for a sword. Hast was that blade. Miphon had snatched the sword Hast even as Hearst, clubbed from behind, had fallen toward the ground.

Again, footsteps.

And voices, yes: a mutter, a curse, a short laugh, a hissed order silencing someone. Intruders were coming down the stairs. This was no menace from the depths of the bottle: this was invaders from without. Miphon gripped the sword tighter.

His enemies came in sight: grinning soldiers dressed and armed like men of the Secular Arm of Veda. But that was impossible! Miphon had scanned the minds of the headman of the Secular Arm, the Grand Master, and even the messenger boy. Everything had been in order.

'Ho, Mister Wizard,' cried one of the men. 'What's with the sword? Curing pox the sharp way, are we?'

'Keep back!' said Miphon, menacing him. Then: 'How did you get in here?'

'The same way you get up your own bum,' said the man. 'By magic, hey. Now throw down your blade, pox doctor, before your arse has an accident.'

There were five of them. Strong, bold and aggressive. Hearst's sword was clumsy in Miphon's hand. Before they could close with him, he tucked the sword under his arm – and turned the ring on his finger.

A moment of darkness as Miphon was swept out of the green bottle. A moment of disorientation as he arrived without. Then he took stock of his surroundings: a large egg-shaped chamber with luminous white walls. In it stood a dozen members of the Secular Arm.

'Good morning, Mister Wizard,' said a man, in Estral. Then, switching from Estar's language to the Galish Trading Tongue: 'Bare blades are bad manners. Didn't you know?'

The stranger had thin lips, set in a line of self-satisfaction. Sharp, hard little eyes. A narrow nose. A narrow face, hard bones showing through the skin.

'Don't you recognise me? I'm Durnwold's brother.'

'Valarkin!' said Miphon.

Given the chance, Miphon would have destroyed him without hesitation. But, as when he had confronted Heenmor's snake in Stronghold Handfast, he found none of his magic worked.

'You shouldn't have found me so hard to remember,' chided Valarkin. 'It's scarcely a year since we parted at the Araconch Waters. Still, your gift compensates for your manners.'

'Gift?' said Miphon, blankly.

'This!' said Valarkin.

He unravelled a length of cloth. Something fell to the floor. The death-stone! Miphon charged forward, roaring. A fighting man lept forward to intercept him. Another thrust a spear-butt between Miphon's ankles. Miphon tripped and went down. His sword was kicked away, and he was seized in a hammerlock.

Valarkin smiled, wrapped up the death-stone, tucked it away carefully, picked up the green bottle, then relieved Miphon of a ring. Valarkin now had both of the rings which commanded the green bottle. He backed out of the egg-shaped chamber. On a signal, Miphon was released; Valarkin's men exited the chamber. Valarkin remained at the entrance, smiling.

'You'll be smiling out of your arse soon,' said Miphon savagely. 'The Grand Master will kill you for this.'

'He'll never hear of it. My organisation's entirely

456

watertight. I've found some good people in the short time I've been here. We had all kinds of plans – we were going to take over all of Veda in a few years. But now you've happened along, we've decided to take over the world instead.'

'You're mad,' said Miphon.

'But very efficient,' said Valarkin, grinning. 'I've got the death-stone, and I've taken Hearst and Blackwood prisoner. One of you must know the spell for working the death-stone.'

Miphon remembered struggling with Ebonair, the wizard of Ebber, at Selzirk. He recalled the injunction which had thwarted the power of the sleeping secrets: Segenarith. What would happen if Valarkin held the death-stone and proclaimed that injunction? Perhaps nothing – or perhaps the experiment would kill him.

'I'll tell you how to command the death-stone,' said Miphon. 'The Word is Segenarith.'

'Is it?' said Valarkin.

'On my honour.'

'On a pox doctor's honour, hey? Well, I'll check. I'll ask Hearst for the right word.'

'And if he won't tell you?'

'I'll persuade him. I've got plenty of time. After all, nobody's going to come looking for you. Nobody even suspects the existence of my organisation.'

'We were supposed to join the convoy. The headman of the Secular Arm was waiting for us.'

'Ah yes, so he was. And now you've failed to turn up. So what's happened? Maybe you've grown wings and flown away through the air. Or become invisible and walked off down the Salt Road. Or found one of the old chasm gates the legends speak of. Who knows? All we know is that our guests have power enough to defeat wizards, warriors, armies, dragons, wilderness. So why fear for your safety? The very idea would be ridiculous. Nobody's going to search for you, least of all in here.'

'I can command minds at a distance,' said Miphon.

'Can you?' said Valarkin. 'Not from here you can't.'

Miphon snatched up the sword Hast and attacked Valarkin, aiming to hack off his head.

But at the mouth of the egg-shaped chamber, Miphon was halted abruptly by what felt like a huge spider-web. It was flexible but as strong as steel. He slashed at the invisible barrier with the sword – encountering no resistance. The invisible net did not restrain steel, but Miphon himself could not pass through.

'Interesting, isn't it?' said Valarkin. 'Back in the days of the Long War, sages came to distrust wizards. Places such as this were built in Veda, refuges proof against magic. No magic works here. Furthermore, no wizard can enter this place.'

'I'm here!'

'You were carried here while you were in the green bottle, thinking yourself safe.'

So he was trapped.

Was there any point in throwing the sword Hast at Valarkin? He might miss. Besides, even if he killed Valarkin, Valarkin's followers would retrieve all the artefacts of power from the corpse, and Miphon would still be trapped. Only suicide could protect the secret of commanding the death-stone.

'I'm going to see if Hearst confirms your version of how to command the death-stone,' said Valarkin. 'I will be back. You can be sure of that. Meanwhile, I guarantee you won't be disturbed. This place lies far underground, far from Veda's life and work.'

Valarkin bowed, mocking his prisoner with an excess of courtesy, and left with his men. They were soon out of sight, lost to view round the curve of the luminous white tunnel which was the only way to and from the egg-shaped chamber where Miphon was imprisoned.

Miphon hefted Hast in his hand. He tested the sharpness of the blade. It could be done quickly – but it would hurt. Oh yes, it would hurt. He remembered the pain when the wizard Ebonair had ripped his flesh open

458

in the struggle at Selzirk. It is hard enough to take a wound in the heat of battle, when the blood seethes with adrenalin, but harder still to administer a mortal wound in the tranquility of solitude. Yet Hearst would have done it.

Not for the first time, Miphon remembered how he had stumbled and bungled in the green bottle after Comedo had trapped him behind the portcullis. It had taken him days to escape, even when he had the means of escape in his hands. Now, if he killed himself, he might be overlooking some obvious way of escape that a common-sense man like Hearst would have seen immediately.

Miphon studied the smooth, glowing white surface of the egg. Would it yield to the sword? A few blows proved the wall unyielding. Would spells command it? Miphon tried three Spells of Opening, with no success; the architecture of sages refused the commands of wizards. There was no way through the walls.

That left the doorway, blocked only by an invisible spiderweb. Material things such as swords could pass through it. And, as Miphon had seen, it did not impede men. Only wizards. Miphon pressed against it and shouted the Ultimate Injunction.

'Segenarith!'

The barrier still restrained him. Why? It had no eyes to recognise him as a wizard – Miphon, in any case, looked just like an ordinary man. He had to think quickly, before Valarkin returned to torture him for the secret of the death-stone. Miphon knew the High Speech: pain would force him to decipher the writing graved on the death-stone's flank. Even his suicide could not safeguard the secret against betrayal by Blackwood or Hearst; even if all three died, Valarkin could go out into the wider world to find someone who could read that writing.

The barrier.

It was made by sages. It restrained wizards. The

459

Grand Master said the sages exploited the natural lines of force supporting the universe. What is the universe? The universe is . . . a pattern imposed on chaos. A pattern created by the great god Ameeshoth: the world of Amarl, in which wizards are an anomaly. Any intensification of that natural pattern would be inimical to wizards, who in any case had to rely on the Meditations of Balance to counter the natural tendency of the world to destroy any anomaly. The barrier must be a subtle form of such an intensification.

Miphon thought his problem through.

And found a possible solution.

By discarding his powers – at least those relating to the world of Amarl, the world of day-to-day living – he might be able to pass through the barrier.

Perhaps.

But even to think of the experiment was almost intolerable. Destroying his own powers would nullify years of work, deprivation, effort, agony. Miphon remembered the Shackle Mountains . . . trials in the darkness . . . the seven tests that may not be named . . . the agony and the loneliness of the long wait.

Above all else, he did not want to lose the power of the sleeping secrets, which allowed him to heal any injury or overcome any evil. That power was incalculable, despite the fact that he had been helpless when kidnapped by Valarkin and those members of the Secular Arm that Valarkin had suborned for his own purposes.

No wizard could ever be invulnerable, for an arrow in the back could kill even the most powerful. With the sleeping secrets, the limiting factor on his power was time. The ten days he had spent in Veda had been busy, busy, busy, as he had treated a succession of patients; he had lacked the time, and indeed the inclination, to search through many of the minds, often unclean or repulsive, that dwelt within the effective range of his powers.

He believed he had the maturity and the spiritual grace to use those powers for good. Yet he had to surrender them. Spells and physical force had both failed to release him from the egg. As a wizard he was trapped, so he must cease to be a wizard, a Force incarnate in the flesh, a Power in the World of Events, a Light in the Unseen Realm, a Graduate of the Trials of Strength, a Motivator of History, a master of lore versed in the logic of the Cause and the nature of the Beginning.

He would miss that.

And there were so many other things he would miss. The exultation in the mind of the hawk as it stooped . . . the night thoughts of the badger . . . the aura of strength in the forest in spring . . . his satisfaction as a fat fish, lured from the depths of a cold pond, flapped in his hands . . .

Accepting the death of his hopes and ambitions, Miphon adopted the pose he used for the Meditations. He would destroy his power in three stages. First, his power to use the sleeping secrets, to read and change minds and heal and change bodies by the application of thought at a distance. Then, his power to read and communicate with the minds of animals. And last, if necessary, even such minor powers as he possessed to read and command the minds of animated rocks, the creatures of the world of the Horn, Lemarl.

Miphon began. Swiftly, he released all the power associated with the sleeping secrets. That power had to go somewhere, but could not escape from the egg, which hummed with a high-pitch resonance as vibrations built up.

Miphon felt uncomfortable. His ears began to hurt. It grew hot. He sweated. His sweat dried the moment it appeared on his skin. His eyes stung. The air took on a violet tinge. The walls of the egg began to vibrate. They cracked: a million hairline fractures appeared.

The barrier blocking the way out of the egg became

461

visible as a web of blue-white energies, pulsing like an eye in which the pressure of the heart's blood is rising so high that it threatens rupture. But the barrier held. Miphon gave a small cry: a dry croak. The heat was rapidly killing him.

He had surrendered all the power of the sleeping secrets.

He refused to surrender any more.

He charged the barrier. He hit it – and a shock of pure energy flung him back, knocking him to the floor of the egg. He lay there, at first unable to move. The air pulsed and sang. Intolerable resonating energies throbbed around him. Bursts of white light sang from the walls of the egg. The walls were warm to the touch.

Miphon knew he had little time left. Unless he got out quickly, he would be dead. He composed himself, and swiftly accomplished the second phase of destroying his power. The heat intensified.

He resolved to charge the barrier again.

He wanted to escape with at least some of his powers intact: those to affect the world of Lemarl, the world of stone. He refused to surrender everything. Yet, remembering the pain when he had last touched the barrier, he was afraid.

Miphon seized the sword Hast, remembering Hearst, and the intensity with which the warrior moved on the attack, committing himself absolutely to the needs of the moment. Wild words came to Miphon's aid:

'Ahyak Rovac!'

Screaming that challenge, swinging that sword, he charged. And went right through the barrier.

He was free!

But, inside the egg he had escaped from, the energies he had released were becoming more coherent by the moment, converting themselves into a pulse, a resonance, a unified power of destruction. If that barrier was to give way . . . looking at the pulsing barrier, Miphon decided it was a question of when, not if. The

462

barrier would not hold for long. So what to do then?

Run!

He turned and fled down the luminous corridor. He saw a doorway: an empty egg. Another doorway: a dusty storeroom. Another: into dead darkness. Then another: opening into a room in which lay Blackwood, bound hand and foot.

'You!' said Blackwood, the word distorted as his mouth was badly bruised and cut.

'None other,' said Miphon, cutting Blackwood's bonds with the sword Hast. The blade slipped, slicing flesh. 'Sorry.'

'It's nothing,' said Blackwood, stemming the bleeding.

'Where's Hearst?'

'I don't know.'

'Come on then.'

They raced on down the corridor. The luminous white curves drew them on. From up ahead they heard a scream. They ran faster, panting. Then they burst into a chamber, a glance revealing: Hearst, tied hand and foot to a metal frame; a young man holding a blood-stained bodkin; half a dozen onlookers, all armed.

Miphon screamed:

'Ahyak Rovac!'

The battlesword Hast took out the nearest. As the rest drew weapons, Blackwood grabbed the tripod legs of a brazier and hurled its burning coals toward them. The torture chamber evoked all the horrors of Prince Comedo's dungeons. Snatching up an iron rod, Blackwood attacked, striking out furiously. Miphon fought beside him, reckless in his disregard for his own safety. He had lost everything he valued: nothing remained to tempt him to make the calculations of cowardice.

It was all over almost as soon as it had begun. Three of the armed men were dead. The rest: running for their lives.

'Are you hurt?' said Miphon to Hearst.

463

'Like a virgin unvirgined,' said Hearst. 'No, don't look for the damage, you blue-tailed pox doctor. Cut me loose! Quickly, man, quickly!'

'I don't want to cut you.'

'Don't worry about that, let's just get out of here.'

Miphon sliced away the last rope. Hearst, released from the metal frame, stumbled, almost fell. Deep-gouped rope patterns ringed his wrists and ankles. Blackwood supported him as they left the chamber.

'This way,' said Blackwood.

'How do you know?' said Miphon.

'The tunnel slants upwards here, doesn't it?'

'Why, so it does,' said Miphon.

They went as fast as they could, Hearst hobbling, Miphon still carrying Hearst's sword.

'Where's the green bottle?' said Miphon.

'Valarkin had it the last time I saw him,' said Hearst. 'That was shortly before . . . before you rescued me.'

Despite their long association, Hearst was reluctant to name a wizard as his rescuer. It had been bad enough at Selzirk, when Miphon had rescued Hearst from magic – a warrior cannot, after all, hope to fight magic directly. Here it was worse: to be rescued from armed men by a wizard wielding a Rovac sword.

'Where did he go?' said Miphon.

'He was called away,' said Hearst. 'One of Valarkin's cronies heard that the headman of the Secular Arm wanted a fellow called Esteneedes, who happened to be searching the red bottle that Valarkin's got stashed away somewhere. So Valarkin went to get the man out of the bottle. Up here?'

Ahead the corridor branched.

'This way,' said Blackwood, choosing at random. Then: 'I've been out hunting with Esteneedes. He's a noted tracker. The headman must be wanting to recruit him for a search party to look for us.'

'Valarkin miscalculated,' said Miphon. 'He thought nobody would try and look for us.'

'Yes,' said Blackwood. 'But obviously they're think-ing of searching the countryside – not Veda itself.'

They came to some stairs. Hearst, now able to walk without support, led the way up. There was the distant boom of an explosion, followed by a protracted roar. The walls shook. Cracks opened. Pieces of luminous white fell from the ceiling.

'What was that?' said Hearst.

The stairs were vibrating under their feet. Miphon knew that never before had a wizard stripped himself of his powers, releasing uncontrolled energies into the world. He had no idea what the consequences might be: but he was learning fast. Quite possibly, the energies he had released might tear Veda apart.

'Come on,' he said.

'But what in hell's name is it?'

'Out!' cried Miphon. 'Out, or we're dead!'

They bounded up the stairs two at a time. More stairs led to more corridors; more corridors led to more stairs. Ever upwards they went. The journey started to become nightmarish. Sweat poured off them. Their legs began to lock with fatigue. Heart and lung strained to their limits. The vibrations got worse and worse. Huge chunks fell from the ceilings. Tunnels buckled and twisted.

They began to pass other people, most of whom were running in the same direction. Some, however, had been trapped or disabled by falling masonry. They could not stop to help these casualities.

There was another explosion, louder than the others. The surface underfoot swayed.

'We're never going to get out of here,' said Hearst.

But even as he spoke, they saw daylight. The sun shone through dust: the way to escape was in sight.

* * *

From a low hillock a thousand paces from Veda,

Miphon, Hearst and Blackwood watched the final stages of the disintegration of the stronghold of the sages. Occasionally rubble was flung high into the air with a shattering roar as blue-white energies burst out from underground.

'What did you do?' said Hearst, watching the dust settling after one of these explosions.

'What do you mean, what did I do?' said Miphon.

'Hearst's not the only one to think you're responsible,' said Blackwood. 'Nobody else has such power.'

'I've got no power now,' said Miphon sadly. 'I used it all in blasting my way out of the cell where Valarkin was holding me.'

'You did what you had to,' said Hearst. 'I only hope Valarkin and the death-stone are buried under that rubble.'

'This is a disaster,' said Miphon. 'The Confederation of Wizards will never believe it!'

'I'll be there to help you make your explanations,' said Hearst.

'And me,' said Blackwood. 'As a friendly witness in the Court of the Highest Law.'

'Now let's get ourselves out of here,' said Hearst. 'Before the survivors organise themselves into a lynch mob.'

The travellers got to their feet. They had the clothes they stood up in, but no weapons except for Hearst's sword Hast. And no tents, pack animals, food, blankets. Not even a change of socks. And no money. It was going to be a hard journey, unless they could improve their position. Hearst looked around.

'We have to go back,' said Hearst. 'Despite the danger. We have to go back to Veda and loot the ruins. That's what I think.'

'I'll trust your judgment,' said Miphon.

'Then I say we go,' said Hearst. 'Blackwood?'

The woodsman stooped and picked up a small, smooth rock. It fitted nicely into his hand.

'When I'm holding a weapon like this, who's going to oppose us?'

'That rock?' said Hearst.

'I'm going to say it's the death-stone,' said Blackwood. 'And if that's what I say, who's going to wait around to find out otherwise?'

'Of course,' said Hearst.

It was a good idea: he should have been the one to think of it.

CHAPTER FIFTY-FIVE

Posing as Galish merchants, they slipped through the Rice Empire, avoiding major centres of population. Miphon did no healing; he could have improvised some basic equipment, but decided healing-work might link them to the tales, rumours and legends that were circulating about Morgan Hearst and his companions.

When the Salt Road was busy, they travelled by night, stealing horses, riding them hard, then abandoning them or trading them for fresh mounts. They knew stories of the fall of Veda would move swiftly along the Salt Road; they wanted to be first to bring the news to the Castle of Controlling Power, so the Confederation of Wizards would hear the truth rather than some garbled distortion.

It was four hundred leagues from Veda to Narba; their sixteenth day on the road ended with Narba in sight. They slept in a corn field, breakfasted on stolen cobs of corn, then pushed on toward the city.

At Narba, much building was in progress. During years of peace, the city had sprawled outwards, so now many houses, taverns, inns, offices, warehouses, shops, temples, tanneries, breweries, bakeries, shipyards, schools, courtyards, mansions and marketplaces lay beyond the protection of the original fortifications. Efforts were now underway to remedy that deficiency by extending the city walls.

Where the Salt Road entered the city, two huge bastions were being constructed to guard what would be a major gateway through the new walls. One bastion, a square structure with walls easily a hundred paces long, rose more than five times man-height. Work on a

468

second was just beginning; men were working waist-deep in a water-filled hole, driving stakes into the ground so the top of each was level with the surface of the water.

'Blackwood,' said Hearst. 'Why are you making your mouth a flytrap?'

'Because,' said Blackwood, shutting his mouth and shaking his head, 'this is incredible. Unbelievable.'

The fortifications were, of course, trivial compared to any wizard castle, and insignificant if compared to Stronghold Handfast. However, the antiquity and inhuman scale of such monstrosities made them seem, to an extent, like natural features of the landscape. The works at Narba, on the other hand, were undeniably the product of the labour of human nerve and sinew; people swarmed over the fortifications like ants over a sugarloaf.

The air was hazy with dust thrown up by the diggings. The bastion nearby, rising high into the air, was topped by arrangements of windlasses and treadmills; teams of men were labouring in unison on this creaking apparatus to drag up block after block of stone.

Standing watching, Blackwood sneezed as dust got up his nose. He touched a finger to his teeth. Bit it.

– This is not a dream.

He scraped a battered boot over the stones of the road, heavily clagged with dirt from the diggings.

– You are here.

– And not elsewhere.

He felt an acute sense of being located in that particular spot at that particular moment. He felt as if he had awakened from a life of dreams, from an insect-habit life of doing things by rote.

– Is this magic?

Miphon and Hearst began to argue about whether they should enter the city or outflank it, and the spell, if it was a spell, was broken. Blackwood joined the argument; they decided to enter the city, not least

469

because they wanted to find out what rumour of war had provoked this outbreak of fortification-building.

* * *

From Veda, the travellers had carried away some glowing fragments of the luminous white interior of the ruined city; they sold these scraps to a jeweller in the centre of Narba, getting a good price; later, no doubt, as trade brought more of the material along the Salt Road, the price would fall.

What they learnt in Narba was confused, ambiguous and ominous. There was trouble amongst the wizards of the castles guarding the flame trench Drangsturm. There had been fighting at the Castle of Ultimate Peace, at the eastern end of Drangsturm. A few wizards, all of the weakest of the eight orders, the order of Seth, had come north to Narba and had taken passage on ships going to the Cold West or the Ravlish Lands. Rumours said other wizards had taken passage on Malud ships sailing the Ocean of Cambria, dispersing to Asral, Ashmolea, the Ferego Islands, the Driftwood Archipelego and the Parengarenga Mass.

The wizards were served by the Landguard, just as the sages of Veda had been served by the Secular Arm. Some of the Landguard, disconcerted by the troubles, had deserted. Meeting some of these deserters, the travellers heard rumours of expeditions to the Dry Pit, of attempts to capture the Skull of the Deep South, of wizards building strongholds in the Ashun Mountains while others, helped by Southsearchers, set up places of refuge deep inside the lands controlled by the Swarms.

At this distance, the truth was impossible to determine.

'But we know this for certain,' said Hearst. 'Narba fears war between the orders of wizards. That's why the city's so busy with these extra fortifications.'

'Small help they'd be,' said Blackwood.

'A war between wizards might lead to other evils,' said Hearst. 'For instance, the Landguard troopers might run wild.'

The men of the Landguard were tough, resolute and dangerous, trained to hunt down and kill any creatures of the Swarms which got round the shoreside edges of Drangsturm or overflew the flame trench. If they went to war on their own account, they would be a serious menace to a place like Narba.

'We'll take your word for it,' said Blackwood. 'You're the warrior.'

'What we have to decide,' said Miphon, 'is what we do now. My duty lies south. The Confederation of Wizards has to be warned that Valarkin may be on the loose with a death-stone. However . . . friend Hearst, the south would hardly be healthy for a Rovac warrior at the best of times. Now . . .'

'I'll see this thing through to the end,' said Hearst. 'A war between wizards could mean . . . perhaps the end of the world as we know it. I won't try to disown my part in history.'

If he no longer wished to be worshipped as a hero, he still wished to be significant; he was still of the opinion that quiet, sheltered lives were for woodlice, not for men.

'You know the risks,' said Miphon, knowing that, actually, if the wizards really did go to war, nowhere in Argan would be safe. 'And you, Blackwood?'

'Once I've bought a bow, a knife and a new pair of boots, I'll be ready to travel.'

'You don't have to come with us,' said Hearst.

'I have to go south to discover my destiny,' said Blackwood.

'Your destiny?'

'Yes,' said Blackwood. 'Why would all these things have happened to me if not for a purpose? Why did I survive when so many others died, if it were not that some destiny is intended for me?'

471

Hearst smiled, amused at this provincial certainty, which was not far removed from the belief traditional in Estar, namely that a peasant was destined to remain always a peasant.

'Chance attends even to falling dice,' said Hearst. 'Much more so to us.'

'That's as may be,' said Blackwood, choosing not to argue. 'But in any case, I've no idea what I'd do if I didn't continue this journey.'

'That's a poor excuse for getting yourself killed,' said Hearst.

'In your company, I doubt any of us will be losing our lives,' said Blackwood.

'I wish I shared your confidence,' said Hearst.

They stayed three days in Narba, spending most of the money they had made from the sale of bits of the substance of Veda – as well to spend the money now, since death might be waiting a short distance down the road – and then they set off south.

Here in the south, the weather was warm; even when winter came, the south would never see a frost. Nevertheless, there was no doubting that it was autumn.

CHAPTER FIFTY-SIX

Twenty leagues from the Castle of Controlling Power, the travellers came upon the skeleton of one of the Neversh. Hearst and Blackwood, who had never seen such a thing, examined it with fascination. From the twin feeding spikes to the tip of the whiplash tail, it was two hundred paces long.

'It's . . . it's a little larger than it looks on a chess board,' said Hearst.

'They grow bigger than this,' said Miphon.

Hearst chipped away at one of the feeding spikes with his sword. The delicate interior structure reminded him of honeycomb.

'I thought these spikes would be solid ivory,' said Hearst.

'That's what many people have thought,' said Miphon. 'If it was, it would hardly be left lying here. Besides, it'd be too heavy to fly. All the bones are light – but strong.'

The arch of the ribcage was huge, bulbous.

'There are sacs inside here,' said Miphon. 'Full of lighter gas. The Neversh find it easy to get off the ground, because of all the lighter gas inside them.'

'What's lighter gas?' said Hearst.

'It's a kind of air that floats within air,' said Miphon.

'I don't understand.'

'If you have oil and water, the oil will float on the water. If you have lighter gas and air, the lighter gas will float on the air. Do you see now?'

'Maybe,' said Hearst.

He examined the thin vein-structure of the wings,

which remained even though the actual tissue of the wings was gone.

'It looks clumsy,' said Hearst.

'You forget the tail,' said Miphon. 'That's very mobile. It's armed with poison. It can move fast as a bullock-whip. It's said the tail's sometimes fast enough to deflect a crossbow bolt.'

'What damage could a crossbow do anyway to a thing this size?' said Hearst.

'With a quarrel through the ribs, all the gas goes out from the inside,' said Miphon. 'Then the Neversh can't fly. It falls.'

'Why doesn't it fly higher? Out of range of crossbows?'

'The higher it goes, the more danger of meeting a high-flying wind that would blow it away,' said Miphon. 'Because they're so light, the Neversh have trouble controlling their own mass in flight. That's one reason why mountains are a good barrier against the Swarms. Most of the ones that live on the ground, like keflos, can't climb very well over rocks, and the Neversh get blown away by the updrafts you find in the mountains.'

'It's absurd for a flying creature to fly so badly,' said Hearst.

'Perhaps,' said Blackwood, 'But we've got an insect like this in Estar.'

'An insect? I didn't see it,' said Hearst.

'It was there to be seen, all the same,' said Blackwood. 'It's called the hubble fly. It has to puff itself up with air before it can fly – though it uses just ordinary air, none of this fancy lighter gas you've been talking about. Then when it flies it's very clumsy. It's about the size of my thumb.'

'There are lots of things that fly that don't do it very well,' said Miphon. 'Chickens, for one thing. Anyway, the Neversh came long ago from the deserts of the Deep South. They've got no trouble with mountains there.'

Hearst struck at one of the ribs with his sword, then sheathed his blade.

'Pity the poor hubble fly,' said Hearst. 'Too big and clumsy to fly properly.'

He spoke lightly, but could not suppress a memory he had inherited from the wizard Phyphor. Twisted shapes against the sky, twisted screams in the noon-day sun. Words of power. A blast of flame. The darkest fears of nightmare animated by the full power of day. Some broke, some ran. Some stayed to stand against the Neversh . . .

If war broke out between the orders of wizards, and they failed to guard the flame trench Drangsturm, the Swarms would spread north as they had in the days of the Long War. They would soon reach Narba, then would follow the Salt Road north. Before long, they would be at Selzirk. The very thought of it was nightmarish.

*   *   *

At dayfail, they camped; they were still seven leagues from the Castle of Controlling Power. Here, close to Drangsturm, the Salt Road ran beside the sea.

'Would it be safe to have a fire this close to the castle?' said Hearst.

'Of course,' said Miphon. 'Landguard patrols are always out and about in the countryside. Nobody will think it odd if they happen to see a fire here.'

They gathered driftwood from the beach in the gloaming then lit a fire. From the shadows of an island to the west, a pinprick of fire answered their own.

'There's someone on that island,' said Hearst.

'That's Burntos,' said Miphon. 'The Landguard keeps a permanent garrison there, because the Neversh sometimes fly out to the west, skirting round the end of Drangsturm, trying not to be seen. Often the Neversh rest on that island.'

Waves from the darkened sea tumbled up the beach, roiling seaweed, shells, barnacles and bones with armoured remnants of creatures of the Swarms.

'Will we be safe tonight?' said Blackwood.

'From the Swarms, yes,' said Miphon. 'None of those creatures moves in the hours of darkness.'

That night, the southern horizon was lit by a red glow; the flames of the Great Dyke, Drangsturm, illuminated the clouds. The next morning, drawing closer to the flame trench, the travellers began to hear its steady, regular, rumbling roar.

Then the Castle of Controlling Power came in sight, a chaotic farrago of spires, battlements and buttresses swirling around the central sky-punching upthrust of the Prime Tower. Hearst, who had previously consulted Phyphor's memories of the castle, had thought them jumbled and distorted beyond belief; he was shocked to find the castle matched the anarchic memories precisely.

'When we get to the castle,' said Miphon, 'let me speak for all of us.'

'Agreed,' said Hearst.

He scarcely saw the blue ocean, the dull landscape, the stones of the Salt Road. All his attention was taken by the bizarre architectural monstrosity ahead of him, the product of eight orders of wizards, each with different ideas as to what should be built, finally raising a monument to ego that would, surely, have been enough to send any sensible draughtsman insane.

'Are you impressed?' said Miphon.

'It would look good if it was made of marzipan,' said Hearst, trying to make some sense out of a particularly confused array of gates, bridges, moats, arches and overhangs.

'So it's not your style,' said Miphon.

'Whose nightmare was the guiding inspiration?'

'It's not that bad,' said Miphon.

'Isn't it?' said Hearst.

'Wizards are not warriors,' said Blackwood.

'When did you find that out?' said Hearst, his tone bantering. 'Certainly wizards are not warriors. No fighting man would build a monstrosity like that.'

'Still, you are impressed, aren't you?' said Miphon.

'Yes,' said Hearst. 'Insanity on a grand scale can be impressive. And this is. After Chi'ash-lan, I thought stonework could surprise me no further. At Stronghold Handfast I learnt otherwise: and now I've been proved twice wrong.'

They marched on to the main gate of the castle. Each of the eight orders had built itself a gate; the main gate, built by the order of Oparatu, was the one which had proved most convenient for travellers coming from the Salt Road.

At the main gate they were met by a detachment of the Landguard dressed in ceremonial skyblue uniforms. They were challenged; Miphon identified himself, naming Blackwood and Hearst as his servants, to get them into the castle without argument. The head of the guard gave them permission to enter.

'I wish to find the head of the Confederation,' said Miphon. 'I have urgent business. Who fills that position this month? And where will I find him?'

'This month it's Brother Fern Feathers of the order of Seth,' said the head of the guard. 'You'll find him in the Chamber of Communal Consent.'

'Why there?' said Miphon. 'Is there a general gathering?'

'There is,' said the guard. 'There has been each and every day for the last forty-two days.'

'Forty-two days! That's unheard of! What's happening?'

'You tell me, then we'll both know. And I'd truly love to be told. Any truth, no matter how bad, would be better than the rumours we're living with. I don't deal in rumours – not me. But I hear them, all the same. The latest, master, says contagious madness is loose in the castle.'

'That's impossible,' said Miphon.

'I know,' said the trooper. 'But many of my men have deserted because of that rumour. We must have a truth, and soon.'

'I'll deliver a truth to you myself,' said Miphon. 'Today.'

'Good. My name is Karendor of the Silk, but if you're asking your way from one of my gutter-mouthed men, ask for Old Bootstrap.'

There was suppressed laughter amongst the men of Karendor's Landguard detachment.

'I'll be in the Meneren barracks if I'm not here,' said Karendor.

'I'll find you,' promised Miphon, and led Hearst and Blackwood into the depths of the Castle of Controlling Tower.

*　　*　　*

The maze within was, in many ways, stranger than Stronghold Handfast, where the travellers had, so many months ago, found Heenmor's dead body. The alien style of Stronghold Handfast had still had a basis in logic, its floors, roofs, stairways and doorways having rational connections with each other. In the Castle of Controlling Power, madness had run amok.

To Hearst and Blackwood, the building at first seemed to have been created for giants. The egos of the makers had demanded huge foyers, immense arches, ceilings rising to giddy heights, pillars greater than any forest tree, and walls built from gargantuan blocks of stone. This inhuman scale was combined with an absence of any appreciation of principles of natural lighting. Everywhere was gloom, dusk, shadows, darkness, except where firestones glowed ochre in the cavernous depths.

The castle had taken seven hundred years to build, and showed the results of wizards arguing for seven hundred years over the design. In places, corridors ran into solid walls, or ended in pits a quarter of a league deep, which had no discernible purpose whatsoever. One arched opening, a hundred paces high, was almost completely blocked by a solid ball made out of millions of bricks held together by mortar.

'If we get separated here, we'll never find our way out,' said Blackwood.

'I can remember the way back,' said Hearst.

'Can you?' said Miphon. 'Now I am impressed!'

Echoes from their voices wandered through the heights of the world's greatest monument to dissonance. It took a long time to reach the Chamber of Communal Consent.

* * *

When, after immense labours, the Castle of Controlling Power had been finished, it had held eight meeting chambers. Any one of them could have served as a common gathering place, but no order would consent to meeting in a hall designed by another order. Yet nobody wanted to go on holding meetings in the open air, which was inconvenient, undignified, and, at times, dangerous.

When the castle had been nominally finished, its centre was a confusion of narrow corridors, tunnels, arches, pillars, walls and cells where the ambitions of all eight orders had clashed. This space was useless. After much argument, the wizards had agreed to demolish enough of the masonry to create a central meeting place. The Chamber of Communal Consent was the result: an irregular hall with three hundred ways in and out of it.

Miphon, Hearst and Blackwood made a quiet entrance, slipping unnoticed into the gloom of the meeting place. In that place, lit only by ochre firestones – it had no windows – strangers could not be identified as such very easily, since a face could scarcely be made out at a range of ten paces.

It smelt, badly, of musty old men, pipe smoke, and the strange, penetrating odour or quelaquire, the keflo-oil used by wizards to help preserve manuscripts. It was filled with muttering, arthritic voices; hundreds of wizards were gathered in groups, arguing, conferring, advising, rumouring; they sounded like a conclave of people many years dead in a limbo far beyond the life of the living.

Hearst and Blackwood wondered what was happening, but did not dare ask; Miphon knew that a meeting must have broken up so members of the various orders could caucus. All had perfect privacy: the acoustics of the place were so bad that it took a determined effort to make oneself heard over any distance in the best of circumstances.

As Miphon led them toward the throne occupied by the head of the Confederation for that month, Brother Fern Feathers, Hearst and Blackwood cast covert glances at the wizards they passed. Such old men! Gnarled, driftwood faces; faded eyes; weathered, liver-spot skin; creaking voices; withered beards. And so many of them!

Drawing near Brother Fern Feathers, they saw that, standing beside him, and talking earnestly, was a fat wizard. The travellers were almost at the throne before they saw the fat wizard was Garash.

'Withdraw,' murmured Miphon.

But it was too late.

Garash saw them.

'Rovac warriors!' roared Garash.

Those two words, like powerful magic, silenced all conversation in the room. All heads turned to see who was in their midst. Garash pointed:

'Rovac warriors!'

'Let's run,' said Miphon, quietly but urgently.

'No,' said Hearst, as wizards crowded in. 'No chance.

480

We'll have to talk our way out of this one.'

'We have, at any rate,' said Blackwood, 'their full attention.'

Some of the wizards activated strange devices which glowed with green and purple fire, illuminating the visitors. The air became hot, dry. It shimmered. The concentrated presence of so many anomalies stressed the very universe almost beyond endurance.

'They're under my protection!' shouted Miphon. 'As a wizard of Nin, I give them my protection.'

He did not try to explain that Blackwood was not a Rovac warrior. He saw fear, hatred, bloodlust in the faces closing in around them. This was no time for complicated arguments.

Hearst put his hand to the hilt of Hast, but knew it would be useless to match steel against the collective power of these wizards. From the look on the faces confronting him, he knew he was very close to death.

'They have my countenance!' cried Miphon. 'They come as an embassy!'

'We should endure this?' shouted Garash. 'Rovac warriors? Here? I say no – whatever their pretence.'

Muttering approval greeted his words. Hearst had faced mobs in the past, in times when cities under Rovac control had rioted, but he had never seen anything like this harsh, muttering, deadly earnest hatred. What to do? Die like a man: that was all he could do.

It was Blackwood who found the solution. Long researches in the memories Phyphor had bequeathed to him had revealed many of their secrets. One chance: one chance only. Blackwood pointed, throwing out his arm so all could follow the gesture. He pointed to Garash.

'You! I accuse! I accuse you! Garash, wizard of Arl, I accuse you of a crime against the Confederation of Wizards. Of murder! Of killing the wizard Phyphor!'

'Lies!' shouted Garash.

'I have witnesses!' shouted Blackwood. 'I name as my chief witness the Rovac warrior Morgan Hearst. Here he stands, a mortal man yet twice a dragonslayer.'

'Rovac warriors!' yelled Garash. 'Rovac lies!'

'It's true,' roared Hearst, in a battlefield voice.

'Kill them!' came a cry. Then:

'Scrag them under!' 'The hooks, the hooks!' 'Claw-bones the raggage!' 'Kala-kola ga!' 'Furrow their kidneys!' 'Batter them!'

'Silence!' boomed Brother Fern Feathers, who had a big voice of his own. 'Silence, by the Rule of Law!'

The tumult muttered down enough for Miphon to make himself heard:

'It is true. The accusation is true. Garash did murder our expedition leader. He did kill Phyphor. By the Rule of Law I swear it.'

'A trial,' said Brother Fern Feathers. 'No, Garash! I rule for your silence. Hear me out. We will have a trial in due course. The Rule of Law must be obeyed. Otherwise, we truly will have war within these walls.'

Miphon allowed himself a sigh of relief. A trial might take months. That would leave plenty of time for negotiations, diplomacy, explanations – or escape, if escape proved necessary. The greatest danger had always been that wizards, discovering a Rovac warrior in their midst, would be tempted to instant murder. Now – or so Miphon thought – the moment of greatest danger was past.

But Brother Fern Feathers was continuing:

'Meanwhile, leaving aside this matter of murder, we must call on these newcomers to make their contribution to our present debate.'

'I'll not be debated over by Rovac warriors!' shouted Garash.

This roused another chorus of angry murmurs, which Brother Fern Feathers quelled with difficulty.

'Only Miphon will speak to our debates,' said Brother Fern Feathers. 'The Rovac warriors will be given no voice until the trial, which is another matter entirely. Miphon here is our fellow wizard. He's the one I'll ask to speak.'

'Speak on what?' said Miphon. 'What are you debating?'

'The propriety of certain actions – quite aside from the question of killing – which have been undertaken by Garash,' said Brother Fern Feathers. 'For days we've debated whether to accept the tales and excuses Garash has given us. Let me review his claims, for your benefit – and also to clarify our own thoughts on . . .'

'I protest!' said Garash. 'I –'

'I have ruled for your silence!' said Brother Fern Feathers. 'Now hold your tongue, while you still have a tongue to hold!'

He stared at Garash until Garash dropped his eyes. A few wizards coughed and muttered, then, when they had settled down, Brother Fern Feathers began:

'Garash says that last autumn, in Stronghold Handfast, he fought the wizard Heenmor, strength against strength, power against power. He claims that Heenmor fled, escaping. Garash then went to the eastern coast of Argan and took passage on a ship southing from Brine.

'His winter southing took him to the Dry Pit. Knowing Heenmor was loose in the world, he took a source of power from the Dry Pit. The death-stone, he calls it. He says Heenmor has one so we must have one. He claims Heenmor represents a danger giving him the excuse to take power from the Dry Pit.

'Garash arrived here at Summerstart with this death-stone. He tempts us with the prospect of limitless power; he speaks of the conquest of the world; he wishes to be made our leader.

'Since Garash came into our midst, many have died. I will not speak of what happened in the Castle of Ultimate Peace. We had thought such feuding over centuries ago, but all the old conflicts and schisms have been renewed by this . . . this death-stone.

483

'We cannot say what danger Heenmor represents. We have only Garash's words to go by. But this I do know: what Garash has done has led to killing amongst us already. It threatens to end our unity, such as it is.

'Though we have debated for days, nobody has been brave enough to prosecute Garash for entering the Dry Pit. But now Garash has been accused of murder, which suggests his tale may need revision.

'We have talked enough. Indecision will destroy us as surely as anything else. If nobody else will act, then I will. I will prosecute. I accuse! Hear me well, for in this matter –'

Then the wizard of Seth broke off, for Garash had taken out his death-stone. His face betrayed his purpose.

'No!' shouted Brother Fern Feathers.

Garash cried out in the High Speech. Hearst lunged toward him, but too many old wizards were in the way. A grinding sound began to dominate the chamber. The death-stone was beginning its work. Miphon remembered the battle with the wizard Ebonair. He remembered the Ultimate Injunction that enemy had used against him. If anything could stop the death-stone, it had to be the Ultimate Injunction. In desperation, Miphon cried out:

'Segenarith!'

Even as he shouted, Blackwood managed to close with Garash. The woodsman drove a blade hard and home. Garash gave a squeal of panic and agony. Blackwood stabbed him again, again, and he fell, dropping the death-stone. Blackwood crushed his throat, stamping down on it, making sure.

The sound of grinding had stopped.

Men drew back from the death-stone, as they might from a poisonous snake. It was Brother Fern Feathers who first dared approach it. He picked it up: and dropped it immediately.

'It's hot!'

484

Even as they watched, the death-stone began to glow. First blue, then red. Hot as a furnace. Wizards stepped back. Miphon realised the Ultimate Injunction had not conquered the power of the death-stone, which was now beginning to manifest itself in another form: heat.

'Run for your lives!' shouted Miphon, his voice commanding the chamber.

A tongue of flame twisted from the death-stone. Dragon-dangerous, it lashed out. A wizard was engulfed by a roar of flame. He spun round, burning, screaming..

Everyone – almost everyone – panicked.

Screaming, shouting, they trampled their way toward the exits. The death-stone began to spin, shooting off bolts of flame. Wizards jammed the major exits, pushing, jostling, clawing for freedom.

Hearst swore.

'We'll never get out!' he said.

'This way!' cried Miphon.

And, running, he led the way to a squeeze-gap in the wall behind the throne. They forced their way through the gap, breaking out into a deserted corridor.

'Follow me!' shouted Miphon.

And fled, the others hot behind him.

Blackwood and Hearst had no idea where Miphon was taking them. He led them through twisting corridors, down stairways, over bridges, until ahead they saw daylight. They came out onto a low battlement where the air was hot, hot and gasping. A sea of flame lay beyond the battlement: the flame trench, Drangsturm. Looking across the flame trench they saw the barren countryside of the Deep South, habitat of the Swarms. The heat so distorted the air that the countryside wavered like an unstable mirage.

'Where now?' said Hearst, sweating.

'This way,' said Miphon, hoping he remembered correctly.

He led them through an archway then down stairs

485

spiralling into darkness. Only an occasional ochre firestone lit their panting shadows. Then they saw light. Daylight! A gateway! Running through the gateway, they gained the open air.

They had exited from the castle at the western end of Drangsturm. Here a buffer of basalt rock, two hundred paces wide, separated the flame trench from the waters of the Central Ocean. The buffer was guarded only by a low parapet: it was designed as a killing ground in which wizards could destroy any attack by the Swarms.

'Come on,' said Miphon, taking a few steps toward the buffer of basalt rock.

'You're crazy!' said Hearst. 'We can't go south! We'd die!'

From behind them came a deep, prolonged roar of falling masonry.

'The death-stone's destroying the castle,' said Miphon. 'But hundreds of wizards will escape. How many friends do you think we've got among them now?'

'We are doing well,' said Blackwood. 'First Veda, now this.'

'The Deep South is dangerous, but it gives us a chance,' said Miphon. 'To stay here is certain death. So follow me!'

And, having little option, they did.

CHAPTER FIFTY-SEVEN

Morgan Gestrel Hearst, warrior of Rovac, woke from sleep and for a moment thought he was in hell. The ground shook; the air roared with dull, continuous thunder; the sky was suffused with the colour of blood; above him loomed a monster with huge underslung lobster claws. The monster had eight legs.

For a moment – and he suffered a lot in that moment – he stared aghast at what he saw. Then he remembered.

Of course.

Hearst lay back, breathing in the smell of cinnamon. He was in the transparent chamber of a keflo, a creature of the Swarms. The red glow filling the chamber was partly from the clouded sky, lit up by the blaze of the flame trench Drangsturm, which was responsible for the thunder and vibrations, and partly from the fireball where the Castle of Controlling Power was melting down.

Hearst remembered how Miphon, quite calmly, had led them into the Deep South, saying the Swarms kept clear of the castle because of Southsearcher raids and the powers of wizards. Toward evening, they had sighted the tall minar housing a colony of keflos; Miphon had led them inside at night, when the keflos were asleep. Finding the hatchery, they had killed embryonic keflos. Miphon had dissected certain sacs from the limp dead bodies; smearing themselves with the contents of these sacs, they had given themselves an odour much like cinnamon.

The keflos, so Miphon said, recognised each other by smell. The Southsearchers used tricks such as this to penetrate the keflo colonies; safe inside a keflo minar, they would not be bothered by any other creatures of the Swarms.

Come morning, they would find out if Miphon was right. How did he know? Hearst suspected Miphon had been a Southsearcher before he was a wizard – but Miphon did not choose to talk of his past. Looking at the monstrous beast bulking over him, Hearst wondered if it really would spare him when it woke. He had his doubts: but there was nowhere to run to. All he could do was trust.

After a while, he went back to sleep.

When Hearst woke in the morning, the keflo was gone. He had expected something that large to make enough noise to wake him when it moved. Miphon and Blackwood were gone. Where? Perhaps the keflo had eaten them – yet surely, if it had started eating people, it would have had appetite enough for three.

Through the transparent curve of the keflo chamber, Hearst studied the landscape. A few keflos were out and about in the countryside. From this height, they looked like discs, for their legs, jaws and organs of sense were slung beneath their domed and multicoloured carapaces. Keflo shell, a valuable product, was traded along the Salt Road; Hearst could see that keflos would not stand much chance against determined Southsearchers.

About three leagues to the north-west was a glowing mass of slag: the molten remains of the Castle of Controlling Power. The death-stone, which still blazed amid those ruins, had melted the ground around till it ran like lava. Clouds of steam were billowing up from the ocean.

'Good morning,' said Miphon, entering the chamber. He held a collection of little sacs.

'More perfume?' said Hearst.

'Yes,' said Miphon. 'For those who don't want to be eaten.'

'What's there for us to eat, while we're on the subject?'

'This,' said Blackwood, coming into the chamber and dropping an armful of eggs.

They bounced.

Hearst, picking one up, found the skin hard and flexible.

'These are keflo eggs,' said Miphon. 'Properly nourished, they develop into the embryos we killed last night and that I've been killing this morning. I think – '

He was interrupted by an explosion which set the chamber shaking. To the north-west, steam was rising, not just from the ocean, but from Drangsturm itself.

'There's a breach from the ocean into Drangsturm,' said Miphon quietly.

When the sea entered a small flame trench like the 'steamer' on the southern border of Estar, the water seethed and boiled. But, when hitting the superheated rock of Drangsturm, cold seawater exploded instantly into steam.

Another explosion shook the world.

Hairline cracks crazed the transparent surface of the keflo chamber. Out on the plain, the foraging keflos stood quite still. High in the sky, flung by the explosion, huge chunks of rock turned lazily in the sunlight. A massive rock, big as a house, crashed to earth near the minar. The floor shook.

'The end of the world,' said Blackwood quietly.

'Maybe,' said Hearst, cutting open one of the keflo eggs. 'But let's not die hungry. Dig in.'

So they breakfasted on raw keflo eggs – which were a thick dark rubbery green, hard work for the jaws. As they ate, the ground near Drangsturm split open. Cracks extended for a league north and south. Flame surged into the cracks as the walls of the flame trench began to collapse.

'Look,' said Blackwood.

They saw, dimly through the crazed walls, a Neversh

wheeling high in the sky in the distance, circling the area of devastation. An updraft from the flame trench caught it and flung it upwards, out of sight.

'The Skull of the Deep South will know,' said Miphon. 'The Swarms will start to march. Soon. Today. They'll forge around through the sea – or their legions will labour rocks to bridge the ruins of Drangsturm.'

There was no stopping it.

They would march north. All of them. Stalkers, keflos, Engulfers, Wings, tunnellers, green centipedes, the Neversh, the blue ants and the others. Hell-creatures from the worlds of nightmare, smashing their way through human civilizations, hunting, catching, killing, eating.

'We have to stop them!' said Hearst. 'If we can get a death-stone, we can stop them!'

'Could we?' said Miphon. 'Remember the effective radius. Two leagues. That's not much. There's few places we could stop them before . . . well, before Estar. We could halt them there, at the Southern Border.'

'Then that's what we'll do,' said Hearst. 'Now how do we get our death-stone?'

'We don't!' said Blackwood. 'After all this time trying to lock away that horror for good and forever – '

'Yesterday was another world,' said Hearst, cutting him off.

'But he's got a point,' said Miphon. 'To let loose that power – '

'That power is loose already,' said Hearst. 'We won't be the only ones making for the Dry Pit. It may bring the world to destruction – but the world will be destroyed in any case, unless we halt the Swarms.'

'From here, it's a fair stretch to the Dry Pit,' said Miphon. 'If we go east, eighty leagues takes us to the Inner Waters. Then another two hundred leagues or so takes us to the Stepping Stone Islands. Then, if we can contact a Southsearcher patrol, we might get passage north to the Chameleon's Tongue.'

490

'And then?'

'Sand,' said Miphon. 'A long beach runs about three hundred leagues east to the Elbow, then about two hundred leagues north to the mountains at the end of the Chameleon's Tongue. There's a harbour there: Hartzaven. If we can get passage to the northern coast from there, we'll still have to march about a hundred leagues inland to reach the Dry Pit.'

'Another journey . . .' said Blackwood.

'You sound . . .'

'Weary,' said Blackwood. 'Leagues of wind and rain. Foraging for meals. Travelling by night, waking to foreign suns. Lurking, hiding, skulking, stealing. After all this time . . .'

'I know,' said Hearst. 'We all want to rest.'

'And we tried so hard,' said Blackwood. 'For what? Our best wasn't good enough to stop this . . . this ending.'

'We're not dead yet,' said Hearst, though he did not fancy their chances for survival. 'Come on, man! Maybe it's at the Dry Pit that you'll find your destiny.'

Blackwood shook his head.

He no longer believed in destiny.

Back in the castle, in the moments of combat, the fate of the whole world had been resolved by the timing of a knife-thrust. If Blackwood had managed to kill Garash just a little sooner, Miphon would never have used the word Segenarith; the death-stone would have fallen harmlessly to the floor, leaving the way open for the future to be resolved by diplomacy between wizards.

Instead: disaster.

It was true: chance did attend to all things. The fate of the world could be changed by the tiniest hesitation at a critical moment.

'We're dice,' said Blackwood. 'And we're rolling. How we fall is not up to us.'

'The will is free,' said Hearst. 'We can act as we choose.'

491

'No,' said Blackwood, heavily. 'Chance settles everything. There's no such thing as free will.'

Hearst smashed him across the face with the back of his hand. Blackwood staggered backwards.

'Draw on me if you like,' said Hearst, his voice cool. 'Kill me if you like. I'll accept the punishment. I performed an act of unadulterated free will. On the other hand, since you don't believe in such a thing, what's your motive for punishing me?'

Blackwood hesitated.

Hearst drew a blade.

'Enough!' roared Miphon, startling himself with his own ferocity. 'We'll go to the Dry Pit. We'll get a death-stone. We'll try. It's our only chance.'

'So you think chance comes into it, too,' said Blackwood, rubbing his smarting face. 'So is the will free or not free?'

'If someone had clouted me over the face, that's the last question I'd be asking,' said Miphon. 'But the answer, since you wonder, is both yes and no. Let me explain.'

*　　*　　*

It was later in the day. Miphon was still lecturing on the nature of free will; Hearst, bored beyond belief, reminded himself never again to raise philosophical problems in the presence of a wizard.

Hearst watched another Neversh high in the sky. Scanning. Scouting. On the ground, the keflos were moving north, picking their way over the shattered landscape.

It was starting already. The Swarms were moving north for the first time in four thousand years. And, his own faith in free will steadily eroding, he thought:

– We are prisoners of history.

An odd thought for a Rovac warrior. Not bitter, but melancholy. Almost philosophical. Almost. He would have to snap out of this mood. He would have to unlearn some of his painfully-acquired wisdom, and think himself back into being a hero, for that was what the age demanded: a man prepared to dare all in a desperate race to the Dry Pit to gain a weapon powerful enough to contend against the Swarms.

Despite himself, he recalled his many failures. He did his best to suppress them, but one memory still surfaced. It dated back to the time at Ep Pass. Durnwold had worked his way behind the wizard Heenmor, had stood at the top of a cliff, had raised a rock . . . had died.

Should Hearst blame himself for that death? Alish had thought up the attack plan, but should Hearst have accepted it? Maybe there had been a better way to do it. The fact was, a man had died, trusting Morgan Hearst. So many men had died trusting him.

Miphon was still talking:

'. . . so you see, the question of free will, is, to a large extent, a purely epistemological question. You do see that, don't you. Don't you?'

'What?' said Blackwood, who had a rather glazed expression on his face. 'Yes, yes. Indeed.'

'Now,' said Miphon. 'If we could return for a moment to Impalvlad's theory for quantifying the stochastic and deterministic elements – '

'Perhaps,' said Hearst, coming to Blackwood's rescue, 'we could leave the quantifying till later, and talk about the Southsearchers.'

'Oh,' said Miphon. 'No, no, not just yet. This will only take a moment.'

'According to Sarla's theory of time, a moment can sometimes be infinitely extended – and I think this might be one of those moments.'

'Who's Sarla?' said Miphon.

'You tell me about the Southsearchers, and I'll tell you later.'

'This person does really exist?'

'Of course, of course,' said Hearst, blandly.

And, by such temptations, managed to get Miphon to abandon the question of free will. They heard all about the Southsearchers, then Hearst told a long – and, alas, unprintable – story about Sarla of Chi'ash-lan, and her very amusing theories about sex, alcohol, time, and the nature of the universe.

They could not risk setting out until it was dark.

CHAPTER FIFTY-EIGHT

'Those are the Needle Rocks,' said their guide, indicating dark shapes in the night which blanked out stars and constellations.

Somewhere a blowhole spluttered as a wave forced its way up its gullet. Paddling, Hearst strained to see their landing ground, which must be close now.

'Those rocks have claimed many ships,' said their guide, his own paddle helping drive their canoe forward even as he spoke. 'Storms make these waters dangerous.'

'It looks calm enough now,' said Blackwood.

'Yes,' said the guide. 'But storms do come in from the Ocean of Cambria. Open water reaches away east to Ashmolea. Storm waves league westward, building their strength.'

And Miphon thought:

– Yes. Yes indeed.

Remembering.

They came in under towering cliffs, where swells, leisured yet powerful, surged onto rocks. A narrow shingle beach afforded them a landing.

'A league's easting along these rocks takes you to the start of the Chameleon's Tongue,' said their guide. 'Nobody will have seen us land, not here in the cliff-shadow. Take care, and perhaps you'll reach Seagate without being seen.'

'Whose eyes should we fear?' said Miphon.

'Any ship cruising the Ocean of Cambria counts as danger,' said their guide. 'Worst are the Alvassar pirates, who sometimes raid this far north – but others can be as bad.'

'What others?'

'Whalers from the Ebrell Islands, who will meet you with a smile then ram a harpoon between your shoulder blades. And the sea traders from Asral, the Malud – they fancy a little knife-work now and then.'

'So much for the dangers from the sea,' said Miphon. 'What about the people living on the Chameleon's Tongue?'

'Nobody lives on this coast for fear of Alvassar slaving raids,' said their guide. 'Over the Lizard Crest Rises, which run the length of the Tongue, there's people living by the shores of the Sponge Sea.'

'What kind of people?' said Hearst.

'Who cares? It's a rugged coast, no good for travellers. I do hear tell that they're poor; I don't know if they'd kill you for your flesh and bones, but I do know this coast's safest.'

'We'll keep to it then,' said Hearst. 'Many thanks for your help.'

'Life is for life,' said their guide, dismissing his thanks. 'All speed!'

'And you,' said Miphon.

The canoe ventured out into the night. Miphon, Blackwood and Hearst began to pick their way over the rocks toward the Chameleon's Tongue. Once they got there, five hundred leagues of sandmarching would take them to the mountains near Hartzaven and Seagate: a twenty day journey, if they made good time.

* * *

While Southsearchers had handed them from village to village on their journey through the Stepping Stone Islands, it had been a blessed relief for Hearst to have all command responsibilities taken from his hands. He had failed so many times that he had come to doubt his own fitness for command.

Now he was reluctant to lead his party away from the

shelter of the cliffs and onto the Chameleon's Tongue. He wished they could have stayed in some South-searcher village, to live out their lives in island isolation while the world contended with its troubles. Yet he carried a guilt-burden: therefore he committed himself to this quest. It was the least he could do.

The tide was half way out; from dark sand dunes, an expanse of beach over two hundred paces wide sloped gently to lines of small surf breaking under the stars; the distances were hidden in the night.

'Well,' said Hearst. 'Let's be on our way.'

Leading them onto the sands, he felt nervous, uneasy: the beach was too open, too wide. But time was important, and they could travel faster along open sands than through the dunes, scrub and rocklands of the hinterland.

Soon they fell into a steady rhythm, tramping over the firm seasand at a pace they could keep up right through the night; slowly the cliffs receded into the darkness behind them. But nothing soothed Hearst, not their steady progress, not the lull of the rhythms of the heart, not the low-mounting seafall of beaching swells. Still apprehensive, he kept glancing backwards, thinking how easy it would be for horsemen to ride them down on the beach.

Suddenly, from the darkness ahead, something huge rose from the sand with a seething, hissing cry. Points of white shone within its expanding darkness as it swept toward them.

Hearst screamed:

'Ahyak Rovac!'

His sword leapt to his hand. His body braced to receive his enemy: braced to meet his death.

The monster broke apart into separate flashes of white which wheeled away into the night, cold cries now clear and recognisable.

'It's only seabirds,' said Miphon mildly. 'Only gulls.'

Hearst stood there, shaking.

'Come on,' said Blackwood. 'Let's be moving.'

*   *   *

League after league slipped away beneath their boots, until gradually the sky began to lighten. It needed close observation to tell that night was drawing to a close, but after so long in the darkness, they were sensitive to the slightest variation in the sky.

They had some darkness left still, but Hearst began to scan the shoreline for a place to stop. There was little variation in the dark line of dunes, but soon they crossed water: one of the streams, scarcely deeper than the thin slick of mirage, that seeped out from the dunes to run down the beach to the sea.

'Halt,' said Hearst. 'We stop here.'

They walked up the beach, treading in water all the way; the waterflow would wash away their footprints before sunrise.

*   *   *

'They're ready,' said Miphon.

Hearst, opening his eyes, sat up to join the others at their meal, which was some triangular shellfish Miphon had recovered from sands near the low tide mark. The travellers had eaten several shellfish meals since they set out along the Chameleon's Tongue. It had been seven days now.

'I think we're better than half way to the Elbow,' said Hearst.

'We'd better get there soon,' said Blackwood. 'Before we die of sheer monotony. I'm dreaming sand, you know.'

'You're lucky,' said Hearst. 'I'm eating it.'

And he spat out some grit which had infiltrated his meal.

'We could use the time,' said Miphon. 'I never did

finish my little lecture on free will. Where did we get to? Quantifying the stochastic and the deterministic, I believe.'

'Perhaps a certain wizard had better determine to leave his lectures to another time,' said Hearst. 'Or a certain wizard might find himself making a personal investigation of some possibly purely stochastic but definitely very cold and vigorous wave-forms.'

'Oh,' said Miphon.

But that was as close as they came to a quarrel.

*　　*　　*

Ten days down the Chameleon's Tongue, Hearst lay dreaming of a struggle on the battlements of Castle Vaunting. In his dream, Phyphor directed a blaze of fire at Collosnon invaders. Then there was a fading glow, like an afterimage, as red-hot Collosnon armour cooled rapidly in the night air.

A survivor, half-cooked, screamed.

The dream shifted to . . . a dragon's mouth, filled with fire . . . Looming Forest . . . Rovac, and then . . . Ep Pass . . . and . . . the Harvest Plains, where Farfalla . . .

'They're ready,' said Miphon.

Hearst let food distract him from his dreams. Without surprise, he found that today's shellfish tasted much like yesterday's. The grit, perhaps, was a trifle finer today.

Having eaten, he lay back and closed his eyes. Through closed eyelids, a blood-red sun. Endless, endless, the sounds of the surf: the thunder of breakers beaching themselves on nearby sands, the moaning surf-dirge of distant waves churning into foam.

Blood-red sun.

Farfalla . . . yes, Farfalla . . . a tent on the Harvest Plains . . . the sun hot through the skin of the tent . . . hot shadows, breathing whispers . . . taste of the sun . . .

499

hot-skin shadows . . . red sun . . . Farfalla, yes, Farfalla had taught him much . . . including how to use a sword, how to fight with a precision which did not come naturally to him.

Farfalla had even taught him how to train when there was no opportunity to exercise his muscles. Now, lying in the sun in a place on the Tongue, hundreds of leagues from Selzirk, Hearst made use of that teaching.

Time and again, Hearst reviewed techniques. He imagined drawing his sword . . . at first slowly, getting every angle precisely right, then faster and faster, till his blade was a blur scarcely slower than thought. Time and again he imagined facing Elkor Alish, remembering exactly how Alish moved: fluid, fluent, supple as a cat, lithe as water, his blade attacking with perfect mastery of speed and timing.

'Timing,' said Farfalla.

He remembered her voice, low, relaxed, persistent, working its way into his mind.

'The greatest mysteries lie in the simplest things,' said Farfalla. 'Timing and speed are the halves of one whole. What is that whole? Language lacks a word for it. That alone should tell you how much we have to learn. There are other mysteries . . .'

Other mysteries. Yes . . .

But think of the training, think of . . .

Timing . . .

In the end he had said to her:

'This watching, breathing, listening, timing, it's all very well, but sooner or later there has to be a moment when you're committed – when there's no reserve, and the only chance is to carry through the attack.'

And she had said:

'I haven't tried to teach you things you already know.'

Sunlight through his eyelids. Blood red. A sword slants through space and time. From moon-bright steel to banner-red blood. Again. Again . . .

500

Someone was snoring. Opening his eyes, Hearst saw Miphon had gone to sleep; Blackwood was nodding. He noted a flicker of movement: a lizard was daring the sunlight. It was darkish green, with bluish spots on top; patterns reminiscent of gills stippled its sides. It breathed in quick puffs though a toothless mouth; its neck swelled out with every inbreath. Slowly the lizard approached the empty shells left from the travellers' meal, where a few flies savoured shellfish remnants.

A quick tongue flicked out, snatching one of the flies for the lizard's maw. Speed and timing. Perfection. The lizard watched Hearst with beady eyes; he wondered if he would be fast enough to grab it.

He would welcome a change of diet.

* * *

Behind them lay three hundred leagues of open beaches, clean and white under the blue dome of the heavens; they had travelled all the way to the Elbow.

In any other geography, the Elbow would have been unremarkable, unless one cared to comment on the way the strata had tilted so they ran diagonally and in places almost vertically. The Elbow was simply a conical rise of rock, no more than a hundred and fifty paces high, upthrust from the sea and connected to the rest of the land by a low spine of rock over which a child could have scrambled.

This piece of rock had been dignified by its own name and marked on maps because it was a major landmark, interrupting the sweep of the sands of the Chameleon's Tongue, and marking the point where the coastline turned north.

The three travellers could see that the Elbow finished in a point deep in the water, but to follow the cliff-edge out to that point would have meant wading waist-deep in water.

'Let's climb to the top,' said Hearst.

501

So up they went, forcing a way through tough, scrawny vegetation, avoiding those parts that were armed with thorns and spines. From the top, they had an extensive view. To the west and north, the sands of the Chameleon's Tongue stretched away to the horizons. Inland, the ground rose to the heights of the Lizard Crest Rises. Out to sea lay the Teardrop Islands.

'That's where we're going,' said Hearst, pointing north.

It was much the same as the landscape they had already traversed; near the Elbow were small cliffs, some with veins of red ore running through them, but further north the cliffs declined and sand dunes ran alongside the beach again.

'We can get down to the point from here,' said Miphon. 'Those rocks might give us good fishing.'

They climbed down, taking care when easing past a sheer drop to the water. On reaching the point, they saw a huge sea-cave was eaten into the cliff.

The water here was deep, the bottom lost in sightless darkness. The tide was low, revealing orange and yellow growths on rocks usually covered by the sea; there was the smell of sun-dried algae. Peering into the water, Hearst saw a few very small fish, nibbling at rocks or hanging motionless in the water until they sculled away with a flicker of orange fins.

'We can use snails for bait,' said Miphon.

From the rocks, they gathered snails, some rounded and black, others living in conical white shells. They pried stones from between crevices and hammered the snails; the sea creatures writhed and twisted as their shells were broken. Blackwood pitied them, their comfortable lives shattered by hammer-stones, their bodies exposed to the harsh light of the sun – yet he still broke open the shells. He was a human being, a kind of creature that must eat to live.

To cut his bait down to size, Hearst bit into one of the white-shell snails. After a few moments, his mouth

502

started to burn. He swilled it out with salt water and spat.

'Don't touch the white ones,' said Hearst. 'They burn your mouth.'

'All right,' said Miphon.

With hooks baited, they let down their lines. Blackwood and Miphon used thin lines and small hooks, trying for the little fish they could see, but Hearst, with stronger tackle, weighted his line for the depths. Blackwood got the first catch, a small fat fish with dark spots on the top and a pale underbelly.

'Did it give you a hard fight?' said Hearst.

'Oh, it was a memorable struggle,' said Blackwood. 'What kind of luck are you getting?'

'Just nibbles,' said Hearst.

He pulled his line up to have a look; steel glistened water-wet. His bait had been stolen.

'The hook's too large,' said Miphon.

'No,' said Hearst. 'The fish are too small.'

He baited his hook again, then pounded the rocks, hammering barnacles to a white scale-paste, which sifted down through the water. More small fish flickered into view, drawn by this manna. Nothing else.

'I felt something,' said Miphon, excited.

'Probably something purely stochastic,' said Hearst.

But, when Miphon drew up his line, his own bait was gone. Miphon packed it away.

'I'm going hunting,' he said.

'Alone?' said Hearst.

'The only other thing on the Tongue is our shadows.'

'I don't think it's safe,' said Hearst.

'I'll be the judge of that,' said Miphon.

He turned and clambered up the steep slope, and Hearst, weary with long leagues of marching, did not bother to call him back. The day was too hot and lazy for anyone to imagine danger on the stalk. Hearst concentrated on catching fish.

Three more snail-baits were taken in quick succession. Hearst gutted Blackwood's fish – there were five of them by now – slicing from vent to gills, drawing out heart-red organs and thick intestines packed with fragments of barnacles. He scaled them, lightweight fish armour spraying up where his knife skimmed the skin. Then he cut off the head and tails.

After baiting his hook with a bit of fish, Hearst threw a handful of guts, heads and tails into the water. They fell away into the depths, leaving threads of blood near the surface. Hearst threw in his line after them. He got no bites except the tiny infuriating nibbles of the little, thieving fish.

Late in the afternoon, Hearst pulled in his line and wound it up.

'We'll come back by night,' said Hearst. 'When the tide's in. The bigger fish might start feeding then.'

'Good,' said Blackwood.

And Blackwood gathered together handfuls of black snails and dumped them in a splash-fed pool above high water mark, where he would be able to lay his hands on them easily by moonlight. He threw a couple of hammer stones into the same pool. Then the two climbed to the top of the Elbow.

Miphon had garnered a brace of lizards, each as long as a man's forearm. They cooked the lizards and the little, little fish over a small, hot fire which gave no smoke to betray them to the watching world.

'We're going fishing tonight,' said Hearst.

'Are you?' said Miphon.

'There'll be bigger fish by night,' said Hearst. 'All fishermen know that.'

'I'll take your word for it,' said Miphon. 'Myself, I'd rather sleep.'

Hearst and Blackwood got a little sleep themselves as the last of the daylight faded; they woke to the light of the moon's declining quarter. The moon rode battle-high, with streamers of black cloud sliding through the sky on a high airstream; down near the sea, the night

504

was calm, but there was a low swell, and as Hearst and Blackwood climbed down to the point they could hear the swells breaking on the rocks, and the glutinous shifting of masses of water within the sea cave.

Hearst stood on the rocks and relieved himself, an arc of urine spattering into the sea, kicking phosphorescence to life in the water. Phosphorescent creatures gleamed on the rocks as each slow, lazy sea-surge rode home leisurely to end in an echoing thud in the depths of the sea cave.

The two men, shadows to each other in the night, broke open snails and baited their hooks.

'I should have saved one of those little fish,' said Hearst. 'That's the best bait.'

'You can have the first one I catch,' said Blackwood.

Soon after, Blackwood handed Hearst a small fish. It quivered in his hand, struggled as the hook went home. Live bait. Hearst swung his line once, twice, three times, then cast it out into the darkness. It fell. The line snaked away as the small fish sprinted in panic. Hearst felt life sing along the line as his bait carried the hook into the depths.

Then the line went weightless. It swayed away sideways into the night. Pulling on the line, Hearst felt a leisurely power bearing his bait-fish away. He yanked on the line to drive the hook hard home. The answer was a sudden jerk that almost had him in the water. The line pulled taut. Cordage burnt through his hands. He swore. Then the line broke.

A larger swell rocked through the dark sea, splashed spray onto the rocks they were standing on, and boomed thunder inside the sea cave. Black clouds swallowed the moon. Something gleamed under water, big, white, far down, turning, gone – what was it? Another wave slammed home against the rocks.

'Come on,' said Hearst. 'Let's get back to the campsite.'

Later that night, waiting for sleep, he thanked his

fates for what had been, in its own way, a perfect day. He knew the dangers that lay ahead: the Dry Pit, the Marabin Erg, and, if they survived that, eventually a battle with the Swarms themselves. He knew the odds favoured his death: he doubted that he would live to see another spring. And so he savoured what was left to him, and found it sweet.

As Saba Yavendar said:

My feet wear down the last of the road
Through scarabshard cities, through shufflerock hills,
Through grey timedwindled mountainscapes.
Insects feed at my sweat
Till a cavemouth swallows me to its shelter.
My goatskin outglubs the last of its bub,
And fills the cup to less than belly-centre:
Yet I drink, for I will not refuse the cup
Simply because the wine lacks the brim.

*　　*　　*

There must have been a storm far out to sea, because for days big swells broke on the shores of the Tongue, each swell rising glass-green as it reached the shallows near the shore, then breaking to churning white spray with a boom of thunder.

As the three trekked north along the sands, the tideline now was littered with shells, and occasional clumps of black seaweed, some with thick clusters of fat pink barnacles clinging to them. Now and then they encountered signs of human life: charred timbers that had once been shaped with axe or adze, and had met fire before the sea brought them to this resting; a fishing float marked with a weather-rune; the cork-buoyed haft of a broken harpoon.

Halfway between the Elbow and the cliffs of Seagate, they found a beachside tree covered with blood-red blossoms. It was, said Miphon, a tree known to some of

506

the peoples of the Ocean of Cambria as yanzyonz, meaning 'autumn fire'. The travellers rested in the shade of the tree; bees were at work in the blossoms.

'Honey,' said Blackwood, listening to the bees.

'That would be nice,' said Hearst.

'These things can be arranged,' said Miphon. 'If you don't mind waiting.'

'But,' said Hearst, 'you've lost your . . .'

'This doesn't need magic,' said Miphon. 'Watch.'

And he caught one of the nectar-seeking bees, tore pieces from its veined wings, then released it. The injured bee could fly hardly faster than walking pace. Miphon followed it, knowing it would lead him straight to the hive.

'I'm going to dig shellfish,' said Blackwood.

'Enjoy yourself,' said Hearst.

Left alone, he decided to gather some firewood. In his search, he discovered, not far from the shoreline, a low bank of old shells, long ago bleached white by the sun. Many were calcined, cracked by heat; there were banks of such shells all along the Chameleon's Tongue, where groups of people had camped for weeks at a time, feeding on shellfish, sometimes cooking them in bulk to take inland. The heap of discarded shells could have been there for years, decades or centuries.

Unbidden and unexpected, a memory surfaced. It was one of the memories of the wizard Phyphor, who, thousands of years before, had stood on the shores of the harbour of Hartzaven, at Seagate, watching a small sailing craft making for the shore.

Phyphor had said:

'Is that them?'

And his companion, one Saba Yavendar, had said, yes, yes, that's them, that's the party come to negotiate for the Dareska Amath –

Hearst remembered.

Remembered the Dareska Amath, as seen through Phyphor's eyes. A wild people, yes, much given to laughter and boasting, fond of improbable stories and outrageous dares, a tough and hardy seafaring folk, eager for the challenge of an audacious venture into the Deep South. Those were his ancestors, and . . . they were nothing like the people who now lived on Rovac.

The Dareska Amath had been quick to anger and quick to forget; the Rovac had developed the capacity for a sour, unrelenting hatred that nothing could appease. The Dareska Amath had possessed a sardonic sense of the ridiculous which tempered their excesses; the Rovac cultivated an overbearing arrogance and a fanatical sense of honour which destroyed their sense of proportion.

Standing there on the sands of the Tongue, Hearst thought of the way Elkor Alish had gone raging to war to revenge a wrong committed over four thousand years ago. The Dareska Amath would have laughed at such a loss of proportion – and at Alish, seeking to honour their memory by destroying the Confederation of Wizards.

Now the Swarms were sweeping north through Argan. That disaster must make Alish re-assess the situation, and see that their world was too fragile to sustain a never-ending feud that threatened the destruction of the strongest and the best. And if Alish would reconsider, then, possibly, Morgan Hearst and Elkor Alish might one day be able to meet again as friends.

*   *   *

The time came when the cliffs of Seagate appeared through the surfhaze: one more march would bring them to those cliffs. Another day would bring them to Hartzaven, where they hoped to be able to find a boat to take them to the northern shore.

Hearst decided to make the march to the cliffs by night, for if they were going to meet anyone on the

Chameleon's Tongue, this last part of the journey was where it was most likely to happen.

They made their way by moonlight. The moon was cold and steel-bright in a clear sky. There was no cloud; every star was visible. The beach stretched away into the darkness; they walked on the wet sand, letting the waves' wash obliterate their footprints.

The ocean had calmed; the waves were less than knee-high, but broke with a series of sharp retorts, each like the crack of a whip. Breaking, each wave curled over, forming a tube in which phosphorescence was stirred to life, so it was as if a bolt of lightning shot along the inside of each tubing wave just before it collapsed into miniature thunder.

Where feet scuffed the wet sand, phosphorescence shone, a speck here, a speck there. Blackwood scooped up a handful of sand. In the centre shone the blue-green fire of one single phosphorescent creature. Its body was too small to see, but its light, in the darkness, held close to his face, was bright as one of the ardent stars of the heavens.

The Rovac warrior Morgan Hearst led them on, into the darkness.

CHAPTER FIFTY-NINE

At Hartzaven, a sheltered harbour in the mountainous upthrust at Seagate at the end of the Tongue, the travellers stole a double-hulled ocean-going canoe from a small fishing village. They also took quantities of dried fish, sweet potatoes and white paste. The paste, extracted from the roots of a type of fern, looked and tasted a little like flour. After living for so long on lizards and shellfish, they welcomed the change in diet.

They ventured the Sponge Sea in the stolen canoe. The seas at the end of autumn favoured them with an easy crossing. They landed on the northern coast, a hundred leagues from the Dry Pit.

Much of the coastline was ancient metamorphic rock, but this was interrupted by dead, cold lava flows, which had run from far inland out to the edges of the Sponge Sea. Miphon said the lava flows had issued from the Dry Pit thousands of years before; to reach the Dry Pit, they need only follow one of the lava flows inland.

It was a hard journey, through countryside that was mostly flat and monotonous, though here and there isolated mountains rose above the barren plains. There was little vegetation, but there were many insects. One afternoon the travellers broke open an ants' nest, a nest of earth that stood half as tall as a man; they mixed handfuls of black ants and white ant eggs with the last of their fern-paste, and roasted the combination over a slow fire. Several times Miphon found small colonies of honey ants, which they ate along with roasted crickets.

Water was a problem. They found a few small pools

and streams, but sometimes ran short and went thirsty. Still, they managed, coping through habit and experience, aided by observation and alertness; they made steady progress through a landscape where others might have struggled just to stay alive. They fed on snakes, beetles, worms and grubs, and did not think that they were suffering.

In times past – including very recent times – the way to the Dry Pit had been very dangerous because of the ferocity of the nomadic tribes that used to inhabit the area. However, so many expeditions of wizards had recently ventured the area that those tribesmen who had not been killed fighting wizards had fled to safer areas.

Once, the travellers met a wandering rock, but Miphon drove it away with ease. Now that his only remaining power was the power over the minds of stone, he found such control very easy. Given the chance to regain all his former powers, he would have done so without hesitation, but he had to admit that life was much simpler now that his power was diminished. The meditation needed to build and control his remaining power demanded much less energy than he had been forced to expend previously. Miphon also found he could control the creatures of stone with much more precision.

Truth to tell, released from most of the demands of maintaining his powers as a wizard, Miphon felt stronger and younger than he had done for years.

On the seventh day they came on the scene of a battle. Fire had been the major weapon used. Scattered on scorched ground were the frayed, tattered remains of the bodies of human beings and pack animals. Morgan Hearst kicked apart the charred remains of a hamper one of the pack animals had been carrying. He revealed books, charts, maps, all ash-black and illegible.

'Wizards,' said Hearst.

That was all he said. The other two made no

comment: none was needed. They went on, leaving the battleground behind them. It did not figure in their dreams, and by the next day they had almost forgotten it; after all they had been through, it would have taken more than a few dead bodies to upset them.

On the eleventh day after leaving the shores of the Sponge Sea, they reached the Dry Pit.

It was huge. Standing on the southern side, Hearst estimated that the northern rim was at least twenty leagues away, if not further. At their feet, cliffs fell sheer to indecipherable depths where thunder rolled, where shadows walked, where strange clouds of purple, umber and orange lumbered out of clefts and chasms, spitting lightning.

'How do we get down?' said Miphon.

'Easy,' said Hearst. 'Jump.'

They shuddered, stepping back from the edge.

'Somehow,' said Blackwood, 'I can't imagine Garash scratching his way down a cliff. Yet he got down there somehow. There has to be an easy way.'

'Or,' said Hearst, 'at least a way which isn't quite suicidal.'

Without further ado, they began to walk round the Dry Pit, but found no way down. They camped for the night; waking the next morning, they found the tracks of a large, multi-clawed animal which had come close to their campsite in the night.

'What is it?' said Blackwood.

'No comment,' said Hearst, who, frankly, didn't know.

As they marched on, they became aware that there were carrion birds circling over a spot some distance ahead. Something was lying out there, dying.

'If it was dead,' said Hearst, 'the birds would have come down already.'

They debated the merits of waiting. Their waterskins were mostly empty, and that, in the end, decided them: they could not afford to wait. Advancing, they began to make out low mounds lying on the barren ground. The mounds slowly resolved themselves into corpses – and low-slung animals which were tearing at these corpses. It was the animals, obviously, which were keeping the birds at bay.

They dared their way forward.

The animals, big lizard-style creatures, turned tail and fled, scuttling over the rim of the Dry Pit and disappearing into the depths. Reaching the bodies, they read the tracks.

'A walking rock was here,' said Miphon, pointing to a huge furrow which had ploughed up some drifting sand, and to scratches on bare lava. 'The bodies . . . well, you can see for yourself.'

'Here's our path,' said Hearst, looking over the edge of the cliff.

A narrow trail wound downwards into the depths.

'Shall we start now?' said Blackwood.

'Eat, first,' said Hearst, pointing to the bodies.

'I,' said Miphon, a little stiffly, 'am not a cannibal.'

'You,' said Hearst, 'are not really hungry yet. No – relax, friend. I'm not suggesting we break out their marrow for a feast. Not yet, at any rate. We'll try their packs, first.'

'Oh,' said Miphon.

Miphon had thought of the dead bodies in terms of human tragedy; Hearst, still very much a Rovac warrior in spite of all the revelations he had experienced, thought of them in terms of loot (and, if necessary, flesh for the pot).

Without the slightest qualm, Hearst rummaged the dead, rock-mangled lizard-chewed bodies, tearing away the wreckage of clothing, uncovering, with pride, a few bits of hardtack, a twist of tobacco and some dates.

Miphon and Blackwood searched the packs. Some had been smashed by the walking rock, but others were entirely uninjured. Clearly none of the dead had been wearing their packs when attacked, which suggested they had been camping – sleeping by night, perhaps – and not on the march.

Turning out one pack, Miphon found a load of maps and manuscripts. Then a tinder box, in much better repair than his own. Then a fire-iron, of the kind wizards of Arl sometimes used for lighting fires. Then a flimsy cotton shirt, which might be good for bandages. Then –

'Skalakala!' screamed Miphon.

It was a cry right out of his childhood. It had served his ancestors both as a warcry and as a shout of surpassing delight. He raised his hand, exhibiting his trophy.

The dead men had already been to the depths of the Dry Pit. They had already risked its dangers. And what Miphon held in his hand now was . . . a death-stone.

It kicked in his hand, like a living heart, and he let it fall. If he had held it any longer without using it, it would have killed him.

CHAPTER SIXTY

They marched from the Dry Pit without delay, carrying the death-stone with them. Their triumph was short-lived; they were acutely aware of the immense distances they had to cover.

By now, the Swarms would already have spread most of the distance up the western coast of Argan. Nobody would say for certain how fast the Swarms would move, but the travellers knew that the distance from Drangsturm to the Dry Pit was roughly equivalent to the distance from Drangsturm to the land of Estar.

If the Skull of the Deep South had sent the Swarms north as fast as they could go, then there was probably no hope whatsoever of the travellers cutting them off at the southern border of Estar. On the other hand, if the Swarms had stopped to kill out each human community they came across, there was still some hope.

A faint hope.

That day, they marched due west from the Dry Pit, putting as much distance as possible between themselves and its unknown and half-known dangers. They camped that evening beside a marginal trickle of water, which – like the dates and hardtack they shared between them – was sweet luxury.

That evening, they began to argue over which route to take. Having at least half-expected to die in the Dry Pit, they had never really talked it out before.

Estar lay north-west, but a direct journey, north-west as the eagle flies, would have meant crossing the Shackle Mountains, dragon country near the Araconch Waters, the Broken Lands, the Spine Mountains and the Ironband Mountains. Such an expedition was out of the question – they would have needed maps, guides, food, pack animals and cold-weather clothing for the mountain crossings.

And it would have been slow beyond endurance.

Their fastest route to Estar, if they walked, lay southwest down the barren and almost waterless coast of the Sponge Sea, then due west across the Marbin Erg to Veda – or, to be accurate, the ruins of Veda – then north along the Salt Road.

'That's if we walk,' said Hearst. 'But I favour the sea.'

'And maybe it favours you,' said Blackwood. 'But there's no way west from the Sponge Sea to the Central Ocean.'

'We wouldn't go that way,' said Hearst. 'Returning to our canoe, we'd go the other way. We'd sail out through Seagate, then travel along the coast all the way to Skua. The sea has its dangers – but I'd rather contend with storms off the Bitterwater Coast than with monsters from the Swarms on the Salt Road.'

In the end, Hearst won.

They would go by sea.

That night, Blackwood dreamt of Loosehead Robert, the mad revolutionary who, according to the children's stories of Estar, came to grief when he was caught in a cave in the hills. Blackwood's dream became a tangled nightmare in which hooks, claws and devouring spiders tore apart Robert's body.

In the dream, Robert bled. Not blood, but long words: stochastic, phenomenological, epistemological. In the dream, of course, the words had the full glory of their High Speech avatars: jonmarakaralarajodo, enakonazavnetzyltrakolii, zeq-telejenzeq. Bleeding, Robert fled down the hill, with the hooks, claws and spiders rampaging after him on a glissando of blue milk.

At first it seemed he would escape. And then:

The hill itself began to move.

'No!' screamed Blackwood.

And woke himself with his scream.

He blinked at dawnlight, at the lava-dark barrens, at his two startled companions.

'Bad dreams?' said Hearst.

'I was chased by a hill,' said Blackwood.

'You're lucky it wasn't a mountain,' said Hearst, carelessly.

'I don't think mountains can move,' said Blackwood. 'Not even in dreams.'

'Oh, there's no reason why mountains shouldn't move,' said Miphon. 'If someone's careless enough to use a death-stone near a mountain – anything might happen.'

'Why didn't the mountains move at Ep Pass, then?' said Blackwood.

'They may well have done,' said Miphon. 'We didn't stay around very long to watch and see, did we? Heenmor would have been able to ward them off with the death-stone if they attacked him, of course.'

'And we could do the same?' said Blackwood.

'We wouldn't need to,' said Miphon. 'I could control the mind of a mountain just as I control the mind of a rock.'

'Then,' said Blackwood, 'why not – '

As he explained what he had in mind, the other two looked at him, at first with patronising amusement, and then, realising he was truly serious, with disbelief, and then, realising it might actually work, with joyous elation.

'We can do it!' shouted Hearst in a battlefield voice.

'Or get ourselves killed,' said Miphon, with a note of caution. 'Nothing could be that easy!'

'Let's see,' said Blackwood. 'Let's try.'

The nearest mountain was five leagues distant. They trekked to the mountain, then climbed its slopes, which rose three thousand paces into the sky. Miphon used the death-stone, while Hearst and Blackwood huddled in the tiny circle of safety surrounding him.

The mountain came to life.

The ground lurched under them, then rolled sideways. The sun staggered. Miphon struggled for control. The mind of the mountain was fierce, strong, turbulent. Breaking loose from stasis, the mountain went raging across the barren land. The horizon bucked and tilted.

At last, Miphon brought the monster under control.

'I have it!' he gasped. 'I have it!'

'Then don't lose it!' said Hearst, badly shaken.

'I won't,' said Miphon. 'It's settling down now.'

'Yes, well, let's hope it doesn't start sneezing or something,' said Hearst.

'And don't let it roll over to scratch its back!' said Blackwood.

'And –'

'Trust me,' said Miphon.

And, having no option, they did.

The ride was far from comfortable. The mountain, even though it was under control, moved in stumbling staggering lurches which kept the sun and the far horizons swaying. Blackwood was soon physically sick, so sick that he swore he'd vomited up yesterday's breakfast; the other two felt indisputably nauseous.

After a while, it became very tedious. There was nothing to do but sit and watch the landscape passing by. Miphon worked on the mountain's mind until it believed it was keeping its heading of its own volition: after that, even he had very little to do.

From that height, everything seemed small and insignificant; instead of making the travellers seem powerful, this made them feel disconnected from the landscape. It was disconcerting, after tramping so many hundred leagues on foot, to discover that there was a way to traverse enormous distances almost without effort.

Riding the clumsy, ponderous mountain, at first they covered over a hundred leagues a day. However, on the third day the mountain slowed, and on the fourth day it halted, deep in the Marabin Erg.

'Is it tired?' said Hearst.

Miphon listened to the mind of the mountain, which raged against resuming stasis.

'No,' said Miphon. 'It would move if it could. Come close to me: I'm going to use the death-stone again.'

Hearst and Blackwood moved into the circle of safety. Miphon took the death-stone and held it. He waited for it to kick in his hand like a beating heart. But nothing happened. The death-stone felt like any smooth stone egg.

'Why are you waiting?' said Hearst.

Miphon shouted out the spell that should make the death-stone work. But nothing happened.

'Give it to me,' said Hearst. 'Let me try.'

Miphon handed it over. Hearst tried, with no success.

'It doesn't work!' said Hearst.

Surrounding them in all directions was the desert of the Marabin Erg. They were unlikely to survive a march across the open desert. They did not have enough water, for one thing.

'Maybe the death-stone needs time to recover,' said Miphon.

'Oh,' said Hearst, thinking about it.

They actually had very little experience of death-stones. Heenmor had used one once near Castle Vaunting, then again, months later, at Ep Pass, later still making unknown experiments with it at Stronghold Handfast. Elkor Alish had used a death-stone on escaping from the green bottle, and again, weeks later, to destroy an army defending Runcorn against his ragtag forces recruited in the hills of Dybra and Chorst. Hearst had used that death-stone long afterwards, to destroy the eastern defences of Androlmarphos, and Garash had activated another in the Castle of Controlling Power.

That was more or less the sum total of the knowledge they had to draw on. They did not know of anyone else trying to use a death-stone twice in the course of a few days. If the death-stone needed to rest, they had no way of telling how long it might have to rest for.

'We could try and walk,' said Blackwood.

'Through the Marabin Erg?' said Miphon.

'If we walk, we fail,' said Hearst. 'We'd never reach Estar in time, quite apart from the chance of dying of thirst. We have to stay with the mountain and hope we'll be able to use the death-stone again soon.'

'If we'd gone into the Dry Pit we might have been able to get more than one,' said Miphon.

'Yes,' said Hearst. 'And we might have got killed in the process, too. Come on.'

'Where are you going?'

'There! Look, a big watercourse, about a league from the mountainfoot. It's dry, but perhaps we'll find water if we dig.'

In the event, they didn't.

However, on the fifth day after they had last successfully used the death-stone, Miphon held it in his hand and felt it kick like a living heart. He used it. The mountain, animated again, continued on its way, stopping once, on command, at an oasis where they drew water.

As the mountain lumbered forward, dust and sand rose up behind them in boiling clouds of amber-umber; they paid no heed to the devastation left in their wake, but scanned the horizons far ahead, watching for the first sign of the Swarms.

On reaching the Harvest Plains, they saw the Swarms moving, not in great armies but in small scattered groups, a dozen here, a dozen there. They kept watch for the Neversh, knowing they had no defence against any Neversh attacking from the sky. Miphon said the creatures of the Swarms had no intelligence to speak of, relying instead on commands from the Skull of the Deep South, but Hearst was not sure whether to trust that.

On the evening of the second day, they passed south

of Selzirk, and saw the Neversh wheeling in their legions above the distant city. Miphon insisted that they give it a wide berth: there was no way they could save Selzirk.

As the towers and walls of Selzirk receded in the distance, Hearst thought of Farfalla, and what might have been – in a different world, a better world. Strangely, he found his memories of his visit to Selzirk were distant, unclear, fading. He was – or so he thought – preparing himself for the end of the world.

The next day, lumbering north-west across the Harvest Plains, leaving a trail of dust and torn earth behind it, the mountain slowed. On the fourth day they reached the shore, and, as the mountain's strength failed, Miphon took it into the sea. It hated the water, which would have killed a mere walking rock outright. Miphon forced the mountain out to sea for a league. Then it halted, its top forming a small island in the Central Ocean.

'We'll have to hug the shore when we go north,' said Miphon. 'Otherwise we'll be walking underwater.'

The day of waiting was hard. They were battered by the cold rains and the biting winds of the beginning of winter. They spent most of their time huddled together for warmth, except when they were fishing; they ate fish raw, having no wood for fires.

Then the wait ended.

Miphon used the death-stone again.

The mountain, liberated in the sea, thrashed in agony as the water tried to destroy it. The travellers were almost flung overboard. Fighting desperately, Miphon forced the mountain to shore. Only half its height reached the shore: the rest was left in the sea, destroyed by the water.

As their journey continued, their mountain smashed its way along the coastline. They went past Runcorn, and saw the Swarms circling above that beleaguered city. They went trampling down the Salt Road, crushing underfoot keflos, stalkers, granderglaws, glarz and other creatures.

They were nearing Estar.

But the mountain's power ebbed before they got there. Knowing they must not halt on the Salt Road – the Swarms would attack them if they did – Miphon forced it into the sea. This time, it fought harder than before, knowing how the water would scald it. But he mastered its will, and finally, sweating, exhausted, drained, brought it to a halt in the ocean.

'Our next move,' said Miphon, 'will take us to Estar.'

There, they would confront the Swarms. And win.

Or lose, and die, and fail – and bring the world down to disaster with them.

CHAPTER SIXTY-ONE

They were on their way again.

The mountain came roaring out of the water. The scream of its hate, pain and rage rocked the sky like thunder. It had started off with a height of three thousand paces: about a third of its height was left.

Miphon brought it to heel, and forced it along the Salt Road. Creatures of the Swarms fled to left and to right as the mountain charged down the road. At last, they saw ahead of them the border of Estar.

They saw, in the distance, the fire dyke. Someone had ignited it, and recently: fresh flame roared upward. North of it was a long mound: a fortification freshly raised. Many creatures of the Swarms were gathered to the south of the flames.

'Men!' cried Blackwood. 'On the mound! Men!'

'The sea!' shouted Hearst. 'Go round by sea!'

The mountain, roaring, fought Miphon's efforts to master it into the sea. It went smashing forward. Creatures of the Swarms were pulped beneath it in their hundreds. On the mound, men scattered like ants.

Miphon screamed:

'I'm losing it! I'm losing it!'

The mountain, running amok, lurched and staggered toward the fire dyke, toward the helpless men beyond.

'Strength!' shouted Hearst.

'You can do it!' cried Blackwood. 'You can do it!'

Miphon risked taking a moment to close his eyes and calm himself, as he would for the Meditations. He opened his eyes again. The mountain was almost upon its victims.

With an almost physical effort, Miphon punched the

523

mountain sideways. It lurched, skidded, crashed into the sea, screamed, spun, blundered blindly through the water, then –

Urged by Miphon, it made for land again.

And swung out onto the dry and hard.

They had made a wild sweep through the ocean, skirting round the flame trench and the fortifications. They had killed hundreds of the creatures of the Swarms, but not a single man.

The mountain began smashing north across the countryside. It was screaming continuously.

'Make it stop!' said Hearst. 'Make it stop!'

But Miphon shook his head. His face was ashen. He was exhausted. At last he said:

'It's gone mad. It's gone well and truly mad. I can't stop it. Nobody could.'

Though he did not say it, his powers were at low ebb. He had used a lot of his last remaining power forcing the mountain through the sea. When he had recovered a little, he settled himself to the Meditations as best he could on that lurching, heaving platform; it was important for him to build his power as swiftly as he could.

The mountain ran on at will all through that day and into the night. When morning came, it was moving more slowly. Miphon did not try to take it under control, but kept working on the Meditations.

Toward the afternoon, they sighted Maf. As the day wore on, the mountain drew closer and closer. Miphon had an idea. He tried it. He used the gentlest of hints to nudge their mountain onto a course that would take it straight for Maf.

It ran on for a while as if it failed to see the obstacle ahead. Then, when it seemed a collision was inevitable, it came to a lurching halt.

Then backed off.

'It sees the other mountain,' said Miphon.

'What now?' said Hearst.

524

'Wait,' said Miphon.

The three of them waited. And their mountain began to speak to Maf in a gruff, growling thundervoice. Only Miphon understood what it was saying. After a while, Miphon began to weep. Hearst and Blackwood watched him, bewildered; they had no way to understand the tragedy of rocks and mountains.

Finally, the voice of the mountain grew slower and lower, then finally ground to a halt.

'It's over,' said Miphon.

As he spoke, the mountain shook. Cracks appeared underfoot. The vibrations began to get worse.

'Come,' said Miphon, quietly. 'Let's get off.'

'What's happening?' said Blackwood, as Miphon led the way down.

'The immersions in water are having their effect,' said Miphon.

He did not wish to tell them that the mountain, driven beyond endurance by what it had suffered, was committing suicide. He thought they would think him stark raving mad.

As they got clear of the mountain, it began to collapse. They ran. An avalanche of rock came roaring after them. But, sweeping forward, the rock disintegrated. Becoming sand. Then dust. Then an unimaginably fine silt. It surged around them.

'Sprint!' shouted Hearst.

They fled, panting.

The silt wafted up around their ankles, surged around their calves, rose to their knees. They found themselves waist-deep in the stuff, wading forward as best they could. It rose to their chests. To their necks.

'Hold your breath!' shouted Hearst.

And grabbed a deep breath, closing his eyes as the silt swamped him. He urged himself forward, felt his head break clear, gasped for breath, coughed, sneezed, heard Blackwood cough:

'Miphon?'

Nobody answered.

'Miphon?'

'Here!'

They had come through. They had survived.

'Have we got the death-stone?' said Hearst.

'I've got it,' said Miphon.

So they still had a chance.

A hope.

That afternoon, they made camp at the foot of Maf. A scouring wind swept the silt in clouds across the countryside, swiftly reducing the enormous pile. Toward evening, they saw a couple of mountains blundering across the countryside in the distance, south of their present position.

'Someone has used a death-stone,' said Miphon, in a sombre voice.

'It must have been used at the border,' said Hearst.

'So it's set mountains walking,' said Blackwood. 'How many will have moved? They're only small ones, by the looks of things. What will it have done to the fire-dyke? What – '

'The only way to answer all your questions is to go south and have a look,' said Miphon. 'But I can tell you this much. The death-stone must have been used soon after we skirted the southern border, otherwise those wandering mountains wouldn't have got as far as they have.'

'If someone's used a death-stone in the south, they won't be able to use it again for . . . for how long?' said Blackwood.

'Work it out,' said Miphon. 'Normally we ride a mountain for four days then have to wait another day before using the death-stone again. That's five days in total. So, down in the south they'll have to wait five days. And us? We used our death-stone yesterday, so we won't be able to use it again until the day after the day after tomorrow.'

'By which time the Swarms may be upon us,' said Hearst.

'How do you work that out?' said Miphon.

'If the death-stone was used at the border yesterday, the Swarms must have been attacking then. If they made a second attack yesterday, they may have broken through. If they can go as fast as a mounted man – which I think is a reasonable assumption – they could be here tomorrow. After all, it's only about a hundred leagues to the border from here.'

'Your mounted man is pushing his horse along pretty quickly,' said Miphon. 'It took sixteen days for us to do four hundred leagues from Veda to Narba.'

'Yes,' said Hearst. 'But you didn't have the heart to thrash your mount to exhaustion. Besides, we were moving mostly by night on a bad road. And skirting round cities, which made the journey longer. And – '

'Never mind!' said Blackwood, thoroughly tired of this theorising. 'Let's stick to what we know. We know for a fact that we can't use the death-stone for three days. We know for a fact – well, we can reasonably presume – that the Swarms could get here by then. If indeed they've broken through. So the question is, what should we do?'

'We can't risk running into the Swarms when we don't have a weapon to use against them,' said Miphon. 'At a minimum, we need to hide out somewhere until the death-stone's ready again. Morgan, when you climbed down from Maf . . .'

'I'd been thinking about that,' said Hearst. 'There's a cave system running the whole height of Maf. I know how to get into it. So if the Swarms come, we can run for shelter.'

The next day was bright and clear, with a stiff wind which steadily diminished the remains of the suicided mountain. They saw, once, one of the Neversh circling high in the sky. But no creature of the Swarms came north along the Salt Road. Night came again, and they slept.

CHAPTER SIXTY-TWO

They woke to find the sky grey, cloudy, moody. The wind had dropped away. Tomorrow, they would be able to use the death-stone; for today, they could only wait. Miphon concentrated on the Meditations; Hearst, half-heartedly, practised with his sword Hast. Blackwood went scavenging amongst the rocks near the mountain, returning, in due course, with a load of snails which he had found glued to those rocks, settled in for the winter.

They cooked, and ate.

They drank stream-water.

They waited.

Toward mid-morning, they saw a body of horsemen coming down the Salt Road. They debated whether to risk talking with them.

'We have to know what's happening in the south,' said Blackwood. 'On the other hand, we can't risk the death-stone. So I'll go. You two stay here. Depending on who it is and how the talk goes, I'll either say I'm alone or else say you're here.'

'Be careful,' said Hearst.

'Trust me,' said Blackwood.

And Blackwood set out from Maf for the Salt Road. Hearst and Miphon eventually saw him intercept the horsemen. There was a long hiatus, and then the horsemen started to make for Maf. Blackwood was leading them to his comrades.

'I hope he knows what he's doing,' muttered Hearst.

'I trust him,' said Miphon.

'Yes, but . . .'

As the horsemen drew near, it became apparent that

528

they were fewer in number than they seemed to be at first. There were, in fact, only a score of horsemen; however, as each had a string of half a dozen mounts – to provide the changes needed for fast long-distance riding – they made quite a sizeable body when they were on the move.

As the riders came closer, Hearst recognised:

Blackwood. And –

Prince Comedo!

And –

Elkor Alish!

Smiling!

And, apart from that, precisely nineteen assorted troopers – Hearst, with a warriors's concern for the odds, counted them. Though it did not look like it was going to come to a fight. Instead, there was happiness all round. Mixed, though, with a fair bit of weariness – these horsemen had ridden long and hard.

'Greetings,' said Prince Comedo.

'My lord,' said Hearst, bowing.

'We understand you can save the world for us,' said Comedo, who looked pale and drawn. 'Accordingly, we have made a treaty with you. Tell him the terms.'

And he nodded at Blackwood.

'The good and gracious Lord Emperor Comedo,' said Blackwood, 'Master of all of Argan, Commander of the Central Ocean, terror of all lands beneath the stars, ruler of Powers and Thrones, deeds to the three of us, as a token of gratitude for the performance of deeds now promised, the suzerainty of the Greater Teeth and of the Lesser.'

'My lord is very gracious,' said Hearst, keeping a straight face and managing a bow.

He urgently wanted this charade to end. He wanted to talk to Elkor Alish. Alish! Really there! On a horse! Just a few paces away! Alish, smiling!

'For his part,' said Blackwood, 'the good and gracious Lord Emperor Comedo will allow us full use of the red bottle which is his by virtue of his treaty with the High Priest of all Gods and all Demons, Valarkin of Estar.'

'Valarkin!' said Hearst, with shock and surprise.

'The High Priest of all Gods and all Demons,' drawled Alish, 'is currently at the southern border with our death-stone. It worked once, then refused to work again. He thinks it'll come to life in due course. I think he's wrong, which is why we're on our way north. With . . . this.'

And he patted the red bottle hanging from his belt.

'We have,' said Alish, 'most of our army within. Including troops from Rovac. They did come, Morgan, I called, and they came. I, you see . . . did my best.'

There was something strange in his voice. What? Tension. Not anger, surely. Not hate? Or was it?

'So much for the red bottle and the death-stone,' said Hearst. 'What about the green bottle? Valarkin got his hands on that, too.'

'Oh, the green bottle,' said Alish. 'Oh, that. I gave that to a pirate as a love-offering.'

'No!' cried Hearst, in shock, pain, horror and disbelief.

'Yes,' said Alish, with a sardonic edge to his voice. 'And I promised that same pirate something else. Your head!'

And with that, Alish drew his sword.

He urged his horse forward.

'Honour the Emperor!' screamed Blackwood. 'Honour the Emperor's treaty!'

A horseman tried to head Alish off. Alish cut him down. Comedo was shouting for Alish to stop.

'Are you with me, boys?' shouted Alish.

Some cried yes, but others – their Emperor was of the Favoured Blood – shouted no.

'Run!' said Hearst.

And Hearst, Blackwood and Miphon fled. Alish, unable to break free from the mêlée to follow them, screamed:

'Run then, Morgan, run! Run, you rat-spawn murderer! You can run, but you'll never find a hole that's safe from me!'

* * *

The Lord Emperor Comedo, titular ruler of all of Argan, ruler de jure of Estar, and ruler de facto of, perhaps, at least some of his own lice, died in the cavalry brawl at the foot of Maf, cut down by a trooper who wanted no part in treaties with wandering vagrants, and who sided instead with Elkor Alish.

He died with a sword in his hand, which was, some might say, to his credit; whatever the merits of his death, Elkor Alish, triumphant, made it positive and final by cutting off Comedo's head.

* * *

The rock chimney was narrow. It led almost straight up to a dark opening in the side of the mountain.

'That's the way,' said Hearst.

It led up into a system of tunnels and caves that could take them all the way to the top of Maf. From that vantage point, they could, on the morrow, command the mountain with their death-stone.

'Are you sure you remember the way?' said Miphon.

'Positive,' said Hearst, hoping.

'How do we climb up?' said Blackwood. 'We don't have a ladder.'

'Watch,' said Hearst.

And swarmed up the chimney, working with back, knees, feet, hand and hook-hand.

'If you get tired,' he shouted, before disappearing into the cave at the top, 'jam yourself in the crack, back against one wall, knees against the other.'

Blackwood and Miphon followed.

Hearst led them on, through the darkness.

531

It was a long, slow climb, with many twists and turnings, but at least they had the comfort of knowing that Alish could not follow them. Someone who did not know the way would soon get lost in amongst the caves and tunnels. When they got to the top, they would be safe. They would have no more worries until it was time to use the death-stone again, and take the mountain south to do battle with the Swarms.

* * *

At last, they saw ahead a glimmer of light.

'That's the dragon's lair,' said Hearst. 'Wait here, I'll go and see if it's all clear. If it is, we'll be able to get into the tunnel that takes us to the top.'

'Of course it'll be clear,' said Miphon.

'It's been seven seasons since the dragon Zenphos died,' said Hearst. 'That's time enough for another dragon to come here. Wait till I've had a look.'

'As you wish,' said Miphon.

'Don't take too long,' said Blackwood.

'I won't.'

Morgan Hearst drew his battlesword Hast and slipped forward through the gloom. Ahead of him the dragon's lair was lit by the fading light of the evening sky; they had indeed been a long time climbing up through the mountain.

Hearst saw the dragon's skeleton in the lair. So there was no new dragon living in this cave high up in the mountain of Maf. Good. He stepped into the lair.

And stopped.

And stared.

'Hello, Morgan,' said Elkor Alish.

'You!'

'Yes, me,' said Elkor Alish, smiling. 'I've been waiting here for some time. An interesting climb, isn't it?'

Elkor Alish had lost some of the skin of his fingertips

532

somewhere on the mountainside, but there was nothing else in his appearance to suggest he had found the climb difficult.

'Alish . . .'

'Here,' said Alish, drawing his sword, 'we have an ending.'

'Alish,' said Hearst, his voice low and urgent. 'We've got to talk. I have to explain. We've misunderstood each other for a long time.'

'You wish to talk?' said Alish. 'Then let steel speak to steel!'

He attacked. Hearst barely parried the attack. They broke apart, both panting already, more from the shock of combat than anything else.

'Alish!' said Hearst, in desperation. 'We were friends once!'

'Were we?' said Alish, his voice rising to a shout as he moved in for the kill. 'Were we?'

Hearst had slipped the toe of his boot under a dragon's scale. He kicked it up toward Alish's face. Alish glimpsed something spinning toward him and slashed at it. His sword shattered the brittle scale into a thousand fragments. Catching that momentary opening, the point of Hearst's sword raked across his ribs.

Alish parried a second blow.

The fighters broke apart.

'Only a scratch,' said Alish, harshly.

Hearst said nothing.

'It was good though, good,' said Alish, bringing his breathing under control. 'You've improved.'

Alish moved in again.

Hearst backpaced, leaping away like a dancer.

Swords clashed, once, twice, three times. Hearst came up against one of the ribs of the dragon. He slipped in under the arch of the ribcage. In amongst the ribs, where Alish would have no room for his fanciest bladework, Hearst would have his best chance.

'There's no place to hide,' said Alish. 'This is the

sword Raunen Song. The bright blade of vengeance. It's all over, Morgan. Ahyak Rovac!'

Screaming, Alish struck.

Metal rang against metal.

Alish beat down Hearst's sword and slashed for his throat. Hearst's right arm swept up. His steel hook caught Alish's blade. His own sword lunged for his rival's heart – but Alish sidestepped then backstepped, withdrawing out of reach.

'Good,' crooned Alish. 'Good, yes. You have, oh yes, my dearest Morgan, you have improved.'

His voice was soft, relaxed, silky.

Then, with a scream, he attacked, fast and furious, driving Hearst out of the rib-cage and into the open ground. Now there was no time to think, only to strike and react. Death matched death in a blur of shadow and light.

Momentarily, their blades locked, hilt to hilt.

Alish spat.

And Hearst slashed him with his right-hand hook.

Alish screamed in agony. His left eye was gone, his face torn open. He took a wild swing at Hearst, who parried the blow.

'Yield,' said Hearst.

Alish swore at him.

Then attacked, striking furious blows in a berserker rage. Though Alish had lost one eye, the best Hearst could do was force him to give ground.

That he did.

Hearst started to manoeuvre Alish toward the edge of the cave. He would force Alish to step back into that gulf of air, if that was the only way to end the fight.

'No,' said Alish.

He knew what Hearst was trying to do.

Hearst said nothing, but slashed and thrust.

'No,' said Alish, desperate now.

'Yield!' hissed Hearst.

'No!' cried Alish.

They were near the lip of the cave. In the air outside, Hearst saw – what? Distracted, he failed to turn a blow. Alish's blade ripped his sword-arm open. His weapon went flying. Hearst dived sideways, making a desperate attempt to recover his blade, and Alish –

Screamed!

Alish screamed like the voice that will scream at the end of the world. His sword fell from his hands and clattered on the rock floor of the cave. Hearst looked up. He saw Alish in the grips of the grapple-hooks of a Neversh. Then the two huge feeding spikes drove home. Alish's body jerked. His mouth gaped open. His whole body shuddered – then was still.

And silent.

Hearst got to his knees and watched as the Neversh carried the body away into the sky. He staggered to his feet, and tottered to the edge of the cave. He almost fell, but steadied himself just in time.

He could not see where the Neversh had gone to.

Helplessly, he began to weep.

CHAPTER SIXTY-THREE

They waited out the next day on the top of Maf. From dawn to dusk they had nothing to eat; there was, however, a little water, gathered in pools on the mountaintop. From time to time, they tried the death-stone, but it refused to work.

Night fell.

Some time during the night, Miphon tried the death-stone again, and felt it kick in his hand like a living heart.

'Gather close!' he shouted.

The other two sat at his feet. Miphon cried out the Words, and the familiar yet still terrifying power began its work.

The mountain of Maf came to life.

And, immediately, began to storm toward the east. Miphon tested its will, and found it strong, savage, ferocious.

'Miphon!' cried Hearst, trying to make sense of the reeling stars in the sky above. 'I think we're going the wrong way!'

'Too bad!' said Miphon.

From the Meditations, he had gathered enough power to bring the mountain under control if he really had to. But he wanted to conserve his strength, not exhaust it by doing battle with the mountain at the outset.

Miphon let the mountain run rampaging through the night. Then, hint by hint, he began to nudge it south. Dawn found them storming south on a course parallel with the Salt Road.

Cold, weary, hungry, they watched the landscape

lurching past. They had no words for each other this morning. They watched the sky for the Neversh. Hearst, after a while, fell asleep; he dreamt of the Neversh, and he dreamt of the shade of Elkor Alish, wandering without comfort or guidance in the darkness of hollow wind.

When Hearst woke, Miphon changed the dressing on his wounded sword-arm.

'Satisfied?' said Hearst.

'I think it'll heal,' said Miphon.

'Let's hope we live long enough to find out.'

The southern border drew steadily nearer. Toward the end of the day, they began to make out the details of how things had changed. A number of small mountains had moved, but most had not gone far. One had made the mistake of blundering into the sea; withdrawing from the water, it had parked itself half-way across the open seashore strip where the Salt Road ran; there was now only a breach some two hundred paces wide to guard against the Swarms.

'No sign of any of the Swarms,' said Blackwood.

'I'm not surprised!' said Miphon.

In the very recent past, they had smashed thousands and thousands of the creatures of the Swarms as they drove a mountain toward Estar. Since then, a death-stone had been used against the Swarms at the border. Obviously the enemy had taken fearful losses; it was scarcely surprising that their advance had been checked.

The fire dyke and the makeshift fortifications the travellers had seen when they skirted the border had disappeared without a trace, obliterated by monstering mountains or the action of the death-stone.

'Somewhere here,' said Blackwood, peering ahead, 'is Valarkin.'

'With a death-stone,' said Miphon.

'Charming,' said Hearst.

'We'll make an alliance with him,' said Miphon, with

537

determination in his voice. 'We have to. He has a death-stone. He may also have the green bottle.'

'Alish said – ' began Blackwood.

'Don't believe what Alish said about the green bottle,' said Miphon. 'Nobody would give away anything like that. Someone's got it right now, and the obvious person is Valarkin.'

'So we find Valarkin,' said Hearst.

'That's right,' said Miphon. 'Then I seal the border with this mountain. Then we wait, so I can be sure it doesn't move away until it's frozen back into inert stone.'

'But if we wait,' protested Blackwood, 'we'll be at danger from the Neversh!'

'We owe our grief a death,' said Hearst grimly.

But, if the Rovac warrior had commitments to death, Blackwood did not. Now that they had come so far, now that they had survived so much, there was no way that he could accept death as inevitable. Well, perhaps the Neversh would not attack them during the two or three days they would have to wait at the border. Perhaps –

'Look!' said Hearst, pointing. 'To the east! Something on that bald mountain-top!'

'Are you sure?' said Miphon.

'I don't see anything!' said Blackwood.

'Bear east,' commanded Hearst.

Miphon hinted to the mountain. His subtle urging made Maf slow, then veer east. He was getting good at this.

As they drew near the bald mountain Hearst had indicated, they saw a tent, a banner, a handful of men.

'Valarkin must be there,' said Hearst.

'We'd better not go closer,' said Blackwood. 'We may frighten him.'

'Frighten him!' said Hearst. 'I don't care if we frighten him out of his breakfast! If we're going to have to bargain with him, let's soften him up first.'

538

'I don't think – ' began Blackwood.

'Good,' said Hearst. 'We've no need for thinking now. Just action.'

They came closer and closer to the tent, which was perched on a sheer cliff face. As they came within hailing distance, men, terrified, stared at them in awestricken silence.

'Hoy,' yelled Hearst. 'You on the mountain!'

Nobody responded.

They seemed paralysed by terror.

'There's Valarkin!' said Blackwood. 'By the tent!'

Valarkin! Yes, Blackwood was right.

'Hello there, Valarkin!' roared Hearst.

Straight away, Valarkin whipped out the death-stone.

'No, Valarkin,' shouted Hearst. 'No!'

But it was too late. Valarkin cried out in the High Speech. And Miphon shouted:

'Segenarith!'

Valarkin cried out in pain as the death-stone grew hot in his hand. He dropped it. His men were running in panic, scattering in all directions.

'Come back!' yelled Blackwood. 'Come back, we'll take you aboard! Back here, or you're dead!'

But, if anyone heard him, nobody obeyed.

'Leave them,' said Hearst, harshly. 'Let's get out of here.'

Miphon began to urge the mountain. Slowly, as the fire of the death-stone grew and grew, the mountain backed off. They watched as a fireball swallowed the cliff-top. Valarkin must be dead by now – unless he had run swiftly, or unless, perhaps, he did have the green bottle in his possession, and had been able to take refuge.

Night was now falling.

By dawn, the southern border of Estar was a sea of flame as the death-stone, frustrated by the Ultimate Injunction, the command Segenarith, released its energies as heat. Steam rose in clouds from the sea where molten rock ran into the water. By now, the mountain of Maf had withdrawn ten leagues from the border.

Miphon made the mountain lie down on its side – a long, slow, difficult manoeuvre. The travellers descended to the ground, then Miphon made the mountain stand again.

Then Miphon used all his skill, talent and strength to work on the mind of Maf, and sent the mountain roaring south. His instructions would take it south into the fire raging on the border. It would stand in that fire. Heat would fuse rock with rock. The mountain would block the way that led into Estar, thus closing the border to all creatures of the Swarms except the Neversh.

'It is done,' said Miphon.

And Hearst, with something almost like disappointment, realised that they had triumphed – and that he was still alive.

Now he had to make a life for himself.

CHAPTER SIXTY-FOUR

On a cold winter's day in the land of Estar, a man named Morgan Hearst found the drained body of a man named Elkor Alish. In days past, they had been friends; they had shared the same shadow down many roads. Then Elkor Alish had betrayed his friend, had tried to kill him and had cost him his right hand.

There had been harsh words and bad blood between them; they had led armies against each other; their swords had crossed in anger, blade against blade. Yet Morgan Hearst stood by the body of Elkor Alish, and said Words of Guiding for the dead man's soul.

Where does friendship end and love begin? Amongst the Rovac, it was a question never asked; they lived close enough to the cutting edge of death to value any human loyalty as an alliance against the darkness.

'Be at peace,' said Hearst.

Then he took a ring and a red bottle from the dead man's husk, and, helped by his friends Miphon and Blackwood, raised a funeral pyre, and burnt the mortal remnants of Elkor Alish.

Then they resumed their journey, heading north.

Reaching the Hollern River, they found, to their amazement, that Melross Hill was now topped by a chaotic disorder of smashed stone and torn earth, through which, at random intervals, fire billowed up.

'What a mess!' said Miphon.

'Positively stochastic,' said Blackwood, nodding agreement.

541

'That reminds me,' said Miphon. 'We never did finish the question of free will, did we?'

'Well,' said Hearst, 'Let's go into town and settle it over a drink or three.'

Whatever had smashed Castle Vaunting – and it could only have been a free-ranging mountain – had missed Lorford, where there were now a few dozen hovel-style shacks. The travellers trudged down the Salt Road toward the shacks.

'We'll build a city here,' said Hearst.

'Will we?' said Blackwood.

'Of course,' said Hearst. 'Who's to rule Estar now, but us? Who's to guard the borders against the Swarms, but us? We've got the death-stone, the red bottle, and an army in the bottle. We've got what we need.'

Blackwood was startled by this. They were to be rulers? Princes? Kings? Well . . .

He had to admit it was possible.

As they closed with the shacks, shouting children roused the people out to meet the strangers. Coming closer, Blackwood saw faces he half-recognised from days past.

Then, suddenly:

'Mystrel!'

A woman ran forward, and Blackwood ran to meet her. A moment later, they were in each other's arms, crying.

'I thought you were dead,' said Blackwood. 'I couldn't get back to you, I thought you were dead.'

'What?' said Mystrel, laughing, laughing and crying at the same time. 'The men all go away and the women promptly drop dead? Not so, mister, not so.'

And then they said nothing more, for they were too busy holding each other.

Shortly, they were all seated round a table of sorts in a house of sorts drinking a liquor of sorts, allegedly made out of fermented fish – 'Hell's grief!' said Hearst, tasting it – and all talking at once at roughly the speed of thought.

And Mystrel told all about her wild times with the refugees in the Barley Hills, about pirates and bandits, storms and famine, mad dogs and toadstool poisoning, and, finally, the return to Lorford.

'But how did you ever get out of Castle Vaunting in the first place?' said Blackwood. 'How, when the mad-jewel was guarding it?'

'The fodden led us out,' said Mystrel. 'Some of us, at any rate. It got us clear.'

'Oh,' said Blackwood, looking around. 'Where is it?'

'I strangled it.'

'You what?'

'It had been feeding on something, in the castle. I asked it what. It was stupid enough to tell me.'

'And what had it been feeding on?'

'You don't want to know.'

'Tell me,' said Blackwood.

Mystrel told him.

He was shocked.

He said so.

'I'm shocked,' said Blackwood. Then, Mystrel's horror story having awakened a certain line of thought: 'But your child? What happened . . ?'

'Oh!' said Mystrel, smacking her forehead. 'How could I? Of course.' She raised her voice to a shout: 'Nickle!'

Shortly, a young woman entered, bearing a sturdy boy-child of a little more than a year's growth.

'Nickle is my helper,' said Mystrel, explaining. 'And the child . . . Blackwood, meet your son, Greenwood.'

Hearst rose to his feet, and lifted his cup.

'A toast,' said Hearst. 'I propose a toast. Ladies. Gentlemen. Girls. Boys. Dogs, rats. And any priests and princes present. A toast, I say. To the future!'

'I'll drink to that!' said Miphon.

As did they all.

('Hell's grief,' said Hearst again, as the liquor clawed at his throat – but that didn't stop him drinking to the next toast which came along.)

That night, Blackwood dreamt that he slept in safety in Lorford with his son and his wife at his side; he woke to the light of dawn, and found, to his relief, that the dream was true.

THE END